THE CALL TO ARMS

Erin bowed her head. Her long warrior's braid looped gently over her shoulder, as it had done many times in the past. Only now, there was no Lady to give the blessing.

She had not sworn the warrior's oath for over four centuries and had almost vowed never to swear it again. But the Lady's betrayal was distant now—a thing of the past. Only three things remained of that past: Erin, her trapped Line-mates, and the Lord of the Empire. All of the others that she had known were dead—dust at the whim of time. But the reason that they had fought still remained.

"Lernan. Elliath. Erin." On the last, she drew her sword; it glowed dimly even in this light. Then she touched Darin on the shoulder, and their eyes met.

They faced each other, the last two descendants of the Bright Heart.

By Michelle Sagara
Published by Ballantine Books:

The Sundered:
INTO THE DARK LANDS
CHILDREN OF THE BLOOD
LADY OF MERCY
CHAINS OF DARKNESS, CHAINS OF LIGHT

CHAINS OF DARKNESS, CHAINS OF LIGHT

Book Four of *The Sundered*

Michelle Sagara

A Del Rey Book

BALLANTINE BOOKS • NEW YORK

A Del Rey Book
Published by Ballantine Books

Library on Congress Catalog Card Number: 93-90873

ISBN 0-345-37949-7

Manufactured in the United States of America

10   9   8   7   6   5   4   3   2   1

This book is dedicated to my mother and my father

because they didn't care what other people's parents did
because they made hard choices so they could both be home while we were growing up
because no matter how stupid, chaotic, or difficult I was (and trust me, I was), they cared enough to stand beside me if they couldn't stand behind me
because they both taught me to fight for what I believe in taught me to believe
helped me build a place that all the cynicism in the world couldn't reach, which is where, after all, the stories come from:

The heart.

I love you both very, very much.

This book wouldn't have been what it is without the help of a number of people. Foremost among those is Deborah Hogan, who continues to answer all of my nitpicky little questions as if they were actually uttered by a sane, rational person. She also knew where the manuscript was in its various stages, and shepherded it along, for which I'll be eternally grateful.

prologue

King Renar I of Marantine was a very tired man.

And here, in the privacy of his richly paneled, windowless study, he was allowed the luxury of showing it. He wore no crown, and his much-vaunted love of fine clothing seemed to have slipped; lamplight flickered disapprovingly over the rough twill of an unembroidered brown tunic.

Four months ago, the Maran House had once again established its right to rule over Marantine; four months ago, less two days, he had taken to the road with the small army that he had raised to visit the villages south and east of Dagothrin. He grimaced, allowing his furrowed brow to sink slowly into hands that would barely support it.

Lady Erin was a warrior; he had seen it proven countless times while she stood at his side, or by it, sword singing the chimes of day or night through the bodies of those who had thought to conquer. He wished in silence that he had her taste for battle.

The soft crackle of paper made him look up again; his desk, or what little could be seen of its polished surface, showed a hint of his face. Papers, all urgent, and all awaiting his signature and his seal, glared up in blank accusation.

He was certain his father had never felt so haggard. His hands curled into familiar fists, and he reached for a quill. Thinking about his father still brought him more anger than comfort.

Ink dripped onto the desk, making yet another stain for its surface. He could hear Molatten's curt sniff, which worked about as well as his first lecture had. Fine furniture, sir, must be treated with respect.

1

Hells with it.

There was a knock on the door; it would have been loud even had it carried over conversation.

"Go away." Fatigue made the words sound as petulant as they were.

The door swung open, and Gerald walked in. He checked his usual stride to avoid stepping on balls of crushed parchment—Bright Heart knew that some of it would probably have to be retrieved, smoothed out, and shoved under Renar's weary nose.

"I'm busy," the king said curtly; he'd enough time to drive the annoying whine out of his voice.

"I see. I won't keep you then, but there are a few more orders that General Lorrence wants you to sign."

The quill hit the desk with an unsatisfying swish. Renar lifted it in a panic, but ink had already blotched the edges of several documents.

With no show of sympathy whatsoever, Gerald neatly added another sheaf of papers to the farthest right corner of the desk.

"Gerald, do you want a job?"

"No."

"Does anybody?"

"Not yours, sir." He thought a moment. "Maybe Lord Cosgrove."

"Ha. I'd see the Hells personally first." He looked at the documents that bore Lorrence's thick, clean writing. They were no doubt urgent. "I don't see the point of this." Renar reached for the documents. "I'm not going to read these—I might try, but at this time of night, none of it's going to sink in. I'm going to sign them, the way I sign everything he sends me, and I'm going to send them back with a courier. Why doesn't he just spare us both and sign them himself?"

"Already has."

"You know what I mean. As far as he's concerned, I'm just a figurehead. Why don't we dispense with the formalities? Oh no. Not that frown. Please. I've had a bad day as it is."

Gerald shook his head. He looked down at Renar and barely managed to keep the smile from his lips. "You weren't trained for this." It was as much mercy as he would show. "But it doesn't matter."

"Why do you only speak when you're about to start a lecture?"

"I say what has to be said." He thought about dragging one of the chairs from the corner, then decided against it. "You're king, Renar. The men who follow Lorrence respect him, but you know that they follow the crest he bears.

"Lorrence didn't take the city; you did. If the king had listened to your warnings in the first place, we would still have a readied army. Women would have their husbands and children, men their wives."

"Yes." The word burned the young king's throat. "And Gregory might now be king. He'd have been the best Maran had ever produced."

"You do better than you know," Gerald continued. He would not refute his king's words; they were undeniably true. "Your presence with the royal guards has strengthened the army; you give them Marantine to fight for, and they need it. We need it."

"Yes." Renar allowed himself a weary sigh. "But do I get any time to be myself?"

"Would you wish the Empire to rule still?"

"No." It was soft, that word, and final. The truth of it kept Renar going as he reached for the red wax and candle.

Darin sat in the two-story bay window that overlooked the main roadway into the palace courtyard. The stone was cool beneath him, but the glass-touched sun was warm enough to take the sting out of early spring cold. He looked up to see no trace of dust or webs and thanked the Bright Heart he didn't have to clean here.

His arm was still swollen and tender to the touch, a gift from the king at their last sword lesson. He sighed; he was abysmal and knew it.

He flexed his elbow gingerly. He smiled. Today Erin and her unit—unit was the easiest word to remember among all of the the military ones that were thrown around—were coming home—for good. She was responsible for retaking the last village. The war was won. Or at least the battle for Marantine.

He had met with the three lords—Stenton Cosgrove, Tiber Beaton, and Tiras Colfeldas, who had given up the name of Brownbur—for daily discussions about the Line Culverne and the future of the Bright Heart in Marantine. It wasn't easy, and it wasn't comfortable, because they pressed him for answers he didn't have.

But they treated him as an adult. At least they gave him that.

Erin, why won't you tell me what you're going to do now?

That question was foremost on his mind as he saw the heavy outer gates roll open and saw the unit march in. From here, the fighters looked dirty, and their step was off—but it was light, almost friendly, if soldiers could be said to be so.

Now that it was over, maybe she'd know.

But Erin couldn't answer the question for Darin, when she wasn't certain herself. And she knew how important it was to both of them.

She sighed as she peeled herself out of her armor. It was dirty, but the blood that had sunk into parts of the leather was old, and more important, someone else's. The quilted padding was worse; it clung to her as if the sweat of the march were glue. She wanted a bath. And here, at the palace, she was finally likely to get one.

Her robes had been laid out across the bed; they were gray and simple, as befitted an initiate. She wore no other now. In a like wise, her room was small and spare. The bed was narrow and unadorned, and beside it sat a small, squat table. There was a modest wood stove, but no chair, no rug. The door was rectangular and narrow as well, and it closed by simple latch; there was no brass here, no luxury.

Well, that's over.

She dropped her armor into a satisfyingly messy pile, then stopped at the one small window that seemed to have been carved as an afterthought. It faced south.

South and east.

She was cold of a sudden; the logs burning in the stove couldn't take the edge off that chill.

Yes, it was over, but what of it? The shadow loomed in the distance, and while the Empire existed, Marantine would always be a target. Renar would not give the city over again, nor his children, she was certain.

But beyond that, who could say?

She shook her head. The braid rapped gently against her neck, and she began to unwind it in nerveless fingers.

The battles for the villages had gone well; better than any expected. Little of the enemy forces had been left there, and those that remained were easily defeated. But two villages had been razed completely before their enemies had realized that they weren't fighting a retreat; they were being routed. Healing the wounds that they left in land and psyche would be hard.

Even for the Sarillorn. For though she could touch the Bright Heart at will now, His power seemed weaker each time she did so.

And why should it not? The lands were almost entirely in the Dark Heart's hands.

Restless, she began to pace the floor, her bare feet taking the chill of stone and sending it upward. Tomorrow she would make her decision. The council meeting had already been called.

Today she would take a bath.

Acolyte Tentarion brushed his forehead against the stone. His hair traced its cracks the way a broom might. He stood slowly, taking care not to catch the back of his robe with his heels; he'd done that once, and it still humiliated him to think about it.

His cheeks were red as he reached for the real broom. One day, when he was older and his power stronger, he would not be wearing just plain, loose black. He would wear red, like a crown. And no one who'd laughed at him would forget that they'd done it. Not before they died.

They'd die here, too, here in this huge, square room, with its majestic ceilings. They'd be strapped down to the floating black altar; they'd writhe under the rippled edge of Karnari blade; they'd see the frescoes, ancient and admired, that adorned the closed ceiling between its rounded beams.

No. That was too good for them.

The broom scratched against the stone floor in the most irritating way. Soon, though, he'd reach the marble, and it would be quiet.

He walked the room from side to side, stepping carefully between the velvet-covered chairs that served as pews for the rich and the powerful. Tentarion had never been seated among them. His family was too insignificant.

But that would change.

The broom stopped its rhythmic motion as he neared the altar itself. The acolyte's hood rustled furtively as his head moved from side to side. Good. He was alone.

The broom came to rest against the dark, carved wood of

the foremost bench, as Tentarion's young eyes looked with yearning at the altar itself.

It was beautiful as it hovered in midair. All around it his eyes could make out the trace of deep, bright red that held it so miraculously aloft. One day, this would be his.

He walked to it, taking great care to plant his feet silently. His black-booted toes left no trace; there was no dust here, now or ever.

As a matter of course, he spit into the pool that lay beneath it.

Here. He spread his arms wide, his fingers turned around an imaginary blade. The red lines seemed to swirl in anticipation, and his teeth flashed in a smile.

The pews filled with ghosts, each face a mirror of his own. *I summon the Darkness.* His hand came swinging down.

And the Darkness came.

Tentarion took two steps back as it pooled in a cloud over the altar's surface. Suddenly, the pews were empty, and the room itself deathly and chill.

No. No, I didn't mean it!

But the shadows that formed paid him no attention. They gathered, growing in density as they sapped the very heat out of the air. Then they lengthened, a moving, roiling pillar.

Tentarion was no fool. He leaped out of the way, taking little care now to see that his footsteps were silent. The broom he forgot as he raced past, hiking the folds of his robe well above his knees.

The doors swung shut; the air cut past his cheeks, they moved that quickly. Terrified, he turned to face the shadow, his face white, his lips trembling.

And the Darkness wore form, almost human, but too gray. Too lifeless. One limb was raised, one claw pointed at his heart.

"Acolyte."

It was no formality that brought Tentarion to his knees; they would no longer support him.

"Tell the high priest that the First has returned."

chapter
one

The room was silent.

The silence might have been less remarkable in one of the small studies or sitting rooms, but here, in the largest conference hall, it seemed to wait for even the slightest restless movement.

Lord Tiber Beaton's gaze remained firmly fixed on the delicately creased vellum of an intricate map, although he raised one tired hand to massage the back of his neck. He wore family colors, the blues and the reds spun round with hints of gold, but these were no longer crisp or fresh.

For Lord Stenton Cosgrove, the map across the pale wood of the conference table held less interest than the people grouped about it.

Renar, his grandson, in Maran colors, cast a short shadow in the pale gray light of morning that filtered balefully through the windows. Both of his hands gripped the underside of the table. Tiras stood at his side to the left, wearing only black, always black; his bloused sleeves curved around his back. If he was tired, he alone in the room chose not to show it; it was, in Stenton's opinion, disgraceful for a man of his age to be so well composed. He sighed.

The patriarch of Culverne, on the other hand, seemed to be nodding off; he could think of no other reason why the boy's forehead would be nearly plastered to the line staff. This, too, Lord Cosgrove disapproved of, but for less selfish reasons.

If his interest hadn't been caught by the look on Lady Erin's face, he might have said something.

She stood alone, her finger trembling over a web of roads on the map. She wore the robes of her lineage, the hood pulled down to gather around her shoulders. Had he not heard reports of her skills on the field, he might have thought the small sword she bore an emblem of rank. But no, he knew she could make it dance, and the grim set of her lips beneath the tight, severe braid told him she wanted to do so now.

"These," she said at last.

"Lady?"

Her eyes met the king's. "These were Cormont lands."

He thought a moment, then nodded sharply. "Yes."

"And this is the capital?"

"Malakar."

Darin tensed at the sound of the word. Erin noticed it and raised an eyebrow.

"I served there," he said, his voice so soft even Erin had to strain to catch it. There were quieter, deeper scars than the one on his arm. She saw them in his eyes now; she had never asked what caused them.

"Would you go back?" And there was more to that question than the four words she spoke.

"Why?"

She took a deep breath. "If this map is accurate, the Gifting of Lernan is there. The second Wound of God."

Darin's eyes grew wide; those words had an import to the lines that was lost on the gathered nobility.

"What is this Gifting?" Stenton asked.

"Old," she answered. "Old. The lines called upon God through it." Her eyes never left Darin's face. They were very green.

Lord Cosgrove was not a man who liked to be ignored. "Lady?"

"Would you go back?"

"Would you?"

"Lady?"

"Yes?"

"The Gifting?"

She frowned for a moment, and then decided. "The blood of the Bright Heart flows through it. More strongly than it does through either Darin or I; it is as close as one comes to God." She closed her eyes. "If it is in Malakar, Darin should have known of it."

"How?"

"We just feel it. If all is well." Her shoulders slumped

downward. "It's old, Lord Cosgrove, and I think the Enemy has used it to weaken God."

"But if the Bright Heart's blood is so powerful, why didn't he strike out through it?"

"He can't. It's only through us"—she gestured at Darin—"that the blood works."

"And is there much power there?"

"Yes."

Lord Beaton didn't like the direction the conversation was taking without his expert guidance; he chose this moment to correct the absence. "It's not going to do us any good; it's at the heart of the Empire. Might we not think instead on how we continue to hold *our* lands?"

"Tiber." Lord Cosgrove held up one ringed hand. His friend subsided.

Erin smiled bitterly. "No, Lord Beaton, we don't intend to march an army there. We'd never make it through Verdann."

"Not yet," Renar said softly. It had the sound of an old argument, because it was.

She thought of the Empire's Lord. Was he watching somehow? Did he know? Did he prepare even now? "Not ever."

"Two years, and we might have some chance."

"Marantine stood on its own for longer than that." Tiras touched Renar's shoulder. "Not even your great-grandfather would have held out much hope of success. Abandon the plan."

"Great-grandfather didn't have either Erin or Darin at the side of his army."

"And if I am not mistaken," Tiras replied softly, "neither will you."

It amazed Lord Cosgrove that his grandson still had the energy to look so outraged.

"What on earth do you mean by that?" He swiveled and met the uncompromising stiffness of Tiras' face. He turned to look at Darin, who looked almost as surprised as he, Renar, felt.

Last, his gaze fell on Erin. "Lady?"

"If you raised an army, he would come."

"He? Who, he?" When she didn't answer, he turned to Darin. "Do you know who she's talking about?"

It didn't help matters when Darin nodded, equally silent.

"Who is this he, Erin? Who'll come? The high priest?"

"The Lord of the Empire." She answered at last.

"Lord of the—" He stopped, thought a moment. "That's a title I've only heard once or twice. In Malakar."

"It is not a title the high priest holds."

"It isn't a title that's used in any practical way as far as I can tell." He shrugged. "And if it is, so what?"

"The Lord of the Empire is the First Servant of Malthan. Nightwalker. Stefanos . . ."

The meeting had adjourned in uneasy silence and exhaustion. Lord Cosgrove and Lord Beaton had retired to their estates; Erin, Tiras, Darin, and Renar returned to the rooms they now kept in the castle.

They slept, deeply and fitfully and dreamlessly.

Erin woke short hours afterward and sat up in bed, her knees beneath her chin. In the last week, no dreams of darkness had touched her; she had not set foot in the dark plains. In the beginning this might have brought her peace, but now—

Stefanos had returned. She knew it. Somehow, he had become the bridge between her world and his God's. The bridge was gone, and there was only one place for it to go. When she thought on it, she could still feel the lingering echoes of his pain call. And that pain no longer existed there. The five who were trapped could no longer be touched by what little light she could bring them.

They waited for freedom.

She rose, casting blankets aside.

They waited for the freedom she had promised them.

In the darkness she found her night robe and wrapped it around her body, belting it tightly. Starlight flickered through the window, distorted by the thick glass, frozen in the night as the five were frozen.

Her forehead pressed against the glass.

I don't want to die. Even now, she could not say the words aloud. The uneasy anger that had grown over the months surfaced here, and she grimaced bitterly. *Bright Heart, for the first time that I can remember, I* don't *want to die.*

Maybe it would have been better to remain a child. The road would be clearer, easier to follow. Her long fingers pressed tightly into her palms; both palms were cold.

The villages were free now; Marantine could stand without her. Isn't that why she'd stayed? Hadn't they needed her help? Might they not still need it in the years to come?

Yes.

But every day that she stayed—every day that she lived—Belfas was trapped in a darkness that ate away at his soul. He had no Bridge to walk across, no Beyond, no peace.

She saw the map almost clearly. She knew that the Gifting of God, polluted and vile as it had certainly become, waited for the blood that would cleanse it.

And around it, Malakar grew like a shell, waiting to be broken. If she could reach the Gifting, she could call the power of the Bright Heart more strongly than she had ever called it at the castle.

She could cleanse the city of the Dark Heart's taint.

She shivered.

I will burn there, she thought. Only once before had she touched the Bright Heart, and that once would have killed her if not for Darin and Bethany's voices.

I will burn there, as Gallin burned.

Death by fire; the white, not the red.

She saw the stars, saw the map, saw the road before her, and knew what she had to do.

Yet one week later, she still dwelled in Dagothrin.

Lord Stenton Cosgrove watched her in the eastern courtyard as she drilled her new recruits. He was not a man easily pleased by anything, but the sight of her, in the gray tunic and leggings that she wore only here, was enough to draw a smile from him. Her voice carried; it was hard to imagine that so small and delicate a woman could have such a cruel tongue, such a loud contempt. It reminded him of his own training; he must be getting old to find nostalgia in that.

"Yes, she's good."

"Tiras." The smile fell into Lord Cosgrove's usual mild frown. With meticulous care, he stood back from the iron-wrought railing and straightened out the pale green and blue of his jacket.

"Stenton." Tiras still wore black. The only time he had given it up was during the abominable reign of the traitor, and this because of the insistence of the Church. He was a stubborn man, but not a stupid one.

Lord Cosgrove turned his attention back to the drill. It was odd; she had built a circle out of small stones, and the style of fighting she chose was her own; light and quick. Better for the time, though; the armorers had work enough for the next two years, and any who could wear leathers and gain advantage were to be prized.

He thought her also diplomatic, if perhaps too retiring, in the councils that had been called; her advice to Renar was solid, and the esteem the army held her in valuable. Indeed, she was an asset, this young woman.

"Put the thought aside, Stenton."

Annoyed, Lord Cosgrove turned again and realized that he was leaning over the rail. "Tiras, is there something you wish to speak with me about, or are you just trying to be annoying?"

Tiras raised an eyebrow, deliberating. There was no jester's face here; no pompous exclamation or appearance of wounded vanity. They knew each other too well. He folded his hands behind his back, a sure sign that he expected an argument.

"It is on the matter of two evenings past that I wish to speak."

"Two evenings ago?" Lord Cosgrove's thick brows drew down in genuine confusion. "The victory celebration?" At Tiras' nod, he said, "Why?"

"The dress she wore, was it Lady Verena's?"

"It was Verena's choice, yes. Why?"

"And the dances chosen, oddly, were Maran."

"The king knows them. Why?"

"The Lady Erin danced with him; you seemed pleased by it."

"Yes. I fail to understand the line of questioning, Tiras. Did it displease you?"

Again, the old man nodded, the movement economical.

"Why should she not dance? It takes the years off her face. She's a young woman, too caught in the ways of war. Were it not for her, we might still be conquered. We owe her this." He could still see clearly the clean, fresh blush on her face, the way her steps, so hesitant to begin with, had grown under Renar's guidance and encouragement. Her eyes had sparkled, but oddest of all was her laugh. It could barely be heard over the din of music and the susurrus of muted conversation, but he remembered it because it was the first time—the only time—that he had yet heard it.

It brought back the dead.

"Ah," Tiras said softly, "and this is the only reason you now watch her at drill?"

Canny, that man. Lord Cosgrove drew himself up. "No."

"Forget about it, Stenton."

"Renar needs a queen," Lord Cosgrove shot back. "Marantine needs his heirs, and quickly."

"I do not argue this point."

"Then you will not argue that Renar is always difficult, head-strong, and apt to be poor at judgment in these matters. We cannot just choose a likely candidate between ourselves for the boy; he would certainly veto it on principle if nothing else. He likes this young woman, this Erin. She likes him; that's obvious to anyone with eyes. He needs a queen that will give him the respect of his armies and his people."

"She is poor in her understanding of statecraft."

"She will learn that."

"Not here."

"And who would you suggest? Tiber's granddaughter? Lilya of Tannisset? There are not many who begin to be as suitable as the lady." He smiled, but it was not a genial one. "I believe if we put this forward to Renar, he would not be too intransi-gent."

Tiras was silent a moment, and then he bowed his head. "I like her, too," he said quietly.

"We are both becoming old men," Stenton replied. "I see the shadows growing in her eyes, on her face. I think not of Cosgrove in this, and not, in the end, of Renar."

That surprised Tiras, the more so because it was the truth. He reached out and gripped the railing firmly in both of his weathered hands.

"Even if Renar would accept the suggestion, I fear the Lady Erin would not. The shadows you see are there, Stenton, and aimed toward Malakar. She has not spoken of all that she knows. I fear that the Lord of the Empire is not so distant a figure to her."

"Yes," Stenton replied, surprising Tiras again. "I also feel this to be true. But here—"

"She would find no safety, not of the type that you hope. She is not your child, Stenton, not like the former queen, ex-cept in this: She will choose her own path, and she will face the consequence of it."

"I see. Have you spoken to Renar of this?"

"He is part Cosgrove," Tiras answered wryly. "He sees much."

"Erin."

Erin looked up from the desk she was working at. Her eyes were ringed with shadow; lack of sleep had taken its toll. The shadows of the flickering oil-lamp highlighted the gauntness of her cheeks as she worked, quill in hand.

Renar stood in the doorway, holding a similar lamp aloft. He wore the raiment of the kings of Marantine; even the circlet glimmered between strands of his dark hair.

"No, you are not the only one to be caught working late." He smiled, but the smile itself was weary. "Haven't we done this before, Lady? No, I forget myself. It was you who came to me, and not I who came to you."

She seemed to shrink inward, her elbows pressing themselves into the leather padding of the large, rectangular desk. The robe of the lines looked awkwardly oversized as it gathered in wrinkles that spoke of its age.

He never quite knew how to feel around her; whether older and wiser, younger and less experienced, protective or in need of the protection she offered.

To acknowledge this, he lifted a hand and removed the circlet from his forehead.

"It's too damned confining anyway," he added, although he knew she asked no explanation. He took a few quick steps across the red, bordered carpet, his feet still light; the training that Tiras had given would never be lost.

Over her shoulders he could see the names that she'd written in her delicate, spidery hand. Road names, city names. He knew them well; had traveled them often in the years past. At the end of that list was Malakar.

She smiled up weakly, and he knew that tonight she was in need of protection; that was the mantle he would wear. It was the most difficult.

"Erin."

"I was just—I've been studying—this is the road that seems . . ." Her voice trailed off, and she set the quill aside carefully. There were no curled up sheets of parchment, no blotches on the desk, no signs of the frustrations that his own servants had become familiar with. But he knew that hers was the greater difficulty. Her hands came up to her lips, and she pressed her head against them.

She was waiting for words. He was always the better with them.

"You're going to Malakar."

"What other choice do I have?"

She hadn't precisely answered his question; this didn't escape his notice. He set the lamp aside and watched it spray shadows across the room, thinking of the last time they had talked this way, with this light, in a different room.

Her eyes seemed brown in the dim light. They searched his, wanting an answer, any answer, any other choice.

She was afraid, in the peculiar way that only she could be. Those who fought with her never saw it; those who were healed by her hand never dreamed of it; those who argued with her in council didn't think of it—but it was there.

No man, no woman, lived without fear. And if the fear did not come out in the ordinary things, it must come out somewhere. In the darkness, in nights like these ones.

"You don't want to go to Malakar." It was not a question.

"No." She shook her head, bitterness mingling with a smile that came out wrong. "So much for nobility. So much for self-lessness."

"What do you mean?"

She didn't even raise her head to meet his eyes. Bad sign, that.

I don't want to face him, Renar. And I don't want to die. Both answers would require explanations that she didn't have the energy or the desire to give.

He sighed and bent over her as if to protect her from the past that paled her face.

"Then stay, Erin. Darin needs your guidance here; he's learning to cope with his magery, but not with the politics of his position.

"The army needs the advice you give; General Lorrence speaks highly of you, and his words are outdone by any who serve in a unit you've led.

"And I, Lady, even I might need you a little. Who else would I dance with?"

She looked up then. He had never seen her look so small. Her hands were trembling.

"Do you know," he said lightly, as if to amuse her, "that there's even been talk of making you queen?"

Slapping her would have been better. Her hands curled into fists; her eyelashes trembled against her cheek.

"Erin—it isn't serious."

She shook her head.

"I'm sorry, Lady. I said it because I thought it would amuse you."

She turned away, showing him the dark glint of warrior braid.

Realization came to him then as if it were new, although he had thought it many times. There was very little that he knew about Erin's past.

Her distance invoked the laws of strangers meeting as if for the second or third time: There were questions one could not ask, no matter how tactfully put or how well meant.

He had no mask to give her.

Very carefully he laid one hand against her shoulder. She stiffened, but did not turn.

"Erin." Knowing it was inadequate, he slid his arms around her and held her bent back awkwardly against his chest. She was cold. "Don't be afraid."

The streets were busy, alive with the hint of spring. Carts moved along the main street, pulled by large horses whose ankles were only starting to shed their overlong fur. People bustled from place to place, stopping occasionally to unfasten buttons on their coats. It was warm, and a brisk walk did much to add to it.

Erin moved through the changing crowd as if she were invisible. She too wore a thick, padded coat, this of wool. It was dark, to catch the sun, and not remarkable; she had borrowed it from one of the castle servants.

The rest of her clothing, gray pants and a white bloused shirt, she had pillaged from Renar's less-ostentatious drawers. The boots were all that remained of her usual city wear.

Even her hair was different; it hung loosely about her shoulders and brushed against her down-turned face.

She didn't want to be recognized.

Two months, nearer three now, had made the city less alien and frightening; the buildings that towered over her in the narrow streets seemed stone trees and hedges; they were no longer remarkable and did not pull her attention from her destination.

The people did.

Out of the corner of her eye, she saw a child slip on the ice, heard his little yelp, and saw the way two others, man and woman, rushed to lift him. An old man, hair white and coarse, roamed by with a thunderous scowl, followed closely by an equally elderly woman whose face bore angry resignation. There, across the walk, a young couple strolled, hand in hand. They paused for a moment, and she heard the low sound of his laughter as clearly as if the crowd had hushed to catch it. He put his arms around the young woman's shoulders, and her laughter echoed his.

She wondered if they were rited, and marveled that the war hadn't scarred what they felt.

But it was spring in the city, the first spring that had touched it in over five years. Everywhere, life went on; normal life, touched by a hope that had been realized.

She could not remember Rennath ever being so. But then, in Rennath she had never walked the city streets so openly; Stefanos had always forbidden it.

Stefanos . . .

She looked around at the buildings; they were not so fine or so clean as those in Rennath; some were still scarred by the fires. But there were colorful curtains in some and plants along the shuttered edges of windows.

In two months, Dagothrin had become home, as much home as Elliath had once been—maybe more so, although she couldn't say why. Maybe it was because she could dance with Renar.

There's even been talk of making you queen.

Queen. That would mean riting.

Her unadorned hands were an accusation. Stefanos must have taken the ring. As he had taken everything else.

Everything? No. Only what she had given.

Stefanos . . .

She shook her head, allowing her gaze to be drawn outward again by the life that moved like a river along the streets. She felt herself moving against that current and wanted to be a part of it; to follow it from beginning to end.

I could never be queen. I can't even rule myself.

And yet, for a while, she had chosen to be empress. For her

people. The slaves of the Empire. They would never walk the streets like this; never have a life of their own.

Air filled her lungs, cold and crisp. She was almost upon the merchant quarters.

"Erin! Don't stand outside in the cold, dear. Do come in!" Hildy's smile was genuine as she moved herself out of the door, giving Erin just enough room to sidle into the vestibule.

"It isn't that cold; the sun's warm."

Hildy snorted. "You're young, that's what it is. When you're my age, dear, you'll think on it differently."

Erin smiled and didn't mention the fact that many of the people who walked outside were easily older than the merchant.

"Have you come for tea, dear? I've seen you and the young man so seldom since the incident."

Always the young man. Never the king. Erin rolled her jacket off her shoulders and allowed Hildy to take it and stow it against the wall.

"Well, we're back for a little while yet, and I thought I'd visit."

Hildy's eyebrow rose shrewdly. "A little visit like the last time?"

The Sarillorn of Elliath blushed crimson.

"Don't you mind my teasing. Come on, I've tea almost ready. You picked an intelligent time in the afternoon to come. Did you walk, dear?"

"Yes."

"Brave. I can't stand the cold myself."

Erin followed Hildy into the small, cosy parlor. A fire was burning in the brick-framed fireplace, and the chairs, all three, had been brought into a semicircle around it. She took a chair, and Hildy did the same, pouring clear, brown liquid and asking her usual solicitous questions.

And then she stopped speaking. The fire crackled in happy silence as Erin searched for the words to say. Hildy watched, but had no intention of helping her.

"Hildy, are you planning to leave?"

"Leave?"

"Leave Dagothrin. I mean, on merchant business."

"Ah." Hildy set her cup down with a sigh. "I was afraid that might be why you came without the young man.

"Are you leaving, dear?"

Erin nodded quietly. "I thought—I thought, if you still took ore out, that you might have room for a guard. I noticed that Hamin and a few of the others are posted at the palace now."

Hildy looked thoughtful. "Where would you be going?"

"Malakar."

"I see." She bent, which was difficult, and began to stir imaginary sugar into her tea with one of her grandmother's frilly silver spoons. "I don't suppose that you'd be open to being talked out of this journey?"

"If you could, I'd be happy." She meant every word.

"More private business, then."

"Yes."

"Well. Well, then." Her brown eyes were sharp and clear. "My caravan only goes so far as Landsfall."

Erin ticked off the distance on her mental map and frowned. Halfway. But it was better than nothing. She nodded.

"And I've not got all of my messages back yet—it's been a little more difficult, although I'll still bless you for it, since the takeover." She lifted porcelain to unsmiling lips. "But there are two houses that've made money off the mines here, and they'll keep trading as long as there are merchants willing.

"Yes, dear, I could use another guard."

"Three days." Darin looked down at the staff that lay across his folded legs. He bit his lip, spread his palms, and conjured fire. It grew easily, crackling against the air and against the restraints of Darin's will. Trapped thus, it flowered, trembling like a blossom in the breeze.

He gestured, and the fire died, leaving his hands cool and empty.

Frowning, he started the more difficult task. He raised his head and focused on the curtains that shrouded the windows of his room. They were a deep, royal blue, although they'd faded; Renar told him these particular rooms had not seen much use in the last several years.

He hadn't asked who they belonged to.

Fold by fold he began to gather the curtains together, both at once. It was hard; much harder than standing and crossing the length of the room would have been. But he caught them, his brow creasing slightly as he began to bind them. Light, and the blue of the open sky, sang in.

His shoulders slumped.

"Three days."

And are you ready, Initiate?

"I don't know." He called fire again, but only because it was easier; it didn't prove anything.

The city, his city, lay outside; doors were opening and closing; market stalls were being set up. The building of a circle over the rough-hewn boundaries of a square had only just been completed.

Line Culverne was gone; its lands had been taken by the Church, and although reclaimed, they would never again be what they had been. Too much had passed. But the city itself was still here.

Five short years ago, he had been so certain he would never see it again.

Do you understand what the Sarillorn will attempt?

"Yes." He stood, allowing his robes to fall to the floor. "I just wish it didn't have to be Malakar." The word still made him cringe. Although most of his dead lay here, the one that slept most poorly was etched into stone and crest in the capital.

She has said that she will journey alone.

Darin snorted, half-angry. "Bethany, why don't you just tell me what you want me to do?"

I cannot decide that for you.

He snorted again and crawled up on the bed, shoving the counterpane aside.

"I have to go with her."

Bethany was silent.

"But what if we fail? What if we die? What happens to the lines then?"

Silence again. He hadn't really expected her to answer. Propping himself up against one of the canopy posts, he continued. "And what if we can't find the Gifting?"

If you succeed, Initiate, the Empire will almost certainly fail.

"I know. I know all that." He sighed. "I just don't know if I can help much. I still can't wield a sword to save my life— never mind hers. I can barely tell direction; I can't really forage; and I'm not supposed to use the mage-craft because it'll give us away.

"I don't know why she wants me to go."

This is the work of the lines, and there are only two left.

He nodded quietly. He had already decided, after all.

* * *

The air was stale. Smoke lingered in its still folds, as did sweat and the smell of too much ale. Conversation, punctuated by the occasional shout and laugh, made it hard to think.

Which was what Renar wanted.

He leaned forward, letting the elbows on the counter carry most of his weight, and glared balefully at his personal guard. Six men, covered head to toe in the regalia of Marantine, stood at a stiff sort of ease that was entirely out of place in the Happy Carp. They didn't move out of the way of anyone coming or leaving, and they didn't allow anyone to get too close. Twice this evening, they'd seen to the death of a promising brawl merely by pulling their swords and wading into the rectangular room that housed the card tables.

"Look, lads," Renar said, for perhaps the eighteenth time, "I think I'm fine here. Why don't you run along home?"

They affected not to have heard him, and his head sank more heavily into his hands as he stared at the half-empty mug under his nose. No lace trailed from his jacket; indeed the jacket itself was a drab brown and white that hung just below his hips. His pants were rough twill, and his boots the type that the lower city markets excelled at dumping on the unwary. His fingers were bare; his brow unfettered. All in all, he'd dressed quite well for the occasion, leaving all pretentions of royalty well behind.

He turned and favored the six royal guards with a glare that slid off them. Almost all pretensions. Somehow, Lorrence and Gerald would pay for this. Very sourly, he downed the mug and thumped it on the counter, empty.

"You could at least," he said over his shoulder, "have a drink. That *is* what a tavern is for."

"Not on duty, sir."

Renar was certain that by the end of the evening his teeth would be ground flat.

"Have another, sir?"

He looked up; the voice sounded suspiciously familiar.

He almost hit his nose on Cospatric's smile, which was a mixture of friendliness—overstated, at that—and malice.

"Yes."

"Very good, sir. Belten—another of the same. But watch his tab."

"Quiet place you've got here," Renar said, his smile much less friendly.

"Aye, sir. Suits the clientele." He nodded briskly at the guards. Walked down the length of the bar. Stopped.

And burst out laughing.

"I suppose this should be good for business—can I get permission to work the Maran crown into the outside sign? Royal approval."

"You lousy son of a whore," Renar muttered, gaining his feet. He wobbled slightly, and the crowd stilled, watching the guards that only a few had associated directly with him.

"Language, sir." Cospatric wiped his eyes. "Set an example, won't you?" But he came strolling back, an ale in either hand. "On the house, your majesty. I haven't had a laugh like this in years."

Conversation resumed, perhaps a little disappointed in tone. Hard to tell. Hard to care.

"Like the place?"

Renar snorted.

"Ah well. Better for me." Cospatric lifted his own mug in a large hand and tilted it back. "What brings you here?"

"Your smiling face."

"In a snit, are we?"

"Cospatric . . ."

The smile didn't leave the tavern owner's face, but it softened. "Problems at home?"

"Problems?" The other half of the glass disappeared. "No. What on earth makes you say that?" Tin hit the counter as Renar nodded at Belten. "I'm stuck in Marantine while my best two counselors go off on a cross-Empire trek like so many babes in the woods. I'm left to deal with the army, the religion, the family squabbles, the state, and enough paper to fire the city for three years. But problems? Hells, this is nothing."

Cospatric's smile completely dimmed. "Worried, then? I haven't talked with Tiber or Stent in a week. What's up?"

"The lady is leaving in three days."

chapter
two

The shadow danced in the twilight that blanketed Malakar. It moved, leaving the faintest trace of red to encompass all, shimmering over the swell of the Torvallen River to the north, spreading long fingers through the narrow streets of the free workers. From there, it stretched on, unfurling like a dying flower to touch the Upper City. Guards on duty in the Upper Merchants Quarter drew themselves up as it passed them, leaving a chill in the air.

Only to the southeast, in the High City, did blood respond to its call; the nobles were waking and watchful. Some eyes could even see the fading film that covered everything before dissipating. They thought it the work of the Church; some were concerned, some pleased, as the politics of the time dictated. Both were wrong.

The Second of the Sundered surveyed the city from the highest spire of the temple of his Lord. No arrogance forced him to the heights; he was not one for gestures of grandeur. It wasted his time, and although eternity stretched out before him, he had always hoarded each moment for his studies.

No; the spire was chosen because it rested at the exact center of this mortal city. Darkness moved as he gestured, melting into the living—and the dead—in the same way. He felt the moon, at its nadir, inch across the sky. It had moved so for each of the twelve nights he had worked here. This would be the last.

After this eve, no power, not even his own, would pierce the veil that lay over Malakar. The spell, twelve days in the making, and months in the creation, had been cast; he was exhausted, but almost satisfied. Like a human mirror, the

23

darkness and blood-spell that could touch the Light—could sense it, could trace it, could identify it—was now reflected inward, returning emptiness to the searcher. No Darkness would touch the light that burned—he could see it so clearly—in the city of Dagothrin.

Let that Light call to Light; let it invoke its pathetic Heart—not even the First would be able to sense it. The Sarillorn would be dead to him, as promised; he would never find her, never sense her presence—should he even think to look. Of the two of them, Sargoth had always been the more deft of the blood-mages; the more subtle. The game would be ready. The net was closing; the last link of chain was in place.

The plan was almost perfect; if not for her ill-timed ward, cast so unexpectedly at the end of the battle for Dagothrin, there would be no question of its success.

Stefanos believed his Empire to be under threat. For that reason, he had returned for war. He would win, for his power was greater than any other being's, save God. He would fight, never knowing who his opponent truly was.

She would come here, to the Wound of the Bright Heart, while Stefanos gathered his human army. And only her death would make it clear, for only her death would undo the complicated spell that now masked her presence. When she died, as Sargoth's Lord had planned, Stefanos would understand all.

Yet he hesitated, as the wind passed around him, shunning his presence. The Light had not moved. Surely, surely the woman that wielded it would be drawn to Malakar; did it not rest on the festering Wound of the Enemy?

Yes; it must happen so. Or God's game would not reach its end. And if there was no end to the game that the Dark Heart had decreed, there would be no end to the service of the Second.

He was aware of the bond that cemented her inimical blood to the blood of the First Sundered. Had he not been instrumental in so great a magic? He knew and knew well that she could linger forever in Dagothrin, aging as the First did: Not at all. And he would be trapped here should she so choose unknowing, in the mortal plane.

Wind called him with its angry rush of voice, its mindless whisper. And water, deep and dark, swirled at memory. These and many other gates awaited his discovery.

Come, Sarillorn.

The darkness slammed shut atop the sleeping city.
We are waiting.

Stefanos gestured, and the last of the large stone bricks fell away. His eyes were dying silver in the darkness as they surveyed the rooms that he had carved out in short days. No light touched them; they were well underground. As his old rooms had been in Rennath, these were carefully sculpted wells in which the shadow could gather in comfort. The floors were smooth now; they would soon be cold, black marble.

He stepped back, looking carefully at his handiwork. Long had it been since he had built, but this, this would be the final time; of this he felt certain. Mortal foibles might enter here; his throne perhaps, and an altar no less fine than the one the priests commanded above. But for now, this would do.

"It is primitive work, Stefanos."

The First of the Sundered stiffened. Without turning, he said, "My orders on isolation here were clear."

"Ah. I had assumed they applied to the mortals." The marked sibilance of Sargoth's voice was muted and softer than it once had been.

"Do you seek to challenge me, Second?"

"Not I, Lord," Sargoth whispered. "Not I."

Stefanos turned, pulling shadow with him. No other eyes but Sargoth's would have seen the gray pallor of skin and the sharp points of teeth in this light. There was no mortal guise, here. There would be no mortal guise ever again. The time had passed.

Abiding fury and suspicion sparked in the red of Stefanos's eyes. An intricate net took form and shape around him. For a moment it resembled armor, but this too was a human conceit, a habit of long years. He needed no "armor" for this, the greeting of a king to a respected but ill-loved general. Thus had the Servants spoken for time immemorial.

"Why have you come?"

"To watch, First among us. To satisfy my curiosity." Sargoth's voice was carefully neutral. His words died in the silence, and after careful moments, he spoke again. "Will you stay in the mortal world, among the mortal cattle?"

"For a time."

"Ah. And do they still hold mystery for you? They are—more strange than I thought."

"They hold no mystery." The words were sharp. "I will rule them; they will follow me. That is all." The shadow shifted around him; the red blazed bright. "Walk with care, Second; speak with more. You tread a thin edge."

Sargoth knew it well. "I have followed your command in all things, Stefanos, save when the dictate of our Lord countermands it." His shields came up, amorphous and pale with disuse. "I have no interest in ruling."

It was true; it was the only reason the Second had never been considered enough of a threat to destroy. It was not as a threat that Stefanos considered his destruction now.

"You alone of our number have resisted His call for long," Sargoth said; it was almost an apology.

"Yes." He was silent a moment before making his decision. "But we have no conflict now. Leave, Sargoth. If you wish to satisfy your curiosity, do so, but stay out of my sight for a time."

Sargoth bowed. "At your command." But his shields remained in place as he drifted out of the rooms.

The burst hit him squarely; his shadow broiled in chaos a moment as his shields absorbed what they could.

"I do not forget," Stefanos said softly to the darkness, to the Dark.

Sargoth left then, and quickly. All things considered, this was better than he might have hoped for. His power, however, had been weakened; he tested the spells he had laid around the temple gingerly, as if they might break.

They were weak indeed. But they held; no glimmer of Lernari light would reach this citadel.

He wondered, as he graced the halls with his shadow, what the First would do if his spell was dropped. Would he search for the woman? Would he find her?

And if he did find her, what would his reaction be?

What would hers?

The questions played at his thoughts, dragging them in a dangerous direction. His hunger to know caused the spell to ripple.

No. God's word was clear; his work clearer.

He raised his spectral head in annoyance. More time had been spent in curiosity than he thought; the dawn was scant hours off. He would have to feed quickly, and poorly, to maintain the power necessary.

* * *

The doors rolled open, and the din of argument filtered out into the hall. It died, but less quickly than usual—not a good sign.

Lord Vellen stepped into the room, nodding at the Swords on either door. They saluted crisply and left. Council meetings such as these were the one place where the guard was not allowed.

The months that had passed had strengthened him. The wounds that the light had left had healed, and the scars, internal, were now invisible to any eyes save his own. He walked with the strength of the high seat; he was, once again, the leader of the Greater Cabal. But the journey to Mordantari had cost him greatly, and the fact that the woman and the boy still lived—and worse—made his rule tentative.

Around the ironwood table, the twelve Karnar of the Greater Cabal sat. They wore their black and red, but three, Benataan of Torvallen, Cortani of Abranthraxus, and Morden of Farenel, had chosen this day to dispense with the formality of hood and sash.

Lord Vellen chose not to acknowledge this; the moment was not right. Instead, he walked to the empty chair at the head of the table and took his seat. Until four days ago, that chair, with its rigid, dark frame, velvet back, and gold detailing, had been the throne from which the Empire was ruled.

What power did it hold now?

Vellen was aware that he was soon to find out.

"You're late," Benataan said casually. He leaned back into his own chair, the picture of casually afforded derision. His ringed hands were carefully folded against his broad chest, his eyes half-lidded brown. Like Vellen, he was a younger man; his hair had only started to gray at the temples.

"I had matters of state to attend to."

"Damion's state?" Cortani asked softly. Vellen noted that his glance strayed to Benataan. Noted the nod that that lord returned.

He glanced around at the rest of the Karnar. Ansellen of Urturas was the only one who would meet his eyes for long, but he expected no help from that quarter; although Ansellen owed his rank to Vellen, he was old now, and the time for his retirement would come soon. No others spoke, but he expected little else; that was not the way of the Karnari.

Morden and Cortani posed little problem; they were teeth that moved with Benataan's mouth. But he stared long at Morden. Morden's shoulders eventually slumped, but slightly. He did not look to Benataan for guidance.

This was better than Vellen expected, but still worse than he had hoped for. "Damion's concerns are not mine. I am not the lord of the house."

"Nor, it would seem, the Lord of the Empire." Cortani's sneer was too self-satisfied. Had House Abranthraxus not been so powerful a block, Cortani would not be among the Karnar. Vellen cursed house loyalty silently.

"That," he said, with just a hint of anger, "was never a title of the Greater Cabal." He too leaned back, his pose almost identical to the one Benataan had adopted. "But you bring us to the point of the meeting I have called."

"Good; we all have matters more important to attend to," Cortani said. Silence greeted his words; not even Benataan spoke.

Vellen's eyes flashed silver for a moment; his hands gripped the armrests of his chair. Then the magery subsided as his anger cooled to ice. He looked carefully at the sunken lines of Cortani's brow, troubling himself to hide his anger.

Cortani's pale hair was neatly coiffed around a face that looked almost gaunt. But his eyes caught the high priest's attention. They were slate gray, but even from here the pupils looked distended.

Sarylweed. House Benataan controlled a majority of the supply that reached the capital.

Lord Vellen smiled gently. It was an unpleasant expression. Sarylweed was addictive, dangerously so, and the course it ran was almost always fatal. He had only to bide his time, and ten of the Karnar would be his.

Even so, Cortani's comment could not be allowed to pass without an answer. His eyes silvered again, fading almost instantly as Cortani gave a shout that was mingled fear and pain. Fire trailed the edge of his face, leaving a red mark in its wake.

"This once, Cortani," Vellen said quietly, "I will not allow the fires to feed." He waited; no one challenged him. "If you have more important matters to attend to, perhaps you have not the time to continue to sit in the council of the Karnari."

The words with which Cortani replied might have blistered the ears of a soldier.

"Cortani!" Benataan cursed. He was embarrassed, a fact not lost on the rest of the council. The man who let sarylweed speak with his voice was a great fool indeed. The man who allied himself with such a one was almost more so.

"If you have finished, High Priest?" Vellen didn't wait for Cortani's reply; it was inconsequential. "I have been requested to present you with the Lord of the Empire's new orders."

"Orders?" Benataan's voice was neutral.

"Indeed, Second. The east wing is no longer ours to inhabit. Should we require the Lord's presence or decision, we may take our message to the grand hall there. If it is urgent, we may descend to the lower levels. Under no circumstance are we to enter the rooms that are being constructed there."

"We?"

"None but the high priests of the Greater Cabal are given access at all."

"So we're to be errand runners for this—this—"

"Cortani." Benataan again, but this time under control. "Be silent. We like it no more than you."

"We're the Karnari! We don't carry messages like groveling acolytes!"

Sorval of Kintassus leaned forward, his elbow brushing black and red along the tabletop. "Cortani," he said with weary contempt, "enough. Lord Vellen, what or who is the Lord of the Empire?"

"Ah. I'd forgotten the briefness of your tenure here. He is the First of the Dark Heart's Servants. The First of the Sundered."

"The Sundered . . . What other orders?"

"The sacrifices of the quarters will be his domain."

Cortani was almost apoplectic; everyone else was silent. Even Benataan.

"The Church?"

"We will run it, as always." *For now.*

"Slaves?"

"Again, as usual."

"Merchant interests?" Tirvale of Wintare spoke slowly, and in the irritating nasal fog that spun the words from his jowls.

"Not yet decided."

"It seems, Karnar, that you preside over the dismantling of the Greater Cabal."

"That is not my intention," Vellen replied evenly. "But the First Sundered cannot be ignored."

"Can he be fought?" This from Telemach of Mordani.

Thank you, Telemach. The leader of the Greater Cabal reached into his robes and pulled out a thin sheaf of vellum. "This is the information that I have been able to obtain about his powers and his weaknesses. I leave it for the council—the complete council—to determine the answer to that."

Sargoth watched from the gallery of the hall. The galleries were very high above the table, and the chairs recessed, but he chose to stand. A pity that the meeting was private; he had no doubt that one or another of these half bloods would be quite annoyed about the deaths of the guards.

Not that he couldn't have faded in and merged with the shadows cast by the cavernous ceiling, but if he had chosen near-mortal locomotion, the half-blood guards should never have questioned him. They had been removed for future considerations.

Curiosity had not brought him here; he knew the Malanthi well enough by now to know that their words would be of conquest, conflict, and death. They took poorly to being ruled and even more poorly to losing power that they thought theirs by right.

They had pathetically short little lives, to lose sight so of the First Sundered.

Lord Vellen spoke, and Sargoth stopped his drifting. What was he saying?

"Should you so choose, I'm afraid I would have to step down from my position as leader of the Greater Cabal." A thin sheen of perspiration made his hands clammy as they lay quiet against the tabletop. But his face was schooled well; it was still, and the ice of his eyes gave nothing away.

The murmuring rushed around the table like a gale, but Vellen was in the eye of the storm; not touched by it, yet not apart from it either.

"Yes!" Cortani shouted, his wrinkled face rather red. Vellen wanted to prolong the meeting to see how far the weed had taken effect. It would be both instructive and amusing. "If he can't protect our interests with his 'magery' we should get rid of him!" One shaking hand stretched across the table, a long finger pointed in the direction of Vellen's chest.

Lord Vellen treated that remark with the respect it was due; he refused to acknowledge it. Instead, his eyes moved around the table, starting from left to right.

Lord Benataan of Torvallen stared down the length of his hawklike face; he was silent, his expression a mixture of anticipation and mistrust. Cortani was already tugging at his sleeve like a pathetic slave. Much of the battle between House Torvallen and House Damion had been won in the Greater Cabal at Benataan's expense. Vellen knew what type of death he would receive should Benataan emerge victorious from this newest of their struggles.

Michaelas of Corcassus and Corvair of Andrellius were exchanging looks and muted words. Michaelas' thin face looked hollow now, all dark brown eyes. Corvair, heavier in set, looked no less pale.

Good; these two were his.

Morden, sandwiched between Telemach and Sorval, was holding his own little court. He was old, but handsome by Empire standards. He was ambitious, and not without persuasive power. Lord Vellen noted the quiet response of Telemach and the less reticent nod of Sorval. One more.

Jael of Tirassus, his round, smooth head catching the light and showing his nervousness, said nothing as he tried to catch and keep Lord Vellen's attention, and failed. Jael was of no concern one way or the other; he warmed a seat; he voted to order. Still, four.

Ah, Dramathan of Valens. One of the oldest houses in the Empire. Grim and dour, he also chose silence as a reply to Lord Vellen's pronouncement. But there was no anticipation on his face, no shock—just cynical skepticism. Dramathan was an old friend and an old adversary, both of which were due to his intelligence and perception. He was dangerous; it was hard to tell which way he would fall.

Tirvale, rotund and sweating profusely as usual, was an easy target for either side: Benataan's or his own. He was of the Karnari, but his interests were almost wholly of House Wintare; whoever could promise more to the merchant family lines would hold him.

Ansellen of Urturas was old, which was a pity. He was also

an oddity—one of the few Karnar who could accept and acknowledge a debt. Were this crisis to have occurred years past,
Ansellen could be counted on. But his retirement was soon,
and he had no wish to end up on the altars as payment for his
years of service.

Marek of Grimfaxos, to Vellen's right, nodded quietly as
they locked eyes. Marek was also dangerous because of his intelligence, but he never ended up on the bottom. Count six,
perhaps—if he could be convinced of Vellen's ability to retain,
or regain, the seat that he proposed to lose.

In an expressionless silence, Vellen damned the First of the
Sundered.

Well, at least this was interesting, if mortal affairs could be
called so. Although these mortals, robed in black with hints of
red that proclaimed their muddied heritage, bore no resem-
blance to his own brethren, Sargoth found himself watching
with an interest no less keen than Lord Vellen's. This politicking was a form of power struggle less raw, but perhaps no
less deadly, than Stefanos himself might have engaged in.

He marked Cortani almost carelessly as one who fit the marble altar. He was loud and stupid; Stefanos had never tolerated
either.

Nor had he ever willingly tolerated the interference of the
priests. And the Karnar that led the Greater Cabal had been in
some wise responsible for the loss of his lady.

Which was a pity. For although Sargoth had no desire to
stand in Stefanos' path, he needed at least one human—the one
in charge. Although he had spent months in the company of
mortals, there was much he did not understand, and too many
ways for information to make its way to the First.

Benataan of Torvallen, perhaps?

But no, no. That one was too foolish. Not so much so as his
Cortani, yet it was obvious that he considered the taking of
what Lord Vellen offered. To keep it, he would have to challenge the First openly, at no behest of God, and win.

In silence, Sargoth considered the plan of action that would
save Lord Vellen's life.

High Priest Vellen sat quietly at his desk. Around him,
books rose like cliffs on all sides save one; this was dominated
by twin doors that peaked in the center. Those doors were

closed and barred by his Swords; no one gained entry here without his express permission or invitation.

One hour ago he had sent the keepers of his vast collection scurrying for the doors in an unusual display of anger, so even the narrow walk of the open second level was empty. His desk, as normal, was clean; the wood gleamed, catching the black and red of his reflection and framing the too-white complexion of his face.

Only one thin sheet rested on the desk. Words, scrawled in uneven brown ink, caught his attention and held it, whether he willed it or no.

He turned, feeling the seldom-used hood brush his cheek. It had been a trying few months.

His own recovery—God curse the slave—had been slow and painful; even now he still felt the lingering effects of white-fire. He had not had the luxury of a peaceful convalescence; by the time he had managed to gain his feet, word had come from Illan.

He was not, by nature, a restless man, so he remained seated while his mind wandered. His eyes flickered briefly over the broken circle at his chest; the red lines embroidered there mocked him cruelly. So much for victory; the Line Culverne had regained its footing. And Renar—who had cost him two loyal members of the Karnari—was king of Marantine.

He cursed again, but silently.

He should have killed the slave boy when he had the chance and risked the Lord's wrath then. How could it be much worse?

Yes, the boy. And Renar, king now. How could three such deprive him of so many years' labor in so little time?

His fingers curled tight around the arms of his chair.

They had had help.

The paper glared up at him, white as the fire.

"Dark Heart," he whispered. The two words were bitter and empty. "Have I not served you well? Without the interference of your general, would you not now own all?"

There was no answer, of course, but he expected none. Somehow, the First was the fulcrum of the Dark Heart's attention; the business with the Sarillorn of Elliath, which was to cost him dearly, had that feel to it in hindsight. Why else would the First have returned, after resisting the will and dictate of the Dark Heart so openly? If not for his actions, the woman and boy would be dead—gloriously dead—and the upstart would not now be king.

His eyes flashed silver a moment and then subsided. His power would need to be husbanded carefully for what was surely coming. If not for that, he might have destroyed this unwelcome missive. If not for that, and the fact that someone would see the ashes; someone would know that he had lost control.

His dignity was important now; it might be all that he would have. Quieted, he rose. There were hours until the appointed time, and he would take them to set his estates in order. Perhaps it was an empty gesture; he did not know and would not guess.

But he did not relish his brief homecoming to the Damion estates.

If his father spoke at all, he vowed that he would not outlive the dawn.

The temple was empty; night was gathering in the wings, but the last rays of sunlight had not yet died at the hands of the darkness.

Yet in these hallowed halls, it was the darkness that reigned.

Lord Vellen walked in silence, as any acolyte might, past the velvet-lined pews to the inlaid marble floors. He had served here in his youth; his first kill had been here, on this altar. Not for him the practice on slaves that was so prevalent among the petulant nobles who yearned for priesthood; he had known he was destined for greater things.

His hand touched the shimmering shield of blood-magic that clung tight to the surface of dark, severe marble. It was cool and dry. It would not remain so.

Dark Heart. He bowed, trembling with resentment at all that had passed. *I will not serve you in this fashion.*

So swore every leader of the Greater Cabal when he took his seat. Yet very few did not find their way here, in the end.

Ansoul, high priest and Karnar, had been Vellen's predecessor. He had engaged in many political struggles and flexed his muscles often in the arena of power. He had lost only once.

A shock of remembered pleasure ran down Vellen's spine; of all deaths dedicated to God, that one he remembered most keenly. The afterimage of blood lingered behind his eyes still.

Ansoul had been small—an old man—but he had lasted long. Death had been the only defeat he would ever acknowledge.

In that, his successor resembled him, although in little else.

If Benataan had chosen an alliance with the First immediately, there would be no hope. Now, however, he did not dare; he would lose the cabal.

"Vellen."

The leader of the Greater Cabal heard the sibilant whisper. He stiffened, recognizing the voice, but did not turn.

"You have recovered."

"Yes."

"You take a risk with your cabal, if I understand mortal politics."

"How may I help you, Second of the Sundered?" he asked, a curt, cold question. Sargoth's power was not in doubt, but Lord Vellen had had almost enough of the interference of the Servants.

"A good question. Perhaps I shall ask it myself. How may I help you, leader of the Karnari?"

Now, Vellen turned. Light, deep red and blue where it touched the stained glass windows, glinted off his winter hair, his silent face. The shadow before him looked almost human, more so than it ever had. The voice gave little away; it was hard to tell if mockery had been meant by the words or not.

He did not answer the question.

"I wonder whose blood runs through you, Lord Vellen. Of a certainty I can only say it is not mine."

"You have been teaching your magery, if I am not mistaken. There was word from Dagothrin."

Sargoth contemplated the mortal before him. A hint of threat was in the words, a hint of question, a veil of power. For a moment, the Second of the Sundered remembered what even the First had forgotten: the Sundering, the separation, and the awareness. Stefanos had then been as like his Lord as existence would permit, a web of power whose boundaries could be felt, but not seen. He had turned to his brethren and first off had destroyed some four of the forming.

Sargoth alone had wondered why, wondered how. He had known—if that was the word—that this miniature Lord was not to be crossed. Yet power, and the search for it, was a strong pull. Knowledge was his power.

He knew who Vellen's forefather must have been. Almost,

he smiled. "I have taught," he whispered quietly, "at the behest of the Lord we both serve."

"I see."

"And that service is not yet complete."

"Am I still required, then?" The voice did not change at all, but Vellen felt the stirring of a hope.

"Yes. And it will not be easy to keep you from the First."

"In return for this?"

"You will help in the game that the Dark Heart has decreed."

"What game is this?" Vellen asked, as if his compliance was in doubt.

"Do you question?"

The Karnar ignored the menace in Sargoth's voice. It was a risk, as was his answer. "Do you not?"

Sargoth's slow chuckle was his reward. "I do not have to, Priest. But I will answer.

"The woman—she is still alive. The First knows naught of it. In little time—at least by my reckoning—he must begin to renew his Empire. She will be his enemy, and he will fight her, unknowing. He will kill her."

Vellen was silent, weighing the possibilities.

"The First of the Sundered will suffer. He has ties to this half blood that we do not understand."

The First will suffer. This was what Sargoth truly had to offer; the risk of a life, even his own, was worth it. The First Sundered had cost him much. It was enough. Vellen nodded quietly. "And I?"

"You will stop any information of her existence from reaching the First through his mortal channels. All of this must pass through the Karnar who heads the Greater Cabal."

"And the Greater Cabal itself?"

"If you are too weak to keep it, the Dark Heart will find a more suitable servitor."

Dramathan of Valens looked up at the soft knock on the door. He brushed his cowl aside and it fell heavily onto his shoulders, the red line of it coloring his pale hair. He had chosen one of two chairs that was not obscured by desk front as a gesture of respect.

"Come."

The door swung open, and Lord Vellen stepped quietly

across the threshold. Gone now was the red collar, but the robes remained to mark his station: rippling black, with borders of crimson.

"You received my message."

Vellen nodded quietly and secured the door behind him. Dramathan was alone. He looked carefully at the older man's neutral expression before inclining his head to the second chair that faced the Lord of Valens.

"Please."

He took the seat and faced the Karnar, wondering how great the distance between them was, and what the price would be to close it.

"The council meeting was interesting, Lord Vellen."

"Indeed."

"And unusual." Dramathan's eyes were dark, shadowed by the line of his brows as they drew together in a faint frown. His jaw, square and narrow, was set firmly, but not in anger.

Vellen said nothing.

"Come, Lord Vellen. We are friends here; there must be some opportunity for even the Karnari to relax."

Vellen's shoulders stiffened slightly, and he leaned forward. "It is difficult to relax when the Church is in such turmoil."

"The First?"

Vellen smiled narrowly.

"You feel he is dangerous, Lord Vellen. I am willing to trust your observations; you alone have worked with him at all."

"Not all of the Karnari are so disposed."

"Not all, no." Dramathan returned Vellen's smile. "Some are . . . undecided."

"Of course. The advent of the First is a new occurrence."

"Not completely new." Dramathan looked more closely at the wall beyond Vellen's left shoulder. "Not for all of our houses."

He waited, and eventually Vellen complied with the unspoken demand. "What do you ask of me, Dramathan?"

"Very well. It is well known that Lord Damion is an older man. You will succeed him, and your house, should your position remain firm, will be a strong one."

"Yes."

"House Valens is not without power, and I believe an association of the two would be to our mutual benefit."

"And?"

"You are not yet bonded, Vellen."

"No." It was a well-known fact.

"I wish you to remedy this situation."

Vellen leaned backward, the ridge of the chair back cutting across his shoulder blades. Dramathan's only eligible daughter was thirteen, and this was young by imperial standards. Betrothed now, he would have two years in which to maneuver. Although he took several minutes to reply, he knew well what his only answer could be. Lord Valens was a powerful individual, and with his support, Torvallen's bid was certain to fail.

"I accept this. Shall we hold the period for two years?"

"Two?" Dramathan's smile was a cat's smile.

"Maia is thirteen, Lord. Two years would give her her majority."

"Ah." The smile broadened. "It was not Maia that I intended to cement our association. Rather, Amalayna."

The only sign of surprise that Vellen showed was a faint raising of eyebrows. Amalayna was bonded to Laranth of Tentaris and had already borne him one child—a son. Tentaris was a merchant family with vast holdings but no power in the Church.

"Repudiation?" Vellen whispered softly.

"I am not a fool, Vellen," was Dramathan's crisp reply. "But Tentaris is already involved in a trade war with Wintare. Many have died. Many more will." He paused and looked down at his hands. "It is rumored that Torvallen has promised Wintare much for his support. A death of such magnitude will almost certainly cause Wintare some trouble, should that death be attributed to Wintare assassins."

"When?"

They both knew that Vellen spoke not of the assassination, but of the bonding. "Three months."

Three months. No time to arrange for difficulties; no time to secure himself enough to be able to slip out of this agreement without grave risk.

"Very well," he said softly.

"My vote on the council then." Lord Dramathan rose. "I believe it would be expedient to wait four weeks before the announcement is made. I must leave now; there is much to attend to."

Lord Vellen watched him go. He was angry, but stilled it with the ease of long practice. Amalayna was not a bad or unsuitable choice, but she was very much her father's daughter—dangerous, unpredictable, and under House Valens' dictate. Perhaps children would change that—and perhaps she would not survive the first few years of her marriage.

Still, he had to admire Dramathan. The Lord Valens knew when he had something to gain, and he was willing to take risks. Of course his hand in his son-in-law's death could not be made public without implicating Vellen in it.

Canny, but that was all the better in an ally.

The Greater Cabal's balance was now in his favor.

News of the death of Laranth of Tentaris had rippled through the High City. It was the topic of much discussion at social gatherings, and the gruesome details grew with each telling, although they needed no embellishment.

Wintare, of course, denied any connection to the assassination, but Lord Tentaris heard little of it; he was busy. In a three-day the death toll of six months of trade war had tripled.

On this, the fourth day, the rumblings of that war, and the consequences of it, were contained in the streets and on the merchant routes without, where life continued apace.

Not so within the vast, stone hall of the house temple of Tentaris, where a quiet silence reigned. Few indeed were the nobles that had chosen to attend the ceremony for the deceased heir of the house, and they had left in their wake of quiet, subdued chatter.

Even Lord and Lady Tentaris were gone.

One person remained. She wore the pale white of mourning, and her hair, dark and long, was braided with pearls and crystal tears. She was lovely, a stiff, exact statue that lingered a moment longer with the body of the man who had been her bondmate.

Her fingers, long and thin, traced the line of his still, slack jaw. In isolation and privacy, the tears came. They were rare in the Empire, and almost never shed in such a wise; they would make the dignitaries of allied houses either uncomfortable or contemptuous.

Lady Amalayna cared little for what they thought. She was numb now, almost empty.

"Laranth."

Her knees folded elegantly, and she rested her cheek against his, waiting for the touch of his hand in her hair. She knew she would wait long.

Her father had chosen this bond-mate for her, and she had complied, as she most often did, with his wish. Only later did she realize how kind his choice had been, even if that kindness had been unintentional and undreamed of.

For Laranth of Tentaris had been astute and canny—the pride of his father's house. He had added to the merchant line's revenue by half in three short years of running the routes, which was no mean feat. He had fathered a son, when fertility in his line had been a known problem. He frightened many.

He had almost frightened Amalayna. Six years her elder, with a sardonic smile that could cut a man's jugular with its cold edge, he had accepted House Valens' suit—her hand, with a sizeable dowry.

He had been pleased with what he had personally negotiated and had wasted little time in investing it. She had expected that.

But he had asked her aid, her advice—and in two cases had taken it, pleased with her judgment. That had surprised her. He had forced her presence to be accepted on the Tentaris House council and had treated her as an equal in matters of state.

It was not for loss of that power that she wept now.

He had become more her family than Valens had been. He had prided himself in his bonding to her—but not because of the power of the house that was her birthright. She had been special to him, in and of herself.

And he—he had become that special to her.

How had he been caught? How had he allowed himself to be killed so ignominiously? He had been the most careful of men, more so than ever since the trade war had been declared. Someone he trusted, and there were few, must have betrayed him, but it couldn't have been his guards; they, too, lay dead.

Only their child remained alive.

She had never dreamed what it would cost her, to sit crouched against the stone of his face and the floor. She never imagined that the death would invoke such a loss, such an emptiness.

"Laranth," she whispered, "I love you."

That was their secret.

She kissed still lips and rose, wiping her eyes. The time for mourning would never pass, of this she was certain. But there was work to do now, with House Tentaris and with her young, young son. Laranth had been lost, but his assassins had not yet been caught.

They would be. By the Dark Heart, she would see them perish slowly.

chapter three

It was chilly in the early morning; winter never forgot the prov-ince of Marantine, no matter how many months had passed. The sun rose earlier to herald spring, and there was no frost—but that was all.

Erin stood beneath it, her breath leaving the faintest hint of cloud. She had breakfasted early, and her power glowed faintly green around the leathers she wore. The cold, at least of the weather, did not trouble her.

Darin was late. She wondered, idly, if he had picked that habit up from her. Bare fingers ran along the hilt of her short sword; it was a comfort to have it at her side. There was so much she would have to leave behind.

"Hello, shadow." Her voice was quiet as she stared at the thin, sparse length the sun made of her height. Faceless and dark, it stared back at her until she turned once again to look at the double doors that came out from the main hall. They were closed and flanked on either side by two of Renar's royal guard. The king's guard.

She marveled at them; they stood stiff and at attention, and she wondered if it was for her benefit, or if even in isolation they kept that pose, flesh statues to adorn the castle.

Her chin tilted upward, and her eyes sought the leaded glass—there was so much glass here—of the main hall. Renar's rooms were beyond it, swathed in dark fabrics, rich colors, thick carpets. Did he sleep?

She felt just a twinge of guilt. She was not due to meet Hildy for another hour yet; there was no reason to leave so early—no reason at all except that Renar habitually slept as late as possible, although these days that was a mere two hours after sunrise.

The two large doors swung open; they were well oiled but even so they creaked loudly—more so than Erin remembered. She gave a little start, then walked quietly up the stairs to meet the one companion that she was to keep with her on the road.

Darin, his eyes lined and puffy with lack of sleep, his coat skewed and buttoned improperly, dragged a heavy pack behind him as he made his way through the doors. His boots were laced properly, but she suspected from the look of the left that he'd have some difficulty removing it at the end of the day; it was knotted.

"Sorry I'm late," he murmured. The last word stretched out into an endless yawn. "It's cold out here."

"It'll warm; it's spring. Let me help you with that."

"No, it's all right—"

"Bright Heart, what's in it?"

"Books. Just a couple."

"A couple of shelves' worth? Darin" —she smiled gently— "where on earth will you find time to read them?" She opened the pack, reached in, and pulled out a leather tome. It was thick and yellowed with age, and the words, scuffed but burned in, were Old Tongue.

"Culverne history."

He nodded, his hat dipping over his eyes. "I didn't have time to read them; I've been studying other stuff."

If Renar was king—and undeniably he was—Darin was just as much patriarch. The titles, like poorly made clothing, fitted both ill. Erin remembered her grandfather and wondered if Darin would cut such a figure of authority and affection when he reached that age. It was hard to imagine.

"You can't take these with you."

"Only as far as Hildy travels. She said she'd bring them back when she came."

Erin shook her head. "If she's searched at the border—and she will be—they can't find these in the caravan."

Darin's shoulders sagged, although it was a little hard to see them beneath the thick clothing he wore. "Hildy said she thought it'd be worth the risk if I thought it was important." But his voice was low and resigned. "I'll take them in. I guess I'll have time to study them when we get back."

Erin didn't bother to answer. Instead she turned her back on the closing doors and watched the sun creep further over the wall. Outside, the market flags would be unfurling, their bright and distinctive colors ringing the three concentric circles that had grown up out of the ground. The outlines of imposed squares were already fading into the winter that had passed.

Elliath had had such a small circle. Winter had been much, much shorter, and spring less chilly. But for all that, this overgrown, crowded city, with buildings passing the treetops, had become home.

She already missed it.

And to sneak out, like a thief or an unfaithful rite-mate, made the loss harder. Few people knew that she was leaving, but those few had already made their thoughts on that clear: silence, gray-ringed eyes, failure to meet the eyes that she averted herself. She was sure that Lord Stenton Cosgrove could not have looked more surprised and more betrayed than if Lady Verena had inserted a dagger between his ribs.

Renar had stopped all argument. She remembered what he was wearing, could see it when she closed her eyes. She left them open. No kingly raiment then; no lace, no velvet, no frills. Just simple brown work clothing, and that in sweaty disarray. He had spent the afternoon in the drill room alone; she had not had the time, when making arrangements with Hildy, to join him for a last bout.

She would miss that—although she would find the lack of bruises a welcome relief.

No time? No. Not to join him for dinner, or afterward. Not to speak and have him ask questions that she would not or could not answer.

Not to dance.

She looked at her feet; they were heavily booted. A smile tugged at the corners of her mouth as she remembered the quartermaster's reaction when they'd been requisitioned—as if small feet were created solely to be an annoyance to his routine.

Think, Erin. Think. Kaarel and Ruth would be here, in safety, no doubt commencing their criticisms of royal rule. Gerald would be at Lorrence's side, or at Renar's; Morgan would be running his cabs in rings around the city and charging a fortune for the privilege of the uncomfortable and harrowing rides to "build up his business to a respectable level."

Stenton would no doubt be plotting in a similar vein, but with different clientele.

She wondered what Lord Beaton would do; the overthrow had left him tired and at an odd sort of peace. Tiras might train, or not; most likely he would stay as one of the king's most trusted counselors.

And Renar?

Oh, it was sunny. The sky was the deep blue that only happens when all clouds are refused and cast aside.

What of Renar?

This time she closed her eyes and let her chin tilt forward. If things were different . . .

She heard music then, the soft, gentle whistling of her first dance lesson. At any other time of the day, the noise in the courtyard would have drowned it out. Turning, she saw the doors to the main hall had opened, and she had missed their sound.

Darin stood in front of two men. Renar and Tiras, both wearing the black shirts and sashes of their earlier years as master and student. And Renar's lips were trembling on a smile and a tune as he walked out from behind Darin's back.

"Erin," he whispered as he approached.

She smiled hesitantly, and he bowed with a flourish. This man, she remembered. She had thought to leave without seeing him again.

"I'm hurt, Lady, that you think to leave without at least saying good-bye, but never fear, I am not so easily sidestepped." He smiled, but they both heard the edge in the words. "And now, we have no time for dancing. The Empire waits."

"Renar . . ."

"I would go with you." He held up a hand, inches away from the no that was forming on her lips. "But Tiras forbids it, thwarting royal whim. He has earned his royal punishment." His arms opened wide, and a breeze ruffled both sleeves. Beneath his shirt, she felt the cooling of his skin as she stepped into his hug. They were of a height, and it was awkward, but it was more of a good-bye than Erin had thought she could have.

He said nothing, sparing her further words, and sparing himself the effort of making them light.

"I'll miss you."

"And I you." He turned almost brusquely. "Tiras."

The old man nodded and bent to lift a pack. "Ready."

Erin looked at him in some confusion.

"Where the student will not do," Tiras said with a dry smile, "I am sure the master will. I accompany you, Lady. With your permission."

"Or without it," Renar added darkly. "He is not to bother returning if either you or Darin do not accompany him."

"Renar, don't say that." Her voice was urgent, her eyes darker than usual.

"Are you afraid of this?"

"Yes."

"I'll never understand why people plot and kill for my rank."

"Would you kill to defend it?"

There was silence and the hint of a subdued smile. He caught her by the shoulders, his eyes darker than her own. "Come home, Erin."

"I—"

His lips brushed hers lightly before stopping to rest against the lines of her forehead. Then he withdrew, bowing deeply, once again the misfit king.

Erin was more than thankful to reach the closed and barred door of Hildy's dwelling. She nearly leaped to knock at it, and the noise relieved the heavy silence that had dogged her since she left the castle. Tiras was not a man for flowery speech when not adopting the persona of colorful buffoon. Unlike his pupil, he saw no need to chatter to pass the time.

Darin, cheeks reddened by the snap of morning chill, was likewise silent, and Erin marked the subtle frown across his lips as concentration. She didn't want to disturb him either.

The door swung open a crack. The servant's frown melted into an almost happy smile.

"Lady Erin! You're here. Good. Hildy can't stand tardiness." He stepped aside and allowed the three to enter.

"Jorrel." Erin smiled as she passed him. "Good to see you."

"And you, Lady. I'd best warn you though, that Hildy's in one of her more sour moods this morn. Waking early doesn't usually agree with her—and never within the confines of a 'civilized city.' "

"Thanks."

"Mind," he added to her retreating back, "she's also

excited—she's got her haven back, and I imagine she'll be smuggling human cargo."

Erin stopped, and Darin bumped into her chin as she turned. She caught his shoulders, although her eyes were on Jorrel. "Someday soon, Bright Heart willing, there won't be any reason to."

His smile showed his age—and his past, which lay beneath the right sleeve of the black and white uniform that Hildy insisted upon. "The Bright Heart," he whispered softly, "and the Lady of Mercy."

Erin might have spoken then, but a loud shout interrupted her, and she wheeled in time to catch Hildy's heavily coated girth.

"Jorrel!" Looking more like a mismatched clothing horse than a person, Hildy stopped. "Oh, there you are, dear. Are we all ready?"

Erin nodded.

"Good. If I can only find my—"

"Here, Hildy." Jorrel stepped past Tiras, his hand holding a small sack.

"You have it!" She sighed as Jorrel tactfully refrained from comment at his mistress' wear. The green coat he didn't mind much, but the pale red boots, the purple scarf, and the black undercoat that hung beneath it, made him shake his head.

"Don't do that," she said curtly as she grabbed her pack. "You *know* I hate the cold."

She stopped for a minute to look both Erin and Tiras up and down. "Dear, it gets cold on the trail. Do you think you're wearing enough?" Without pausing for an answer, she added to Tiras, "And you sir, should know better—at your age, you've no excuse."

He raised a pale eyebrow, but forebore comment.

"Well, luckily I also travel prepared. Come, come, we must be off."

"Papers, Hildy?"

"Of course I have them, Jorrel."

She swept out of the house.

With a sigh, Tiras followed.

"Now, dear, I'd best introduce you to the— Darin, are you paying attention?"

"Yes, ma'am."

"Good." She patted him on the head, then frowned. "You're getting taller, dear."

"Yes, Hildy."

"Right. Boys?"

There were one or two murmurs, and eight men stepped forward.

"Where are the rest of you?"

"With the wagons, Hildy."

"Oh. Yes, of course. Be a dear, Marek. Come here."

"Dear" Marek stepped forward and nodded. His head cleared Erin's by almost a foot, and his face was both lean and scarred. His uniform was in good repair, with a gray crispness that Erin knew was Hildy's dictate. The weapons he carried—two swords—were in better shape; his own choice.

"Marek, this is Erin, Darin, and Tiras. They'll be traveling with us."

He looked down at Erin.

"She'll be part of the caravan guard, dear, so mind that smile."

"Ma'am."

Corman, Luke, Trent, Sanfalis, Eric, and Amahl followed, each with a varying degree of respect. Amahl, the youngest, was positively bridling at Hildy's use of the word "boy," probably because he most lived up to it. His face was half-covered in a red-gold beard that did nothing to add to his age. Erin shook his hand and found the grip just a little too tight.

"I think you know the last guard, dear."

And Hamin stepped forward. He'd added two small scars to the broad line of his face and a small beard that was darker than the rest of his hair. His teeth showed white as he smiled; through some miracle, he still had all of his front ones.

"Hamin!"

"At your service, Lady. It'll be a pleasure to travel with you again."

"But I thought you'd rejoined the royal guards."

He laughed, the deep-throated laugh that came with a chest his size. "I did." The laugh faded to a chuckle.

"But—"

"I've been given leave to rejoin Hildy's ranks for a time. To be specific, the time you'll be traveling with her."

"Renar?"

"Aye, the king." His smile faded. "He was in quite the

mood when he gave his orders, too. I don't think he likes being here overmuch—not when the three of you are traveling. I'm to report at the end of it."

On impulse, she hugged him, not minding the chain links that cut into her cheek. "Thanks," she said softly.

He blushed and pulled back.

"I know, I know." She laughed as he tried to find words. "Battle is easier to face."

But she felt good for the first time in days. Darin was with her, but she hadn't thought that Tiras and Hamin would be coming, too. Less to leave behind; less to say good-bye to.

They traveled out toward the south gate of the city. Already the roads unfolded in a semblance of life, and they were among it, their quiet group one of many. The colorful clothing of the market vendors was a little splash of vibrancy among the grays and browns of the city buildings; Erin could see the flags were already at full mast.

Some nodded at Hildy, and a few stopped to wave in a cheery fashion. At least Erin thought it was at Hildy; with her gaudy winter clothing she was easily the most visible member of the caravan.

The children would be out later; Erin was sorry to have to miss them. She sighed. The lines had taught her better than this; warriors were always saying their farewells.

Yet it was Darin's feet that dragged the most, sliding over cobbled stone with a growing reluctance.

This day, he held his staff firmly in one hand. Bethany's voice was silent, as it was when there was no crisis or danger to contend with, yet he felt her all the same. He looked at the slightly knotted wood and smiled; either Bethany had grown shorter, or he taller, in the time here.

Buildings grew more squat and less dense as they neared the gate; the walls cut into blue sky with their white, impenetrable face. Before they reached those gates, those walls, Darin knew he would have one last chance to see the gently sloping hills that had once belonged to Culverne. They were Marantine lands now, although Renar had said he would hold them in trust for Culverne when the time came to rebuild.

Rebuild? The grass was new, and drops of dew, like cold sweat, glinted in the sunlight. What could be rebuilt? Huts, houses, perhaps a small church. But they'd be empty of the voices and faces that had made them home.

He turned slightly to the east and stopped for a moment. He didn't notice Hildy call a quiet halt to the caravan progress, although he should have—she had been quite anxious to leave.

Later, he would thank her. But now, his back to his companions, his eyes sought and found the single structure that graced Culverne lands.

It was stone—pale, thin, and tall as it stretched toward the endless sky above. A closed circle, with a tall unadorned spire. It stood as a testament to the fallen, above the clean earth. He hadn't designed it, but he had requested that something be built in place of the graves that didn't exist for him to find some peace at.

Very slowly, he lowered himself to one knee.

"Lernan." He touched his forehead.

"Culverne."

"Darin."

He placed Bethany on the ground a moment and touched his forehead for a third time. It was all the blessing he had to give; all the promise.

Someone knelt beside him then, and he turned his head to catch a glimpse of Erin, who had also assumed his stance. She stared at the spire in silence, then bowed her forehead. Her long warrior's braid looped gently over her shoulder, as countless warriors' braids had done in the past. Only now, there was no Lady to give the blessing.

She had not sworn the warrior's oath for over four centuries and had almost vowed never to swear it again. But the Lady's betrayal—if, in that most revered Servant's mind, it was betrayal—was distant now; a thing of the past. Only three things remained of that past: Erin, her trapped line-mates, and the Lord of the Empire. All of the others that she had known were dead; dust at the whim of time.

But the reason that they had fought still remained. She closed her eyes, and her lips began to tremble.

"Lernan. Elliath. Erin." On the last, she drew her sword; it glowed dimly even in this light. Then she touched Darin on the shoulder and their eyes met.

They faced each other, the last two descendants of the Bright Heart. Their eyes went, as one, to the south and east. In silence they made their own pledges, and in silence they rose to join the caravan.

The wagons rolled out of Dagothrin, and only Darin remembered the last time he had left, on foot, behind wagons. He looked at the right sleeve of his jacket, seeing beneath sheepskin and linen to the white network of House Damion's crest.

It sunk in then, fully and finally. He was going back to Malakar.

Lady Amalayna stepped down from the carriage that was only used for the most important dignitaries of House Tentaris. The coachman, Pentar, held out one gloved hand, and she gripped it firmly as her feet gracefully found the ground. She stared at him a moment, taking in the crisp, clean velvets of the red and the gold that blended into the sunrise of the crest of House Tentaris. Then her eyes moved, above the folded collar, to catch a glimpse of his face.

It was round; old now, she realized with a start, but his brown eyes were steady.

She saw her distorted image in them; her delicate nose suddenly severe; the beaded length of her dark hair melting almost exactly into his pupils. Half-embarrassed, she let her hand fall into the folds of black silk skirts. Bordering the black was a ribbon of white; these two were the colors of post-ceremonial mourning. She wasn't sure why, but it had always been so for those who cared to wear it.

She so chose, on this morning a week after the death of her bond-mate. She felt, at this time, that she would never choose any other colors. Let their presence be a testament to Laranth and the gift that they had achieved together.

Still, she was nervous. She lifted her head and saw the vast stretch of the two-story mansion that held the House she had left when Laranth had accepted her. At the center of the building, one large, square tower rose to dominate the mansion and its grounds; the shadow it cast was long and solemn. At its peak, burgundy and gray flew in the wind. This was House Valens.

She wondered, as she walked unescorted to the peaked double doors, why her father had summoned her here. Perhaps he had news on the whereabouts of Laranth's killer. It was a possibility; her own sources had yielded nothing but frustration.

Still, she doubted it. The tone of his carefully worded message denied the hope.

Her fingers folded into a steeple as she walked; her steps grew smaller and came less frequently. It was not only Lady Amalayna who had received word from the lord of Valens; the lord of Tentaris had also taken a sealed message into his study. He would not divulge the contents, and as he was preoccupied with the search for his heir's assassins, Amalayna had not seen fit to press him beyond a few simple questions.

She regretted that now.

Either the house guards had grown lax, or had been previously instructed. They bowed, as if she were still of Valens, and stepped quickly to either side to let her pass in silence. She paused with one foot above the threshold and then looked back to see the Tentaris carriage pull away along the drive. She almost retreated before she could be cut by the sharp edge between the door and the open courtyard. But no; she was Lady Amalayna; such cowardice, such timidity, did no one proud.

The house master greeted her at the door beyond the courtyard, the tower's great base. He, too, looked older. If possible, the white wisps of hair that formed a semicircle around his head had retreated farther, and his cheeks looked gaunt as the circles beneath his eyes.

"Lady Amalayna." He stood stiffly. "Lord Valens requests your presence in his tower chambers."

"The tower?" she asked, her voice deceptively soft.

The house master nodded quietly.

"Lead, then." She waved quietly. "I will follow."

As he had always done in her life here, he obeyed her command, turning his back upon her before he could see the trembling of her jaw. She looked at his upgraded slave's clothing as if it could anchor her and followed lightly behind, taking care to lift her skirts above the clean stone.

She was wary and weary both as she climbed the stairs without aid of the brass banisters that lined them on either side. She did not pause to stare out of the windows that vaulted precisely toward the ceiling—she might once have, but then she had been a child. It was not as child that she had been summoned, and not as child that she had returned.

The house master reached the fifth floor landing and paused, clearly out of breath. Had she been feeling cruel, she might have pointed this out, but she kept her silence; he was a slave of House Valens, not of House Tentaris, and his condition was not her concern.

"The lord awaits within; you are to continue on your own."

"Thank you." She took a deep breath, then opened the maple doors into the short, thin hall. Alone, she paused to steady herself before continuing the length of the hall to the grander double doors that waited, bearing the crest of Lord Valens himself.

Once she reached them, she paused again, wringing her hands behind her back. Then she nodded, and without knocking pushed them aside and entered into the quiet, carpeted room.

Lord Valens was waiting. She expected that he would be seated in his customary chair behind the desk and in front of the fire, his hands folded neatly before him, his expression impenetrable. But this was to be an unusual interview, for he stood, his face to the rounded window, his hands clasped behind his back.

Nor did he turn as she entered.

"Amalayna."

"Father." She waited.

"Be seated, child."

She wasn't certain whether he gave the order for her comfort or his own, but in either case she obeyed it, folding her skirts neatly beneath her legs and placing her hands in her lap.

Only when the rustling of silk stopped did he at last turn to face her. He did not speak, but his eyes traveled over her, taking in the white beads nestled so carefully in near black hair, the severe white collar that framed her chin, and the long, black gown. For a moment he frowned, his brows drawing together as if in pain. Then, the lines of his face stilled and smoothed themselves into his unreadable and undeniable expression. He shook his head.

"This is foolish, Amalayna."

She had not expected less, and her chin began to tilt upward. She did not answer.

"The merchant women of unhoused families wear garb such as this for their common dead. It is beneath you."

There were many lessons that Amalayna had learned from this daunting parent, and chief among them was the use of silence. She only wished that she could school her face so carefully.

"Do you think it does your rited mate a service to be so seen? Do you think it aids House Tentaris?"

"Lord Tentaris does not seem to mind." Each word was spoken slowly and distinctly, as if it were part of a separate sentence.

"I see."

She waited, knowing that she should not have spoken. Her eyes traveled around the room, and she thought it smaller than it had ever been; the walls pressed inward, exerting her father's pressure, although to what end she did not yet know.

"Very well," he said at last, a hint of satisfaction in the words. "It has been a week; enough time for this"—and he gestured at her clothing—"to pass.

"I have been in communication with Lord Tentaris, and he and I have reached an agreement."

"Agreement?"

"Indeed." He paused a moment, and then continued, his voice sharper. "These colors—they do not belong here. Wear the burgundy and gray, Amalayna. They are your colors now."

"P-pardon?"

His eyes grew darker. "I see your stay in House Tentaris has not helped you to gather your wits. Very well. I have paid House Tentaris a portion of your rite-price, and Lord Tentaris has agreed to release you from that house. You are to return to Valens; you are to once again be Lady Amalayna of my house."

"B-but—" the beads in her hair rattled gently as she shook her head. "My son?"

"He is of House Tentaris. He shall remain there."

She paled then, until her skin was white; white as the lace that framed her skirts; white as the beads in her hair. She was exactly the spirit that mourns for the dead. All black, all white; undisturbed by the colors of life.

"You will, of course, be given leave to see him, and I have retained some rights, in your stead, for his education. But he is the line now, and in no wise would Lord Tentaris be parted from his sole grandchild."

If the words were meant to comfort her, they failed.

"When?" she whispered at last.

"Three days."

For the first time in her life, she almost defied him. Her cheeks began to warm, and her jaw grew tight.

"Amalayna, it is not a matter of pride. You did well by House Tentaris; you provided that line with an heir, and in time. It was purely a question of capital. House Tentaris has seen its resources severely depleted in this war with Wintarc. If it eases you, think that this is the biggest service that you may do for Tentaris and be proud of it."

She rose stiffly and nodded, not trusting her throat to form words.

"I will see to your clothing while you set your things in order. Your old chambers in the east wing have been restored."

Her shadow touched the flowers that had been laid in front of pale, green marble. The grass, cropped short and precisely, set off the hues of red and gold petals, freshly cut and left here.

She had done this. Numbly, as if by routine of long years, she had walked in the grounds of Tentaris and snipped each blossom. They were flowers to her; she didn't know their names or their season, and she didn't care either—as long as they served their purpose.

The marble piece had been Lord Tentaris' decision, although she knew that it was more a gift to her than a necessity. His life had continued; his war had grown—his son was now a thing of the bitter past.

After today she would never again have the tending of this site. No doubt it would be removed, or at least left in stark isolation. For a moment she started to stand, then she changed her mind and knelt forward, letting her head touch the cool stone.

There was so much that she had been warned of, growing up. Assassination was not unfamiliar, even to her house; she had lost one of her brothers to it. She knew the cost; it had been drilled into her extensively. First, there were political instabilities; second, there were monetary ones; third, there were shifts in alliances.

No one had thought to warn her of the worst; of this emptiness, this rage.

She didn't hear the footsteps in the grass behind her and only became aware that someone waited when the gathered shadows shifted slightly. She knew enough to be embarrassed, and strove to gain her feet quickly, straightening out the folds of her dress.

To her surprise, Lord Tentaris awaited. He had no slaves

or guards in attendance, which was unusual, and the clothing he wore was sparse: red and gold seen only in the sash that crossed from left shoulder to hip. His shirt was black and simple, even the hem unadorned as it cut above his knees. No white, but then again she expected none. This was as close to mourning as Lord Tentaris would ever be seen in. In his arms, blanketed in simple linens, was her son. Their son.

"I thought to find you here, Lady," he said, and held out the child.

She gathered him into her arms. He was sleeping.

"I regret that I have been unable to see you." He did not meet her eyes. "House matters have been pressing."

"I understand," she whispered. And she did. But it surprised her, knowing that he found it difficult. "Will you answer one question?"

"If it is in my power."

"Why?"

"Amalayna, you loved my son. Not all knew it, but many did. He was less obvious; more careful. Still, it was a weakness. Had he many others—" He shook his head. "Between us, I will say that I held my son in esteem. I did not question his choice, and it proved to be a good one."

"Then why?"

"Laranth is dead." The words were harsh. "I have seen for myself what this has done to our house. We will suffer more for it yet. I cannot afford to have a child raised with such a weakness at this time."

Ashamed, she nodded and turned away, still cradling her son.

"Amalayna, I am sorry. Perhaps later—"

"Later?"

"You are intelligent and not without your own resources. If not for the straits we find ourselves in, I might have made another choice, even given this risk. You have done this house proud, and I shall not forget it."

She kissed her son on the forehead, and he stirred.

"I understand," she whispered, and her lips turned up in a gentle smile. "May I still see him?"

Lord Tentaris nodded quietly. "In a few years, Lady, you may yet have the raising of him."

He did not mean to be cruel by giving her that hope, but the hope cut her nonetheless. She gave her son to his grandfather's keeping in silence.

chapter
four

*Morning, with its crisp, clear chill, had held sway over the hori-*zon for two hours when the caravan finally made its way to the Empire's border post. They traveled along the open road, touched by the shadows of trees that were displaying the season's new green to those below too preoccupied to care.

Erin rode alongside the caravan's mistress. She wore a small version of Hildy's cold-weather clothing, which was both cumbersome and ugly, even to Erin's admittedly ill-trained eye. She had never much favored the color purple, and certainly not so many yards of it. She sighed and locked her hands together; it kept them away from her sword. Tiras had been forced to change as well, and he had accepted it both more silently and less gracefully than Erin had. Luckily for all concerned, Hildy was adept at ignoring small outbursts of "unpleasantness."

"If I didn't, dear, do you think I'd ever make it across the continent with a caravan intact?"

Erin smiled and glanced over her right shoulder to see Tiras walking among the guards. He looked out of place there, she had to admit, but not by much. He was an older man, true, but long years of training and practice kept the full toll of age at bay.

The wagon hit a rock on the road, and her smile vanished as she righted herself. She had thought the carriages in Dagothrin had been uncomfortable and wondered how Hildy could manage to sit for so many hours of each day.

"One gets used to it, dear," Hildy said, as if reading her companion's mind. Erin hoped Hildy's age and wisdom, rather than her own transparency, was the cause of this.

"Around this bend we'll reach the outpost. I expect that the

58

soldiers there will be unpleasant—they usually are. Hamin, dear?"

"Ma'am?"

"Do be ready in case their boys get a little rough."

"Ma'am."

Erin sighed and played with the hem of her coat. When Hildy had said she could travel as a caravan guard, she should have known it was too good to be true. She wanted to be on her feet and on the ground, watching and waiting with the rest of the guard.

"Darin, dear, do get into the wagon now—and do put away that staff for a moment, won't you?"

"Yes, ma'am."

"And be careful, dear."

He was already doing so; her warning wasn't necessary. Beyond the border post he was still an escaped slave; his life was worth very little, except perhaps as fodder for the altars. He hoped, as he crawled into the wagon that housed their tents, that the weather wasn't going to get warmer; in the new spring chill, his scarred arm was never exposed.

The wagons creaked—wagons weren't supposed to sound so rickety, were they?—as they rounded the rather sharp bend in the road. A bend such as this, Erin thought as she ground her teeth, was a foolish place to put an outpost. There was no easy way to see the length of the road, or to see what lay beyond. Whoever had designated this as the—

"Bright Heart."

Hildy's "around the bend" was hundreds of yards off, but it didn't matter in the slightest. If anything, the distance gave Erin the scope to appreciate the size of the fortress that sat, with two huge gates beneath a squat, square tower, over the road.

Trees had been cut to clear the area around the fortress, and in all, there were eight of these towers, evenly spaced. Each held four men. In times of war, they could easily hold twenty—and at that, mostly archers. Nor would it be easy just to fire it; they had built this at some cost, judging by the stonework and the size of it. The wood that had been cleared had been used in some areas, but not many.

Flags flew atop each tower; black and red.

Erin turned to Hildy and forced her lips to work.

"Outpost?"

"Well, dear, what else would you call it? All the way out on the border and such as it is."

"Fortress," Erin managed. She swung her legs around to the edge of the cab.

Hildy caught her shoulder by one mittened hand, the other held firmly on to the reins. "Don't get down, dear."

"We can't just walk through here!" Erin shrugged the hand off. "Not after the recent war!"

"We can do exactly that." The older woman patted a layer of coat above her left breast. "Trust me."

Although she knew it wasn't, sitting still felt like the hardest thing Erin had ever been called upon to do. The fortress grew larger and larger as the horses continued their steady pace. Arrow slits in the ground and second floor became evident; they were well spaced; well planned. The flags shivered in the wind like dark clouds—storm clouds. She could see people in long, black surcoats pointing; she could hear their curt shouts and orders.

"Hildy," she whispered. "Please."

Hildy didn't appear to be listening. She let the horses go forward, and the other wagons followed. The clip-clip of horse hooves and the groan of wheels were the only noises that filled the silence.

By the time they stopped in front of the closed gates, eight men were arrayed to greet them. The black surcoats covered a patchwork of different armors; some leather, some dinted breastplating, and some chain. Weapons, though, were standard and in good repair. Swords were readied in the hands of four men; two carried bows, and two held spears. Their shields were Empire standard: rounded at the top, peaked at the bottom, portable fields of black. There was no red on any of them, though; at least they weren't Swords.

"Halt!"

As the wagons had already done just that, Hildy didn't see any need to respond and sat waiting on the cab almost impatiently.

"This," she said half-fretfully, "is where we lose time."

Time? Erin wanted to scream. But she said nothing. She didn't even reach for her sword, although her hands were sweating.

One of the men, armed with a sword, stepped forward, ignoring the guards around the caravan. He approached Hildy at the lead wagon.

"Dismount," he said curtly.

She sighed and began to do as he asked, her muttering muffled slightly by her scarf. This she unwrapped and handed in an unceremonious heap to Erin. She followed with her mittens and her gloves and even went so far as to unbutton her coat.

"There's no traffic between Illan and Senatare," the guard said, but he held out his hand nonetheless.

Erin stopped from bridling at the word Illan; she wasn't, after all, a stupid woman. She turned, expecting to see Darin's face in a crimson flush, and was disturbed by just how white he was.

"I'm a commissioned trader with House Boradil," Hildy said, matching the soldier's curtness. She unfurled one battered scroll and put one thick finger beneath the seal and date.

With a noncomittal grunt, the soldier took the scroll in one hand and held it almost under his nose, which was wide and oddly angled.

"Citizenship papers?"

Hildy sighed. "Just mine, or all of ours?"

"All of 'em."

Another wad of curled papers made an appearance from beneath her coat. She handed them over in a chunk; Erin caught the gleam of red seal at the corner of the foremost one.

With annoying leisure, the soldier looked them over. Obviously he was in a position of authority—he could read. His eyes traveled down the length of each paper, pausing only once to meet the green of Erin's eyes. She froze slightly and forced her lips into a shy smile.

"My niece," Hildy said curtly. "I'm taking her out of Illan; it isn't safe for her alone since the fall of the city."

There was more silence, and then the guard handed the papers back to Hildy. But his eyes didn't leave Erin's face. He walked over to the wagon, and she clenched her hand, hearing his steps as if they were shattering glass. He paused beneath her, his head not quite level with her knees.

"Down."

Jaw clenched, Erin began to descend. She didn't trust herself to speak. Her hands ached now for the feel of hilt—she couldn't steady them.

His fingers bit into her jaw.

"Pretty girl," he said softly. To Hildy, in a louder voice, he added, "There isn't much traffic between Illan and Senatare at the moment."

"And not much iron work in Verdann." Hildy's voice was ice. "You had best examine the date on the Boradil papers."

He looked back at his men, and then let his eyes travel up the gates to the tower where four men with readied bows looked down.

"There're bandit problems on the road now. House Boradil wouldn't be surprised if you didn't make it this far."

Hildy's voice was no less icy, although it became slower and softer. "They wouldn't be surprised, no. Lord Boradil would be very angry."

The soldier said nothing, but rather yanked Erin forward by her face. Her feet stumbled, but she had no time to right herself before his lips bit down on hers. Before she could throw him, he pulled back and spit to his left.

"Open the gates." It was a snarl.

Shaking with anger, Erin mounted the cab once more.

"I'm sorry," Hildy said softly, her voice no less angry. "It's why we don't often travel with younger women in the caravan."

Erin took a deep breath and forced herself to ease forward. She longed to pull her sword, remove the soldier's lips, and leave them lying in the wake of the caravan. "Boradil must be a big house."

"A rich one," Hildy answered as she urged her horses forward. "They politic in the merchant trade; they've won two trade wars in seven years, with the help of their allies." She smiled grimly. "They don't give a damn about the state of the Empire unless its instability interferes with their trade. I bring them ore and metals, some gems and precious stones. They give me safe passage and keep me free from most of the border searches that might reveal more . . . sensitive cargo returning to Dagothrin. As a partnership, it works." The tone of her voice made it clear what she thought of her partners.

"Why—" Erin took another, deeper breath. "—do they accredit you? Those papers are—"

"I'm accredited because they tried unsuccessfully for years to keep a caravan intact long enough to reach Dagothrin." She smiled, but it was grim and unpleasant. "And if the caravan got to Dagothrin, no one would trade any iron that wasn't a Sword with them."

"Do you make money?"

"Rather a lot," Hildy answered unapologetically. She looked sideways at Tiras, and her smile warmed slightly. "It comes to Marantine and stays there in two ways. Sometimes by fabrics, other wares, and information, and sometimes through slaves. Not all of the ones I transport are escaped."

She was silent then, thinking. "We set it up almost thirty years ago." Her voice was quiet. "I purchase those who might have been raided from our villages and return them to their country.

"At least that's how it started. But every now and then I've taken more contraband materials. Some slaves know me, or know how to reach me. I don't ask how. But I take them when I can." The wagon halted, as the second set of gates was opened to allow them passage. "I'll introduce you to one of my links when we get to Verdann."

Lord Vellen sat, idly twirling the stem of a small gold glass between his left fingers. A deep amber liquid swirled within, catching glints of daylight in its eddies. He lifted the cup to his lips and smiled; it was warm and smooth, but it certainly had a bite.

Lord Valens sat across from him, occupying the second of three velvet-lined chairs drawn evenly around a dark, flat table. For once, neither man wore the red and the black. Dramathan was resplendent in his lord's role; his jacket was a mix of burgundy and gray velvets, domed at the shoulders and traced with silvered thread. His pants, velvet, also, were gray over supple black leather.

Vellen wore his house colors, as well, but as he was not lord, he chose against the added warmth of heavy velvet. No, his jacket was deep blue silk over black laced fringes at throat and wrist. He wore no circlet, and the modest hat had been left at the door with one of the slaves.

High priest or no, here he had come as Lord Vellen of Damion, and no other rank intruded. He glanced out the window almost impatiently and then relaxed; the sun still held high afternoon—evening was hours away.

It was curious, though. Dramathan looked edgy and in ill humor. His smile was one of steel, but it was not aimed at

Vellen—it couldn't be. Lord Valens had successfully negotiated all that he desired; Vellen was in the lesser position.

As he would be later this eve. The summons that he held in his breast pocket—no other word but summons could apply—seemed to writhe there like a living, burning thing. It had been some days since he had spoken with the Second of the Sundered, and he had had no word from the First. A poor choice, to assume that the Second had somehow prevailed.

There were no ceremonies slated for the evening; the quarter was in midsession, and no deaths were demanded. But it would not be the first time that one of the Karnari had died in midquarter.

He took another sip of the liquid and let it play across his tongue before swallowing. There was nothing he could do, of course, and that rankled. He would have to wait upon the First Servant's word.

Lord Valens lifted the silver decanter and poured himself another drink. His hands were steady, but his brow was cut by the lines of a severe frown. They eased somewhat when the knock came at the closed door.

"Enter," he said brusquely.

Vellen turned his head to catch his third glimpse of Amalayna of Valens as she entered the room. Even his brows rose a fraction as he saw the colors she had chosen to wear: black and white. The colors of war and death—the colors of mourning.

He couldn't help himself then. He smiled broadly. This was the secret of Lord Valens' annoyance, and he knew in a like position he would feel no different. He relaxed for the first time in two days and looked the lady up and down as she walked across the carpet, her eyes on her feet. She was quite lovely, in a pale, thin sort of way. Her age she wore well; he might have thought her just turned twenty. No colors had been added to her eyes, lips, or cheeks—and even in his opinion, this vanity would have served a purpose. No doubt Lord Valens had already made this clear and to little effect. He thought he might almost enjoy this interview.

"Amalayna."

"Lord Valens." She raised her head for the first time and met her father's eyes. Her own were dark and heavily ringed.

"We have a visitor, Lady. Comport yourself accordingly."

Her cheeks flushed, whether from anger or shame it was

hard to tell—but if she were her father's daughter, Vellen would guess the former. She said nothing, but turned to look at him.

He could see her pass through images that she carried in memory as she sought to place his face and was pleased that he had chosen his house colors, his house crest. He saw his house come to her and waited as she tried to place his name. The reward of the slight astonishment she let touch her face was enough.

"This is Lord Vellen of Damion," Dramathan said almost wryly. He knew his daughter would have already picked up the unspoken second, and by far more important, title.

She curtsied, holding the bend for just as long as his house title required and not nearly long enough for his Church rank. This, too, amused him.

"Lord Vellen." Her features were all smooth indifference and polite interest as she turned to face her father. "Lord Valens, you called me here. How may I be of assistance?"

"You may be seated." Cold were those words, a veil of frost over anger.

She sat crisply, almost regally, either arm pressed gently against the rests.

This was the type of obedience he liked least. Tentaris had not been as ideal a house as he could have wished if it had wrought such changes in her disposition. Tomorrow he would have slaves dispose of all of her current clothing. Only the burgundy and the grays would remain; she could choose among them until she learned that she was once again of House Valens.

She asked no further questions; did not offer to refill either of the lords' cups, although both were empty; did not attempt to join in pleasing conversation. How dare she wear her black and white here?

No matter, he thought. No matter. All would go as planned, smoothly or no. "Amalayna."

"Lord?"

"Lord Vellen of Damion has not come to see me; rather, it is you he pays court to."

"P-pardon?" She turned suddenly to catch the glint of Damion teeth and arrogance. Turned again to see her father's impassive face. "Court?"

"Indeed."

Vellen thought, at that moment, that the black and white she wore were superfluous. Her hair, against the pale ice of cheeks gone white, made her almost beautiful—a statue to commemorate mourning and loss. Perhaps Lord Valens did not drive too hard a bargain at that.

He rose, offering the lady a steady hand.

She rose as well, but there was little gracious in the movement. Her eyes were wide and dark, her hands light where they pushed him aside.

"Amalayna!" Lord Valens' roar filled the study, but it could not contain his wayward daughter; she was gone before the word could even echo, the doors swinging forcefully behind her.

Lord Vellen of Damion smiled.

Amalayna stared sightless at the adorned walls of her rooms. She had fled there because there was nowhere else to run. Her ribs, thin and sharp, cut into her lungs with every breath she took.

She stood in front of a full-length portrait of Cessalia of Valens, resplendent in the burgundy and gray, the moon above her head, the body of a slain deer beneath her feet. Her hair, near as dark as Amalayna's, was wild with wind and the hunt; a single diamond ensconced in a tiara glittered at the watching world. Night had taken the sky, and even the stars seemed small and weak in Cessalia's presence.

Amalayna bowed to her ancestor and wiped her cheeks uselessly with the back of her hand.

Mother of us all. She couldn't speak, but her lips moved over the words. *I know what the house demands, but I cannot do this.* Cessalia looked back, unmoved.

My child . . . I will lose my son.

But she knew that it was not for her son that she had run; it was not for the living and the breathing that she truly cared. That weakness made her cringe. It was Laranth, and Laranth's memory. How could she rite with any other, take any other, bear any other's children?

There was no knock at the door, but she could not help knowing that someone had entered the antechamber to her rooms. The walls resounded with the slam of the wood against them.

Only one person would dare to enter so.

The tears stopped, but their stain was evidence that spoke of her weakness when she could least afford it. She turned away from Cessalia and faced the door moments before her father made his way in.

He was alone, and his face, as hers, was flushed crimson. She had never seen him so angry. He strode across the room, his heels grinding the carpet. One hand gripped her shoulder, and the other struck her face. Hard.

Silence descended over the ringing in her ears, and she met her father's gaze squarely. She had no words to offer him.

"How dare you?"

Tears filmed her eyes, and she held them in check. As a child she had learned what tears bought. But her silence was no gift to Lord Valens either. His hand caught her hair, twisting it in such a way that it held her face up.

"I do not know what you did in House Tentaris, but you are not of that house any longer. Do you understand?"

"Yes. Yes, father."

"Lord Vellen is leader of the Greater Cabal, and he is here to bargain for rites. To you." He released her with a shove, and she stumbled, her back catching the edge of the frame that bound Cessalia. She caught it with her fingers, praying for strength.

She knew well why her father was angry and knew that she had given him just cause. She knew even that he was probably right: Her relations in House Tentaris had weakened her severely. She would never have embarrassed her father so badly before she had lived there. Before Laranth . . .

"Amalayna!"

She forced her eyes open enough to see the contempt in his. Those damnable tears had started again, and they wouldn't stop.

"I'm sorry," she babbled. "I'm sorry."

"You will give your apology to Lord Vellen, Lady, and you will do so now."

She nodded.

"And you will take off that dress—those colors will not be seen in my house—not by a member of my family!"

She nodded again, but this time it was harder.

"The house will lose or gain by your actions, Lady. Remember it." He turned and stopped at the door. "Gather yourself."

His voice was chill. "You have shown enough weakness for this day."

She nodded again and felt wood splinters in her palm.

If Laranth were still alive, she would be spared all of this. Lord Vellen could not court her, and her father's rage wouldn't touch her.

The tears stopped then, as if a tap had been wrenched.

If Laranth were still alive . . .

No, she thought. *No . . .*

"Stefanos."

The Lord of the Empire did not even raise his head, bent as it was over the steeple of his fingers. All around his feet, shadow pooled. Beneath it, he could see the slick surface of cold marble. His chambers were now complete. Or almost complete.

Stefanos.

His gaze slid away easily, finding walls that were the best example of mason work in his Empire. His work. It had taken time and power both, but still he was not satisfied.

For the walls were bare.

The time had come to alleviate that problem. The high priest would come to relinquish his hold on the council of the Karnari. Soon.

"Stefanos."

He rose slowly, a glint of red in his eye. Around him, as around the marble, shadows whirled: He was the eye of their storm. He cast his glance out one last time, following the stone arches into their peaked dome. He had returned to his kingdom in darkness, in silence. From here, he would rule.

"Stefanos."

"Sargoth, you annoy me."

"Yes," the Second of the Sundered whispered. There was no triumph or caution in the word; that should have been warning enough.

Stefanos was no fool, but he was angry, if so small a human word as anger could express the rage he barely contained. He was still; even the shadows around him became as cold and hard as ebony. But his eyes glowed a brilliant bloodred that haloed the room.

"Our Lord," Sargoth whispered, "has been calling."

Almost imperceptibly, Stefanos relaxed; a hint of his teeth showed themselves to Sargoth's vision.

"You may answer His call," he replied. "I shall not. But whatever you choose, Second, you *will* leave to do it elsewhere."

Sargoth drifted backward, but his shadow did not diminish.

Stefanos. Like a thread of fire, it wound its way around him, burning bright and cold. It was sure, the word, more of a command than any order. The Heart of the darkness; the voice of God.

Stefanos pushed it aside, but he trembled in the doing. Only once before had he ever ignored his Lord's summons.

"First of the Sundered, there is no war between us."

"There is a death between us, Sargoth. Yours would ease it. *Leave.*"

"Only once before did you seek to turn away from God. Remember it. You lost the rim to the Light."

The rim . . .

For a moment there was no ground beneath his feet, no roof above his head, no stone or marble, no smell of dust and earth—no altar, gleaming and untouched in the center of an obsidian dais.

But Light, there was Light. It was around him, seen in ways that human eyes could not conceive of. It was hideous; the sight of it unforgettable. Everything in him fought against it, fought to extinguish it.

He remembered the rim. Clearly, as only a Servant could do, he called up the image of nebulous ribbons of entwined light and dark. Standing, drifting, so close to the body of the Light he could almost see it; darkness above and below, a shield and armor to wear gladly; red down his hands, red along his eyes. And she, opposite, a tiny figure pulsing with the green of her deity, her Lord; her shield more obvious, her power no less.

There, the Lady named herself: Alariel.

And there, he in return named himself: Stefanos.

Hideous? No. Stark, and beautiful, as the war was.

It was there he had defied God to answer the call of the Light with a cry of his own. The first cry, the first name the Sundered of the dark had ever taken.

It was that name that bit into him now, twisting and turning as even the Light had never done.

Stefanos. First of the Sundered. Answer.

He fought against it as it grew; fought against himself as his blood answered. Only here, there was no Light to anchor himself against; no war that was more important than the Dark Lord's order.

The room dissolved around him; the shadows, no longer his own, closed inward, obscuring even his vision.

And when they cleared, they fell away like fingers unclenching. This was the Hand of the Dark Heart. He stood in it, knowing how much his power counted against his Lord's.

Stefanos.

"Lord."

You have been building.

There was silence. A human might have been choking here, in frustration and rage. No mortal was the First of the Sundered.

I have felt the power ebb.

"Lord."

You may use it.

For a moment he wanted to. He held his peace, waiting the time necessary before his return.

But use it only in my name and only in my work.

"Your ... work, Lord?"

There is one among your mortals; he is to be left alive.

Mortals? The air around the First of the Sundered grew red. "Have you not interfered enough? The mortal plane is—"

It is yours as I will it. Shadows writhed like captive dancers in the plane. The Dark Heart's anger was no less than that of his Servant's. The shadow grew almost solid in substance.

Stefanos felt the wave wash around him cleanly. Pain, too minor to be acknowledged, flowed through him. He felt no fear; even his anger seemed to have passed. The fury of the Dark Heart could only destroy one separate from His essence. Perhaps it could a lesser Servant, but not the greatest among them. At least, not here. Not in this plane.

But in the mortal plane, His given power would be strong indeed. Who then to wield it? Sargoth? He thought carefully: No. There are two others. And he would be damned before he saw his Empire fall to either.

"Which mortal?" He knew the answer before it came.

The one the Second calls Vellen.

Very well. Stefanos seemed to relax. The Dark Heart's game was entwined with Sargoth's somehow. "And in return?"

The plane.

Nothing more, nothing less.

"As you will it, Lord." He stepped back and began to unfurl the shadows.

Stefanos, the Second is useful to me. His voice is not as strong, but you will not take him.

Sargoth? "No, Lord."

He said nothing else; he had no need to. They were kin, these two, and they both understood well that this was not the last time they would meet, nor the last they would clash.

But only the one knew what the outcome could be. And He was well satisfied.

chapter
five

But Stefanos was angry.

Here, in a velvet imitation of darkness upon his mortal throne, that anger twisted. If there were games to be played, they would be *his* games.

Fire flickered around his fingers; the fire of Sargoth's plane. His eyes silvered, a glint pale and cold, as the blossom bit at his palm. With a shake of his head he clamped down on the gate, and the fire guttered.

It was almost time to think of other things.

He gestured, and a map spread itself out in the center of his audience chamber. From perfect memory he drew its thin red lines, contouring them for mountain or valley, twisting them for lake or stream.

Veriloth. He formed her cities carefully, placing them exactly as they stood, with their nebulous boundaries and outlying farmlands. He knew them well; they were his, part of the red net he cast.

Last, he drew Marantine in lines of white. The borders here were pink and imprecise, but the mountain ranges were crisp and clear, almost as much so as Dagothrin. Its cursed walls were once again secure against him.

He paid a bitter salute to his bygone foe. What she had built, she had built well. He was certain that she had not built it alone; not even she could have contained all of the power necessary to do so.

It mattered little. He had centuries, should he so choose, in which to discover its secrets. Perhaps he would order Sargoth to those very walls, and when they were his again, he would somehow have them dismantled.

He rose; he found his throne tiring. Black marble passed quietly beneath his feet until he stood facing this miniature creation of his world.

There was a knock at the door.

"Enter."

It didn't creak as it slid open, but it disturbed the air enough to catch his ear. Very slowly, the map a glow at his back, he turned to face his visitor.

The high priest stood, resplendent in full ceremonial garb. A red, high collar rose above the back of his head, and a simple tiara encircled his brow. His shoulders, padded and pointed, were also red; silk fell to the floor like a liquid, ending in a black hem above his feet. Red was the color of power in Veriloth; only the black, dark sash and the hem at foot and sleeve spoke of the source of that power.

Almost without thinking, Stefanos' gaze slid over to the pale, blank wall. There it was that he had intended to hang his trophy as a warning.

His eyes grew silver, and noting their color, Vellen's followed, becoming an opaque and uneven mirror. Neither moved.

Once before, standing in front of exactly this map, Vellen had entered Stefanos' chamber. It had been a chamber less grand and less lasting than the one he stood in now—but no less threatening. He had never come before in the full garb of the Karnari.

Stefanos smiled, if the movement of lip over teeth could be called that. His teeth were pointed and sharp, his lips almost gray. It was fitting; they both wore their guises of power. But Lord Vellen's could be removed easily; a claw to shred silk, and all that would remain was a frail, mortal body.

Fire split the air; no human fire, but no red-fire either. And fire answered, circling Vellen like a wall.

It would be easy to kill him; none of God's power was required. Just will and a way to Sargoth's magical gate—he had both.

The fire grew at Vellen's feet, licking the hem of his robe without quite consuming it.

"It was the Dark Heart's will," the high priest said; they were the first words that he had spoken, and their utterance ceded some small victory to the First of the Sundered.

That was not enough. The fire grew taller and brighter;

Stefanos could almost hear its hissing voice. He let it go a little, and it folded inward, to stop an inch from Vellen's face. The high priest didn't even flinch. He faced the fire squarely, his eyes still silver.

Stefanos felt the shifting of the fire and let a little more spill out of the gate. He began to tighten the circle around the high priest.

And felt another presence enter the fray as the fire halted dramatically.

"Sargoth."

There was no answer, but the fire was reply enough.

Stefanos.

Lord.

He called back his power; he closed the gate. Darkness burned through his Servant's body. By effort of will he did not clench his hands or jaw; no visible sign of the Dark Heart's words could be read by an observer.

The fires died. At a gesture, the torches in the walls flared up, and the First of the Sundered returned to the throne he had built. If his hands gripped the gold inlaid armrests too tightly, the shadows hid it from Vellen's eyes.

"You have lost Illan," he said softly.

Vellen nodded. There was a faint tremor to his jaw, and his eyes were still filmed the silver-gray of Sargoth's magic. But he felt only a touch of fear. Stefanos could barely hear its music.

"Report."

"Lord." Vellen bowed deeply. It was an unusual exercise for him, but he performed it well. "Our reports indicate that the Lesser Cabal that ruled that province was ambushed; I do not believe any survived."

"Ambushed?"

"Lord."

"By who?" There was more of a threat in those two words than even the fires had held.

"By Renar of Marantine." Vellen took a deep breath. "And his companions."

"Renar?"

The soft voice was always the worst. "The youngest son of the former king."

"He was to be assassinated, along with the rest of that line."

"Lord."

"Kill him."

"Lord." The high priest didn't even bother to say that Renar was now on the throne in Dagothrin; he knew how little that would buy him. Instead, he repeated his bow and then began his retreat; he knew a dismissal when he heard it. But his eyes were still silver as he reached the door, and only when it closed behind him did he acknowledge any sense of relief.

"Sargoth," Stefanos said to the shadows. "How long do you intend to protect a half blood?"

There was no answer.

"How long do you intend to interfere with my affairs?"

Oh yes, the soft voice was always the worst.

"For as long as the Dark Heart commands." The sibilant voice was cautious and neutral. "Do you think I would choose to remain in this gray and uninteresting place? It has little mystery for me."

The anger and frustration in those last words were all that stayed the hand of the Lord of the Empire. For a moment these two were kin again, under the command of the darkness. Both stood tall, and both were unbent by the anger and frustration that ate at them even now.

But now they fought across the fields, aiming at different targets.

"Play then," Stefanos said softly, still softly. "I have my own game to attend to."

"Sara."

Wind passed him by; the air around the spires was restless. Clouds, like gray velvet, lined the face of the shadowed moon. His fingers touched brass and steel as he bent to survey the entirety of the city that lay sleeping beneath him. Here and there a light flickered, or a fire; there was some movement in the streets. Not much of it.

He smiled grimly. There would be less in months to come. What passed for winter in these parts was vanishing quickly. He straightened himself and took a step onto the railing; it was strong, although it took only a part of his weight.

Let God keep one mortal for the moment. It would not be for long.

He rose until he hovered an inch above the rails and then began his descent. But he paused before a foot of the tower

had passed his eyes. There was still something undone,
unfinished—words that must be said just once and then buried.

He took a breath, although breath was not necessary. Cold
air pierced him cleanly enough that he almost felt a shiver. He
spread his limbs like wings of shadow, hovering a moment.

Memory. But he was no mortal, to be sapped by it; it was
his to call up in infinite detail; his to hold in abeyance should
he so choose.

"Sara." There, her name again. Two syllables, the merest
movement of air over lip and teeth and tongue. Still he swallowed, as if that single word were solid enough to choke on.
For a moment his throat remembered the water that she had
blessed when she had made her promise—it burned him even
now.

Enough. It was gone. It was past, like so much mortal history. This evening he meant to be free of it as she had always
been meant to be. She had gone the way of her mortal kin because she hadn't the strength to stand at the last by his side.
She had been very weak, and the time for weakness had
passed.

Ah, the shadows hid their lies. But his eyes, with their reddened glow, could pierce them easily. Had she a grave, he
might wander there to speak to what remained of his chosen
empress. Weak? No, not Sara. Not the Sarillorn.

"Sara, you have weakened me."

There. It was said, it had been acknowledged. He began his
descent again.

"You have no grave, Lady." The wind took his feral whisper
and shattered it against the stones above and below. "I will
make one for you." He drew his arms in, and his feet brushed
the ground.

He would never be weak again. He felt the lives in the
sleeping city in anticipation. Centuries had passed since he had
taken mortal blood to replenish power spent. Never again.

Closing his eyes, he let loose the hunger.

None of the slaves heard the screaming.

House Damion, as all houses, kept the slaves' quarters in the
lower level beneath the ground. In darkness, surrounded by
earth and stone, they had slept away the day's exhaustion.

Lord Damion and Lord Vellen had both done likewise, each
in his wing of the manor. Their rooms were large and solid—

spacious, elegant tributes to their titles and their powers. Velvet curtains drawn shut beneath heavy canopies had kept stray hints of breeze from open windows at bay.

Even their guards heard nothing amiss in the hours of early morning.

Not so the guards of Lady Cynthia. To them, her voice had carried like a word of doom. They had paused, perhaps to look at each other in askance, before throwing the doors open to enlarge the incoherent cries.

At least so the rumors went.

Two of the lady's personal slaves, on their usual early-morning errands, had found the guards missing and the doors to her sitting chambers thrown open. The sitting room was prim and perfect, each piece of furniture neatly and exactly placed. But the door from that room to her boudoir was also open. They had walked through that and stopped at the double doors to the bedchamber.

These were open. One was off its hinges.

And beyond that . . .

A sword lay across the threshold, attached to an arm that was no longer attached to anyone. Lady Cynthia had always favored pale colors, and the powdered blue of her carpet heightened the blood that had been spilled. Nearest the bed, a headless body, with one leg missing and the other at an impossible angle, matted the carpet. The other guard, his uniform dark and wet, hung from the brass wall fixtures that had once held a lamp. His feet dangled above the floor, casting a shadow in the streaming sunlight. His face, smooth and unwounded, was twisted inward in frozen pain.

On the bed itself lay what remained of Lady Cynthia of Damion.

The youngest girl froze. In her pale pink shift, with its pale blue belt and hem, she looked a part of the deathly tableau; the tips of her shoes were nestled in the blood on the carpet.

The other slave screamed.

Only this time, in the hours of daylight, the house itself was alive with the buzz of busy slaves. Those who heard came at a run, leaving buckets, mops, and dusters aside.

"Peg?"

The older girl shook her head. "S-Stev?"

"What's the—" She could almost hear him snap to a stop. "Lady of Mercy."

Others came crowding in.

"Briana—get the house mistress. Now. Take a care with your words and who you address—the lord'll be about soon."

He walked over to Peggy and Marla, putting an arm about either's shoulders. "Come on, we can wait in the outer rooms."

Peggy allowed herself to be led. Marla was still too frozen, and Stev eventually had near to lift her off her feet to move her. It wasn't hard; she was small and young. Her hands were clenched tightly in the pale, pink skirts of the uniform that Lady Cynthia had chosen.

"Easy," Stev said softly in her ear. "This wasn't your fault."

She nodded almost convulsively, but couldn't tear her eyes away from the corpse of her mistress. Stev snapped it by wheeling her around.

The house mistress came and went without speaking a word. Her face was gray, however, the lines of it more pronounced than they had ever been. Those slaves that had come to see what the screaming meant returned to their tasks, melting into anonymity and silence.

Stev waited nervously for her return. Neither Peggy nor Marla spoke at all, nor would they meet each other's eyes. They were as demure and pale as new slaves.

When the house mistress returned, she did so at the back of a unit of guards, all clad in the grim crispness of the black and the blue, with only the glint of steel to alleviate their darkness. They were armed for trouble; each of the eight bore a naked sword.

At their head strode Lord Damion. A robe of green and gold fell from his shoulders to the floor, catching the shadows as it swirled around his slippered feet. A black sash cut across his left shoulder and around his waist, the only sign that he'd been attended to at all.

He dominated the halls, and although the peaked roof towered above him, it in no way diminished his presence. He was lord of one of the most powerful houses in the Empire, and even unprepared, he showed it.

Stev drew Marla and Peg to the side of the hall and allowed the lord to pass. The house mistress took up her position beside them; it was a grim vigil they each had no choice but to perform. They were furnishings, maybe less, and accorded that much attention by their lord as he swept past them.

Lady of Mercy be blessed.

The hindmost house guards took up positions at either side of Lady Cynthia's door. They were younger, their faces cold and pale as they watched the four slaves huddled in the hall. Those slaves didn't need even that much warning; they didn't move.

But Stev sent silent thanks to the Lady, all the same, for this one small mercy: None of them were present to witness Lord Damion's initial reaction. Few indeed were the slaves privy to any expression of his weakness—and fewer were those who survived it.

Still, he listened. He could hear the tread of heavy boots against hardwood and carpet; he could tell the exact moment that they stopped. The guards were intelligent—not one of them made any sound of exclamation or surprise. Even for the free, life was not guaranteed.

Stev averted his eyes as Lord Damion came once again through the white of the open doors.

"Who discovered this?"

Marla and Peggy both tensed.

"The lady's personal slaves, Lord," the house mistress answered. "They were—"

"Enough!" He stepped forward and caught pale, pink shoulders in either hand. "Let them speak, house mistress."

"Lord." She curtsied, acknowledging the command. Even a noble would have; it was that strong.

"You were there first?"

"Y-yes, Lord."

"Did you touch anything?"

"N-no, Lord."

"You, girl?"

Marla was shaking. Stev wanted to speak, but not more than he wanted to live. He tried very hard not to notice his lord, although their faces were mere inches apart.

"Answer me!"

"N-no—no I couldn't—I didn't—I—" Tears slid down her cheeks, punctuating the quick, sharp intake of breath.

For just a moment, Stev's heart fell. Lord Damion's face was the mottled gray of a lord who wants a death.

Marla. He didn't move.

The lord released Peggy's shoulder. He raised his free hand as his grip on Marla tightened. His lips were almost white; anger chased the lines of his face into grim, cold definition.

And then it was gone.

Lady, Lady, thank you.

Miraculously, it was gone.

"House mistress. Assign these two elsewhere."

"Lord."

"And you," he added, deigning to notice Stev for the first time, "back to your duties."

"Lord."

Lord Damion turned away. If he had been almost anyone else, Stev would have been moved to pity at the bend of his shoulders and the lines of his face. "Haleth."

"Sir?" The captain of the guards was at his lord's elbow, as if speed or attention could somehow erase the failure of his unit.

"Send for my son."

"Sir."

Stev waited until the guards had left the hall before unlocking his knees. He nodded shakily at the house mistress and made his way back to his duties—cleaning the gallery's many frames and railings. Sunlight, pouring through windows that were two stories tall, warmed his back as he bent into his task.

Ah, it was warm here; the sky was clear and blue where it passed through clear glass instead of colored window; Marla and Peggy had been spared their lord's wrath.

But Lady Cynthia returned to him, her lifeless body framed by the matted wreckage of her bed. He scrubbed at near-spotless brass and finely oiled wood as if the motion could clear the bloodstains from his mind.

Hours later, the sun at high noon, he allowed himself to ask the question, but in silence, only in silence.

What did this?

The chill was all around him. Even the strength of the Lady's song held no comfort.

Lord Damion, now dressed in the sober colors of his office, had only to see the tired visage of his heir to know the answer to his question. He was not, by nature, a kind man. He asked it anyway.

Lord Vellen, all dressed for the hour in the finery of his Church position, met his father's eyes across the desk and the distance that divided them—all of the distances.

The lord of House Damion and the lord of the Greater Cabal

had, between them, much of the power of the Empire of Veriloth.

Of the Empire as it had been.

"The First." His voice was a whisper, as if his power were already dead, and only a ghost lingered.

"What does he intend?"

"I don't know." After a moment, he added, "I didn't foresee this." It cost him, to put that in words.

Sharply, his father said, "This is not a matter of the Church."

Old anger flared to life—red glints that were never far below the surface of the eyes. But even that anger died. It was a house death, a house loss.

"No, Father."

Again, uneven silence descended upon them. What course of action was open? No counterassassination, no political penalty, no shift in alliance. The First of the Sundered stood alone.

"Vellen, was this in response to an action of yours?" Lord Damion seldom used such a tone. Nonetheless, Vellen knew it well and knew what it presaged.

He began to grope for an answer when the knocking, frantic and loud, began at the study door.

"Enter," his father barked, the lines of his brow darkening.

A slave nearly fell across the threshold. By his clothing, he was a door slave.

"Lord Vellen," he gasped, "your presence is urgently requested at the temple." He reached out one trembling hand, and Vellen took the piece of curled parchment that shook there.

He read it quickly; it lost none of its import.

"It seems," he said, meeting his father's eyes, "that this is a matter for the Church after all." With some relief he rose and left the room at the heels of the slave.

Lord Damion sat alone in impenetrable silence as the doors swung shut. His aged hands curled slowly inward—the fists of a powerful man. He did not raise them to strike; he was old and wise enough not to need to make a futile gesture.

His memory had always been good. He had used it to great advantage to increase the power and standing of his house. But now . . .

Cynthia's face, frozen in a silent scream, had burned itself across his inner eyelids. Such a death not even his slaves met at the altars.

What use power now?
Cynthia . . .

Thirteen houses. Thirteen deaths.

Vellen glanced impatiently at the back of his driver. He clamped back an order and tried to settle into the padded carriage seats; the rough movement of wheel over stone told him that the horses could not be pressed much faster. The streets emptied at his passing; colorful glints of fleeing merchant-wear and market slaves told him that none so far had been foolish enough to remain in the path of his coach. All the better; he could not afford any delay. If any were idiot enough to get caught beneath his wheels—never mind it. The thought of the death he'd evoke had no glamor or distraction for him at the moment.

Thirteen houses.

And no coincidence that the Karnari numbered thirteen, either. No coincidence that the slaves had slept untouched and untroubled while members of the house proper bled their lives away to feed a walking Servant.

He looked around from side to side as the market stalls moved past his carriage window.

Was there not life here to take? Many of these stalls fronted houses, where the so-called free slept closeted with their abundant families in their mundane, thin little homes. Was there not enough in the north city near the docks?

He closed his eyes, shutting the city out for the moment. Perhaps, perhaps he could use this to his advantage. Perhaps, in the council meeting that he drove so speedily to, the loss of each house would be a bargaining tool for him. Perhaps he would be allowed a graceful exit from his dealing with Lord Valens.

If the council still existed at all.

Vellen, was this in response to an action of yours?

Yes.

The leader of the Greater Cabal clenched his jaw in silence. In anger.

All this, all of it, for the sake of one half-blood woman.

Red light eddied in the shadows near the pillars, a spill of liquid from a dark communion. The First of the Sundered watched it in silence, well satisfied.

This peace, this warmth—he had not known it for centuries. Even perfect memory had denied him this satiation.

Twenty-seven dead.

Twenty-seven splintered souls, broken and lost in the wash of his power. His power; not God's. He smiled, and the light crept up the pillars like a flag.

Not for years had he been at the zenith of his strength. That had changed, and much would change with it. Was he not the Lord of the Empire?

He stood stiffly, his hands still touching the armrests of his throne. Claws, sharp and cold, left their mark as he at last stepped away. His arms he threw wide in a fan of red glory. Even the acolytes levels above would feel this and know that he had truly arrived.

Shadow bubbled up in dense clouds before him. A red lattice danced around it as the door opened to starred and clear sky.

He told no one where he was going.

He barely thought about it himself.

And his feet made no trace in the darkened grass beneath them as he trod through the careful construction of hedgework that was the maze. Flowers and grass he could barely smell, so strong and cloying was the scent of his Enemy's blood.

Yet he stayed, to begin his search anew before the hours of dawn.

He did not see Sargoth, for the Second was skilled indeed in the use of God's power. No sound of Sargoth's curses reached his immortal ears. No trace of Sara's presence was caught in the intricate strands of the web he wove, no matter how long or how far it stretched.

He could not say why he wanted her body. But he searched for it anyway.

chapter
six

Getting into Verdann was surprisingly easy. The guards at the gates gave them no trouble—they didn't even bother with a cursory glance at the various citizenship papers that Hildy carried, invisibly, upon her person. Not that Hildy had them ready; it only encouraged the boys, as she said, to be bullies.

Erin looked at the "boys" a little doubtfully and wondered just how the Verdann city guards would feel if they heard her. Their armor, for the most part, was in good repair, and the scars along the exposed skin of their hands and faces showed that the weapons they wore weren't decoration. She almost smiled in spite of herself when the captain of the gates came out from the guard post; he was nearly Hildy's age, although he didn't come close to matching her weight, and he wore his authority like a mantle. His armor was black, but there was no red to mar it. Light glinted off the chain of his arms as he waved them through.

"I can't believe it," Erin whispered to the older woman as the wagons began to lurch and roll. "They didn't even inspect the cargo."

Hildy smiled. The smile was a rare one, for there was a hint of genuine malice combined with amusement in it.

"House Boradil owns half the guards at the north and east gates, dear."

It was the northern gates that they passed under. These gates were not so high or fine as those of Dagothrin; designed and built by mortal hands, they had weathered time poorly. There were cracks in the mortar that held the stones together, and the wood was warped in many places.

The main thoroughfare was almost deserted; those farmers

that had goods to bring had long since passed this way, but it was still too early in the day for them to leave.

Erin looked at the streets as their cobbled stone passed beneath the wagon wheels, trying to remember if they had looked the same on her previous visit. Here and there the road was cobbled solidly, but there were large stretches of dirt flanked by rocks and early weeds. The horses seemed to prefer the dirt.

"Darin, dear," Hildy called.

Darin looked up, and Erin was shocked at the expression on his face.

Seeing it mirrored in her reaction, he struggled with a smile. "Yes?" His voice was very quiet.

"I think you'd better come up here with us. You can ride in the wagon, if you'd prefer."

He frowned slightly. "Why?"

"We'll be heading to the compound in the warrens." She paused, then pulled the wagon to a slow crawl. "Darin." Her voice was very soft. "We aren't going to the market."

He closed his eyes and nodded, the lines of his jaw tense. "I know."

Erin slid off the wagon and walked around its back. She didn't remember the roads here clearly, but she knew now that Darin did: the roads and more.

She put an arm around his shoulder and gently drew him to the cab. "Ride with Hildy, Patriarch of Culverne." She said his title lightly and gently. "I've been lazy long enough."

"But you're a—"

A firm finger pressed against his lips very quickly. "Don't say it. Say: 'You're a warrior,' or I'll think you've spent too long in the Empire." The words were sharp, but again the voice was light and gentle.

"You're a warrior." His hand trembled slightly as Hildy reached down to help him up.

Erin looked down at her hip self-deprecatingly. "Without a weapon." She sighed. "Do you know what a weaponsmaster would say if he could see me now?"

"No, what?" Tiras asked.

Erin laughed and went to retrieve her sword. "Never mind. I couldn't ever get the voice right without destroying my throat—to say nothing of the words."

* * *

The compound looked every inch a prison camp to Erin's eyes. Wire, barbed every eight inches, was wrapped quite tightly around thick, wooden poles and pulled taut in seven evenly spaced rows. There was a gate, large enough to pass the wagons through, that would open onto the grounds that fronted a small but well-kept building.

Erin gave Darin a quick, sideways glance, but he seemed relaxed now; wherever he had been kept in Verdann, it was not in a place such as this.

Hamin caught her staring as they approached the compound. He grinned. "Quite a sight, isn't it?"

She nodded.

"It isn't just for show—you need security in the warrens."

"Why does Hildy stay here?"

"The warrens aren't well patrolled, at least in practice." He walked over to the gates and raised his hand to catch a short, thick rope. Bells clattered in the quiet street, and the horses skittered nervously. "Sorry about that; you need it to catch Burrows' attention."

The door of the low, squat building burst open, and an elderly man, with an expression as grim as his holdings, hobbled out toward the gate. He held a dark, thick cane in wide, bent fingers. As he approached, Erin could see the lines of a squint around his eyes—the day was very bright.

"What's this, then?" he bellowed, in a quavering, low voice.

"Knock it off, Burrows," Hamin said curtly, rolling his eyes. "It's just us."

"Oh." Burrows seemed to look momentarily deflated. "Well, then, let me get the gate." He straightened out, losing years in the process. At this distance, the gray in his hair was suddenly suspect, as were some of the darker lines of his narrow face. Even the clothing he wore seemed to lose the patina of age that Erin had noted at a distance; they were brown overalls with carefully placed patches that now seemed superfluous.

"Early, aren't you?"

"A couple of weeks."

Burrows grinned and opened his mouth to display a broken row of teeth. Not all of his age was mimicry.

"Don't even think of asking us for papers. It's been a long day."

"Right." The gates swung open. "Any problems getting here?"

"Not today."

Burrows looked out. "Ah, well." He scratched the side of his face absently. "Maybe it's because you look too well armored. I could take care of—"

"Burrows!"

"Right." He stepped out of the way, and the wagons began to roll forward. Hildy leaned slightly to the right, her hands still holding the reins.

"Burrows, dear, do be a good boy. We have three new friends with us, and I'd hate them to think that I choose inappropriate warrens."

His sigh was quite audible and quite genuine. "Yes, Hildy," he offered meekly.

"Have you had any trouble, dear?"

"Some from Milford; nothing I can't handle."

She shook her head. "I thought Milford might grow out of his dangerous precociousness."

Burrows rolled his eyes as he began to walk alongside the horses. "He isn't exactly dangerous, Hildy."

"No, I don't suppose so. But he's very—" She shrugged, searching for the right word. "—well, rude."

"Rude. Right." Burrows reached for the reins.

"Still, dear, you were rather rude when you first came to work for me. Maybe he'll change after all."

Burrows muttered something under his breath.

Darin, missing it, found himself stretching forward to catch whatever else Burrows would say.

Hildy caught him by the shoulder. "Don't fall off, Darin." She grinned. "If you want to know, I'd bet gold that he said 'It's a good thing Hildy only manages the money.' "

"Bad bet, boy," Burrows called out. "Hildy's ears are better at her age than most are at yours."

Hildy beamed. "A compliment. How nice." She pushed herself off the cab and hit the ground with a soft thud. "Burrows, dear." Her arms, still bundled for cold although the day was distinctly warm, swept out to either side.

"Aw, Hildy—not in front of—"

She gave him a bear's hug, or the next best thing to it. Darin had a suspicion that Burrows would have preferred the real thing.

Especially when Hamin began to laugh loudly.

* * *

The inside of the building—Burrows' house, or Hildy's Verdann headquarters—was as spare and solid as the outer walls. There were windows that let in the light, but these were heavily barred—as if anyone could get to them in the first place.

A large kettle was beginning to bubble over the wood-burning iron stove, and cups had already been laid out across the length of a simple rectangular table. Chairs had been hastily gathered from the other three rooms, and although they didn't match the table particularly well, they were taken quite gratefully by Burrows' visitors.

"Sorry about the tea," Burrows murmured, as he tended to the kettle. "It's Iverson blend."

Hildy sighed. "Well, it is that time of year after all."

Tiras nodded his agreement in silence.

But while Tiras and Hildy might commiserate in their knowledge of tea drinking, Erin found the brew offered by their host to be quite good. It wasn't fragrant—no hint of perfume or flower scent touched it—but it was heavy and solid. It reminded her of her early life; she could almost hear the echo of Katalaan's voice rippling between the kitchen shutters—shutters that had been forever swinging in the wake of Katalaan's presence, passing the scent of baking bread, cakes, or meals into the whole of the house.

But Katalaan's table had never hosted such a fellowship, and with a sigh, she turned herself to the matters at hand.

"Are there any newcomers?"

Burrows' smile was a weary one. "Three this time. Word of the 'fall' of Illan has been slow to spread. You know that the Church doesn't encourage rumor-mongering."

Hildy touched his arm gently. "I've brought a few papers—Boradil seals. I think they'll cover three. And dear, there will be more; news like this can't be supressed forever."

He smiled again, but this time the expression was caught somewhere between hope and indulgence. "Thanks, Hildy."

"Where are they?"

"At the usual place; I've told 'em to expect you, but not for two weeks."

"Well, we'll be there in a few hours—I'm sure we can get an introduction without too much pain."

* * *

The Servants, whether of Light or Dark, had always possessed the ability to memory-walk. Every scene that they had passed through, whether briefly or at length, could be called up and examined in minute, silent detail. Any scent, any color, any conversation, all could be brought back whole and exact.

Even two mortals could not agree on all the details their own lesser memory held—but the Servants, no matter their number, could speak and nod in total assent.

Erin wondered how it was that their descendants often missed receiving that gift. Especially now.

The streets of the warren, with their high, thin wooden buildings and their narrow thoroughfares, had wound their ways into the warren's center, following Hildy's steady lead. The wagons, left at the compound under Burrows' scrutiny, would barely have maneuvered many of the sharper turns and potholed roadways, so it was just as well they were left.

People passed them in the streets, but few indeed were those who stopped to speak or nod hello; for the most part, seeing the armed escort that walked with Hildy, people elected either to cross the street or melt into the shadows of the alleys.

Erin wondered where they were going, but felt it wasn't her position to ask; she walked with the guard, weapon out and readied in a steady hand. Only when Hildy called a stop did she begin to recognize where they were.

The dilapidated sign of the Red Dog hung undisturbed over her head. Erin's eyes widened, and then she smiled at her reflection in the dusty glass of a large, flat window. Almost hesitantly, she reached out and touched the distorted image; her fingers came away dirty.

"Looks better than the last time we saw it," she heard at her shoulder. She turned to look at Darin and realized for the first time that he was almost her height.

"You've grown," she said, before she could stop herself.

He still blushed.

"Sorry. I sound like a grandmother." Then she stopped and looked at him more closely. "Darin."

He nodded.

"Have you— Is your voice cracking?"

"Not much," he answered shortly. He was embarrassed.

"I hadn't noticed. Is that why you haven't been talking?" The instant she said it, she truly wished her foot could fit into her mouth. "Uh—maybe we should go in."

He caught her arm. "Erin—it is, a little. Why I haven't been talking, I mean." Each word deliberate and controlled.

She knew what the other reason was and hugged him, hoping that wouldn't embarrass him more.

"Well, dears, are you going to go in, or are you going to stand here blocking the door?"

Erin laughed. "We'll go in. There's someone I want to say hello to." She caught Darin's arm in hers. "Someone we both want to say hello to."

"Uh, Erin?"

"Yes?"

"The sword, dear."

"Oh." Metal slid into the scabbard, but the lack of a weapon didn't make her feel nervous. Not here.

The door swung open before her, and she looked into the dark, noisy den of the Red Dog. At midafternoon, it was still well over half-full, and the charming assortment of round tables and mismatched chairs was spotted with the customers that the warrens attracted.

Halfway into the tavern, a barmaid was busy dropping an empty tray on the unadorned head of an older customer while his cohorts laughed loudly. She herself was laughing, although her smile was anything but blushing; she was not a young woman, just a very competent, attractive one.

The injured man seemed to take it all in stride, and if he looked disappointed, it was obvious even at this distance that he was completely familiar with such a feeling.

Which was good; Verdor's inn didn't allow for much other expression of disappointment when it came to the availability of his staff.

"Hey—are you coming in, or are you just holding the door for the flies?"

That voice, Erin felt she would recognize anywhere. But she hesitated on the threshold, as if just remembering all of the trouble that she—they—had caused the last time they had stayed at the inn.

The bartender stepped out from behind his counter, his large, square hands already forming fists against his hips. He wore a soiled apron over a heavy, brown shirt that had been rolled up by obviously dirty hands.

"Verdor?"

His frown froze and then began to unwind as his eyes widened. "Is this who I think it is?" He smiled broadly, and the men at the bar stools relaxed, more because they could hear his tone of voice than see his expression.

Erin nodded, her own smile both friendly and uncertain.

"So it is!" He strode over, covering the distance in four large strides. "Lorie—and who's this giant beside you?"

"It's me, Darin."

"Impossible—I remember him. He was just a small boy." Then he laughed, that deep-throated, friendly roar that was so unmistakable. His arms came out, and he caught them both in a bear of a hug.

"Astor!"

"Dad?"

"Go tell your ma we've got real guests!"

"Real guests?" someone shouted. "Does that mean they don't have to drink this swill?"

That someone was elbowed in the ribs by his drinking partner before Verdor could find him.

"So, how's the half-wit? I've heard rumors that he's got his backside stuck to the highest chair in Marantine." He chuckled, turning them around without releasing them. "Let's head into the back rooms."

"Well, we're here with someone."

"Who?"

"A merchant from Marantine. I think you might—"

"Hildy?"

Darin nodded. He edged out of Verdor's hug as the bartender turned, yet again, to face the door—and to face Hildy, who stood patiently blocking the path, her mittens in her hands.

"Hildy!"

"A nice man," Hildy said to Erin, "but not the most observant."

"Hildy . . ."

She sighed, looking very much like a put-upon older relative. "Hello, Verdor dear. I see you've met my friends before."

"Astor!" There was no answer. "Now where has that boy gone?"

* * *

"Well." Hildy leaned back into the comfortably worn cloth of the love seat that she occupied by herself. Her fingers played gently against the twirling patterns of delicate china that held a much better tea than Burrows had been able to offer.

Verdor was smiling. He took a swig from a large, thick mug and set it down on the table. It contained tea, but as he had reasonably explained to all present, a man his size could barely get his fingers around the handle of a teacup. "So you *have* been busy."

She nodded at Erin, Tiras, and Darin. "These three have. Putting Marantine into proper order hasn't been easy. It's a good thing the Empire was only there for five years."

"And half-wit?"

Erin smiled.

"Half-wit, dear," Hildy admonished sternly, "is not a fit appellation for a king."

"He really did it?"

"Oh yes." It was Tiras who spoke. Erin wondered if her memory played false with her; she remembered his strutting pose as Lord Brownbur and couldn't easily reconcile it with his grim silence here. Gone were frills and rich-hued velvet, gone was the jovial wordiness.

Verdor didn't blink. "Does he like it?"

"As much as one would expect."

"Ah well. I expect I'll see him this way soon, then."

"You had better not."

"He didn't want to stay," Darin added. "But someone had to watch the throne."

Verdor's smile gentled. "So this is how kings are made. Ah well. If you can keep him there, he'll do a good job."

"I'm sure he will, dear." Hildy set her cup aside firmly. "But we've all got our work to do."

Verdor grew more somber. "Business already?"

She nodded. "Burrows tells me that you've three here that need help."

"Three." He nodded, setting his own mug aside. "But to be honest, Hildy, it may well be two by the time everything's said and done."

"How so?"

He grimaced slightly. "One of them's pretty bad. Older man—almost my age. He had some trouble getting down here.

Aquitted himself well enough to make it." He leaned back in the chair. "We've had a doctor in twice, but he's got two wounds that're infected. He's fevering now."

"Oh." Hildy's face developed a few more lines, giving those who watched their first true impression of her age. "Are they staying here?"

Verdor nodded quietly. There wasn't very much left to say. And words couldn't have captured the expression on either the innkeeper's or the merchant's face as they turned to look at Erin.

She had already half risen, but those looks stopped her with her hands on the table and her knees half-bent beneath it. Verdor's expression she could understand; his life had been the first step on the path out of shadow.

But Hildy . . .

As ever, Hildy understood the unspoken confusion and smiled gravely. "They talk of you often, dear. King's friend, king's captain. The royals in particular—the guards, mind—have nothing but praise to sing of you." She too rose. "Of you, dear, and your skill."

Erin stared awkwardly at her hands, unsure of what to say in response.

"The royal guards don't place their affections on nothing." Hildy offered a hand.

After a pause, Erin took it, surprised as always at the strength in its grip.

"You aren't used to being complimented, are you? Probably just as well. Verdor?"

"I'd best lead. They're all a bit jumpy."

Tiras rose, silent, and Darin rose last. Very carefully he picked up the staff of his office and glanced at Erin's retreating back.

She will be fine, Initiate.

He barely heard Bethany's voice. Instead, Stev's jaunty whistling returned in a slave's song. A song to the Lady of Mercy. Somehow it wasn't out of place here, and that worried him.

The uncarpeted halls of the third floor of Verdor's inn were narrow and tall; clean, unadorned wooden doors punctuated them every few feet. All were closed, and all were silent. At the end of the hall, a large rectangular window let daylight in through the bars of a thick grill. Even this high up, the warrens still had some effect.

Darin noticed all of this, but to Verdor it was part of the everyday business of running his inn. He walked down the hall toward the light and turned at the third door from the end. There he gestured for quiet, then knocked very precisely; five times, three short and two long, each blow echoing dully behind him.

There was the sound of shuffling, then the door creaked open a few inches.

"It's Verdor," the innkeeper said quietly. "I've come with another doctor."

Someone nodded—that much could be seen, although little else—and the door swung more fully open.

A woman, dressed in simple clothing, stared apprehensively out at that company gathered before her. One slim, callused hand fell into thick, brown folds of linen, the other remained glued to the door. She wasn't old, but her face was lined, and her hair was silvered brown. Along one cheek the remnants of an old scar lingered.

"Maya."

She smiled hesitantly up at the much taller man.

"How's Horvath?"

"He's better . . ." She stepped aside almost helplessly.

"It's all right. We'll see for ourselves. Is Gareth—"

"I'm here." A younger voice came, male from the sound of it. Looking into the room, Darin could see someone nearly his own age. He wore familiar clothing—Astor's regular work tunic—and sat in the room's single chair. It had been pulled up beside the bed, as close to the man that slept there as possible.

At least at first glance, it appeared that he slept. But even to Darin's untrained eye, it became readily apparent that that wasn't the case. Horvath's skin was sallow, almost green, and sweat beaded his brow. His hair, which was thin, whether from age or illness, was plastered to forehead and pillow in damp, greasy curls.

Erin's sharp breath made Darin move out of the way to let her pass. "I'm sorry," she said softly to Gareth. "I think I'll need the chair."

He had already gotten to his feet. He started to walk to his mother, then stopped as the lady sat down. He watched her push her sword hilt to one side and forget about it.

"What're you going to do?"

"Gareth."

He knew the tone well. It was the shut-up-and-get-over-here voice that his mother only used when there was a chance of danger. He shut up. But he lingered over Erin's shoulder, watching as her hands, smaller than his, reached out to cup his father's face. They were, it seemed, very gentle; he had trouble believing they could hold the sword at her side.

She murmured something clearly, but he didn't understand the words she used. Her hands fluttered a moment, then came back to touch his father's cheek and brow.

"Can you—can you do anything?"

Just like a mother. She could talk; he had to be quiet.

The lady in the chair nodded quietly. "Verdor—maybe you should clear the room."

"What're you going to do?" Gareth's voice was distinctly louder, and the words more urgent.

"Gareth!"

He swung around, to see his mother edging her way past the burly innkeeper. With quickness that spoke of experience, he dodged around to the other side of the bed and wedged himself between it and the blank wall. He bit his lip and caught the bed frame between clenched fingers.

"We came this far together," he said to his mother, between equally clenched teeth. "And I ain't leaving yet."

"Verdor, I'm sorry," Maya began, as she walked over to her boy. "It's just that . . ."

"Don't worry about it." Verdor caught her shoulders in one arm, letting her know again the strength of the comfort he could offer. "My own son's none better behaved than yours."

And Erin looked up. Her eyes were glowing with the green, living light of the lines.

Neither Maya nor her son knew the lines. In a silence uncomfortably stretched between fear and awe, they both stopped moving.

"Stay, then," Erin said softly, her voice low. "I mean this man no harm and will help him if I can."

Maya nodded dumbly.

And Darin, silent until now, knew what Erin intended to do.

He walked into the room, but not to her. The floorboards creaked loudly, unnaturally so—no one else was moving.

"Maya," he said, trying to lower his voice as much as possible in an effort to be adult in her eyes, "I've traveled with her for a long time. She's saved many lives."

Maya looked down at him and saw him as he was: a boy maybe a year older than her son, walking with a staff, wearing a cream-colored shirt that was a little too large for him. She nodded, and her eyes flickered away, to be held once again by Erin.

"She's special," Darin continued, although Maya did not look down again. "And what she's about to do may seem odd."

His words, if they might have had their desired effect, had no time to sink in before Erin reached down to her leg to pull out a simple, unadorned dagger in a slim, steady hand.

Both mother and son stiffened, and then Gareth began to crawl up on the bed, his mouth wide with shock.

"Gareth!" Verdor's voice had the effect that Darin's did not. "Hold!"

"What are you doing?" he demanded, his fists clutching thick wool blankets.

But the light in her eyes was growing still, and she had no answer to give.

"She's trying to touch God," Darin answered, and then bit his lip. Had it been so long? Had he forgotten so much of life as a slave that he could say this without realizing immediately what its effect would be?

He reached forward, staff in hand, and swung it lightly into Gareth's chest. Light limned staff and boy as if they were one single object, but it was light that Gareth's eyes would never see. Yet he felt it still, as Bethany's power enveloped him, giving peace in almost equal measure to his fear.

Maya swiveled to Verdor with a look of horror and betrayal writ large across her gaunt, angular face. Her hands came up to frame her cheeks as she shook her head from side to side.

"Hold, Maya," Verdor said again. "This God is not the God of Veriloth. Trust us."

Trust a free man. As a slave.

This, this Darin understood. And he knew what he might do to help her. An act, not of power, but of powerlessness. With only a thought of Bethany, he dropped his staff and began to fumble with the buttons on his long, right sleeve. He rolled up the linen past the elbow, then shouted her name— the name she had given in trust and hope to a free man.

This time, when she looked at Darin, she saw him as he had once been. The white lines of House Damion curled around the soft inner skin of his arm like a bracelet.

They were kin, in a way. They had suffered the same small deaths, and the same losses; the same helplessness and the same dying dreams. "Please," he said. "I'm Darin. Trust us."

And she bit her lip and turned to face Erin again.

To face the Sarillorn of Elliath.

Blood dripped from Erin's palm to splash the worn, scuffed wood of the floor and the rough, pale brown of blanket. The dagger stayed suspended in Erin's left hand a moment and then fell, gently, to the bed. She released it and brought her arms across her chest. Her throat rose suddenly like a pillar of human fire; her hair, dark without sun to glint along its copper edge, seemed to crackle in electric wind. For a moment her eyes were too green, too bright to countenance, and then they went out beneath the curtains of lids and lashes.

Darin felt the stirring of blood at the sight of the Sarillorn. He had never met a Servant, but knew now, again and as always, that this is what they would have looked like—living, burning statues in the hand of God. He reached for Bethany and held her tightly.

Maya's trembling lips began to stumble over words that sounded strangely familiar to Darin. Her fear was suddenly guttered, gone as if it had never had the time and the years to grow so large and all-encompassing. She was singing.

> *"Lady of Mercy, please hear us*
> *Lady of Mercy, be near us*
> *We who have toiled, still wait*
> *The hand that will free us from fate."*

Another voice joined hers, lower, younger, but less tremulous in its hope. Youth did that.

> *"Lady of Mercy, you sleep*
> *In darkness, yet faith shall you keep*
> *We know, we who wait, that you'll come*
> *Love and Mercy, your will will be done."*

She moved to the beat of that chorus of two as the last of the ward was done. Her hands, one clean and one bloodied, came to rest upon the brow of the dying man.

Three people were healed by the hands that touched only one. Power, Lernan's, flowed through the vessel she had made of herself. Life answered His call; infection withered and died as she weeded it from his system like a master gardener.

And when she was done, she slumped forward in the chair as if strings had been cut at the shoulder. But her image remained, both in the room, and in the markets and squares of the Empire.

The Lady of Mercy returned and triumphant.

She smiled wanly, and her voice was impossibly human, impossibly tired as she met Maya's eyes. "I think—I think he'll be all right now."

Maya fell to her knees. There were tears streaming down her cheeks, and she did nothing to check them, even though they blurred the edges of the woman who had saved her husband's life.

"Oh Lady, Lady." She whispered it again and again, giving the words the tone and timbre of the litany that they had become in her life. "Oh Lady, thank you, thank you."

Even Gareth half bent to the floor, but his mouth was wide and still.

Erin's brow creased in confusion. "He'll be fine, now. Are you all right?"

Maya laughed, and the laugh was a girl's laugh, a child's laugh. It was that open and that vulnerable.

The eyes of the man on the bed flickered open at the sound. "Maya?" the man whispered. "What's going on?"

It was Erin who answered. "I'm not sure."

He swiveled his head to look at her with suspicion and confusion. "Who are you?"

And Maya laughed again, sweeping herself to her feet in such a lithe motion that she left the years behind. She ran to the bed and threw herself across her husband's chest. The wound that had been there was now a thin white line; the body's memory of something painful in the distant past.

"The Lady of Mercy," she said softly.

"Girl, have you been drinking something?"

"Oh Horvath, don't you understand?"

"Maya? Why are you crying?"

"We're free," she said, and then the tears became too strong to let words pass.

chapter
seven

It was Darin who explained things to Erin.

He was young enough not to be able to find the right words and close enough to his past not to want to try too hard. But he knew, in the sleepless dark of a night with Tiras' snores for company, that until he made her understand, he would see her a little as Maya and Gareth now did: too distant. He had to make her see what Maya and Gareth saw. There was an easy way to do it, but he would have to brave the market of Verdann. The very market that he watched the last emblems of his free life be sold away in. He didn't want to go.

In the morning, tired and drawn, he avoided breakfast and spoke with Verdor for a few minutes.

That afternoon, Erin, Darin, Tiras, and Verdor headed out to the West Market Square. They dressed much as they had for their journey; like travelers, still a little dirt-stained from the toil of the road. And they carried the grants of House Boradil as protection against unwanted inquisition.

"But I don't understand why we have to go to a market—isn't that more visibility than we should have?"

"Lass," Verdor said easily, his arm around her shoulders, "I go there all the time on errands from the wife. It'll be safe; you're with me."

But it wasn't Verdor she asked the question of, and Darin would only look away and shake his head. He looked younger and older both, and he had left his staff behind at the inn. It troubled her; he seldom left Bethany's voice anywhere that he couldn't see her.

The warrens melted away, to be replaced by buildings with

more land and less height. These too were replaced by larger buildings in better repair, and the road beneath their feet was distinctly, neatly cobbled. Merchant money paid for it, so there were seldom any missing stones or holes to trouble wagons, carriages, or careless feet.

The market square opened out before them, although its edges had been blurred by actual storefronts and a few straggling stalls that could find no room in the square proper. At just past midday it was cool, although the sun was warm and the air dry.

Erin followed Darin, making her way past the growing crowds of people wandering briskly to unknown destinations. She had no money and very little worth stealing, so the thought of thieves didn't make her as nervous as the sight of Darin's stiff, trembling back.

Market vendors shouted, some at Erin, and some at people on either side. The cries were normal market cries, mock-anxious, mock-friendly, and all aggressive. Once or twice she turned and almost headed off the main thoroughfare—she had not been raised to ignore direct questions.

Verdor, on the other hand, had no problems doing so. His grip on Erin grew more sure as he walked, and his scowl somewhat more pronounced.

The stalls suddenly opened out into a sky clear of colorful eaves and poles. People grew more sparse, but Erin was short enough that she didn't see Darin's destination until it was almost upon her.

Yes, it was Darin who explained it to her.

He stopped at the foot of the iron-wrought fence that surrounded and protected the statue that loomed in its center, with only birds for company. He bowed low in front of it, partly through habit, and partly for Stev, who had seldom been sent on market expeditions because he looked too awkward and gawky and would be a slight embarrassment to the house.

The statue didn't notice his small deference. It stood, arms extended, head thrown slightly back. Alabaster hair flowed with chiseled power to cut the breeze.

"The Lady of Mercy," Darin whispered, looking at Erin's booted feet.

Erin stared in silence at some sculptor's careful mirror.

"The Lady of Mercy," Darin continued, "came once to aid us." He shook his head. "We all know of her. All of us. There are songs—like children's songs—that we all sang sometimes. Stev taught me. In—in House Damion.

"She's going to return." He still could not meet her eyes. Whether for his sake now, or hers, he couldn't be certain. "And when she does, we'll be free forever."

He looked up then, but her eyes were thankfully turned to the statue. She didn't really resemble it; not now. She was mortal, and this—this was the evocation of God, whether or not the one who had worked it realized what he had captured.

But Erin knew herself in it. Knew God. Knew blood and the call to battle it had always sounded. She understood Maya and Gareth then, with complete clarity, knew what they saw, and knew why Darin had taken so much trouble to bring her here. These people did not know God, and the one hope they had of Him was . . . her. She was Lernan's Hope, the Lady of Elliath's Hope, and now, also the Hope of the slaves.

Dry-eyed, she spoke one word. It cut, to say it.

"Stefanos."

Darin sat quietly at the small table in the back room of the inn. It was night; fire burned in the grate, and dinner was set before him.

Tiras was off with Verdor and Hildy discussing God only knew what; Astor was working the front. Only Erin remained in the back room with him, staring at her dinner in uncomfortable silence. The fire was at her back, so the shadows had free reign to darken the contours of her still face. Neither had eaten much.

He had thought it would be easier to talk to her if she could see the statue in the market square. Now he knew it wasn't going to be.

Why so, Initiate?

He jumped a little, and his fork slid out of his grip.

Erin didn't seem to notice as she pushed peas listlessly into a swirl of gravy and potatoes.

Why what?

Why do you find it so difficult to speak with the Sarillorn?

Why? Because he didn't know what to say. He had expected that she would look shocked, confused, surprised—something *normal*.

And how did she react?

Tired, he thought. Tired. Hurt. Bitter.

You cannot address these things? The Sarillorn is not only comrade, Initiate, but friend, also. Can you not offer her your support?

How was he supposed to support the Lady of Mercy?

As you always have. As much as you can.

But it was different. He picked up his fork and experimentally lifted a cube of boned chicken to his mouth. It was cold and wet. With a grimace he began to chew.

Then stopped. *Gervin knew her.*

Yes.

He had not thought of Gervin for months.

Why didn't I?

Bethany was quiet, her silence a telling one.

I didn't want to. He put the fork down. He knew it was true. Gervin had recognized her both as an initiate of the Circle and as some promised Lady returned. He hadn't been afraid of her and hadn't stopped being able to talk to her. But he hadn't treated her like a person, either.

He was afraid, he realized, of being like Gervin. He was afraid of losing Erin as a comrade and the only other living initiate of the Circle that all lines held in common.

"Erin?"

She bit her lip and looked up at him; in the flickering light her eyes seemed almost brown. "Yes?"

His throat was dry. "Are you the Lady of Mercy?"

"Yes." Her voice was flat and weary. She looked away, her eyes trailing the stone fireplace and the battered heirloom plates that rested on the mantle.

"Oh." Great, just great. Oh. How helpful. But what else was he supposed to say? Something else. He had to find something; Erin had always said she wasn't good with words.

Maybe she knew what he was thinking. Maybe she wanted to help. "Darin,"—her voice was very low—"*I* didn't promise them anything. I didn't write their songs; I didn't come up with their legends."

He thought of Stev, who had tried so hard to help him adjust to House Damion. "Our legends."

Her eyes grew red around the edges. She stood, pushing her chair quietly back from the table.

"*Yours*, then. But it wasn't me. *He* wrote them. He built the statues. He did this."

"He?"

"The First of the Enemy."

"Lord Darclan." It wasn't a question.

"Yes. But I don't know why." She was half bent, her hair shadowing her face, the strands of it bars to a welcome cage. "I don't know why he did this."

He spoke without thinking. "What are you going to do?"

Her hands spread out before him like a plea. "What else can I do? I stayed with him, in the beginning, because of *hope*. Not just my hope, but their hope. Your hope." Her fingers began to shake, and she curled them into fists. "And I— It cost so much. Too much." She bowed her head, and water splashed onto the tablecloth, darkening it. "I thought it had cost everything. I didn't know that he would—do this for me. Keep hope alive. I don't know why."

"He loved you."

Her head snapped up, and for an instant Darin thought she would scream or shout at him. But what she did was infinitely worse. She straightened herself out and faced him grimly.

"And I loved him." There were tears, but they seemed more crystal than liquid; he could almost hear them shatter as they fell. "It wasn't enough."

"Erin, I didn't mean to say that. I didn't mean it."

His stricken face was a convoluted reflection in her eyes. "It's the truth, Darin." Her voice was quiet without softness. "But we've made our choices." She turned slowly, seeking both the warmth of the fire and the shelter of her back against his eyes. "And now he's left me with this legacy, this one gift." She laughed as if struck by something new; it was a shiny, hollow laugh. "I'll accept it. After all—isn't that what we've come for? To free the slaves? To have an end to the darkness?"

"Erin—"

"I'm sorry." She shook her head, and the hardness was gone from her stance. He still couldn't see her face. "I just feel as if I've spent all my life trying to be what others wanted. And failing.

"They want a Lady of Mercy. A Lady of Light, Darin." She looked down at her sweat-stained shirt, her grayed, callused hands. "They want all love, all care, all gentleness." Those hands became fists. "What would they feel if they saw these hands hold Gallin's sword? How would they react if they saw me kill?"

"Erin—"

"I want—I want them to want *my* help. I want them to want me. Is that so much to ask? No, don't answer that. Do I have the right to ask them for anything?"

He walked over to her then, stood close enough to touch her.

She laughed weakly. "And anyway, I'm not so sure I know who this *me* I'm talking about is."

"I am."

She turned and then jumped a little to see him so close.

"You're Erin." He bit his lip. "And I'm Darin. I'm trying to be the patriarch of Culverne for the lines. But you, you're trying to be a—a God."

And as soon as he said it, the distance was gone. He meant every word, more so than he had realized even as they left his lips. They weren't so different, not right now. He couldn't just set down his staff and quit, even though he wanted to sometimes—he couldn't live with that, even if he didn't feel he had the right, or the knowledge, to claim his title.

And Erin couldn't just say "No, I'm not your Lady" or "No, I'm not your Sarillorn."

"And we're never going to be those things—not the way we'd like, maybe not the way everyone who depends on us would like." It was true, all of it. Admitting it wasn't as hard as he thought it would be—not when he could share it as he did now. "We're never going to be perfect. But we're going to try—isn't that the best we can do?"

She held out her arms then, and he hugged her, or she hugged him; it was hard to tell who took more comfort from it.

"What if we make mistakes?" she said into his hair, fear in her voice; his fear, and hers.

"We will. But we'll fix 'em. I'll help with yours, if you help with mine. And I won't forget that you're only Erin."

"I won't forget that you're only Darin."

"Blood-promise?"

"Blood-*vow*."

"Right. Vow."

"Yes." Her arms grew tight. "Yes."

So it was that a little blood was shed in the peaceful, small room. But more was shed and taken on anew than blood alone. The prophecy of the slaves, forged in darkness and shadow, took the first, and the biggest, step toward the light.

* * *

The long line of men began its procession out of the peaked, twin iron gates of the temple. The sun had finally set, but the night, clear and moonlit, had not fallen hard enough to obscure them fully. Black robes swirled against the cobblestone of the street, picking up dirt, dust, and mud from the previous day's rain.

Each man bore a pickaxe or hammer over his shoulder; one or two of these was new enough to gleam as they passed the oil lights of the High City streets.

They were, to a man, acolytes of the temple—no mere slaves, no mere guards. They had made a life of study and education, not one of heavy labor; nonetheless they found themselves called after dinner to do this night's work. And to a man, they all resented this forced march and leave from their seat of power. But they said nothing of this at all.

For at their head walked the Demon of the Dark Heart. They had all been present at the blood ceremonies of God and had seen men and women die in the most exquisitely painful of fashions, but they knew that those deaths were nothing compared to what this shadow could do. Rumors—with bodies to substantiate them—had grown within the Church, and not even the lowliest of acolytes was not now privy to the deaths this Lord had caused in the past weeks. Nobles had died at his hand—nobles, and one or two priests. That there were others who had also died did not concern them; the fact that he could take highborn lives with no fear of censure or threat told them all they needed to know about his power.

Stefanos knew what they were thinking; he could see it in the stiffness of their backs and the awkwardness of their hands around his chosen implements. Indeed, it amused him mildly to taste the scent of their fear, mingled as it was with their pathetic anger. He thought of taking one of these here and decided against it. He was not hungry.

But the walk bored him.

Habit alone confined him to the ground, and the minute he realized this, he shed it. The cloak of his shadow spread wide and fine; he took to the winds and the air. Those closest to him stopped their move forward in fear. He ignored it.

He knew all of their faces, having seen them the once, and would deal with any who chose not to arrive at the ordered rendezvous.

The market square opened up beneath him, low, flat, and empty save for the statue that adorned its center.

It was for that statue that he had come. A thing of the old days, it irritated him. He was not now what he had been, and the future that the statue heralded had been irrevocably destroyed. He had returned; he would rule. And by this action, in the darkness of his night, he would begin his reign.

Alone, he descended to stand before it, much as any slave would stand if he had a spare moment.

And he faced her again, as he had once or twice faced her in the past at the zenith of her power; the Dark Lord, to her Lady of Light.

The Light was gone now.

It had been fully a month since he had confronted even his memory of her. He stared unblinking at the hands that curved so strongly and so delicately, in the twinned gesture of supplication and power so peculiar to the Lernari. She had been the best of their number.

Sara . . .

How long he stood he could not say, and later not even memory would supply him with the answer, for his eyes did not touch the night sky to see the passage of moon or stars. All that disturbed him was a stray breeze, and this he ignored until it carried the sound of footfall.

The acolytes were coming.

He stiffened and turned away, his resolve hidden in the gray lines of the face that none of these men could meet.

"I have summoned you here," he said softly, "to remove the statue at the market's center."

There was a susurrus of muted approval. The Church had never been fond of the Lady of Mercy.

"I wish your work to be completed by evening's end."

No one moved.

"Go!" His left arm swung wide, and the acolytes began to surge around him, taking great care not to touch their Lord. He watched with a thin smile; they would have their work cut out. They had brought no scaffolding or platform with them, and the statue was high.

They surrounded the statue, levering their weapons off their shoulders, and staring at it uncertainly. They would never have dared so open an approach had that statue been flesh.

Sara . . .

One man, round but tall, stepped out of the group. His tool was a large, pointed pick. With only a nervous glance to the side, he readied it.

And time slowed for an instant.

The statue took on a hue of life and color, almost a semblance of motion. It hurt much, much more than he would have imagined.

He had called her the Lady of Mercy, but there was no mercy she could grant him now; she had left, the Beyond of her kind swallowing her. These monuments were all that remained, and he did not care to have them as constant reminders.

The pick came swinging down.

And his hand shot up in a straight line. With an inarticulate shout he called his power and let it leap out of him in one red, ugly blur.

A scream sounded—there was almost always a scream—and the pick clattered, useless now, against the statue's foundation.

The acolytes panicked. Their bodies flew in all directions, carried by legs. Most dropped the hammers or picks they had brought so grudgingly this far.

One or two were foolish enough to remain. These, he killed quickly. She was watching, after all.

In minutes, he was alone again with the legend that he had built. He almost wanted to be a mortal slave—he would believe, then, that she would return.

He floated upward, carried by blood power, and reached out to touch her outstretched hands. They were cold as he gripped them. Cold and hard.

I have failed. His own hands stroked inanimate ones reflexively.

Even this much of you, I cannot destroy.

Ah, Lady, Sara, we betray ourselves in ways that even we cannot comprehend.

He stayed with her until the sun began its ascent.

"You're leaving us again, lass."

Erin nodded.

"That's what you get for running an inn, dear," Hildy said. She straightened out her overcoat, which didn't work well because the three layers beneath it were wrinkled and bulky, and then smiled. "Erin, dear, are you certain you're warm enough?"

"Yes, Hildy."

Hildy looked quite doubtfully at Erin's leather jerkin, with thin but ample padding underneath. Her boots, also plain leather, weren't lined with anything, and she insisted on having free use of her hands, so she wouldn't wear mittens. Hildy sighed and clucked a little, both of which Erin was quite used to.

Verdor, for his part, was dressed for the bar. This meant one already-dirty apron over a large, thick shirt and dark breeches. He looked at Erin very carefully, his face unusually thoughtful. Then he cleared the expression with a familiar smile.

"Well, then. Don't stay away as long, this time."

"I— I'll try." It was almost a whisper. Then her smile strengthened, as well; it was hard to feel the shadows when Verdor was around—even if he was saying good-bye.

"Where is Darin?"

"Outside, Hildy. Waiting."

"Good. We've a stop to make before we leave the city."

"Burrows?"

"Well, him, too. I don't suppose we'll do much good without the wagons."

"Where?"

"We usually pick up a few extra guards for the next leg of the journey."

Erin nodded; it did make sense. She wondered that Hildy hadn't hired more before they'd left Dagothrin.

"Don't worry, Erin." Verdor slid an arm around her shoulder. "I send her to a friend of mine just on the outskirts of the warrens. You can trust the people she offers for hire."

Erin nodded quietly, and Verdor caught her with his other arm in a bear of a hug.

"Lady of Mercy," he whispered into her hair, "have a little mercy for yourself."

You can trust the people she offers for hire.

Erin looked dubiously at the six men that waited in a scraggly, not-so-patient line in front of Hildy. They each had papers, although some of those papers were almost tatters and were nearly illegible into the bargain.

If Erin looked dubious, Darin looked worse, but he kept it

to himself by wandering around the "lobby" of the building. It was an old tenement, which had obviously seen some fire and some repair. A desk, thick, plain, and solid, sat a few feet away from the doors, behind two armed men who were obviously bored.

Candy sat behind the desk, drumming her fingers against an open ledger and cocking her head to one side to catch Hildy's questions and comments. Her peppered hair was cropped very short, and a scar ran along the edge of her jaw, ending about two inches from the gray of small, round eyes.

From where Darin stood, he could see the hilt of a sword at Candy's hip; he had no doubt that years ago she herself hired out to caravans. Why she was called Candy he couldn't say, and he knew better than to ask.

Hildy said something to the last man in the line and then nodded. She walked over to the desk, gesturing Candy's guards away.

"Well?" Candy said.

"Only six, dear?"

"Hildy." Candy leaned forward. "I am nobody's dear."

"Yes, dear, I know," the older woman replied. "I remember when you used to run my route with me."

They both smiled then, the tall muscular woman behind the desk and the round, matronly one in front.

"Six." Candy's smile was wry. "You're early this time." She nodded to the men. "They're good; they've all had experience. If you want to wait about three weeks, I can get another six, maybe eight."

Hildy shook her head. "We've a tight schedule. We don't want to wait. How have the roads been?"

The scar across Candy's face twisted with her lips. "Not great."

Hildy was silent a moment. Then she pursed her lips and glanced at Erin.

Erin said nothing.

Hildy sighed. "No, dear. We still can't wait. Come, Erin, let me introduce you to the new boys. Darin? Darin, dear, do come here."

Jeren, Corfaire, Ferdaris, Carcomack, Boris, and Sudenir joined Hildy's caravan as it made its final preparations to leave the city. They had obviously been informed of their hire, for they took no time at all to get ready.

Not one of the men was younger than Erin; indeed Jeren and Carcomack were in her opinion on the old side. But all had seen battle of one form or another, much of it on the routes during merchant house wars. They came with their own armor and weapons, and these were in good repair, if little else about them was.

Erin looked at them all carefully, trying to remember the names that matched faces that would grow familiar over the weeks to come. She tried to remember Verdor's assurances, but she felt uncomfortable nonetheless, probably because these were not men that had yet proved they could be counted upon.

But it didn't help to know that the only other person who seemed to be uncomfortable with the newcomers was Darin. It didn't help at all.

chapter
eight

Corfaire watched Erin as if she were the danger that the merce- naries had been hired to prevent.

He was afraid of her. Not in an obvious way, but all the subtle signs were there; the way he spoke, or didn't, around her, the way he drew slightly inward when she approached, the way he avoided even brushing against her when the road narrowed enough to merit a tighter formation. He wore his fear well, as well as any who has learned to live with it, and she might not have noticed it had she been anyone else. In fact, she didn't notice it immediately, for she rode with Hildy for the better part of three days before Hildy deemed it "safe" enough for her to join the guard.

But she was Lernari and very sensitive. So she began to watch him.

His hair was dark and a little too long in the front; had Erin been in charge, she might have ordered him to cut it. But as no one else seemed to notice, she didn't mention it. Besides, he wore the back of it long, in one loose but coherent braid. Much like hers, in fact—although she wasn't aware that it was an Empire tradition.

His skin was rather pale but flaking around the tip of his nose where he'd managed to catch too much sun; his eyes were a dark, deep brown, which was disconcerting because it was hard to tell where his pupils were. His cheekbones were high and seemed a little too fine, but his nose had been broken at least once and had mended on an angle, so he didn't look too out of place among the rest of the guards.

* * *

The sky was darkening but clear, and the stars, faint and pale, mapped its length and breadth completely. The moon shone at half-mast, its glow sharp and hard. A mosquito flitted lightly from arm to arm seeking purchase in exposed skin. Hildy slapped her hand down without looking up from her dinner.

"That's the worst thing," she said, raising her hand again, "about travel at this time of year."

He sat between two of his city comrades, eating noisily for the most part, but talking little. The fire added color to his face, but it also added shadow, as well as a red glint to the surface of his eyes.

"Who is that man?" Erin asked Hildy softly.

"Corfaire, dear. Why?" Hildy could ask why in the softest tone of voice, but it never removed the edge of the question.

"I'm just curious."

"He's traveled with the caravan before. Knows the route well enough. We've seen some raiding when he's been around, and he's always held fast."

Erin nodded, only half-listening.

"He's never caused us any trouble, dear."

Erin nodded again and moved back to her place around the fire. She had eaten quickly but neatly, as habit dictated. Now she bent down and unlaced her boots, giving her feet a much-needed chance to breathe.

Darin wrinkled his nose and made a face.

"Don't assume yours smell so much better," she shot back. She reclined on her elbows and tilted her head forward. Her face was clean, but her hair had escaped the braid she wore and lay in wisps about her ears and cheeks. She looked least like the Lady of Mercy at the end of a long day and knew it well.

"I don't. That's why I'm leaving mine on." He swatted ineffectively at an insect that was buzzing uncomfortably close to his face. For some reason, they seemed to like him best, and one of his eyelids was swollen from the previous night's sleep, even though he'd made sure that the net was properly tied over the entrance of his tent.

Still, he felt relaxed. For a moment he could almost imagine that Erin and he were once again traveling the road alone. He started to lean backward, and his elbow banged into a rock. Why was it that everything always happened to him? With a grimace he tossed the offending lump aside and moved nearer to where Erin was.

"I hate the road," he muttered.

She laughed quietly. "It isn't easy on you, is it? How's the eye?"

"Itchy."

"Well don't—Darin! If you keep scratching it, it's only going to get worse."

He mumbled something under his breath, and she laughed again.

This laugh was louder, and her laughter was rare enough that it brought the attention of those gathered round the twin fires. A dozen people cut their conversation to look back at her, some smiling, and some wearing expressions of barely veiled curiosity.

One of those men was Corfaire.

She met his eyes, and her smile froze the corners of her lips. Her fingers danced up in the Lesser Ward before she could still them.

He smiled then, an odd, quirky expression, and turned to murmur something to the man beside him.

The moment broken, Erin gazed down at her hands; they were shaking. She realized that he was not the only one who was uneasy. Tomorrow, though, that would have to change.

For perhaps the hundredth time, Erin wondered why her power could warm her in the winter, but did nothing to cool her in the sun's heat. The armor that she wore was light, but she'd been walking for hours now, and little beads of sweat were rolling down her forehead.

She took a perverse comfort in knowing that all of the guards were also hot and a little irritable. Only Tiras seemed cool and refreshed, and that mostly because he managed to walk in the shade of the wagons; the guards were not quite so lucky.

"Can you use your sword?"

Erin turned her head slowly to the side, measuring her words carefully. She lost them when she realized it was Corfaire who had spoken. He was two feet away, but she'd last seen him at the rear of the caravan.

"Yes."

"Well?" There was a hint of uneasiness in his eyes, and he kept his distance firmly.

"Well enough. And you?" She wondered if that's what frightened him, and it bothered her, as did much of the Empire's custom.

It was disconcerting when he flipped between seriousness and laughter without warning. He laughed now. "Well enough. I've been at it for years."

An arch of auburn eyebrow greeted his answer. He wasn't that much older than she herself at her best guess.

"As," she answered curtly, "have I."

He was silent a moment, taking in the heavy leaves of the overhanging trees and the muted twitter of birds. The path here twisted and turned often, much too often for the comfort of those that guarded. But it was the safest route to Hillsdale, the second largest town along the route through Senatare, and Hildy always chose it.

"You don't live in Veriloth, do you?"

"I'm here." Almost grudgingly, she added, "Why?"

"There aren't many women who fight in Veriloth."

"There's Candy."

"Candy, as she calls herself, didn't originally hail from Veriloth. She was born and raised in Marantine—I believe that's what you call it—and came south when she was older." He shook his head. "I believe it. Besides, she's at least a head taller than you and somewhat heavier."

Erin said nothing. Instead of feeling uneasy, however, she now felt annoyed. Which of the two she would have preferred didn't matter; she felt as she did.

"I don't imagine that even in Marantine you got much training."

She still said nothing, but her hand slipped to the hilt of the bright sword and held fast. For a moment she wanted to challenge him, but she bit her tongue and pushed the foolish impulse aside. She had been away from the war for a long time if a simple taunt could anger her so. If it weren't so hot, she was certain that hairs at the nape of her neck would be standing at rigid attention.

"I had," she replied, in clipped, even words, "better training than most."

He shrugged, giving her words the attention he felt they merited. "As you say."

"And were you raised in the Empire?"

"Oh yes," he answered softly. "I was." He looked past her for a moment, seeing God only knew what, and then shook himself. This time it was his turn to be silent.

"You were talking with Corfaire today."

Erin nodded. Once again it was dark, and once again, outside of the light of day, she found herself relaxing. Darin's face looked somewhat better; he'd made an effort not to notice how itchy his eye was and the swelling had gone down.

"What did you say?"

"That I knew how to use the sword I carry."

Darin looked confused for a moment, then his eyes widened.

"Don't bother. I'd forgotten, too. The Empire's a different place." She brought her chin forward until it was touching the edge of her shirt. The fire crackled and lapped at the air inches away from her feet. She wiggled her toes and watched the shadows, remembering other roads that she had traveled. Other roads, and other companions.

Like the dead, he returned to haunt her.

His face was a twinned one. The lines of his lips curled around a human smile and a human pain. But his skin was gray, and the teeth that glittered in the red light were sharp and feral.

Stefanos.

She shook her head, and the image retreated for the moment. "Sorry, Darin. What were you saying?"

His eyes flickered over her face, then he too shook his head. "I was saying that I'd talked to some of the others. Candy's people. They all think Corfaire is, well, fine." He shrugged. "Doesn't really stand out—except in a fight."

"Meaning?"

"He isn't really quiet, he isn't really loud, he isn't really funny, he isn't really big or small—he's just one of them." He leaned forward and wrapped his arms around his knees. "But when they've been in trouble, he's supposed to be good with a sword. And he's never afraid; he doesn't panic at all. At least that's what they say."

Erin nodded. "I could believe it. But I wonder . . ."

"You might ask."

Erin looked at Darin, and he at her, before they both turned to look over their shoulders.

Corfaire stood less than three feet away, the shadows gathering at the feet that were planted firmly in the ground. His left hand was on his hip, his right on his sword hilt. One corner of his mouth was turned up slightly, but it was hard to tell in this light whether it was in a smile or a grimace.

Darin heard the echo of the Grandmother's voice. That, it said, is what you get for idle gossip. His cheeks flared in a blush, as did his ears. It had been months since he'd heard it, and he had begun to hope that he'd outgrown it forever.

Then he looked at Erin, and even that hope died, for her face was colored with almost the identical blush, and he had no doubt that in spite of her experience and age, she, too, heard the voices of the past.

"Have I interrupted something?"

"Uh, no." Darin stood up. "Can we, uh, help?"

This time it was obvious that Corfaire was smiling. He shook his head in mock regret and stared down at Erin, who had not moved. "No. But I thought, perhaps, the lady had some questions I might help her with."

Erin was certain that he was thinking no such thing. Her lips became a tight, white line.

"No," Corfaire whispered intently, "I don't suppose that you do need my help. Or anyone's."

She raised her head at that and finally took to her feet, uncurling slowly before the blazing fire. Her shadows, stiff and silent, were thrown back over the man who waited in attendance.

"What do you mean?" she asked softly, turning at last to face him. Her hand mirrored his as it rested against the pommel of her too-bright sword, and the breeze seemed to eddy in the few loose strands of her hair.

Darin was the third point of the awkward triangle that had formed. He held Bethany in both of his hands, but his stance, unlike either Erin's or Corfaire's, was uncertain as he glanced from side to side.

"Oh Lady," Corfaire answered, the inflection in the word unmistakable now, "do you so poorly recognize one of your own?"

She was silent, but her eyes widened.

"Yes." That smile still tinged his lips. "Lady of Mercy. My mother would have been . . . disappointed. She took such care to teach me all of your prayers and your songlets." There was contempt in the last word.

"What would you know about her?" Darin asked, as uncertainty gave way to anger.

"What would you?" Corfaire countered, his eyes never leaving Erin. But his words hung in the air like a sword or a bitter challenge.

Only Darin could answer them. "I have no name in the Empire," he said softly. He lowered his staff in one hand, surprised at how easily the words came. The last few weeks had been hard, and the steadily increasing heat of the evenings had done nothing to stem the rising chill of the death this land held for him. But he was no longer the child in chains—and the last link fell away as the truth, perversely, freed him.

"Isn't that interesting?" Corfaire turned to meet Darin's eyes. "Neither do I."

They stared at each other, seeing so little that was similar in the past they both claimed obliquely.

"What house?"

"Damion."

At this, Corfaire raised an eyebrow. "And you're here? That's almost remarkable." The lines of his face altered subtly. "Or did you have help? Did someone make a sacrifice to free you?"

Darin froze for an instant as memory snapped shut around him. The years melted away, dwindling into the sounds of screaming that had never quite died and would never do so while he lived. There was too much to say, too much to explain, and not enough words to contain it. So he said, quietly, "Yes." That was all.

It was enough. Corfaire nodded, his eyes half-lidded with some shadow of his own. "And you follow this woman?"

"Yes." Stronger, that word, and older; he was back in the present.

"Why?" It was a rhetorical question; he didn't expect an answer, as was obvious when he turned to Erin. Even so, some of the fire in his eyes was banked. "Make me a miracle, Lady." His voice was a fine twist of muted anger and bitterness.

"What miracle would do?"

He laughed; it wasn't pleasant. "Call back the dead."

He didn't wait for her answer; instead he turned and let the night take him back to where he had come from.

Erin was left alone with shadows and not a little anger. She mastered it outwardly, but even that with difficulty, and bent her head to stare at the hands she stretched out before her.

"You see?" she said softly to Darin.

"He's just one man," Darin answered. "And he doesn't really believe in you."

Her smile was crooked. "Maybe he's right."

Darin shrugged. "I don't know. For some, belief is all they can have." But he remembered how, for five years, he had labored without it on the stones of House Damion.

The sky was darkening again; sunlight had been broken into bands of multicolored clarity that ringed the horizon. There were no clouds, and the moon was at its nadir over the stately manses and the moving streets of Malakar.

Although the Empire was in service to the Dark Heart, most of its citizens still scurried through life to the rhythm of the day, but for many this eve marked a turning point, whether they realized it or no.

For it was not yet end of quarter, and the time to start anew had not arrived, but the streets to the temple were lined with carriages and palanquins, each jostling in its finery for a position in the crowded roadways. An impressive array of house guards was out in force, adding somber color to the cobbled streets; here and there, weapons were drawn and steel flashed under the odd lights of the High City, punctuating the tension, but not quite breaking out of it into violence.

Slaves, also bearing the colors and marks of the houses that claimed them, attended their lords and ladies as if nothing were out of the ordinary. They were no regular slaves, these, but rather the best of their number—were someone to be killed in front of them, they would not so much as blink without leave from their master or mistress. For the most part, they were older men, with the bearing and dignity of the almost free. More important, they had the experience to carry themselves with grace through any situation.

Tonight it would be tested.

Within the well-oiled and well-guarded gates of the temple complex, black robes swirled like frenzied shadows, carrying chairs, benches, books, and wine into the open cathedral. Flashes of red and silver could occasionally be seen on some of those who ran these errands; the signs of authority stooping low indeed. If the acolytes or the lesser priests noticed the presence of their betters, they were too busy or too cautious to make any comment; they had at best half an hour to prepare the cathedral for more than full capacity.

Slaves also worked among those who served the Church, carrying the heavier items and working more quickly, although hardly more diligently. Gray was the color of their "office," and often that word was shouted by one anxious priest or acolyte across the length of the great hall. It was said that the temple slaves were the best behaved of their kind, and on this night they proved it true, answering immediately, with no sign of question or nervousness.

Indeed, thought Vellen, as he surveyed the crowded floor of the cathedral, they were as perfect as slaves could be; perhaps he could train his house slaves under such circumstance.

His robes were the color of fire as they rippled to the floor; shadow curled around his waist in the form of a black sash. He crossed his arms as he watched, wondering if the priests would have the room in order at the prescribed time.

No. There was no question of it; they would be finished. And then what? The corners of his lips turned down slightly.

"Thinking, Lord Vellen?"

"Some of us do, Benataan."

The lord of Torvallen, and the Second of the Karnar, was dressed in robes identical to those that Vellen wore—the only thing missing was the tiara, with its small but startling ruby.

"Indeed." Benataan inclined his head, failing to notice the lack of title with which Vellen addressed him. A taut smile lurked at the corner of his lips, but little else. "What does the evening hold?"

"Watch." The leader of the Greater Cabal said curtly.

Benataan raised an eyebrow, nodded, and then sauntered over to his place among the thirteen. His chair was empty but in readiness, and he took it, resting either hand against the curled thickness of velvet-covered armrest.

Vellen spared him a glance, no more.

Still, it irritated him. This meeting had been called by the First of the Sundered for reasons that he alone knew. What would unfold by evening's end was hazy and uncertain, both of which made the high priest uneasy. His own chair, at the center of the half-circle that stood nearest the altar, awaited him—but for how long?

The Karnari slowly filtered in, some wearing openly worried expressions that did nothing to ease Lord Vellen's temper. He kept his peace and waited until the last of their number, Dramathan, had assumed his seat.

The Lord of Valens was in many ways a staunch ally. No concern touched his features; indeed, the set lines of his forehead seemed to speak of boredom, if anything. He nodded to Vellen. That small, silent gesture was not lost upon the lord of Torvallen.

Vellen stepped down from the dais, moving with a regal confidence that became his office. He took his chair, looking neither to the left or right.

An acolyte scurried across the floor and bowed quite low in front of him, casting a slight shadow.

The leader of the Karnari let him hold his stance for a moment before nodding. "It is time."

"Lord."

Behind the arched, high back of the Karnar's chair, the doors swung open. Three slaves stood on either side, pushing them with care and moving silently enough that the slight creak of well-oiled hinges could be heard echoing throughout the chamber. Those same slaves would lead the incoming nobles to their places for the duration of this unusual audience.

Vellen's eyes surveyed the altar that glittered smoothly. As of yet, no one stood behind it, but that in no way detracted from its dark glory. He pitied the eyes that could not see the red lines that traced its length and breadth, for those eyes would never know, truly, the power and the beauty of the God all now served.

Almost, he bowed his head in contemplation. But now was not the time, even if no better place existed for it, and he caught himself.

The silence of the temple was muddied by the muted whispers and chatter of the nobility as they pushed and shoved their way into seats. Yet even this annoying background noise died away into the silence of waiting.

Vellen knew that all eyes fell upon the back of his chair, but he was powerless to answer the questions that the nobility barely held in abeyance. He too waited.

Not for long.

The doors swung shut behind the assembly, guided by no living hand. The shadows seemed to lengthen until they touched the very height of the arched ceilings.

And entwined in those shadows, for those who could see them, were lines of red so deep and so pure that Vellen's heart contracted with a bitter envy. He knew whose signature they were.

Darkness formed a well above and behind the altar of God, darkness that coalesced into physical shape and form. If widening eyes could make a sound, the temple would be full of it and nothing else, for it seemed that all those who watched had forgotten the delicate art of breathing.

The First of the Sundered stepped forth from the shadows, treading on air.

It took no special vision to see his power.

"Welcome," he said softly, his voice filling the cathedral.

No one dared to answer, as if a word could draw his attention.

He smiled then, looking down upon them all. His eyes swept the arc of the Greater Cabal, and the smile sharpened for an instant, no more. "Welcome to the cathedral of the night." He gestured with both hands, and the shadows pulled away, to reveal one man and one woman who stood rigidly on either side of him, their cheeks nearly brushing the edge of his cloak. They seemed to strain at some bonds, although none were visible, and the aura of their terror reached out to touch even the weakest of blood in the audience.

"It has been long since I have traveled among you." His eyes were red, with such a depth of color and light that the ruby that Lord Vellen wore seemed flat, poorly cut glass—a fitting comparison of their powers.

"But my business elsewhere has come to an end." His arms he raised high, and from his hands pillars of red fire exploded outward, crackling through the air without quite finding living purchase.

"This is not the quarter, but the Dark Heart knows no mortal time." Very slowly he began his descent, the shadows slowly flattening and gathering beneath him. "Nor do I, any longer.

"But the daylight does not please me, and you who are among the most ... powerful of my subjects, you live too much within it. This will end."

Like tendrils of smoke, his hands reached out now, one to

either side. Claws, gray and human enough to be disturbing, clutched the shoulder of the man and the woman at precisely the same instant. The grip was not gentle; blood fell in four red lines, staining the white, linen robes that either wore.

"I am the Lord of the Empire. The Church that you have served serves my whim, my will. The laws that you have followed are my laws, and should I choose to change them, you *will* obey them."

His gaze, bright and burning, fell upon Lord Vellen.

This, this was why the meeting had been called. Vellen's question had been answered, and the answer was bitter indeed. Here, in front of too many enemies, he was to be called to divest himself of the power that he had struggled for most of his life to earn. And what other choice was left him?

The leader of the Greater Cabal rose from his chair, his hands leaving the armrests reluctantly. This was almost worse than death—almost. Rigidly, he bowed, the movement low and precise.

"Lord," he said.

"I cannot hear you, High Priest."

"Lord." Vellen's voice was stronger. "The Greater Cabal stands ready to obey."

"Tell them."

Vellen stepped away from his chair and the shelter it provided. He walked toward the altar until the First of the Sundered shook his head. There he stopped—before the altar, rather than in his customary place behind it. His face was pale, his eyes glittering blue ice.

Shadows shrouded the First's face, but Vellen saw clearly all that was in it. He swallowed, choking down anger, not fear. There was no contest—not here, not now. And it was the Malanthi way to respect the greater power. As long as it was too close to be challenged.

"The Lord of the Empire has returned."

"Louder."

"The Lord of the Empire has returned."

"Tell them, then."

Vellen swore softly that any who derived amusement from his humiliation would pay for it in the future. He swiveled, his red robes suddenly both hollow and heavy.

The faces that lined the pews disappeared into darkness as they grew distant; he scanned them, searching for even a hint of a smile. Shock he found; dismay and fear. No amusement. He drew his shoulders back, standing the straighter for it.

"The Lord of the Empire has returned."

"Good enough," Stefanos said. "You may take your seat."

That seat stood empty, a forlorn, dark chair that had fallen somewhat from grace. Still, it had power. Vellen walked toward it steadily and resumed his position as the head of the Greater Cabal. His hands were shaking; he couldn't still them, and that angered him more. He was no acolyte, to be so ordered, and yet in front of all of the nobility of Malakar, he had come and gone at the whim of this darkling ruler.

But he would think on it, over and over again, at a later time, worrying the wounds he had suffered here. The Lord of the Empire was speaking.

"Do you understand?" His voice was velvet, sibilant in the subtlest of fashions. There was a caress in it, the softness of snow with a hint of the ice beneath it.

The congregation nodded, wordless, almost breathless.

The Servant's smile was red. Nightwalker eyes washed across wan faces.

"Good. Then let the evening truly begin."

He made no further movement, but the two that stood on either side of him opened their mouths in wide, startling unison, their voices the melody and harmony of agony.

Vellen heard it, *felt* it, as he had no other death. His agony was of envy, for the Servant, the Lord, wielded no blade, and no obvious hint of God's power. Yet with two hands, two immortal claws, in a grip firm but hardly cruel, he elicited the full range of human fear, human pain.

Lord Vellen had long prided himself on his control; with such self-discipline he had carved for himself an Empire at the head of the Church. There was no alcohol for him, save on celebratory occasion, no drugs, no excesses of indulgence that marked the weak who accidently stood in power.

Yet he had his weaknesses, and to his shame, they were exposed fully here. He knew beauty when he saw it. And as the twin sacrifices writhed, yet stood, as they screamed and twisted in the face of the inevitable, as they danced between the edge of insane hope and mere insanity, Vellen walked the rope between sweet, sharp joy and utter despair.

He wondered, as he watched, wondered as the hours drifted

past, unnoticed and unremarked upon, if this was what God felt.

Tears trailed down the sides of his face, signature to the awe he felt. Never, never would he forget this ceremony, for the darkness had suddenly come alive in his blood; the night was, indeed, a complete cathedral—everything was holy. And he knew that try as he might, he would never have the gift to create so perfect a sculpture with the chaff of human life.

Lord Vellen of Damion knew true grief for the first time in his life.

And the Lord of the Empire knew it well and was pleased.

chapter
nine

Erin had slept poorly. Some nightmare fogged her mind and dogged her step, and it was more potent for the fact that she could remember naught but shadow. The day was too new and too young to pull her away from it.

On the road, she remembered the darkness.

Belf. She shivered. *What are you doing now?*

She knew the answer already; it hid in the shadows, awaiting her. Each step she took beneath the awkward bower of towering treetops brought her closer to it.

Mornings were often like this—gray, even though the sky was brilliant, and small shoots of wildflowers dusted the tops of her boots. The green of leaves also cast shadows, both the obvious dappling of ground, and the darker, personal ones. She felt the fading fingers of the Lady's wood in every oak she passed, and although she saw none of the Lady's trees here and none of the smooth, bright birches, she felt her grandmother's presence more for their absence.

Birds twittered above, their little high voices carrying a hint of alarm at those who passed safely beneath. Erin heard the life as it moved and looked up to catch the blue flashes beneath briefly spread wings.

"Come, dear, I think you'll find Coranth quite an interesting village."

Erin looked up to meet Hildy's eyes—eyes that were crinkled, but warm and brown. The lines in her brow softened and slowly vanished. "Coranth?"

"It's quite small."

"Was it on the map?"

"Well, no dear, but it is on the route." Hildy raised an eyebrow. "You did read the route itinerary, didn't you?" She shook her head as Erin's cheeks turned pink, happy to see a little color in them, even if the source wasn't completely laudable. "Never mind, dear."

"Coranth is an odd name for a village."

Hildy nodded. "It's a newer name."

Breeze blew around Erin's face; shadows cast by leaves played against her dusty clothing. Grass and wildflowers played at her ankles as she took what care she could not to crush them. She smiled as she watched Darin's odd step, knowing that he too sought to mar as little as possible.

The shadows were gone; their grip suddenly faltered and vanished as she looked anew at the surrounding land. The sun was out, and the sky was an impossibly deep, clear blue. Empire or no, these lands were beautiful.

Something skittered through the undergrowth, leaving a green whisper in its wake. For only a moment, Erin wished that all of the body of the Twinned Hearts could be so peaceful. No Light, No Dark, no war—just the little wonders of undisturbed life.

"Halt!"

What a futile wish. A child's dream.

No—as a child she had dreamed of war and glory. And what a dark war, what shadowed glory.

Her hand already rested upon her sword, although she did not draw it. The rasping of metal against metal that sounded above the creak of wagons coming to a halt told her that not all of the guards were so circumspect.

Very slowly she turned her head in the direction of that sound.

Light gleamed off the naked blade in Corfaire's hand. It seemed as natural there as his fingers, and it took her a moment to realize that she had never seen him wield his weapon before. He met her eyes with a nonchalance that belied the supple expertise of the stance he had taken. And yes, even now, a sardonic smile folded the corners of his lips up.

She had no doubt that he would wear just such an expression should the men ahead on the road force a combat. And those men, she told herself sternly, merited more attention now than Corfaire did. For the moment.

There were four altogether, at least in plain sight. Each wore an uncrested chain, and three carried swords, holding them with considerably less skill and ease than Corfaire did.

The fourth person carried a crossbow, which was not in itself remarkable. What was, in these lands, was the fact that this fourth, grim-faced young fighter was female.

She was younger than Erin, her skin made dark by the sight of the sun. Her hair, where it could be seen under a leather and iron helm, was fair—almost white. Her eyes were large and brown as they met Erin's—but seemed larger due to the way they widened.

The crossbow wavered and fell a fraction, even as Erin's hand fell away from her sword. Their smiles, which started at the same instant, were those of equals acknowledging that they might, one day, be friends, should they meet in less unfortunate circumstances.

"Bretnor! Aeliah!"

The young woman and the dark-haired man beside her both looked up to the cab of the lead wagon. Bretnor's sword began to fall.

"Hildy? Hildy, is that you?"

"Unless there are other old, fat, female merchants on the road to your tiny little village." The words themselves sounded wry, but that didn't fool Bretnor—or Aeliah, for that matter, who all but dropped her weapon in her rush to point it elsewhere.

"Put them away!" she hissed to the other two guards. "Now!"

"Hildy?" Bretnor said again, but this time with a good deal of evident embarrassment.

"Yes, dear." She smiled; if she had had feathers, they would have been unruffling.

Metal scraped metal again, and Erin turned in time to see the last of Corfaire's sword being swallowed by his scabbard. His smile was gone for the moment, and Erin was almost sure that a vague air of disappointment skittered across his fine features.

"Does your father know what the two of you are up to?" Hildy asked as she picked up the reins. "And dears, you haven't introduced your friends."

Those friends numbered eight; four had taken to the trees with crossbows.

They came out wearing the shaky stride of relief, and Erin realized that they were all younger than she—perhaps five years Darin's senior, if that.

"Hi Hildy," one said quietly. He started to wave, realized that he held the crossbow in both hands, and lowered it slowly.

"Take the bolt out," Hamin said. "Or you'll forget it's readied and shoot off your foot."

"Don't mind him, Randy," Hildy said, glaring at the captain of her guards. As a leader he was good. As a judge of, or handler of, those in transition between youth and adulthood, he was decidedly lacking. "I think it's very brave of you to be out here. That is, if you're out here for a good reason."

Randy smiled, but Hildy noticed that he did take Hamin's rather blunt advice. What had been a rather dangerous weapon became just another piece of well-crafted, molded wood. "Yeah," he said. "We're out here for the right reason. But aren't you early?"

"I hadn't realized," Hildy said wryly, "that being early had become a capital crime."

Bretnor blushed. He did a lot of that—maybe it was why Erin found herself liking him. But there was a shadow in the affection, and she wondered if everyone who even remotely reminded her of Belfas would cause this quiet pain.

"Hey," someone said, and Erin turned, nearly bumping into Aeliah. "Do you know how to use that thing?"

Erin didn't even bother to follow the direction of Aeliah's fingers. "Yes."

"Where'd you learn it?"

"Home."

If Aeliah noticed the tremor in the word, she gave no sign of it. But she didn't ask where "home" was. Instead, she sighed. "Did it take as long as they say it will?"

"Probably longer." Erin smiled, shaking off the shiver so simple a word as home could bring. "I think, let's see . . . eight solid years to start, and a few after I'd seen my first battle."

Aeliah pursed her lips and brushed a lock of hair out of her eyes. "That's longer."

Erin had thought that Aeliah was close to her age, but she revised her estimate down by a few years. She knew what Telvar would have said, but Telvar was a very different man from the woman that she had become.

Woman. How odd. She had spent so long telling everyone

who would listen that she was adult, yet this was perhaps the first time that she had really felt it, not as a passionate struggle or statement, but as a simple, unchangeable fact.

"Are you learning?"

"Sword? Yeah. Yes," Aeliah corrected herself. "Can't you see the bruises?"

Erin did laugh then. So did Aeliah, sure evidence of the fact that she'd been at it for a little while.

"It could be worse. Dervallen had eighteen different arguments with my father about it, and I think he still goes easy on me. I'm sure he does. Bretnor *always* looks worse than I do after a lesson, and it isn't that I'm any better than he is."

"Why was Dervallen—oh. Yes. Why are you training?"

Aeliah's face lost its bright wreath of friendly laughter. "We've been having trouble lately."

"And we'll leave it for Father to tell," Bretnor added curtly.

Aeliah nodded, but felt compelled to add, "There aren't enough of us—everyone's got to be allowed to do what he or she can." She glared pointedly at her brother, who glared, if possible, more pointedly back. "I'm not rited yet, I've got no children, and Dad's too young to need care. So why shouldn't I fight?"

Bretnor didn't answer her. It was obvious that this argument had been had many times before.

Erin heard echoes of her own words in Aeliah's. "She's right."

"She doesn't know what she's asking for." Bretnor's cheeks were flushed.

"Yes I do," Aeliah said firmly. "The right to defend the people I love. And I can't do it by sewing or cooking the enemy to death!"

Little lines jumped in Bretnor's jaw as he met his sister's eyes. "Well you got it past Father, and you're here. Be happy." With that he stomped away, to stand closer to the wagons.

"Sometimes," Aeliah said, glaring at his retreating back, "I hate my brother."

"Don't," Erin said. To her own surprise, she found herself sliding an arm around Aeliah's slender shoulders. "He doesn't hate you."

Aeliah's face lost the stiffness of anger. "No, he doesn't." She frowned bitterly across at Erin. "But if he had his way, I'm sure he'd just love me to a helpless death."

* * *

The village of Coranth was named, not after its founder, but after a lord who had been sent this far west in disgrace. Exactly what the disgrace was, Erin didn't know, but she knew that none of the eight here felt anything but pride in it.

This Lord Coranth had governed his house and the village around it for just shy of twenty years now; the land was fertile and green enough to grow food for all of the villagers and leave some for export and trade besides, and the distance was not so great that cattle and the like could not be led to the city.

There was, Aeliah said with affectionate pride, the best blacksmith in the province of Landsfall, and two good carpenters besides—and the wool got hereabouts was well worth any merchant's journey. And Lord Coranth was a wise and gentle ruler, judge, and counselor.

Of course, her accolades weren't all that surprising—she was his daughter.

From Aeliah's fond description, Erin expected Lord Coranth to be rather portly—fond of food, as Aeliah had taken pains to point out—rather peculiarly, if practically, dressed, rather elderly although not indisposed, and rather bald.

He was bald.

As to the rest, the fondness for food didn't show, and the clothing bore the faintest hints of the city style that he had left years before. Erin learned, with mild chagrin, that Aeliah's sight was the forgiving one of youth, with all of the affectionate exaggeration and blindness that that entailed.

Lord Coranth was tall, at least a head taller than Erin, and what there was of his hair was peppered and short. His eyes were those of his daughter's, a cool blue that spoke more of refuge from summer swelter than of winter, but the rest of his face was his son's—long and angular, with broad cheekbones that softened it somewhat. As for age—Erin just shook her head. He was twice hers at most, and that certainly didn't qualify him as "elderly"—at least not in the lines.

"Hello, 'Narion," Hildy called, waving one large arm with a happy smile.

"Hildy!" Lord Coranth placed a book down on what was presumably an end table; it was so covered by curling papers it was hard to tell. He crossed the room in two long strides, already holding out both arms instead of the usual proffered hand.

Those arms were long enough easily to encompass all of Hildy's considerable girth. "You're early."

She returned his hug and then pulled back, nodding. "I've brought a few friends with the caravan. I'd like you to meet them."

"Friends of yours? With pleasure."

"This is Tiras—he's from Marantine. You did hear about that, didn't you?"

Lord Coranth smiled. "Not enough, though." He held out a hand, and Tiras shook it firmly.

"Bennarion of Coranth." The lord's smile was an odd twist of lips. "The village, not the house."

Tiras raised an eyebrow, but it was obvious that he felt no threat here, for he demurred from formal speech—indeed, any speech.

"This is Darin, also from Marantine."

"Not one of your guards?"

Darin shook his head. "No—I'm just a traveling companion."

"Do you need that cane?"

"Cane?" Darin looked around in some confusion, and then his jaw dropped slightly. "The staff? Uh—"

"Yes," Hildy answered, putting a considerable amount of gentle order in the single word.

Lord Coranth looked mildly confused, but nodded and moved on to stand in front of Erin.

"This young woman *is* one of my guards for the moment."

"I see." The lord held out his hand for a third time, and Erin took it, not surprised to find his grip firm.

"I'm Erin," she said, before Hildy could speak. "I'm also from Marantine—although I lived in the southeast for a long time before that." She didn't know why she said it, and regretted it almost before the sentence was finished.

"Malakar?" Lord Coranth asked, his brow folding into many neat lines.

"No."

He was silent a moment as a map of the Empire unfolded in memory's eye. "Southeast?"

"I believe it was Mordantari." It was Tiras who answered, and his voice, though soft, had an edge of warning in it.

The word should have been enough.

"Mordantari?" This time, when he looked at Erin, there was nothing social or welcoming about his eyes. They were clear and piercing, and the coolness had hardened. He caught her by the shoulders, and Tiras stepped forward quietly: another warning.

"Those lands were claimed by the Lord of the Empire. No house has any hold on them. Were you a slave there?"

"Not—not in the . . . no." She did not know, could not know, the way her eyes flashed and her lips suddenly trembled over the answer; she could not know how that look transformed her face in the eyes of the man who watched so intently. But she had never been good at hiding, and if she had not always spoken her thoughts, they were in her face to read for those who had learned the skill.

"Father—" Aeliah began, but Bretnor stepped quite neatly, and quite forcefully, on her foot.

Her father was a better judge of character than she was of him. He let his arms fall to the side and stepped back, the intensity already dying out of his eyes. "Lady, maybe you could tell me something about the rumors that have passed this way from Malakar."

"Rumors?"

"They say that the Dark Lord of the Empire has returned to rule."

Erin was very, very still.

"What else do 'they' say?" Tiras asked casually. He had crossed his arms, and his hands rested beneath the draping black sheen of his sleeves.

"That he walks. That he is the foremost of the demons of the Dark Heart. That he has taken sustenance from both the free and the housed."

It was impossible for Erin to grow more still, and yet she seemed to, each word forming the links of a chain that held her tightly in place.

"Hold."

Lord Coranth swiveled his head to the side and froze as much as Erin had.

Tiras stood, two inches from the far wall, the glint of daggers adorning either of his slim, sure hands.

"Tiras!" Hildy shrieked.

Bretnor's hand flew to his sword, and Tiras' left arm rose

with blinding speed. The lord's son froze, and the dagger remained in Tiras' hand, but barely. No one who watched doubted the skill with which it would be thrown.

"If you would be so kind as to step back from the Lady?" Lord Coranth did as bid.

"Hildy!" Bretnor shouted.

"Tiras!" Hildy shouted in response. Yet even she did not move toward the black-garbed man.

How much, Erin thought in bitterness, fear, and wonder, *how much do you know, Tiras?* But she said nothing; even her breath seemed to have deserted her.

"Lady of Mercy," Aeliah whispered.

Erin wheeled to face the young woman in surprise, feeling a sudden threat, as if her armor had suddenly dissolved into shadow around her.

But Aeliah wasn't looking at her; indeed the words were a mixture of curse and invocation to some unknowable being, uttered in a voice that only the lowest, the slaves of the Empire, might have used in a time of stress or panic.

Yet she was Lord Coranth's daughter, no slave. There was more here than Erin had thought. The village, as Hildy promised, was "unusual."

"Tiras," she heard herself saying. "It's all right."

He hesitated for a moment, then the daggers disappeared.

Bretnor's sword left its scabbard in that second.

"Bretnor!"

"He was going to kill you!"

"Bretnor."

"Hildy—who are these people? How could you bring them here? Do you know who they're working for?" The young man's voice was a mix of anger, fear, and a deep sense of shocked betrayal.

Hildy threw Tiras a look. It said much, and Tiras was only barely able to ignore it. But it was Bretnor she spoke to when she answered.

"Yes, dear." Her voice was resigned, almost gentle. "I *do* know who they work for."

"Bretnor, Aeliah." Erin spoke now, turning to face them, her hands spread and empty. "I'm sorry. Tiras means no harm to you or your father—he was, he was afraid your father meant to kill me."

Bretnor snorted, and Aeliah looked shocked.

"There are many houses in the Empire that would."

"My father's no Empire house!" Aeliah said indignantly.

"I think—I think we know that. I'm sorry." She turned then to face Lord Coranth, and her voice grew softer, but no less sure. "Lord Coranth?"

He nodded carefully, still keeping one eye on Tiras.

"I cannot answer your question about the first rumor. But if it is true—the others almost certainly are." And then she bent her head.

The plush crimson of carpet caught her tears. As they fell, they seemed transformed; the blood of a wound that no eyes could see.

Darin walked over to her and put an arm around her waist; the staff he held out, although whether it was to warn the others off, or to give her some privacy, no one was certain. Yet it worked on neither level for Lord Coranth, who now approached Erin both cautiously and openly.

"I offer my apologies as well," he said gently, touching her with words, as Darin would not let him closer. "It has been a habit of my life to ask inappropriate questions. And Mordantari is not a known, not even in the capital. Those lands no one has dared to claim in our history." He held out a hand. "I will not ask again."

Erin shook her head and looked up, adding a smile to her pale face and finding, oddly, that it fit. "I—I do it all the time. Ask stupid questions, I mean. It's—never mind it."

"Well then, if that's decided, maybe Bretnor could tell us who he thought we were working for." Hildy said, trying in her inimitable fashion to smooth over—indeed brick over—a "rough" patch in the conversation.

"Hildy, maybe we can discuss this over dinner. Let me send for Sorrel; she'll have rooms made for you and your guests. You've no doubt been traveling the day, and perhaps you could use some rest."

Erin nodded gratefully.

But in the silence of her modest room, which she shared with no one, she saw the dead, their slack faces lining the folds of pulled, blue curtains, their frozen fingers locked stiffly against the worn and faded carpet. She dropped her pack on the floor and closed the door firmly behind her back. She rested for a while, her eyes unseeing as they stared through the leaded glass of the room's twin windows.

"Stefanos," she whispered, "why?" Must it happen, if she were not there? Did no change take place in him that did not pierce the surface? Her hands formed fists, but they were useless, they shook so. He was in Malakar. He ruled the Empire.

And to him she must go, as always.

But this time, it would be different—had to be different. There would be freedom, and for a moment, the price of that freedom was not and could not be too high.

"I am not your Lady of Mercy," she whispered again. "I never was." She saw the dead and imagined vividly those who would yet feed a nightwalker's deathless hunger. "I never was."

No one in Malakar heard her words. And oddly, if they had been heard, those they had been meant for would not have believed them.

The blood ceremonies that had begun continued, and many were the nobles of Veriloth's houses who had begun to lead a more nocturnal existence, in accordance with the Lord of the Empire's wishes. Gone were the quarters, at which the Church had performed the most glittering and cruel of its duties—but the house stones still had to be bloodied.

And the numbers of the dead had risen. The whisper on the streets was one of open fear—for any who walked, whether free or slave, could now be taken by the shadows the night cast. There was no recourse, no protection. The Lord of the Empire walked where he would.

Yes, much had changed in the Empire's capital, much that would be felt as its effects rippled outward to touch all of Veriloth. All of it was black, evil news.

And yet . . .

The slaves still slaved, bending back and arm to tasks appointed; they still died when their errors were too large or glaring, still bloodied the stones, still lived in the hidden depths of the houses whose mark they bore.

But their songs were louder.

The Lord of the Empire had returned.

". . . and we're not to take any offerings to the Lady."

Stev looked up from the railing of the main gallery, taking

care first to deposit his cleaning rag in the appropriate bucket. He swept a quick glance across the floor a story below, but no one walked it.

"Ayc," he said, as the two maidservants walked past, "I'd heard it myself."

"Oh, Stev, there you are."

He rolled his eyes. "Why?"

"House mistress's looking for you."

He nodded, bent, and picked up the bucket, his lips forming a familiar circle as he began to whistle.

It was the Lady's song.

"Sing it softly," Tarael said.

Stev almost laughed. "What does it matter, now? The Dark Lord has returned, and you know he loved the Lady. Can her return be far from his?"

Tarael frowned. "Remember Lady Cynthia," he answered grimly.

Stev nodded, breaking his tune a moment. "Aye, but his coming hasn't harmed us—it's just made the rest of them a little more familiar with what it's like to slave."

"Stev, he's been killing our number as well."

"I know," Stev answered softly. "But remember your legends, Tar. He did that before she came. She'll take those dead into her own fold now. And she'll come to bring light to the Dark Lord, but this time, when it all changes, she won't leave us." He started to head down the hall and turned, his face still grave, although his eyes were shining.

"She promised."

Tiras held up a weary hand, which did nothing to stop the flow of Hildy's angry diatribe. He felt his age, here in this small village in the province of Landsfall. He had not felt his age since the Night of Fires had extinguished so much in Dagothrin.

What was most annoying was the fact that she was, in her own way, completely correct. By way of apology, he had gone to some length to defer to what could understatedly be called Hildy's strong opinion; gone were the draping, black shirt and pants in which he both hid and announced his element. Now, beneath his chin, the ruffle of a complicated white shirt protruded; over and beneath it he wore blue velvet.

Ah, good. It looked as if she were, for the moment, finished.

"Hildy," he said quietly. "I have apologized to both you and Lord Coranth. I have agreed that I will no longer take such a cautious, or careful, stance when dealing with either of you. Is there more that you could ask?"

She snorted. "You could pay more attention when I'm speaking."

He rolled his eyes, but forbore from pointing out that she had repeated herself some eight times in the course of this long half hour.

"Why did you even mention the area in the first place?"

"It is," Tiras said, through a stiffening jaw, "on the map. I didn't realize that the demarcation of that province was so strongly kept." And, although he would never admit it to Hildy, he had been curious. Of Mordantari, very little information had crept back to Dagothrin.

"But did you have to pull the daggers when—"

"Hildy, I believe I have explained, or tried to, at least nine times." He stood. "Are we not called to meeting now?"

"Not yet," she answered, folding her ample arms together and standing in front of the door. She eyed Tiras the more suspiciously for his change of clothing, not the less—for the clothing itself was fine, and finery in the Empire always required caution. Her own dress was almost a tent of sturdy linen in a lovely shade of mauve that was completely unflattering to her coloring.

"Very well, if you must hear it again. The Lady Erin's mission is of utmost import—and the goal that she seeks no other can accomplish."

She did not look enlightened. "And?"

"Really, Hildy, I think—"

"And?"

In anger he spoke, but it was quiet, as much about him was when he did real business. "I do not myself understand all that the Lady Erin has been privy to. She has not troubled herself to explain it either to the king or his counselor." He drew breath. "But I have chanced to hear her talk to the patriarch of Culverne. The connection between herself and the Lord of the Empire, the most powerful of the Enemy's nightwalkers, is a strong one that has lasted a long time.

"In no wise, and in no place, not even Marantine, is it safe to have that revealed, and unfortunately, whatever else her skill may lie in, it does not lie in subterfuge.

"Were she to make more clear than she did, in my opinion foolishly, this day, I would be in the position of having to—"

Hildy waited, but Tiras did not continue. She was old and had been in the business for a very long time. Her voice carried none of her age and all of her experience when at length she replied.

"You will not kill Lord Coranth, regardless of what he finds out. The Lady's business is for herself to decide."

Tiras did not bother to nod; he had his own peculiar code of honor. But he knew that Hildy understood him well. Too well, perhaps.

Lord Coranth wore a simple gray tunic that was finely tailored, but not overtly fancy. No frills or lace for him; even the signet ring that a lord of his house would rightly bear was absent from his fingers.

At his right sat Bretnor, son and heir; at his left, a contemporary, a thin man with a long, straight nose and dark eyes that never seemed to blink.

Aeliah sat beside Bretnor, her fingers drumming idly against the surface of the long, rectangular table.

The table itself was not fine; it had seen many years, and most of them had been unkind to it. Chips and stains tarnished the wood, which was in need of some oiling, and it was obvious that much water had been spilled that none had thought to clean.

At least, so it looked to Darin.

He took a seat at the table, facing Lord Coranth; the chair beneath him had uneven legs and creaked against the floorboards. Erin nodded at Aeliah as she entered, performed a half bow in Lord Coranth's direction, and also took a seat. She had removed her armor and the boots that had carried her down the road; her clothing, like Lord Coranth's, was a pale gray. But around her hips, the sword still hung.

Lord Coranth did not fail to notice it; although he had allowed his daughter to enter his old friend's tutelage, he was still not accustomed to the sight of women bearing weapons of war. Even so, he nodded and smiled pleasantly.

"Are the others to come?"

Erin started to answer, and the doors at the end of the mess hall flew open.

Oh no.

Hildy looked thunderous, which was underlined by her silence; Tiras looked bored. Tiras seldom looked bored; it wasn't a good sign. Still they both took their seats—Hildy waiting until Tiras had seated himself before she chose.

Given the expression she turned on the older man, it was surprising to all that she sat squarely, and firmly, beside him. Hamin made way for her.

"Ah, good." Lord Coranth ignored the tension between these two guests, ever the gracious host. If his gaze lingered a little over Tiras, that was to be excused. "Will either of you take anything?"

"No."

"Tea."

Lord Coranth smiled. "Tea then. Aeliah?"

Aeliah nodded and left the table. Lord Coranth sat in silence until she returned.

"Good," he said softly. "I believe we have matters of concern to discuss; they affect us all, and I would appreciate any aid that you might offer. Ah, but first, let me introduce Dervallen to those of you who haven't met him before. He is my arms master."

Tiras raised an eyebrow, and the man called Dervallen favored him with a measured and cold look in return.

"Well then," Hildy said, lifting a delicate silver spoon and trailing sugar along the table to her cup, "what is this news? Something to do with the way we were greeted?"

Bretnor was reddening.

"Yes," Lord Coranth said softly. "We have had some trouble in the village recently. An odd trouble; farming accidents, and a fire at the mill."

"Oh, no." Hildy's voice was almost hushed.

"We got the fire out in good time."

"And you don't think these are accidents."

"No. You see, they come on the trail of a message from Sivari."

Hildy set her cup down; the steam rose from the liquid like a thin, weak cloud in front of her face. "Sivari."

Darin whispered something, and Hildy looked at him. "The capital of the province of Erentil, dear."

He nodded and she turned to look at Lord Coranth once more. "I suppose it's House Vanelon?"

"How did you know that?" Bretnor broke in.

Lord Coranth looked slightly pained.

"Vanelon is the only house with a large mine, and mining interests, in the Empire. A few other houses dabble, but Vanelon keeps them in line." She smiled almost grimly. "We had some trouble with them recently—just prior to the liberation of Marantine." Her expression made clear what that had cost. "The mining interest that comes through Boradil strengthens the west; Vanelon would be as happy to see it entirely destroyed."

"They intend you some harm now," Lord Coranth said, equally quiet.

"How serious is it?"

"Lord Erantos of Vanelon arrived personally."

"Erantos isn't the heir?"

"Second in line."

Hildy was quiet again; so much silence from the large woman was rare, and not to be treasured.

"Erantos offered my house a return to its former glory for my aid." He smiled, and that brought a similar expression from Hildy. "A return to the capital; a return to power; escape from the confines of this—" He waved a hand around the room. "All for the simple service of assassinating one merchant who has traitorous connections in Marantine."

"And the accidents followed your reply."

Bennarion nodded. "Still running your monopoly on the resources north of Dagothrin?"

"More so than ever. But there's more?"

At this he seemed to sag. "Two caravans coming from the east have failed their passage. A few escaped from bandits on the road."

"Bad. How many bandits?"

"Hundreds, if you listen to them talk; I would say forty, but that may be conservative." He was silent for a little while longer, then leaned forward. "You are a creature of habit, Hildy. I believe they expect your arrival in the village three weeks from now."

"Very bad." It was Tiras who spoke; Tiras who rose quickly and quietly. "Do you have a map of the village?"

"The only question is when." Tiras looked up from the map that he had marked. There were four hundred villagers, but many of those were too old, too young, or lamentably too untrained to be of use; these did not merit individual pins. All others stood as slim, straight poles that cast tiny shadows against the parchment.

The map was an older one; Lord Coranth had been quick to point out additions to his village, and Tiras had already etched in the newer buildings that had been put up along the one cobbled thoroughfare the village possessed.

"Forty?"

Lord Coranth nodded tersely, then shook his head. "I don't know. Forty is my guess, but it could be off by half again." His face had been made unusually gaunt by lack of sleep and worry. In his mind's eye he had been confronting the situation for almost two months, but the terse, sharp immediacy that Tiras showed brought home the reality of it in a way that imagination couldn't capture.

"Lady?"

"I don't know." Her fingers traced the underside of her jaw. "Lord Coranth has a total of six people who can fight, but it means that both he and his heir *must* front on the line—if the attackers feel they need to have a real line of battle.

"And we've got fourteen. Not including you, Darin, or myself."

Lord Coranth marveled at her composure. None of the strain that she must feel showed in either her face or the way she carried herself; indeed it seemed to him that she was more relaxed now than she had been before he'd relieved himself of the burden of his news. He had not thought it in her and wondered where she had come from. His glance strayed to Tiras, and he decided abruptly against the asking of questions in the older man's presence.

"Twenty-three trained men against forty. Not auspicious; there are too many noncombatants in the path."

Hildy raised her head from the map. "Count on sixty," she said softly, no hint of lilt or jovial humor in her voice.

Erin looked at Tiras.

Tiras closed his eyes.

"Maybe they haven't noticed you yet—maybe you can leave." Aeliah's face was white and tense, but her eyes were sparkling.

Did I look like that? Erin wondered. *Did I, before my first real battle?* "No." She said aloud. "If they've been causing your accidents, they'll already know we're here. We made no secret of our arrival."

"If we leave down the east road," Hamin said quietly to Hildy, "perhaps they'll contain their attack. There are quite a few good places along this road to plan an ambush."

Hildy weighed his words very carefully. Then she turned to look at Lord Coranth. The knowledge that she was the cause of his trouble was written clearly in the lines of her face; she looked her age, or older. "How did they react to your refusal?"

Lord Coranth gave an elegant shrug of his shoulders. "You mean besides the deaths and the burning of the mill? Not well, but certainly not as poorly as might be expected."

"Father," Bretnor said tightly.

"Bretnor." There was a caution in the words.

His heir ignored it. "I think the only reason they haven't razed the village is that someone might escape up the west road to give you warning."

"Then we stay," Erin said softly. "And we plan."

"I think Erin's right, dear."

Lord Coranth's shoulders sagged suddenly, whether in relief or surrender, it was hard to tell. "Thank you," he said. He reached over and placed a hand on Dervallen's shoulder.

Erin spoke: "Aeliah's right: You aren't a normal Empire house. If you had given what was asked of you, your village would be safe. You didn't. That alone means more than I could ever tell you."

"But we're still twenty-three against sixty." Lord Coranth laid his free hand, palm up, against the table.

No one spoke.

And then Darin, patriarch of Culverne, set his staff lengthwise across the table and took to his feet. He hadn't Bretnor's height, although he had gained a few inches since he had first been chosen to serve his Lady Sara in a different world, a different time. His shoulders were still slim, and it was obvious that he would never have the breadth or depth of chest that most warriors claimed. But true strength is measured by more than stature, and there was a dignity in his stance that, though newly found, already served him well.

He cupped his hands together; they were smooth and still, and betrayed none of the nervousness that he felt. He closed his eyes, then forced them open; the gate that he sought, he would have to seek later in awareness of his environment.

Very slowly, and in dead silence, the staff of the Line Culverne began to rise. No hand touched it, and no visible line chained it to him.

When it topped the tallest standing member of the impromptu council, it stopped, hovering in the air as if freed from gravity.

Sorry, Bethany, Darin sent to her.

I understand, her voice said, a comforting and comfortable presence. *But proceed cautiously, Initiate.*

Now he spread his hands in a fan, more for show than strict necessity. And Darin called fire in earnest. Fire came, in a heady, sweet rush, tingling along his arms and spine, whispering a deadly, pervasive music in his inner ear. This time, this time he held it all, hoarded it like a secret. A hint, an echo of its words, escaped him at his desire, and the staff of Culverne was suddenly haloed by a deep, red light.

"Twenty-three." He formed each syllable with deliberate care. Each one cost him much. The fire died out as he forced it back through the gate he had formed. The staff fell lifeless, to clatter against the wood. His might not have been the path of the warrior-priest had another way been open to him. But circumstance had issued this single challenge, and he accepted it.

Erin dropped lightly to one knee, her hand touching, but not drawing, the sword that she wore. "Patriarch," she whispered, bowing her head. Her eyes were dark but sparkling when she raised them, and for a moment she could not see the child that he had been, only the adult that he had chosen to become.

Even the taciturn Tiras bowed his head. "Against sixty," he offered, but those two words had lost a little of their patina of menace and death.

"Lady of Mercy," Aeliah whispered. Then the corners of her lips turned up in a fierce, heady smile.

It was many minutes before they returned to the map that curled along the table.

chapter
ten

"So how come you carry a sword?"

Erin looked down into the impossibly round face of the child who had succeeded in accomplishing the difficult conquest of her lap.

"I guard Hildy's caravan against bandits," she answered; it was easier than explaining the whole of a life. She looked up to see that her compatriots were still absorbed in the details of dining. Lord Coranth had no formal conference room; at the dinner hour, people had come in, dragging either chairs or trays, and the map had been hastily rerolled and put aside.

There were servers here, as there had been in the great hall of Elliath, but there were no slaves in the truest sense of the word; the brand counted for nothing, although many bore it.

The child in her lap, already outgrowing the little coveralls that she wore, was the daughter of one so branded. Her mother had disappeared for a few minutes on one errand or another, or Erin was certain the child would not have been so bold.

"But you're a girl."

"Well, yes." She met the eyes of her inquisitioner with a friendly, patient smile. "But so are you."

"Do you got a rite-mate?"

"I had one once."

The child wrinkled her nose. "You don't got one once. You get 'em forever. That's what Ma says." Then her eyes widened, with much the same pleasure as having discovered a secret. She tried to stand up, but found that an adult's lap didn't offer much purchase, and she flailed around for a moment before grabbing the front of Erin's tunic. "Did he die?"

145

Innocence could be so guileless and so cruel. Erin tousled the tangled mop of brown curls.

"I lost him to a war," she answered quietly.

"Melissa!"

"Uh, oh."

Children were born cute for a very good reason.

"What do you think you're doing?"

"Talking to Erin." But Melissa was already old enough to begin the slide off the guest's lap.

Erin didn't have time to concur. The doors to the hall flew open so quickly they hardly had time to creak. The child, her conversation, and her annoyed mother were forgotten, as a boy of ten seasons threw himself across the threshold, clutching his sides and drawing deep breaths.

"Bandits! Bandits!"

Lord Coranth started from the table, his face gone suddenly pale. "Where?" he shouted at the young boy, who stood gasping for breath in the doorway.

"East," was the reply. "East at Hepley's."

"Bretnor, get the wagons going! Aeliah—"

Tiras grabbed Lord Coranth by the shoulder.

"Belay that!" he shouted, and Bretnor froze in half step. "How many?"

"I don't know! We saw them from our farm. Da sent me— he's arming up with the crossbow." His eyes, wide and dark, found Lord Coranth. No one had moved. "Are you going to just stand here?"

But Lord Coranth had already shrunk six inches as he followed the hand at his shoulder to meet Tiras' eyes.

Wordless, he stared as Tiras nodded grimly.

"Boy, were they—did they look as if they were attacking the farms?"

The boy shook his head nervously. "No. Dogs're setting up a racket, though." He rubbed the sweat from his forehead with a swish of a night robe. It was simple enough, but it left no doubt that he hadn't been given time to dress properly.

"Which direction were they headed in?"

"West," the boy answered promptly.

"Here."

"Hildy," Erin said, her voice hard and quick. "Get Hamin and the others."

Hildy nodded and trundled out of the dining room, side-stepping the messenger of such ill news.

"Darin?"

"Ready."

"Bretnor, Aeliah—weapons. Get the house staff who know how to use them."

Aeliah nodded tensely and left at a run.

"This—this is it, then." Lord Coranth put both hands on the table.

"My fault," Tiras answered shortly. "I was certain we'd have more time."

"Let's assign blame later." Erin had already unfurled the map; two tea mugs and a beer stein held three corners down, the fourth curled forlornly. "Where is Hepley's farm?"

Taril was the name of the boy who had been sent with word of the bandits. Taril, Harper's son. He sat at the edge of the table, his hands beneath his legs, his face white. He'd run all this way in bare feet, but he didn't seem to notice it.

Indeed, he noticed little of his surroundings; only the words of battle and death seemed to catch and hold his attention. For his father, and his two elder brothers, were even now preparing to defend their land. Ma hadn't been happy about that; Susan and Cherylin had gone with her, but he wasn't sure where; they'd left in a hurry.

He'd never seen a map before in his life, but he was quick, and if couldn't read the words in the small, square boxes, he could understand what they meant.

He started once when the men began to enter the hall, dressed in fine links of chain, and carrying swords. Only the lord carried one openly, but never had he seen it drawn. Men only carried drawn weapons for a reason.

There were a lot of them, and Taril recognized only three. Raul, Bretnor, and Kaanis. It was to Bretnor that he turned his white, desperate face.

"Tar," Bretnor said, reaching out with one hand. His face was tight and drawn; anger shone from the surface of his dark eyes. "I'm sorry."

"But what about—what about Da?"

Bretnor looked away.

"We can't just stand here talking—we gotta go!"

Tiras turned a grim stare in Taril's direction, and the boy

suddenly sprung up, knocking his chair aside. The worst of his nightmares, undreamed of until this moment, had just come true.

"If you won't help 'em, I will!" he shouted, lunging for the closed doors.

Darin caught him. Darin, with Bethany upright in one hand, and the other empty and shaking. He was only slightly taller than Taril, but not so wide; nor did his muscle speak of the fields of farmers and the way they labored over them. Still, he barred the way to the door with determination.

"They'll die!" Taril shouted, barely stopping himself.

Darin brought Bethany around in a tight, decisive arc. The staff hit Taril just below the right shoulder, and a light that only Darin and Erin could see leaped from it to encircle the boy.

"I don't want them to die. I have to help."

"We'll help," Darin said quietly.

The tears started then. Darin took care to keep Bethany in contact with the younger boy as he himself drew closer. "These men," he said, pointing at Hamin and Hildy's caravan guards, "are armed and well trained. They've come to help the village."

It was hard just to say the simple words, for Darin knew exactly what Taril was feeling. Who better to know it? By a night like this one, in the Dark Lord's shadow, Culverne had fallen. No warning had been given of the treachery that had opened the gates to Marantine's deadliest foes.

But he wasn't a boy anymore, and this village was not so helpless, so friendless. He was Darin, patriarch of Culverne. And if the enemy chose fire as a weapon, he would take his fire against them to save the village. And to quiet the memories that rose now, like acrid smoke, to sting his eyes.

"It isn't your parents I'd worry about, boy," a new voice said.

Darin looked over Taril's shoulders and met Corfaire's eyes. There was a smile in them, one harder and colder than the steel he held.

"Those men aren't worried about farmers."

"Enough, Corfaire," Hamin said. "We've no time."

Corfaire shrugged, the motion both economical and elegant. "The armory, then?"

"All of us." Hamin shook his head wearily. "There's not

enough light, and not nearly enough window cover, but at least there are only two entrances. Erin?"

"The front." She unsheathed her sword and held it a moment aloft, gazing down the ancient blade at a play of light that held too much meaning for her.

"Tiras?"

"Back, then. I'll take Marek and Corman."

"Not enough."

"Luke and Trent."

Hamin nodded. "Corfaire? Ferdaris? Good. Everyone else take a window seat; you know when to come down." He paused for a second. "Lord Coranth, it's best if you and your son are on the upper level; when it comes to it, there'll be fighting enough, but there's no point in the risk until it's absolutely necessary. Hildy, gather the household staff and wait in the cellar. Send someone to set the horses loose." He drew a breath and turned, last, to face Darin, who waited in quiet patience.

"Patriarch," he said, and the word held no command, "the front northern window is probably the best position for you to take; it overlooks the front doors. They're solid, but not impassable, and that's where the gathering of so-called bandits will probably be strongest."

Darin nodded and turned to look one last time at Taril. "Don't worry," he said, and knew it was useless.

The manor was no grand manse, and the windows it boasted, while solid, were small. Only two of these might allow a grown man passage, should he have the time to remove the leaded frames that held the glass. No self-respecting noble would have so small, and so quaint, a family house; most country estates could boast more finery and grand space than this. But it was stone, and stone didn't burn; nor did it easily break.

Inside, the halls were the width of two grown men, and Erin thanked the Bright Heart for it. Only at the front door did it open up into a wide, high-roofed space; the upper hall looked down upon its vestibule, and both Bretnor and Aeliah had chosen to crouch beneath the rail between the solid oak pickets, their crossbows drawn and ready. They could see the four silent soldiers beneath them take up their stance in a quiet and a calm that neither could master.

"Do you hear anything?" Aeliah whispered.

Bretnor shook his head.

"Do you think they'll come?"

He nodded, and the nod was all his hope. What if Tiras and Erin were wrong? What if the bandits had chosen to kill the unguarded villagers and raze their homes? Even now, they could all be dying, and anyone capable of defending them sat crouched in the manor. Waiting.

Waiting had never seemed such an evil choice.

"Well, Dervallen?"

"Lord?"

"Oh, cut it out." Lord Coranth rested his elbow upon the window frame of his personal chambers, looking out at the grounds from one side. He had wanted, at the very least, to douse the lights—but Tiras had forbidden it; he wished to let the enemy think they had some measure of surprise.

More than they've already succeeded in? He was weary, but a strange tingle coursed through his veins; this would be the end of it. After tonight, one way or the other, there would be no unexplained accidents, no little fears.

"Well?" he said softly again.

"Well what?"

How like Dervallen.

"You could have had a house, man. One of your own, not one that you served."

"Yes." Dervallen's eyes did not stray from the window.

"Was it worth it? You never earned the epithet. You were never a 'slave lover.' "

"No, I wasn't."

"You never told me why you came. Never made it clear."

"You never asked."

"I'm asking, then. Tonight. If we fail here, I would like to die knowing why. Was it for her?"

They so seldom spoke of his departed wife. Tamissen of Reydoc, the hawk of her house, and the pride. She had had so much power, had danced the political quadrille with such grace and such skill that many, many houses had courted her, and not all for alliance.

He had had no love of the city, no love of Malakar with its grim, distant glitter and its expensive facade. Yet now, even now, he regretted that her death could not have been there; for it was there that she had conquered much in both of their names. Her funeral should have been all that her life was—an exercise in power and triumph as well as loss.

"Why do you speak of such things?" Dervallen asked. "They are passed. They are not our concern now."

"No," Lord Coranth replied, and he let the matter drop. But he had his answer, and it was bittersweet. Even in death, she still had her power, and the good that she had brought to him remained.

And perhaps, in the twilight of the longest night of his life, he might find the passage he desired, just to see the little quirk of her proud smile when he told her of what she could still do.

Darin waited. He was alone; Taril had been taken by Hildy to join the rest of the servants in the cellar. He sat in a plain, low chair that had been taken from under a narrow desk. Staring out of the window in Aeliah's bedchamber brought him the ghost of his own reflection, mingled with the darkening sky beyond. The moon itself was full and bright as it watched the empty grounds and the street beyond the gates.

Bethany rested in his lap, her voice was stilled; she had no advice to offer. His fingers curled around her. Despite the urgings of Hamin, she was the only weapon he would carry.

Why do things always happen at night?

He pressed his forehead against the glass; it was cool. If his nose weren't in the way, he might have pressed the entire length of his face there.

Stars stretched out across the horizon, mounting the banks of the sky until they were past his sight. His eyes followed them along the edge of the window's frame, and then plummeted back to the earth.

In the heavens, the stars were flickering points of cold, white light. And flickering beneath them, evenly and precisely, were small, red torches.

The enemy had almost arrived.

Darin rose, setting the chair clumsily to one side. Bethany rolled off his lap, and he righted her, leaning a little upon the burled knob of the hard wood. They stood together, watching as much as Darin's eyes could catch from the side of the window.

He looked down at the grounds surrounding the lord's house, but there were none upon them; no servants, no guards, no one going about any house business.

The torches drew closer, and beneath them, glowing red-orange, the armor and faces of "bandits," walking almost in step. True, he could make out no insignia, no crest—but they were well prepared for this encounter. All carried swords, although as yet they were sheathed, and some bore bows. As the torches came up the main street, they split into four groups; two large, and two seeming very small.

Ah; that would be front, back, and the windows.

He tried to smile, but it would not come. They were in for a surprise; the only window in the house that had no crossbow-men at it was this one.

He tried to count the men, but lost track of which was which and gave up, hoping that most would come frontward. It seemed that they might, for a large group of men approached the double doors at the front of the house.

But three stayed behind; they bore no torches and quickly became a part of the landscape. Observers? Darin wondered. Maybe, or maybe not that alone—for he observed now; a prelude to entering the fray.

He thought there should be more noise, for he remembered the noise of his youth; the sound of metal against metal, or infinitely worse, against flesh—the sound of many heavy boots, the sound of crackling wood, and the shouts or screams of the soon-to-be-dead. But here there was silence, punctuated only by the ripple of his tunic where his chest rose and fell in a semblance of normal breath.

He darted behind the drawn curtains, losing sight of the attackers; it would do him no good to be seen just yet.

Steady, Initiate.

Bethany's voice soothed him; if he closed his eyes he could imagine that she stood beside him, flesh not wood, arrayed in the armor of the warrior-priests of Culverne as she had been at the dawn of the line.

He felt the hint of her smile, both warm and grim, telling him that he did not need to stand alone—indeed could not, while he was patriarch.

A wordless shout pierced the heavy stillness. Darin chanced a stray look in time to see a torch waver and half fall. The crossbows had sounded their quiet call to battle.

And in answer came the solemn, loud lowing of horn; one clear, deep sound. Darin was not so foolish as to hope it a call to retreat.

He ducked back again, but this time he had work to do; he crawled along the floor, dragging Bethany with him along the bare hardwood, until he reached the pale oak of Aeliah's bedside table. He clambered up then, sure that no one would spot him from without, and guttered the flame of the oil-burning lamp.

Darkness descended, broken only by the glimmer of like lamps in the inner halls. It was odd that he could feel the darkness as a cloak of security in the middle of an attack, but he could dwell on this later; the window beckoned, and the war.

Erin heard the shout from beyond the doors. Her hand gripped her sword more tightly, and she pulled her shield down from over her shoulder. The horn followed, and she stepped forward; it was almost time.

Her armor was leather, a heavy stiff jerkin dyed in the gray of the lines. Lord Coranth had offered her "proper armor" and had been a little upset when she declined to wear it, and even more so when she did not explain why.

Corfaire had only looked at her out of the side of an eye; his eyebrow had formed an arch both familiar and annoying to her, but he had offered no comment. He stood beside her now, his sword no less ready.

"They are upon the door," Erin said in a soft voice. The softness was a deception; all who waited could hear each word clearly. "Be ready."

"You hear well," Corfaire said, the tone mocking.

She didn't waste breath on a reply.

"They have a small ram. They will start now."

And the crash came. The doors shivered in their frames, but they held for the moment.

"Back," Tiras said softly.

"What?"

"The door will not hold. Luke, Trent—stay behind the kitchen door for the moment; Marek, Corman—behind those of the dining hall."

Luke's jaw seemed to spring open, but Trent caught him by the shoulder and began to drag him to the kitchen.

"You're out here on your own?"

"You'll know when to come out, I trust," Tiras said wryly.

Luke started to speak again, then thought the better of it. He was used to taking Hamin's orders in times of battle, but in any other situation he answered to Hildy. A quiet old man, a noisy old woman, what was the difference? He smiled, even as he drew his sword and flattened himself against the wall as much as his size would allow. Hildy was certainly more than she seemed—which was saying quite a bit—and from what he had heard, so was the old man.

Marek looked relieved. He'd stood with Luke before and knew that Luke could be counted on to take orders about half the time. If he'd been serving in the regular army, he'd have either been cashiered or, well, best not think about it yet.

There was plenty of death in the air as it was.

The door shivered again, but this time there was an audible crack at its center.

Tiras bent as if to check his boots. One. Two. Three.

The ram came through. He remained crouched, the lights of the oil lamp gleaming off his head and face. Four. Five. Ah, there.

Tiras had his first look at the bandits. Chain, of course, but this man carried no shield as he stepped through the breach.

"Clear!" he shouted, seeing only the man on the floor. He raised his sword, and the light flashed off it as he stepped forward. The smile he bore was singularly unpleasant.

No crossbows. Idiots.

Tiras rose in one fluid motion, and his hands flew out, a gesture more of greeting than denial. Sparks flew from them; two large blurring glints. They took the soldier in the throat and the eye.

He bent again, rose again, and another man fell.

A shout rose from beyond the door, and as the third man came barreling forward, Tiras stepped back. His face was calm, smooth; there was no hint of anger, fear, or triumph in it.

"Gentlemen," he said softly as he backed between the twin doors that led to the kitchen and the dining hall. He crossed his arms, cursing Hildy quietly, for the linen shirt was not nearly so concealing as the clothing he normally chose. Then he stopped, and the soldier before him charged.

He had time to cross his arms before Luke leaped out of the kitchen, bellowing wordless nonsense. The sword caught the fool in the chest, and he toppled with a gasp of surprise.

Then the battle was truly upon them. Tiras had time now to

pull the swords he seldom used, long in the right hand, short in the left. This style he had taught the king, but between the two, the older was still the master.

The first two men through the doors went reeling back before either Erin or Corfaire could reach them. They were not dead, but the bolts that Bretnor and Aeliah had fired had made their mark.

Two more crossed the threshold almost immediately, and Erin heard the cry for bowmen being raised behind them. That was bad, but she'd not the time to think of it now. She stepped forward.

Months had passed since she'd been called upon to use her skills so, but the things learned in youth were never forgotten. The Sarillorn of Elliath fought now as she had fought under Telvar's guidance. Indeed, the pale walls of the manse seemed to melt into starlight and forest cover. The man before her, armored and helmed in unfamiliar colors, was still her enemy, trace of taint or no. He was tall, bearded, and deep of chest. He was also surprised to see her fighting. It cost him an instant. It cost him his life.

No matter, the man behind came forward, armored in like manner. She lost sight of his face, but battle did that—no one man was memorable as a person until some time after the fact.

Her sword flashed up to block, and down again to catch a clumsy feint. She heard movement behind her and to one side, and knew that Hamin had come to take her left, should she be forced to abandon the door. This vestibule, curse it, was at least four men wide.

Curse it she did, but quietly; her teeth were clenched in the silence of concentration. When she lunged forward, the weapon was part of her arm, and in no wise could the two be separated. It pierced a rent in the hauberk of the man just to the left, and for a moment, he too was inseparable from her intent and action. Then his blood spurted out, a thin red wall that became a barrier between them—the living and the newly dead.

She moved quickly, gracefully. The magic-carved runes that ran down Gallin's blade glowed green beneath little runnels of red. No one noticed that she was female, not anymore. They saw the splay of thick, auburn braid as she moved back and forth, snapping herself out of the line to avoid the thrust of

metal. They saw someone pale, even through the flush of exertion; someone small whose eyes glowed green and fey as if
they saw every enemy move, every thought.

And then their line parted a moment, and Erin stepped forward to man the breach, stepped forward to see that the first
of the bowmen had made his way through the soldiers.

She opened her mouth as if to speak, but less than a gasp
escaped; she was too close, and the range too sure. The bolt hit
her, traveling above the center of her breastbone to lodge in
her throat. A heavier man would have been thrown back; Erin
near flew.

"Erin!"

If she could have answered, she would not have tried; her
mind turned inward, to the Hand of God. The blackness closed
swiftly around her, but it was here that she could reach Him—
the darkness of the beginning or of the end.

Darin started as the shudder went through him; ghostly fingers prying at his heart.

Steady, Bethany said.

He shook himself and looked once again into the folds of
the night. All grass was black and dark, even under the light
of torches. On such a night, the day was forgotten, and no one
would have been too surprised if someone had told them it
would never come again.

The men were huddled below; he could see their helms
where they caught the light and sent it scattering up to the sky
above, could see their swords drawn and readied as they stood
in wavering lines, awaiting their turn at the small front. He
could not see their faces. He was glad of it. Faces lent them a
semblance of humanity and life.

Why are you here? he thought, his hands clenching his staff
until his fingers were whitened and cold.

They are here, Bethany answered, the words ice and steel, *to
kill you all.*

But why do they serve the—

*Now is not the time, Initiate. In this, life has its imperative.
Think later, think long if you will.*

He nodded, but the question lingered like a bad taste in his
dry mouth. He knew that if he ever found an answer for it, it
would come too late to make a difference.

* * *

The blackness felt thick and turgid; it clung to her ankles, but worse still, to her hands. No gesture, no matter how old or how strong, would easily tear away these webs. She was hurt, and she felt the throbbing at her throat as if some drummer played there—the last beat of a difficult song.

Lernan. The call was weak, and no Light sprang to answer it. *Lernan!*

Still there was no response. She felt the blood trickle down the sides of her throat and pool in the hollow above her chest; it was warm and wet, but it held no power and told no story.

Not so the blood that flowed through her veins. This brought her the tale of twilight, the state between the living and the dead. She knew the gape and tear of flesh, knew the shattered pipe that drew no breath, and knew the exodus of blood from her prone body.

It frightened her.

Many times before had she used the thrust of enemy sword, spear, or bow upon the field of battle to call her to the Hand of God. Not once had she fallen from the fight; not once had she hesitated for more than an eye blink before God was with her.

Lernan! Bright Heart, please, please . . .

She had no eyes that could touch the twilight. Thus had she been taught, and she knew it well. Yet she thought she saw a faint, pale glow in the distance; not white, nor red either. Not even green, although why she could not say. It was blue, a pale nimbus of sparkling mist.

Twinkling, it grew larger, and in the distance she heard the soft murmur of water on the rocks.

Now, he thought. He called on the gate, and it came, pressing in at him, a force of its own with its own will. He opened the gate—that took no strength—and felt the rush of a heady, familiar tingle sear his veins. If anything it was stronger, no matter the care he had taken. The music of the fire was a silken whisper; it caressed him, twining around his stiff, upright body. No other sound had ever been this strong.

He opened his mouth, and the song began.

Fire leaped to life among the helmets below—tongues of flame, multifoliate rush of heat and bitter salvation.

Was any red ever so deep and perfect as this?

Darin looked down upon the press of men. For a moment

they stopped, as if the fire were cold enough to chill the marrow and freeze the blood. And then two of their number, caught in the maw of flame, were devoured. Helms fell to the untouched grass, rolling beneath the heat.

There was screaming then, a cacophonous harmony to the fire's music. The door was abandoned—no mortal foe could hold them in the face of this strange and deadly apparition.

Darin watched on, pale and still; his eyes misted, and all color was leeched away by the very real, very detailed beauty of another plane. In his eyes alone was the fire reflected, and they shone a deep red, should any look up for long enough to see him standing, unguarded now, in the window.

Initiate.

Bethany. He did not think he could speak; Bethany's voice was the only one that could have reached him so clearly here. It was calm and wise and pale compared to the murmur of brilliant flame. *So soon?*

Yes. Yes, Darin. Two are dead.

Dead. The chill that rose up his spine found a place in his heart and held fast there against the warmth. He sought the gate and sought the fire both. With pained skill he drew them together.

The fire, as ever, did not want to retreat.

But this time, Darin was the master of it.

The last refrain of fire echoed into the night, leaving a trace of chill longing.

Is all power like this?

Is ours? Bethany asked quietly.

He remembered the very first time he had held her and nodded quietly.

It was time now to see to the back.

Lernan?

There was nothing, no sound but the splash of water, a tinkle of nature's music. She drew closer still, and only a small part of her mind was left to wonder how she moved, or whether indeed it was not the light that reached for her.

And then she saw it, and she stopped, her eyes wide in wonder. Fear she felt, but that was mortal, and even it began to slip away.

What living being could know fear here, on these banks?

She took a step forward and felt something cool and soft at

her feet. Looking down, she could see nothing but simple wooden steps.

Why? Her brow furrowed, but that felt wrong here, and the question slipped from her before she could answer it. She would ask someone later. There was time, she was certain, for all the questions in the world.

"Well met, daughter."

That voice—her heart lurched and fell in her chest, and there was nothing to stop it. Tears pricked her eyes, and she looked up wildly.

No.

Fear touched her then; something was coming suddenly upon her; she could feel its breath on the back of her neck. She squinted her eyes, searching the sudden mist that surrounded her face like a halo.

Great-granddaughter.

A darkness began to close over the bridge, eating away at its edges. The voice, that hidden glimpse of something too peaceful to be memory, was destroyed.

Child, I have come. I am sorry; the way here was hard, and it grows harder.

No . . .

My power is not what it once was even mortal months ago. A darkness has entered my wound, and an evil blood festers there, of a strength I have not felt for a very long time. I fear I will not be of help to you ere the end, but I will do as I can. Great-grandchild, return to the living.

Erin curled up in the Hand of God and wept bitter, bitter tears.

They coursed down the sweat-lined grime of her cheeks to mingle with blood that was already drying. The hall of the Coranth House loomed above her in blank, austere white.

"Lady?" Hamin's ash-gray face was at her side.

Erin reached down and yanked the bolt out of her throat, throwing it far. God's green light cocooned her and warmed her.

Hamin's eyes were wide, but he nodded and rose.

"The battle?"

"Over, for now. At least here. There is fighting at the back of the house, but it won't last long."

She nodded. This was what they had planned.

"Lady, you came close to death. I thought—"

"I know." She reached out and gripped his mailed hand in a gloved hand of her own. The tears fell, but she ignored them. In minutes, she could not be certain why they fell. It was not from fear, although fear underlay them, and not with pain—for physical pain alone had long since ceased to bring tears; Telvar had seen to that.

No, beneath the tears, she felt a longing, a yearning, something elusive and yet very, very strong. That longing would not leave her, not now, and not ever again while she lived. But she did live, and as that life returned to heart and body, so did duty and the vows she had sworn.

She had almost died. She had summoned the True Ward, and God had reached her faintly, and only just in time. If God's Light was so weak, what chance had she of accomplishing her mission?

Tomorrow she would think on that, long and hard. Tomorrow she would take the time to plan, to think of planning. Tonight . . . ah, God's Power had come. Let her see now to the injured here, and to the wounded.

chapter
eleven

"Hey, Erin?" Amahl said, wincing as a damp cloth was applied to his forehead. *"Let's not do this again."* He was the youngest of Hildy's guards, and it showed in ways other than his injuries; more skilled men lay here, in the cots rigged up in the dining hall, than he—and all more calmly.

"Amahl, didn't I tell you *all* of your clothing?"

He blushed, and his pale face looked healthy for a moment.

Erin was too tired to think it very amusing, although later she might. She turned her head to glance down the row of cots; there were four more beds to tend to here; four more men. Sanfalis and Sudenir were already beyond her; Hamin had said he would see to their bodies.

Darin had offered his services in that regard, which left her free to work at the postbattle healing. She frowned, and Amahl removed the last of his underclothing, revealing the jagged welt across his chest.

She touched it carefully, killing the infection that had already started there.

"Bad?" he asked.

"Not so bad. You're still alive," she answered, rising. "I'll come back." She had to husband her power carefully; little enough of it remained, and she wasn't certain how badly injured these last four were.

She stretched, trying to smooth out the kink that had developed between her shoulders. The ceiling, well over ten feet in height, seemed low and uneven; too much time had been spent in this one room over the last day. Still, she wondered how they were going to bring the dining table back in.

161

Never mind. Why was she thinking about trivial things now? She walked over to the next cot and knelt beside it.

"Hello, Luke," she said quietly, touching his face.

He had no answer to give her, and even his chest rose and fell in an irregular, shallow manner.

"I hear you saved Tiras' life."

His lips curled up in a smile as she sent her power out, tracing a net the length of his body with its strands. He had been twice hit with crossbow bolts, and once with a sword, but each wound had been clean. Only the sword wound had bled much.

Big ox, she thought, as she felt the power leave. *It's a wonder you're still alive.*

"How is he?"

Erin started at the sound of the voice, even though it was familiar. She withdrew hastily and looked up to see Hamin's drawn face. Luke was one of his men.

"Nearly dead," she answered pertly.

"Erin—"

"He's lost a lot of blood."

Hamin raised an eyebrow, but the grimness of the question was already dissipating. Erin never made jokes when a life was truly in question.

"How are things outside?"

"We didn't have enough men to catch the ones that ran."

"The leader?"

"Long gone."

"Damn." She rose and staggered slightly. Hamin caught her arms. Her voice was weaker than her smile. "Maybe we'll talk about it later."

He nodded and helped her to the next bed. He nearly had to catch her again as she gazed down at the pale, slim figure beneath the thin coverlet.

"Corfaire."

The last time she had seen him, he had been fighting like a man possessed. If he had had any injuries, he had given no indication of them—perhaps they served as a goad rather than a hindrance.

"Ah, Lady." His eyes blinked open, and he struggled to rise, casting the coverlet half-aside to reveal the white, scarred chest and the three new wounds that marred it. Nothing came of the effort, but it was not in his nature to resign himself quietly to helplessness.

Any other patient would have been forced back into the pillows, but not this one. Erin felt hesitant looking at him so disarmed. She did not want to touch him yet.

Hamin was not so reluctant. He caught Corfaire by the shoulders and pushed him down. "Enough movement, man. You'll open them further." His eyes narrowed. "That's an order, Corfaire. And here, you answer to me, not Hildy."

"Hamin."

"Erin?"

"It's all right. I'll be fine from here." Her cheeks were slightly pink. She knew her duty; she had no business letting it rest, for however short a time, on Hamin's shoulders.

"Well, Lady?" Corfaire said softly as soon as Hamin had moved away. "Have you a miracle for me?" Even here, in a sickbed, that sardonic, bitter smile matched his face perfectly.

Erin was heartily sick of it. "Yes," she said, through clenched teeth, "I do." She spread her shaking hands, noticing that they had become fists only by uncurling them, and leaned forward to spread them against his chest. It was cool and slightly clammy. There was no sign or feel of infection here.

Corfaire's smile vanished at the pressure, and he gritted his teeth. "Then do so. I wait."

Still she rested thus a moment, fighting with herself. She did not want to heal this man, and she didn't know why. Certainly he was abrasive, even rude, yet he had fought no less surely than she, and with no less dedication. He was a comrade-at-arms, and if he was not one she would have chosen, that changed the fact not at all.

Her power curled above her fingers, and she caught it, weaving her net. Very slowly it spread out to envelop him.

I'll give you a miracle, she thought grimly.

And Corfaire did what he had not done during the long battle. He screamed.

A second after, Erin cried out and fell over into her low-backed chair. The thick, cedar rest caught her in the back, but she didn't notice. Corfaire's scream cut off abruptly, and he lay staring at her with wide eyes, his chest heaving.

She hadn't the breath to do likewise, but her eyes met his; they were green now, glowing in the pale light of her face.

And his, his were vaguely red in the oil-lit shadows of the infirmary, in the equally pale light of his face.

"Malanthi," Erin whispered, drawing the Greater Ward as a

silent shield between them. She forgot the last bed, forgot the battle that had passed and the men that had escaped, forgot that she was a healer here. Her hands reached down, and she found her sword. It flashed up, near whistling with speed, to rest in her hands like a gaudy, perfect plume above her head.

His eyes glowed anew, and now he found the strength to roll from the bed and crouch, scrabbling at his side, opposite her. He had no weapon and no armor to offer her. Blood left its signature down the front of his chest; the letters there were writ large. But his hands made no gesture, as he met her eyes with bitter resignation.

Any other expression, any haughtiness, any fear, any anger, would not have had this effect. Erin slowly lowered her sword. The room came back in a rush, and she fought herself and her blood to keep hold of it.

"Who are you?" she said, her words quiet and dangerous.

"Corfaire." His answer was neutral still.

"You are Malanthi. Blooded."

"Yes." It was a bitter, cold word in the ice of his face. The blood was flowing more freely now. He could not stand thus for much longer.

Erin pointed her sword at his chest. The runes along it seemed to twist and pull toward him. "Lie down, Corfaire."

He did not move.

"If I wish to kill you, I'm less likely to do so if you're prone. That is the way of my line. Lie down."

This time he nodded and very stiffly made his way back to the cot. Erin offered him no aid.

"Why are you here?" she asked softly, when at last his shoulders touched the padded cotton and wool.

He didn't seem to hear her; his eyes were staring up, straight up, at the flat pale ceiling. What image he saw there was made clear by his words. "Ah, Mother, can you see the irony of this?" They, too, were bitter and resigned.

And Erin felt the unforeseen undertow of his pain. She found herself setting her naked blade to one side, on the floor. Her hand stopped two inches away from him.

"Who are you, Lady?" he asked, and there was no sarcasm in the title. He flinched as he saw her hand hovering, but made no move.

"I am Erin of Elliath."

"And that?"

It was a night for surprises, although this was a small one. "Don't you know the line name?"

"Is it a house?" Erin bristled, and sensing it, Corfaire searched for other words. "No house, then. A family? I do not know it. These things were not studied by me." He raised his hands and brought them into range of his eyes. Erin could see the pale white bracelet of slavery that adorned his arm.

"How did you come by that?" she asked. "What crime did your house commit?"

Corfaire laughed, and in that laugh was the first hint of anger that he had yet shown.

"My house?" If he could have thrown back his head, he would have, but the pillows caught all of the motion and damped it. "Lady, I have no house! What crime? I was born. That was enough." He turned from her then, his voice quieter. "I was born to a slave. What matter the father?"

"No slave fights like that."

"No *untrained* slave." He grimaced, staring at shadow. "Did you think we were all quaint, ignorant little housekeepers?"

Silence. Erin cringed. How many warrior-slaves had there been in the halls of the palace in Rennath? Not one, to her knowledge.

"Who trained you?"

The smile that curled the corners of his mouth up was a familiar one—and not on his face alone. It was cold, hard, and very, very cruel. "My father."

Erin swallowed and looked away. Her hands were curling again. "Why do you fight here, Corfaire?"

"Why does Darin?" he answered. "Why do you? No—answer only the first. I don't know why you fight. I don't know what you are."

"Darin? Darin fights because—did they teach you nothing of your blood?"

"What use does a slave have with the gestures and pretenses of nobility? I was taught to fight. I was the best. And I fight to hurt the Empire. I fight to hurt my father." He looked beyond her, and his words had the feel of an old vow, oft repeated. "There is no peace between us until one of us is dead." He turned and caught her hand in a tight, fevered grip, unmindful now of the power that had been such agony. "But you, Lady of Mercy, did you ever hear my mother's prayers?" His fingers bit into her, drawing blood. His eyes were wide now and dark, not red. She felt certain his consciousness would not outlast this exertion. It was suddenly important for him to rest. Why?

Because she believed his answers, the words, but more important, the emotion behind them. Pain call thrummed quietly within her mind. "Corfaire, rest," she said quietly. "I am no God. No prayer that is spoken can reach my ears in any way other than normal speech."

"Yet you know the blood—and you turn from even me, who makes no use of its power." He coughed. "Except in combat, and where I can, in combat against the Empire."

She reached out and smoothed the hair from his eyes and forehead, gentle now, and only a little repelled. *That's blood, not me,* she thought, *and I am my own master.*

"Will I see her?" he asked, as his lids fell shut. "Will I see her?" He coughed again, and his eyes fluttered weakly open. "It's been sixteen years. But I never forgot. I kept as much of her as I could."

"Yes," Erin answered. His grip relaxed, but she held on. "Yes, Corfaire. At the Bridge to the Beyond, she will be waiting for you."

She waited until she could see the rise and fall of his chest, then rose to get bandages and a needle. This healing she could not do with power, but she had spent a number of years on the front before she had been given the power of the Sarillorn of the line, and she remembered the old, bloodless ways.

As she worked, all that he had said gnawed at her. How many more of his kind lived in slavery in the capital? How many more had his blood, which could feel the lasting Light of God, and perhaps be destroyed by it? How many more of her people were so divided?

She shook her head and continued to work.

"I don't like you," he said, above the crackle of the fire in the small sitting room. The great arms of a well-worn high-backed chair framed him loosely. His skin was tinged orange, and the pupils of his eyes caught the flame and held it, flickering. He wrapped an old wool blanket more firmly around his shoulders and legs; his chin rested on his knee. He turned to look at her, losing the reflection of fire, and taking the shadows instead.

Erin nodded quietly, watching him. She was tired and a little chilled. The only blanket she had was the grime of the day, which she would just as soon be rid of. Breeze blew in through the leaded window, where panes of glass had been deliberately broken, by which side, it was hard to say; nor did it matter. Lord Coranth had already seen that repairs would begin in a three-day.

"I don't like you," Corfaire repeated, his voice soft. "I don't know why. I haven't liked you since the first moment I saw you."

"I didn't like you then either," Erin replied. She leaned down and picked up a mug of cooling tea. "But I do know why."

"The blood." He looked back to the fire.

"Yes." The mug settled back on the low, plain table. "But not just yours."

That caught his attention, and once again his face was half covered by shadows. The room was poorly lit. "What do you mean?"

"The Dark Heart is not the only God."

"No." He smiled, the characteristically unpleasant lift of lips. "There is the Lady of Mercy."

"She," Erin said archly, as a well-experienced teacher to a novice, "is no God. Have you not heard of the Twin Hearts? The Bright Heart?"

"I studied no Church doctrine."

She sighed. "It isn't just doctrine; not from my understanding of it."

"Then what?"

"The blood that you bear flows from the Dark Heart. And the blood that I bear, from the Bright."

He raised an eyebrow in question, and she sighed more deeply. It was already late, and she was very tired. In an hour, the sun would make its presence known, and no doubt she would be called to the table again.

"Lady, tell me about the Twin Hearts."

She did, hesitantly at first, and then more quickly as memory supplied a steady narrative she could cling to. It felt odd to sit so, explaining both her own power and the power of the Enemy, however dilute, to one who bore his blood.

Or did it?

No. Here, in the darkness, she remembered other evenings,

and other explanations. She spoke until at last Corfaire seemed satisfied, and then rose, retrieving the cup that was now cold.

"Lady?"

"Yes?"

"What do you do now?"

"Sleep." She brushed strands of stray hair out of eyes that were darkly lined.

"When you quit this place, I mean. What will you do?"

She took a breath, held it, and then slowly exhaled, deciding. "I go to Malakar."

"To free the slaves?"

His sarcasm still riled, especially at this time in the morning. She bit her lip, containing an equally sarcastic retort. He watched her quietly.

"No," she said at last. "But maybe afterward, the slaves will find their way to freedom with no one to hinder them. No one of any blood."

He nodded then, and seemed to be satisfied.

The last meeting was held, once again in the dining hall. The table had new chips and scars along the worn face of its surface, but somehow the servants had managed to fit it back through the doors. They had brought the high-backed chairs from the sitting room as well, and arranged these as best they could in the stark environment of the hall.

Lord Coranth nursed a scratch that he was ashamed to say came not from battle, but from breaking a window; otherwise he was whole and looked a good deal more at home than he had mere days ago. Dervallen sat, as ever, by his side, and in silence.

They had eaten, but no servants came into the hall to clear away the remnants of dinner, and crumbs remained on plate and table, keeping company with crumpled napkins and half-empty glasses.

Erin smiled as she looked around in the after-dinner quiet. This room, messy and occupied, looked lived in. No lord's manor, this, but rather, a large home.

"So, Hildy, you're leaving us already?"

Hildy nodded and lifted her teacup. It was delicate and fine—and the only one of its kind in the room. Everyone else drank from large, earthenware mugs.

"I'm afraid so, Bennarion dear." She sighed. "I'd love to stay, though. Mera tells me the berries are almost in season."

"We'll have some made into jams; you can pick them up on your way back through." He sat back into the cushioned rests of his chair. "Tiras tells me not to expect any further trouble. Not for a while."

"I know," Hildy answered. "He made that quite clear to my boys." Hamin, the only representative of her boys, grimaced.

"But what of you?" Lord Coranth raised an eyebrow.

"We should be safe for the time. At least on the road."

"And you?" Lord Coranth turned to look at Erin. She smiled and nodded. "Then I must thank you all."

Tiras sat alone, listening as the conversation broke up into small groups and passed from one person to another. Night had not yet fallen completely, but it would come soon. Looking out of the small window in the dining room, he saw the gardeners begin to end their day.

He was tired, and his muscles ached abominably, a sure sign of the age he would rather ignore. Just a little longer, a little farther . . . He glanced at Erin, saw that she was speaking to Hildy with a hint of twinkle about the lines of her eyes, and looked away.

They had not managed to locate the house lordling and his advisers; night had swallowed them rather effectively. No doubt they would wend their way back to Sivari with word of the difficulty on the road. Word and fear.

He looked now at Darin, whose cheek was fastened to the dining table by either gravity or sleep—Darin, who wielded both the staff of the Line Culverne, and the fire of the Church of the Dark Heart.

Only the fire had been seen at play the previous evening, and Tiras had no doubt that the Church would be blamed for the failure of the raid. No doubt that Church power, or threat of it, would keep the merchant House of Vanelon at bay. He wanted to laugh and wanted to cry at the same time; his lips were still as both desires pulled him in different directions.

For although he would never say so to the patriarch of Culverne, he still hated the fire, if not the hands that wielded it. Oh yes, he was getting old—too old, if he could not be happy with the justice that the fire had wrought. But the smell of burning wood and seared flesh lingered like a ghost, an acrid taste touched his mouth and burned at his eyes.

The dead haunt us with no will of their own. No will? He wondered if Terrela would still be waiting in the halls of judgment, and if she would accuse him of doing nothing, or open her arms to one who had been too long from them.

He rose restlessly, hating war, hating the Empire, and wearying of life. In the morning perhaps he would remember that they had won this battle. He turned and walked out of the hall to seek the silence of his chambers.

So great was his self-control that the Lady Erin only looked up once at his passing and felt no call to him.

In the morning, when sun had barely crested the horizon, the caravan was ready to move. The guards stood in clothing that had been freshly cleaned and, to some of their chagrin, starched. They were silent; even Hildy's tone was subdued. She kissed Lord Coranth and hugged his two children, tousled the hair of some of the small ones that had come to play, one last time, under the wheels of the wagons, and made her usual promises to return with goods and news.

"Hildy," Lord Coranth said, as she turned to leave, "it wasn't your fault."

Hildy smiled sadly. "Doesn't make it feel any better, does it?"

He sighed. "No. It never does."

"Look after the graves."

"You know I will."

She mounted the cab of the wagon with Hamin's silent aid. The reins were slack in her hands as she looked over Lord Coranth's small estate. Two of her boys were buried there, including one who had made this journey many, many times.

Well, the merchant-voice said, *that* is *the risk they're paid for.* She frowned, angry at the thought, and even angrier that it was hers.

"Come on," she said aloud. "Rennath is waiting. There're a lot of houses to fleece there, and they won't keep forever." With a billow of sea-green sleeve, she set the wagons rolling.

The voice returned in the darkness, an echo all the worse for the fact that the speaker would never come again. Night was chill, even so close to the fringes of dawn. Sleep, when it came, would last through the dawn and into early afternoon—by edict of the creature who now ruled the land.

Lady Amalayna sat shrouded in a thick counterpane. It was burgundy, but the darkness hid that fact mercifully. It was the only mercy granted.

Her fingers gripped the quilted, tasseled edges so tightly the twine made its mark in her palm. It was over. She had done the right thing. She had done her duty to her house, there, in the ballroom of House Damion, that long, grand room that was the envy of smaller houses. Lights had lined the walls, cupped in long, cut crystal; in the center of the room a chandelier threw multicolored shards against the hand-knotted carpets. Those carpets were a deep, dark blue, with hints of indigo along the borders of stylized flowers with hearts of blood. She knew what they looked like; she had spent much time in silence examining them.

In the hollow of her neck, in blue and silver, she bore the crest of House Damion, publicly given and publicly accepted in the cold glitter of noble fanfare. Her father had stood to her right, his hand on her right shoulder, as was the custom. Lord Vellen had stood on her left. He knew that she had shrunk, if only a little, from the hand that he brought down. Still, her smile, cool and rigid, had not altered in the least.

Lord Tentaris had been invited—as had most of the lords of the houses of Malakar. He had stood near the back of the audience resplendent in dark, rich velvets and gold, and behind him, not so far behind that Lady Amalayna could not see, stood a slave in his house colors, bearing a young child.

Lord Parimon, the heir apparent of Tentaris. Her son.

She would not embarrass her son on his first major occasion, even if he would not remember it. She was certain his grandfather would tell him, when the time came. So she had borne all that had happened with the cold grace of House Valens. She had been known for it, once.

There had been some murmuring in the audience, but little shock. One or two of the ladies had issued forth a smattering of polite applause.

Even here, in the quiet darkness of her room, she could feel their eyes upon her, cold shades of blue, brown, and green. She could feel their envy of the position she would one day hold. Take it, then, she had wanted to shout. Still, she'd felt a little spark of pride at their envy.

It was gone now, completely guttered.

For she heard his voice, and it cut her deeply.

Would you accept rites to the man who murdered me?

She had not been idle. Although Tentaris had had few contacts within the hierarchy of the Church, Valens had many. She had used these ruthlessly to find out what position Lord Vellen held there. He was still leader of the Greater Cabal, but not by much; Lord Benataan of Torvallen was swaying the lesser players of the council.

Her father had no desire, or so he said, for the leadership, but she knew that he was among the most powerful present. Lord Vellen needed power. And what better ally than Valens? It was not arrogance that guided her thought here; she knew what her house was worth.

But it left a question hanging, and she didn't want to ask it. *Father . . .*

The skin of her shoulders was burning with some unnatural heat in two places, each the size and shape of a man's hand. Her shaking fingers reached out and fumbled with the clasp of the necklace. Three times she tried to remove it, and on the fourth she gave up. It was a symbol she held meaningless. Did it matter what others thought?

But her breath came in short, sharp gasps. She trembled too much to contain herself. Had she any clothing, she would have wrenched it off and thrown it in a pile on the floor for the slaves to comment on, if they dared. She felt unclean; dirt and shadow seemed to cling to the parts of her that no soap and water would reach. Her spirit roared; her mouth whimpered. She bit down on the counterpane to stop the sound from traveling.

Darkness was not complete. Even here, a hint of light filtered in, although the doors were shut and sealed, and no human torches burned. He sat on his ebony throne, still enough to resemble the gargoyles that alone dared to stand on the dais at his side.

The passing of time was a mortal habit, a mortal measure, and he wondered if the centuries he had spent here would ever be cleansed entirely from his mind. Memory was too deadly and bitter a trap.

Yesterday evening he had fed, and fed well. He turned his mind to it, reliving all the details in the slowest possible way. He could see fear in the face of the old man who had run through the streets—that fear was a carpet that marked the passing of the First of the Sundered as he followed. High City or Low, it mattered little. Who dared to tell the Lord of the Empire where he might walk?

He had been slow to catch the man, drawing out the hunt until the last possible moment. This was a dangerous flirtation, for the sun always waited and always rose. Perhaps with time he could cure that.

Perhaps not, for only in light did shadow take form.

No. He turned his thought more forcefully to the hunger and its end. Yet although he remembered each detail of the nameless man's death, he felt none of the immediacy of his former pleasure in it. The hunger was a stronger memory.

Rising, he let it become more substantial.

For years he had turned aside from this—by his choice he had been restrained. That time had passed, and it would not come again. Yet still . . .

No. No. He was the First of the Sundered. Let the mortal world tremble and die in the wake of his passing.

Peggy hated the night. That would never change, and it was only worsened by the fact that many of her duties, which could just as easily be performed during the day, were now started at the set of the sun. She rose as the bells began their sonorous toll. The sound was taken by the stone and made both hollow and cold. House Damion, like any other house, followed the new edicts of the Church.

What slave could hope to do less?

Still, if she dressed quickly and hurried to the housekeeping station, she might catch the rays of setting sun through the front windows. It was well worth it; the pinks and blues and golds that scattered through the leaded glass windows were like a kiss of the light upon a brow it seldom saw.

She considered fetching her daughter but thought better of it. A few moments of privacy and peace surely weren't too much to ask. And she so seldom had the chance. She hesitated only a moment more, then hurriedly buttoned up her dress. The skirts swooshed across the clean, bare ground as she walked briskly through her door.

The gallery was silent when she arrived, and blessedly, also empty. She dared not sit, or look as if she were not already involved in her chores, but she could linger just as well on her feet.

Sun's glow was already fading; the moments spent considering her day had counted more than she thought. But she paused anyway, feeling the lingering brush of its warmth. She wished she were a farm slave. Then she might rise as usual with the dawn, and not the dying dusk.

But in some ways, this encroaching blackness was her morning. She bowed her head briefly and began this day as she had done for all of her life: in quiet prayer.

The prayer had changed over the years—how could it not?—but the peace and hope it brought her had never faded. *Lady of Mercy, hear me now.* She paused, and silence answered as it always did. *I give you thanks for preserving me in this Dark world. Help me do the same this day.*

And Lady, guard my daughter. I know well your kingdom is the better place, but I ask it nonetheless. Let her come in the fullness of years. I need her with me.

There was no time for more. She could hear the creak and swing of five different doors as the slaves began their labors.

She thought of her daughter and sighed, knowing the child would barely be out of bed and would certainly have left off prayer. Well, Peggy could say enough for the both of them until the girl had grown into it, which had better be soon. Peggy's mother would never have allowed her the luxury of rising without them.

But her mother was dead. If she had any lectures to give, she would have to save them for the Bridge. The thought turned her lips up in the first smile of the coming evening. She was certain there would never have been a noisier crossing in all of time.

She was almost into the heart of the slaves' quarters when she heard the shouting. It was hoarse and thick, and many voices carried it, all in deathly terror.

Footsteps came thundering up the hall and turned the corner as she stood, frozen. Stev. Face white with fear, he could look no more poorly if he had just seen his own death. Without thinking, she reached out to stop him. His chest hit her hands and drove her back.

"Stev!" she shouted, rising quickly to her feet amid the blue mess of her skirts.

"He's come! He's come again! Oh, Lady, he's here!"

"Stev!" She drew her hand back to slap him and stopped when his eyes met hers. "Who?"

"The Dark Heart's demon!"

She almost ran then, yet she held her ground for one more question, even as another, younger slave ran past them both, mouth wide, voice hysterical.

"Where?"

"Sleeping quarters."

Those two words were the most horrible thing that had ever happened in her life, and her life included the fall of Culverne. She found her feet then, and her voice harmonized with the strains of the terror of the rest of her companions.

There was only one difference. She ran toward the quarters, and the shout that she mustered was a word.

"Terry!"

Ladyladyohgodohgodplease

"Terry!"

When had the halls grown so long and so tortuous? When had they become so empty and so tall? She felt that she was shrinking at each step she took, with the world growing too large around her. But not so big that she couldn't find her way to the sleeping quarters.

Another slave passed her, hardly noticing where she ran. Two doors were flung open and clattered against the walls. On a normal eve, no one would have dared such carelessness. Tonight it didn't matter. No guards would make their way down to these rooms, and certainly no lord or no lady would.

Peggy didn't stop to check any of the rooms that passed her by, doors ajar. She did not look at the fall of shadow and did not care that the darkness grew deeper where two torches lay in black ruin. She knew where she was going.

Breath deserted her. She had none left to shout or scream. But her footsteps echoed the beat of her heart, preternaturally loud in the stillness. Her fingers skirted the wall as if for support, but even then she did not stop.

Not until she reached the door of the room her daughter shared with three of the other children. Children were always separated from their parents after they had been weaned, and the rooms put aside for them were small even for two adults.

The door was closed. In this empty hall, doors still swung with an ominous creak. All of them were open, save this one.

If she had had time for prayer, she might have pleaded as she had never done before. There was no time. She was terrified, and the face her fear would be answered by rested just beyond the door. All she had to do was open it.

Trembling, her hands caught the simple latch. It clicked, and the door flew open.

Her fear was dark and black; not even a glimmer of light shone through its center as it stood in the confines of four stone walls. Two rough-hewn beds, stacked one upon the other, lay against the west wall; one was empty. One was not.

Neither belonged to her daughter.

In the silence the darkness moved like a snake curling in upon itself. She could almost hear its sinuous whisper. She stood very still, as a mouse might, hoping not to catch its attention. Lady, what was she doing here?

In answer, a young voice whimpered.

She closed her eyes, although it made little difference. She drew a breath that was sharp and cold.

Sometimes courage is only a choice between the greater of two fears. And for Peggy, just another slave in the Empire, the choice had been made the minute she had started running.

With a wild, strained cry she launched forward, throwing her weight ahead of her feet and letting it carry her the last few inches. Her arms flailed about as if they were swords wielded by a true novice. But they hit their mark, as she did.

The darkness had a form, one solid enough to move. There was a small comfort in that, for she felt it give ground. Her teeth were clenched tightly, as if to form a snarl, but only a whimper came out, almost a twin to the sound her daughter had made.

And then she was through it; the cold of the darkness was gone. Her arms hit the east wall just a little too fast and the shock of it traveled up to her shoulders. She wheeled, crouching, and heard—peace.

"Mommy?"

All of the wild strength that had carried her this far deserted her, and she knelt, shaking as she groped in the darkness. Her hands touched wet cheeks, and she recognized the feel of them, round and smooth, beneath her fingers. Her arms shot out, encircling small shoulders and dragging them forward as if she had just found her life.

The smell was right—a little mixture of soap and sweat. The skin was warm as it pressed against her cheek. She could not speak for a moment. Words could not convey all that she felt.

"Mommy?"

"Terry."

She felt something grab her right sleeve and started.

"Peggy?"

"Corman." Peggy uncurled her knees, although she held on to her daughter. "Is Neil with you?"

"Here," Neil said. His voice was weak now, although whether with fear or relief it was hard to say. She didn't ask about Scott. Even in the darkness, she knew a corpse when she saw it.

"This is very touching."

Hair, short and thin, rose on the back of her neck and arms. She stood and put her daughter very firmly behind her back. "Stay there," she said quietly. She felt a nod as it rustled against her dress. "Neil. Corman."

They didn't have to be told twice. The shadow in the room was a demon that all children dreamed of—and who better than a mother to drive it away? Peggy knew what they felt, and it almost broke her heart. She had long outgrown her childhood. Very stiffly she turned in the direction of the almost-human voice.

It didn't sound so terrible, really. Maybe it would be satisfied with the life it had taken. Maybe it would leave.

"Little human, do you know what you dare?"

Before she could answer, she saw the red rising from two twin points that the shadows had concealed. It flew out, more sure than archer fire, and lanced through either shoulder.

My arms! She threw back her head and bit down on her lip; blood flowed freely down her tongue. Almost wildly she swung around.

"Not yet, little slave."

The pain was gone.

"Do you know who you have dared to strike?"

Shaking, she raised her head.

"No answer? Very well. But I promise you, you *will* know by evening's end." The shadow surged forward, and Peggy turned her head.

"When he touches me," she whispered, as quietly as she could, "run. All of you. Don't look back. Don't—don't listen to anything you hear. If Mommy—if Mommy sounds hurt, don't come back. It's just a—a trick."

She wanted to say more, but she didn't have the time. Courage was a choice between two fears, yes, but with every step he took, one fear grew larger and stronger. Let her daughter know that she was loved in more than words. If she didn't understand it now, she would come to know it clearly later.

He heard every word precisely and clearly. He saw, as she could not, the uneasy looks of doubt cut across the faces of the three children that stood behind her. He watched their heads bob in the direction of the door—the only source of light in the room. It amused him to let them run; they would have to go past him, after all, and they were small and easy to catch. Or perhaps he would just hunt them later, drawing out their individual fear into a fine, clear strand they could not cut away.

Already, one death was past him; he basked in its dark afterglow. There was peace in this—the drink of the immortals. No human could know it, and their decayed berries and grain were a poor, pathetic substitute. How would she feel, this slave, should she hear her daughter's bones snap? He waited, motionless now, for the answer, although it was easy to guess.

Yet she surprised him.

She stepped—lunged—forward, her arms wide as if to embrace him. And as she drew close, he could see the look upon her face. She was terrified.

And her terror had two faces. One for her death, and one for her daughter's. It was the second that held him the moment necessary for the first of the children to break away.

He knew the look. He had not recognized it immediately on so foreign a face.

The second child, another boy, slipped past, feet beating against the floor.

Had not recognized it, so laden with fear for herself as it was. The third child skittered by, and he reached out a claw to grab her.

He caught, instead, the mother's hand.

It was warm, almost hot, as it clamped around his. His claws, almost of their own accord, burst through her palm. Blood dripped onto the floor. He could hear it as it fell.

He could hear more.

Her voice. Her words, here, even in the wake of his feeding, the pain in them heavy, clear, and ugly. The warmth of the dead was gone in that instant. The strength of lifeblood had turned to ash; the feeding of hunger, a concession to weakness.

She turned, her ghost hands passing through him. Light glimmered, caught by the tears on her cheeks. He could kill her and cause her less pain.

His head shot up wildly, as he tried to hold on to his peace, his last refuge, his one pleasure.

"No!" His voice was a roar. *"You are dead!"* He swung out wildly with his free hand, and bone splintered where it struck.

She was.

He stopped for a moment, and his eyes were a color that no living person had ever seen; brown and dark and opaque. With a snarl, he threw Peggy's body aside. It crashed into the bed and fell to the floor. Blood began to pool beneath it, and the dry floorboards drank greedily.

He stood in a well of shadow, the light at his back flowing over his shoulders, but never quite reaching the body. She was warm; he could see the lines of fading heat as he watched. He stood looking at the ruin of her skull, the lines of her slack face, the shape of her body.

Nothing of Sara was in it.

It had been an illusion then, a hallucination. His anger shrank back beneath the hardening lines of his face, but it was a wild rage that barely stayed below the surface.

He swung around, gathering his shadow, and walked through the door. The other three still wandered the manse. He would send them after their protector.

The halls were cold and lifeless as he entered them. Almost casually he doused the torches as he passed. His hand touched the wall at his left, and unaware of it, he made a long, deep, gouge in the stone.

Where, where were they?

Sara, you are dead. Do not trouble me here.

The words were less an order than a plea, and he hated that. Angrily he stopped and bent his mind to the task of tracking his prey. Other fears lingered in the air, older ones—they were more complex, but less primal.

Where?

Ah. His teeth glinted in the remaining lights he had not yet passed; no smile there.

It was an early night yet; it had just begun. He needed much now to satisfy the hollowness that was growing. He was the First of the Sundered, the Lord of the Empire. What he desired was his.

The halls grew wide as the slaves' quarter melted into the darkness behind him. The ceilings grew tall, and the lamps more fancy, but no less easy to extinguish. He let the twilight in as glass tinkled against the marbled floor.

Up ahead, he saw house guards, and they saw him. Like the slaves, they fled, drawing no weapon, and offering no resistance. His anger grew smaller, and the wildness more contained. This, this is what he was seeking.

He mounted stairs, not bothering to touch them. Meager starlight filtered in through the gallery window. At a toss of his hand, shadow plastered itself against the glass, sealing out light and announcing his presence for all who were not yet aware of it.

He was close now. He could smell them, cowering. There were others with them; three—no, four. Their fear was not yet strong. He would change that; they would pay him his tribute yet.

The peaked, twin doors were shut at the top of the stairs. He put his fingers through them, crumpling detailed inlay work as if it were paper. The doors resisted only a little as he pulled them off their hinges and threw them over the balcony.

There were screams, then. Pain song writ large and shrill upon the air. He tasted it, and it felt dull—almost alien.

No.

"I want the children." His voice was soft. If there was a tremble in it, not one of the watchers noticed. They were busy with a wild fear of their own.

Four adults, dressed in the common gray and blue of the house. Three of them, two old women and a young man, shrank back, trying to burrow into the paneled walls that were covered with frames and mortal likenesses. If he had seen them before, he did not recognize them. A beautiful fear had transformed, almost transfixed, their faces. They were already the white of blood-drained death.

And they did not concern him, not yet. If they ran, he might even let them pass. His eyes, twin points of muddied red, turned toward the children.

And to the one adult who stood, shaking and white, in front of them.

"I want only the children," he said again.

The man's mouth trembled, and no words came out. Perhaps he stayed because he was too petrified even to find his feet.

No. Stefanos knew the feel of that fear well, and this was not right for it. He stayed, in the end, out of foolish choice. Twice in one night? It was unthinkable. The wildness bucked and pulled at him. He shuddered, and his hands flew out.

The man gasped, and the child named Terry screamed.

Why? In a haze of confusion he looked down to see hands that were covered in blood. Hands.

He looked at them as if he had never seen them before. These he wore for her. He had rarely felt her presence so strongly when she was alive, yet she was not here—not even a glimpse of her memory flashed before his dark, human eyes.

A new hunger opened within him, and he understood it, fully and finally. He had given Sara much more of himself than he had ever realized, and she had taken it with her when she left. She would not return; he would never be whole as he had once been, and feeding the ancient call for pain would not, could not, fill the void.

There was no light in his darkness—only the yearning for it. He opened his mouth, his lips running along the edge of sharp, feral teeth as he threw back his head.

No howl escaped him, but rather a keening, a wail of bitterness, pain, and loss. He had to leave this place, these people; they were still, in some way he did not understand, hers. Her hand, invisible and internal, gripped him tightly, and would not let go. The protection that she had once offered, she offered still.

He raised his arms as the slaves cowered before him, mistaking the gesture. Their fear held no allure now; it was distasteful, and he would as soon be gone from it as partake of it.

The room vanished. All sign of House Damion was left behind in a swirl of red darkness. But the blood on his hands remained wet and sticky—a tribute, a sign that life had not been given in vain.

Your people, Sara!

He gazed wildly around at the new halls, the familiar ones. The temple of the Dark Heart opened before him, its secret ways known and disdained. No one whom she loved was here. No one who loved her.

Perhaps here he could feed and find peace. He began to move, a substantial shadow beneath the vaulting ceilings. He caught a Sword at guard, and then another, and another after that—but they died too quickly, offered too little. This new thing, this new feeling, it grew wilder and wilder still; demanded more and more and was satisfied by less and less.

This place, this temple, this hollow shell of cold stone and dead wood, held all the things that she had fought against. He turned, seeing the grooved, carved pillar that was the heart of the open walkways. He grabbed it, twining his arms around it, and taking in as much as he could.

The snap sounded distant; it was too small a thing. Even the rumbling up above was not enough.

The priests lived here.

The Swords lived here.

The worship of the Dark Heart was renewed daily.

Something else crumbled in his hands, his claws; something creaked against his back. He threw it off and continued to wander forward.

All that she had hated was represented, yes.

Priests, Swords, God—and the Servant of the Darkness.

The last was too much to bear. He moved forward, it was effortless now. He could not see the trail of red that spread all around him, burning brightly. Stone gave way before him as if it were no more than water, flesh, as if it were air.

He continued to walk, descending slowly into darkness, falling into shadow, into blackness.

The Hand of the Dark Heart closed around him so tightly he could almost ignore the pleasure that resounded throughout it like waves from the center he represented.

chapter
twelve

She did not wake, yet awareness took hold of her and shook her,
hard. The webs of a dozen different dreams fell away, bowing
to the greater shadow that stood above, beneath, and all around
her. She was a ghost here, one who bore the stigma of the living, when life never truly touched these lands.

She shimmered to her own sight, if sight it was, and hovered
above the ground that was alien to her feet, just as the Servants
did in the waking world. That thought had never occurred to
her before—that the Servants hovered so because the land was
alien.

Yet they had power in her world; here she had none. She
trembled, a shudder that came from within. The pain call
echoed throughout these dark lands.

This time she knew it for what it was: a bridge.

"You are bound yet, you and he."

The voice came from the blackness, but it was not a dark
voice. She smiled, or rather, felt a smile, and sad though it
was, it was more than the Dark Heart could understand.

"Kandor."

Here and there the land bucked, and the very air seemed to
coil as if to strike. But it passed through her now; she was
calm. Only the pain disturbed her—it was so very, very strong.

Still, she had come a long way from the days of her early
adulthood. She chose her course, not the blood. And she chose
to stand.

"We thought you might come to us."

Erin nodded as the darkness shivered and shattered. Kandor
stood at its heart. His feet, she noticed, touched the ground;

here he seemed more human than she herself, and he seemed old, changed by experience, even bent a little.

"Kandor," she said again.

"Little one. You have grown." They were words that might be said to a child. "Where are you?"

"In the lands? I am on the road to Rennath." She was aware of what the word meant; the echo of it pleased the plain.

"Rennath." A different voice.

"Belfas?"

"Yes." He came from the darkness as well, but not so easily or cleanly as Kandor had. Still, his face, the lines of it drawn subtly in shades of mourning, was familiar. Welcome.

"Why do you return to Rennath? It was the beginning of all the evils."

"I don't return to stay," she answered. She moved forward, and he back. A little shock of hurt traveled through her. She stopped. "I travel the road with a merchant. You—you would have liked her, I think." Swallowing, she answered the question she thought she heard in his voice. "He isn't there now."

"We know. We hear his voice, as you must."

"I mean that Rennath isn't the capital anymore."

"Then where?"

"They call it Malakar. It is over the heart of the August lands."

Kandor moved, coming forward now with difficulty. "The August lands. Ah—the Gifting ... Erin, what do you seek there?"

How to answer? She did not know, and he mistook her silence.

"Do you still seek only death?"

"No." That much she could say with confidence. "But I—I want to free you all."

It was his turn to be silent. He turned from her, hiding his expression a moment, before he started speaking again. "Sarillorn, what a road you have been asked to walk. You do not seek your passage anymore, but you must know that this is the only way to gain our freedom."

Did his voice tremble on the last word? Did it contain a hint of hope, of desire? She would never be certain, for she had never heard a like thing from him before. It unnerved her; it laid bare the end of her journey.

"Belf?"

"Yes?"

"I want you to wait for me. At the Bridge. I promise I'll try to explain." When he didn't answer, she added, "I miss you."

"Oh Erin—"

She held out her arms, moving quickly forward to catch him. The net of her light went out, a prison and a balm both, and they stood together as they had not done for a long time. A tenuous peace, a tremulous promise, existed between them. For a moment, Erin felt happy.

And then he was gone, suddenly she embraced no more than shadow and darkness. She pulled her arms up in surprise, and drew back, if direction had meaning here.

The roar sounded through her; she heard it, but not with her ears. Pain call reared up, almost tearing the curtain of light that she had become here. She cried out, whether in fear of it, or in welcome, even she could not be sure.

He was here. Turning, a blur that scarred the air, she could see where a deep red-fire took hold of the shadow, driving it away. That fire had arms, legs, and torso, but all else was obscured. It pulled away from the darkness, and stood—the Lord of the shadows here.

The Lord of the Empire.

He faced her, tall and proud, with a grim, fell wildness that crackled in the air. For just an instant, the red flickered; it seemed a dying fire, or at least a cooling one. He was silent, and the pain that throbbed between them was almost solely his.

Then he laughed; it was strange and reckless, an act of defiance. "Do you think to trick me, even here?"

She did not answer, but even against her will she began to move forward.

"Do you think that my grief blinds me to your shadow?"

He was not speaking to her. She reached out and saw her hands glow dimly and impossibly delicately before her.

"Where did you learn this, Lord? Where did you capture this likeness? Was it Sargoth?" His laughter was an ugly rupture of air and sound. "You shall have no Servant but me, if it was. I alone will stand, and I will serve *no more*."

Erin gasped as he lunged forward, his claws raking through the air—and through her. They passed, little red triangles that left no mark. She barely felt it at all.

"What is this?" He turned now, to look at his claws, then

to look again at Erin as she hovered, untouched by his power. "Do you still dare this facade?"

She shook her head; she couldn't help it. All the words that she had said, all the vows that she had sworn—what did they matter here? She knew why she had been afraid to face him on the field. She knew it too well.

"Stefanos."

The red light melted away, running down him as if it were water—or blood.

"Sara."

They were silent a moment, and then he began to speak in a rush, as if time mattered to him. Time had always been his enemy, and he would never forget it. "Have you come, Lady, to return that which I gave to you?"

"Stefanos." Her voice broke, and she held out her arms. She had never thought to hear the wildness or the pain so exposed.

He continued, as if he had not heard the single word.

"You have returned to no avail. Sara—I would not know how to accept it back. I do not even know what it was that I gave." He bent his head into his hands like a broken man. Thus did the slaves go to the markets all across his Empire and kneel before her likeness.

She could not watch him so without trying something— anything. She reached out for him, as she had reached out for Belfas, and her power flared from her fingertips.

His reared up in answer, and the red and the white flowered bitterly before lapsing into empty death.

"Stefanos," she said, her throat too tight and too swollen, "I loved you."

"I know it," he answered. "You are the source of all pain."

"Would you have changed it?"

"Yessss." The ancient voice arose in him, the darkness of the beginning. "Yessss. For I would rule all in peace; I would feed where I chose, and when. You have infected me, divided me." He rose. "You are dead, and yet even here, I have no peace from your memory. Even another's pain has lost its hold, its thrall."

It hurt, to hear that. She was surprised at how much. She turned from him. But not before the ghost of a glimmer lighted her ethereal cheek.

"Lady?" His voice was quiet, almost confused. "Have I hurt you?"

But the daylight had already claimed her. She woke with tears coursing down her cheeks as the sun broke across the horizon.

And even his roar was not enough, in the daylight, to draw her back.

Lady Amalayna drew up to Vellen's house by carriage. The carriage bore two crests, each the match of the other in artistry and execution. House Valens and House Damion had equal part in her life until the rites, and every observer had no choice but to acknowledge it.

The grounds, glorious and green, threw blossoms and trees in her path, but they were dark; night limned and hid them. Perhaps if she waited long enough this eve, she would see them in full glory. Oil-lit lamps only glinted off their surfaces, presenting a teasing hint of what they truly were.

She had never thought that she would miss the daylight. Her fingers bit into the cushioned seats as the gates flew past; she counted quickly to the clip of hooves on the cobbled path. The Vellen estates were magnificent—and the thoroughfare to them long. Too long by far.

Tonight she meant to speak with Lord Vellen, to speak in earnest, as she had not once done since accepting his troth and his symbol. Cold metal burned at her throat. It was heavy; she thought it would cut off all breath with its weight.

Impatient, she leaned out of the window, gripping its edge for support. They were not there yet. The manor, lit by all types of lamp and torch, glittered white against the darkness, a dramatic relief of stone and glass against the sky. The center tower rose high, and even now she could see the crest of the house fluttering in the wind above it.

She sat back, forcing her shoulders to touch the seat. Her chin was tilted slightly up, and her face was calm but pale. Too little sun, she would have answered, had any been fool enough to ask.

Anger had two colors: red and white. This night she chose ice as her implement and her strength. She meant to have her answers from Lord Vellen, one way or the other.

The carriage rolled to a stop, and she waited impatiently for the sound of the driver. Ah, there. He had disembarked. She saw him, his uniform of Valens, crisp and impeccable. A burgundy glove reached out, touched handle, and twisted it. The door creaked open. Absently she jotted it down in memory as something that must be attended to; no door of a carriage in her service made a noise like that.

Her chin lifted a hair's breadth as she waited for ritual to be over. The driver bowed low and offered his hand. She was loath to accept it, for hers were shaking, but she knew manners and form well enough. Let him think it the cold; he would never ask.

Still, it annoyed her as she found her feet. She had never liked to share her weakness with anyone—anyone but Laranth, and he was gone. She did not speak, not even to thank the driver for his speed. Instead she liberated her hand as quickly as was suitable and hastened to the entrance of the courtyard.

The guards knew the symbol that glittered between the clasps of the cape she wore. They bowed low, their faces a study in attention and strength in servitude. While Lord Vellen would one day rule them, Lady Amalayna could still make their life very difficult. A gesture of respect cost them little now and might be rewarded by a smooth transition to a new lord in the future.

A slave stood to the right of the double doors that led into the grand hall. Chandeliers—were they everywhere in their ostentatiousness?—glittered fractures of light from above. She stood impatiently as the slave took the cloak from her shoulders.

"Shall I announce you, Lady?"

She nodded gravely. "Tell Lord Vellen that I seek an audience with him."

She caught the way his eyes flickered over his feet.

"Is there news?" she asked, her voice cold but not yet sharp enough to sting.

"Lady." The slave bowed. "Lord Vellen has departed the house."

"Where has he gone?"

A flicker of eyes again. Still, if the slave were nervous, he showed it in no other way. It was a good sign; it spoke of good training, not a lax master—not in this house. "He is on business, Lady. Please, I am not given leave to say more."

"When will he return?"

"I do not know. Perhaps Lord Damion may be able to help you further. Shall I announce you to him?"

She took a deep breath and straightened herself out; her shoulders had started to slump. Disappointment, mingled with relief, hollowed her out. "Yes," she answered curtly.

The slave bowed again and turned to his task. His strides were quick and sure as they took him to the left of the hall. He was a little old to be on door service, but Lady Amalayna could well understand why Lord Damion chose to keep him here. He was not easily flustered, and she was certain that had she pressed him for more information, even under threat, he would have yielded none. If the rites were completed, she would have to remember this slave.

Lord Damion was prompt with his reply, although he did not come in person to greet her. She nodded briefly to the slave and followed him as if the way to Lord Damion's personal study were not familiar to her.

The slave paused to knock at the door.

"Enter."

He pushed it open gently, then stood to one side to allow the lady to pass. She met his eyes, and he continued to look straight ahead. With a small smile, she walked into the study.

Lord Damion stood with his back to the fire that was burning merrily in the frame of an old, finely crafted mantel. On either side, little diamonds of glass caught the orange light and reflected it outward. Behind the doors, small, perfect cabinets held books that looked impossibly old. One or two of them were faded enough that Amalayna had to stare to catch their titles. She was surprised to find that they were not in the tongue of the Empire—surprised and a little shocked.

She hid it well; either that or the lord forbore to comment. She couldn't be sure which.

"Lady Amalayna," Lord Damion said. "Please be seated."

Had he been Vellen she would have demurred, but in truth she felt tired and was glad of the opportunity to fold her legs and let something else carry her weight.

"I ask my son's pardon. He is absent on business at the moment, and I fear he will not return before dawn."

She shook her head. "Not at all. I didn't have an appointment."

"No? Then what brings you, Lady? Perhaps I might help."

"Is the business Church business?" That was direct, and a bit chancy.

"It is not house business," Lord Damion replied.

She was silent a moment; there was really little else for her to say. Church business, though, and in a hurry, from what she could tell. An emergency?

Her skirts rustled as she shifted uncomfortably in the chair. Lord Damion's benign expression did nothing to hide the fact that he watched her keenly. His smile smoothed out so slowly she didn't notice the change of expression until he spoke. "Lady Amalayna, was there some emergency that brought you here tonight?"

Only then did she look at him carefully. He dressed in the same manner as his son did when at home—blues and silvers dominated the black background of velvet and embroidery. He wore no lace and no obvious finery, but the ring on his finger was platinum—almost a year's worth of the house annuities. He was shorter than his son, but not by much—and his eyes were the same clear blue, a piercing, cold light.

"No," she answered, neither too quickly nor too slowly. What had she been thinking? She hadn't; that was plain enough. To come here like this, prepared for war, and to think that her only enemy in the house was Lord Vellen, was the reckless act of a child. "Yet we are promised, and I have not seen my lord in over a week." Her voice was cool now as she remembered clearly where she was. The why didn't matter.

"You did not seem overanxious to see him when he gave you the crest."

"Lord Damion, I am no young girl and no untrained one, to react so obviously and with so little dignity in front of other houses." She paused, letting her voice chill further. "But perhaps Lord Vellen is reconsidering his decision? I assure you, if that is the case, you will find House Valens in a particular position to tender you the only viable response."

If she hoped to catch him off guard, she failed. He was after all an older man and well versed in the political skills of conversation. His face gave nothing away. "Meaning?"

She drew breath, letting an expression of anger and uncertainty, both of which she was feeling, flit across her face. It was important to be genuine in your lies. And it made her look younger than her years, which had always been an advantage.

"I had heard, through my sources, that Lord Vellen has been

seen with Lady Eveline of Morganth. It is said that they are
... close."

This, too, was true.

The smile that Lord Damion turned upon her took none of
the edge out of his eyes. Still, he was pleased; this much was
obvious. "My dear lady," he said, with just a slight inclination
of his head, "in a few short weeks I will ask you who your
sources are; they are good." To her surprise, he bowed. "Very
well. But do not think the heir to my house so foolish or so
lacking in intelligence. He is well aware of the merits of association with your house. He will not endanger or risk a breach
war. I will see to that myself. It is, after all, my house that you
are questioning." The smile that he tendered then was not for
her; its malice was turned elsewhere. "If it helps, I assure you
that he is not now with her; his business is of a more practical
nature."

She let the relief she felt show and took to her feet, carefully
straightening out her skirts. "Thank you, Lord Damion. I shall
let you get back to your house business then. Please forgive
me for being so headstrong as to interrupt you." She meant every word. Funny how the truth could be so neatly twisted to
serve any purpose the user deemed fit. She turned to the door.

"Lady Amalayna."

"Lord?"

"One other thing."

"Yes, Lord?"

"I was at the last rites for your former bond-mate."

She froze.

"You wore black and white. You looked quite elegant—and
very, very much the foolish, sentimental girl you claim not to
be. Whatever business you have with my son I will leave to
your discretion. I believe that I understand its nature, and I am
pleased with your cleverness in hiding it; you are not respected
for no reason. But do not think to endanger my house. The war
would destroy yours."

She turned again, to see the eagle's smile on his face. She
should never have come to him. "How much do you know?"
Her words were flat.

"That, my dear, is a very foolish question. Not up to the
standards of the rest of your conversation." He did not lose his
smile, though; it became sharper, sweeter. "But perhaps I will
answer a little of it. I do not think this business is my son's

alone. Why don't you speak with your father?" His voice was
a purr.

Amalayna looked directly at his eyes and caught just a glimmer of red about them. The blood ran strong in the Damion
line—and strong enough that she was unable to rob him of all
of his victory. She turned and left the room, knowing what he
looked like, knowing that he would chuckle and turn back to
the fire or walk to his desk.

But he had, perhaps, made one mistake in judging the lady
his son had chosen. He had seen her at her bond-mate's funeral
rite in the gaudy, sentimental colors she had chosen and had
felt a certain amusement and a little scorn for the weakness she
showed in wearing them. Not even for the death of his heir
would he humiliate himself so in public. He was not a weak
man. And Lady Amalayna was; weak enough, certainly, to
grow too fond of her rite-mate.

What Lord Damion would never have considered was this:
She was too close to the loss of the things that had become her
life. She did not think of her death, but did not fear it either.
Any threat he had made this eve had become just another
weapon in her quest for vengeance and peace.

Jagged edges of wood and stone cut into the darkening line
of sky mingled with torch. Rubble adorned the foot of the central column, which was all that remained of the tall, grand pillar that the priests had ordered carved two centuries ago. The
walls had been leveled to their base, and breeze flew through
them to stir the dust in gray-white clouds.

It was like this everywhere. The whole of the south wing
was gone. And layered among the rubble and the broken
beams were the crushed remnants of dead bodies. Here and
there black robes fluttered in the wind when they were not too
heavy with blood.

Lord Vellen had taken no slaves with him and was glad of
it. He could not contain his expression of disbelief and horror.
With great care he mounted an opening in the wall itself. His
fingers came up sticky and red—he had discovered the edge of
a window. The careful handwork of multihued glass, lead, and
crystal was gone. He could not see even shards of it, except for
the one his hand now contained. He curled his fingers around
it, grimacing. The air was dust-heavy and dry, his lips were
cracking, and he had not even been here long.

"High Priest?"

He did not bother to turn; the voice was an irritating chitter, but enough of the priesthood had been lost this eve. "Yes?"

"Shall I have an acolyte send for the rest of the Greater Cabal?"

"Wait my word," he answered. He had to have time to absorb it all—and there was much damage. What had caused it? There was no sign of fire, no blackening of walls, no charring of wood, no molten rock. Nor had there been sign of lightning; such a strike would have been seen for miles.

He crossed over another body. Legs alone were exposed. But these legs were jointed and mailed—a Sword. He wondered if his weapon had ever left its sheath.

The air grew still of a sudden, and Vellen stopped his aimless wandering.

"Karrick?"

"Lord?" The voice was caught by the twist and turn of splintered stone. It did not echo as grandly as it once might have within the south hall.

"Leave me. Come back in an hour. Speak to no one yet."

There was no answer, but none was expected, and Vellen did not so much as turn to see the acolyte bowing. He waited until the footsteps had left him alone in silence. The silence was thick and heavy, and the shadows that pooled beneath the open sky seemed thick and hazy.

"Who did this?" he asked, his voice very soft.

Sibilance twisted itself around the words that came from the darkness. "The First of the Sundered."

"Why?" There was more in that word than many ears would dare to catch: anger, fear, and a burning hatred.

The answer to this question was not so easily delivered. Vellen cast a little spark of his personal power outward. It flew like red moth to black flame, and Sargoth became suddenly visible. He stood cloaked in shadow, so much like the First that Vellen's hands clenched into fists, driving the splinters further into his flesh.

"Sargoth. Second," he added, remembering himself.

"It is an interesting question," the Servant said, even more remotely than was his wont. "I do not have the answer. I would ask him, I think, but it would do you no good."

"What do you mean?"

"He is in the Dark Heart's hand."

He was not here then. Good. Vellen felt the muscles around his jaw relax. Without question, he knew he was no match for the First of the Sundered. What the nightwalker had accomplished here in short hours, he could not do with a team of mage-trained priests in days.

"It is odd," Sargoth continued. He looked straight at Vellen, but it was not to the leader of the Greater Cabal that he spoke. "I had not foreseen this difficulty."

"*Difficulty?*"

"High Priest, it is merely wood and stone. Blood your altars well, and call upon God's power. This wing of the building can be redone." He turned and looked around him. "Not, perhaps, with complete ease, but certainly not with great trouble." It was hard to tell in the shadow, but it appeared that the Second of the Sundered shrugged. "I have never liked this architecture anyway."

His cloaked form drifted above the ground, as if caught by the breeze that had started once again. Then he stopped.

"High Priest, perhaps you can help me."

Lord Vellen did not reply.

"The First went to only one place this eve. I followed him from afar."

"Yes?"

"House Damion. If memory serves me, that house is yours."

"Yes." The answer was curt.

"What did he accomplish there?"

"Nothing," Vellen replied. "He killed two slaves. No more, no less."

"Killed?"

"Fed, then. What difference does it make? The Church will find me others." The entire south wing lay before him, a maze of rubble and death. Gray stone, brown wood, pale white marble—these distinctions were meaningless. Perhaps they had always been so to the one who ruled.

"I see," Sargoth answered. Stefanos would have been pleased, but the irritation in the Second's voice was not so clear to Vellen. *Why, Stefanos? Why destroy this place? This is the seat from which you rule the Empire you built out of these half bloods and their kin.*

He reached for the Dark Heart's whisper and found it absent. The God was feeding.

* * *

No homecoming could have been more welcome than this. The night air was chill, and Vellen the high priest had been too wise to use his power to take the edge off its bite. He was weary, and a fine powder clung to his boots and the hem of his robe. The bleeding in his palm had stopped, and the priest who had tended it thought no infection would take in the wound, but the hand still ached.

House Vellen loomed above him beneath a sky that was turning to pinks and blues. Gardeners were already about their tasks—they were among the few who had been spared the Church dictate of rising with the dusk. The grounds seemed preternaturally silent.

He shivered, but knew that this was not from the cold. The vast expanse of the south wing still lay before his mind's eye like the shattered body of a treasured friend. Vellen had few enough of those, and he took the loss poorly.

He should have waited until tonight to call the council. It angered him that he had not, but there was no one to take that anger out on—the house had lost a number of slaves over the past months and could ill afford any more. His father, no doubt, was already in bed, along with most of the staff.

He thought of rousing the cooks and decided against it; although he was hungry, the thought of food displeased him.

Had he not enough to contend with? Oh yes, the Greater Cabal could have waited.

He could still see Benataan of Torvallen standing in full robes, his back to the lowering moon. He could hear clearly the precise ring of the first words he had chosen to speak.

"Lord Vellen. I see that your actions have displeased our Lord." No more, but he hadn't needed to say more. It was obvious that he had been forewarned of the disaster and had had the presence of mind to turn it properly.

Vellen would find the acolyte that had delivered the information on the morrow.

He walked in silence through the gates of his house. Guards snapped to attention and held it crisply, chancing nothing but the most formal of behavior. Their eyes did not even follow their dust-covered, tired master.

The stairs seemed impossibly long, and Vellen passed them in mounting anger. The door to the gallery had been removed from the marbled floor below, but the hinges and cracked wood of the frame still sullied the entrance to the empty hall.

He paused a moment to stare, remembering Sargoth's questions. Tonight he would, perhaps, begin questioning the slaves about the nightwalker they had encountered. Then again, he might not have the time for it.

Dawn stretched out, illuminating the stained glass windows that followed him as he made his ascent. He was weary indeed.

If not for the presence of Lord Valens this eve, he might have been tempted to a foolish display. But Lord Valens had done what he might to take the edge and power from Benataan's words.

"Benataan, do you not recognize a threat to the Church when you see it? Save your petty politicking; if the whole of the Greater Cabal cannot address this, it will avail you nothing, even if you win." They were wise words, said with the right mix of warmth and coolness. Vellen was keenly aware that he should have been the one to speak them.

The doors to his chambers were closed, and there were no guards at them. He paused one last time before them and let a little of the tension dissipate. In moments he would let sleep claim him, and when he woke to darkness again, he would have the answers to the predicament that had absorbed his evening.

Dark Heart, he thought, *let me have those answers.*

The minute he reached the safety of his sitting room, he began to remove his robes. A little cloud of dust stirred round him as the sash peeled away. He walked to the door of his room, swung it open, and stopped.

Lady Amalayna was seated in the only chair the room held, her arms laying calmly over the blue velvet-covered wings, her ankles crossed demurely beneath her skirts.

Her face was pale, and her eyes were accented by dark rings that lent them a bruised appearance.

"My Lord," she said quietly.

"What-are-you-doing-here?"

"Waiting for you." Her eyes cut through the dust and the sweat that covered him; they were cold and sharp.

He let the robe fall back into place, aware of the advantage her gathered, crisp appearance lent her.

"I will have to ask you to leave," he said, forcing the anger out of the words, but barely. Lord Valens had been instrumental this eve; he could not risk too large an offense. "I have had a very busy evening and am not in any condition to answer any concern you might have come with."

The words had no effect at all; she did not even bother with the pretense of rising. Instead, she continued to regard him intently.

"Amalayna," he said, "I am warning you. Do not press me now."

"You are warning me?" A delicately shaped eyebrow rose askance. White fingers held on to the rounded fall of the chair arms a little more tightly.

Not since he had been a small child had he wanted so dearly to strike someone. He gestured, and a crackle of energy enveloped his hands. Filaments of flame, delicate and burning, came from them.

She raised an eyebrow again, but her face, already white, did not pale further. She did not even blink; this game she understood well. "My Lord," she said, in her most demure voice, "not even for the sake of an alliance would you offer your promise to a fool. This does not impress me."

No. No, it wouldn't. Her value was in her life, and he knew that she knew it well. The fingers of fire that he held forth could not be allowed to caress her. He held the flames a moment further, unwilling to grant her the point, and then relented. The fire died at his hands, but it grew in his eyes; they were red and palely luminescent.

"Why have you come?"

"For the truth."

"My Lady, enough of your games. I am not in the mood for them at present. If you have a point to make, make it and be done."

"Very well." She inclined her head as if accepting the most graciously offered invitation. "I want to know who you hired to assassinate Laranth of Tentaris."

The weakness that he showed then was a weakness that any man would have showed—shock, smoothing out to incredulous silence. He opened his mouth as if to speak, then snapped it shut; the lines of it molded into an exquisitely unpleasant smile.

"Laranth," he said, and the word was a thrum that pulled her forward in her chair. "Your former bond-mate."

Her nod was stiff, but it was still under control.

"I had heard rumors, Lady." He shook his head in a mockery of disapproval. "I had not credited them with truth."

Still she waited.

"Did you really let him mean so much to you?"

That struck; she flinched. His smile grew sharper, his eyes more red.

"Why would you think that I would have any hand in his death? Tentaris had declared its war. There is always a price to be paid in battle, especially among the merchant houses."

"He was not killed because of the trade war."

"No?" Vellen feigned surprise that would have fooled no one. Nor was it meant to. "No, I suppose you are right."

"My Lord." Her eyes were wide and dark; no light seemed to touch them.

"I don't know who, little Amalayna." The words grated. "I would have settled for your sister, although it would have been a longer wait." He laughed at the expression that turned her face from white to a mottled pink. "Oh yes. I cannot answer your question. Only Lord Valens has the information you seek."

She rose then, no longer seeing him, although he stood only a few feet away. She had suspected that her father might have known of this, but to find it on his hands . . .

"But at least you offer one advantage."

She turned her eyes to him almost blindly, following the direction of his voice.

"You have proven that you are able to bear children. Every house covets that; it is not always common among the nobility."

She said nothing, nothing at all, but the veneer of her control was weak and close to breaking. He grabbed her shoulders and drew her close.

All smile was gone from his face. "Amalayna, you will learn that I am not crossed often. You have what you wanted; do not be a fool now." He wheeled her around and used her body to shove the door open. He released her, and she fell back, her elbows scraping the carpet. "Never come here unannounced again."

She gathered the shreds of her dignity about her and stood shakily. Lord Vellen was a strong man. "My Lord," she said, bowing her head so that stray strands of hair touched her cheek, "I will not."

The words, even and sure, forced a grudging respect. She had some strength about her, certainly more than her sister had ever shown. The decision that the Greater Cabal had forced upon him had not been a poor one.

Her skirts swished by in a formal curtsy that was all that his rank demanded, and then she righted herself and walked quietly out of his rooms.

The sky was blue and clear and naked as it glared down at the empty streets. No people crossed the cobbled walk of the High City; no hollow, booted step announced the presence of the guards on their patrols. Everywhere the buildings and gates of the manored houses stood silent and closed.

Lady Amalayna walked these streets alone. She had no guards or slaves to attend her, and her fancy, heavy carriage had been sent back to House Valens empty to allay the suspicions of Lord Vellen.

Habit forced her shoulders straight. Habit kept her chin up and her feet moving in the delicate, arrogant gait of her lineage. No anger showed, and no tears fell. She was, after all, Amalayna of House Valens.

She walked like a ghost that had lingered beyond even its time. Echoes blew past her ears, carried like breeze by the memory that was shouting all of its useless warnings.

Laranth . . .

She struggled to find any understanding or any resolve that could support her as she walked, but they were too hard and too solid to be contained by the ethereal being she felt she had become.

Drifting, helpless, she continued to walk the path to House Valens in the silence of screams that she could not utter.

chapter
thirteen

Rennath had changed much over the centuries. What had once been a simple dirt track through farmland was now a wide, packed road through squat, low buildings that were densely concentrated even this far from the city's center. They were rectangular for the most part, but one had a curving hall that seemed to be built into a sloping hill. That house was thatched an awful shade of green, and the doors were gaudily painted. In fact, many of the buildings here were painted; it seemed that color had seeped over the gray of the city she remembered. Rennath.

Erin walked in silence toward it. The murmur of guards, both in front and behind, was lost to the breeze and the clip of horses. Instead of torchlight, sunlight glinted off helm and corselet. The sky was bright blue, not deep and dark. She was armed, armored, and quite alone.

But she still walked free.

"Look at those spires." She caught the words clearly although they weren't spoken to her. Only when she heard them did she realize that she had been averting her eyes, and she looked slowly to the heights of the city to see the black spires, arrayed now with banners that were blacker and cleaner. The road curved into what must be the outer city.

The sharp crackle of paper told her that Hildy must be readying their passes. No one looked nervous; the documents, with their spidery writing and bold, red wax seals, were perfunctory. No trouble was expected here.

In fact, almost everyone looked relieved to have arrived at last. There were no more stops on the journey; from here they could return home. Hildy already planned to pick up a few more guards from her usual sources, or so she had said, to replace the ones she would leave behind here.

Erin alone felt no relief. She looked ahead, to see Darin walking closely beside Hamin. He was chattering away, but she didn't listen carefully enough to hear what he was saying. His smile was light enough, and his tone held no fear.

Rennath.

She wondered how much of it she would recognize. She wondered how she would feel when she walked past the place of judgment in the market—if the market itself had not been moved. She wondered what those spires would mean to her now.

All she felt was a peculiar numbness. That twisted sprawl of streets and buildings, those people moving quickly or slowly among them carrying their burdens, seemed a waking dream. Perhaps they were; she had slept very little for the last few nights. Sleep and darkness had intertwined into a painful, harrowing pattern. Each night she fought anew the urge to comfort him, telling herself it was only the blood, knowing, as she kept herself steady with the thought, that it was a lie.

She had never come to this city without him.

Her chin rose a fraction of an inch, and her eyes became unwavering. She did not even see the city guards that called a halt to the caravan, and if they spoke at all, their voices did not reach her ears. She heard only *his* voice, saw only the home that they had shared.

"Who lives there now?" To her surprise, the voice was hers. But it was strange to her ears.

"In the palace?" someone asked.

She turned then to see Corfaire. His face looked familiar to her on two levels, and it was the deeper one that resonated. The long, thin lines of his face belonged to this city's nobility. To Rennath. Were he attired differently, he would be part of the landscape of hostilities that had been home to her.

"Erin?" he asked. It was rare that he used her name, and the surprise of hearing it pulled her a little closer.

"I'm all right. It's—nothing."

An eyebrow arched askance. When she returned no answer, he turned to look at the spires as well. "In the palace proper?" He shook his head. "No one."

"None at all?"

"The dead, maybe."

She shivered. "But—it's still standing."

"Yes." He fell into step with her as the caravan began moving forward again. "I forget that you don't know much about these lands."

She could have stopped him, but she smiled instead. Or at least her lips turned up at the corners. "No."

"The grounds themselves are tended, and the walls and spires maintained by some imperial dictate that no one understands. I don't believe even the Church does."

"The Church?"

He nodded, and if he heard the pale tremor in her voice, he made no sign of it. "It is an estate that they covet, but they've made no move to touch it. Odd, isn't it?" His eyes narrowed; her expressions changed so fluidly he could not identify them.

"Do you think that we might see it?"

"Yes, in a manner of speaking." He watched her eyes trail down to the feet that she moved mechanically forward. "We'll pass it on the market route to the merchants' quarter."

She was silent for a few moments, wrapped in thought and distance. Then she turned to him suddenly, and her eyes were sharp and brilliant.

"Is it guarded?"

"Against whom?" The words were measured. "No one will enter it. Why do you ask?"

"Just curiosity."

Corfaire nodded blandly and turned his attention to the road. But he shook his head slightly as he walked. The lady was a very poor liar.

Things were different in the outer city. There were very few trees remaining, and those were old and grand. Their lowest bowers topped the buildings that nature had not made, lending shade and dropping leaves as the season turned.

"Hey Erin!"

She smiled as Darin caught her arm.

"Hildy says the Church isn't really powerful here. It's why we don't have to worry about the passes so much." His face was brown and not a little dirty; his clothing was whole, but travel worn. He, too, could have been a part of this city years ago—if not for the staff that he carried so blithely. Looking at the staff, she wondered what its presence presaged; the lines had not been in the city for centuries.

Better that they had never come at all.

No. She shook her head, and her braid batted ineffectually at her shoulders.

". . . and Hildy says that the best bakers in the Empire are here. We'll meet one of them before we lodge in for the night."

That seemed to be the last item in the litany of "Hildy says" that Darin had been practicing. He waited a few minutes and then wandered back to Tiras.

Erin wished she had had something to say, but she was glad that he was gone. Without him she could continue to look around the city, to feel the strangeness of it, and to recognize herself as an alien.

Perhaps Corfaire knew how she felt. Perhaps not, but he walked now to join her in her welcome solitude. Ignoring him had no effect; he continued to keep pace with her.

"See, Lady. We come to the old gates. Soon we will enter the old city." He pointed, although there was no need for it; Erin could see the walls well enough.

"They aren't guarded, but you can see what used to be the post; it's off to the right." His finger shifted a fraction. "You can tell the age of it."

She wanted him to leave, but couldn't bring herself to say so.

"See, those arches beneath the gate? Those must have taken years to build, and they stand well. The wall is solid stone. There was a curtain wall of some sort—that's gone now."

"Do you know the city well?" She had never asked a question that sounded less curious.

"Fairly. When I left the capital, it was to Rennath that I came."

"Why?"

He didn't answer for a moment, and the silence stretched between them like a wall. For once, Erin wasn't interested in breaching it.

"Why?" he repeated, the word slow and deliberate. The tone of his voice changed; it was bitter now, and the mockery in it was turned inward.

Against her will, Erin found herself listening intently as the walls grew closer. There were some cracks in them, some spots where the stone had weathered poorly, and some where the stone, ringed by new mortar, had been replaced.

"Rennath is a place of legend to us."

"Us?" The word was out before she could stop it, but for once Corfaire did not bristle. She noted, however, that he did not answer, either.

"If you can reach Rennath, or so the stories go, you will find the freedom you seek." He laughed. "You'll find safety."

"Why?" This time the question wasn't flat or lifeless.

"Do you really not know?"

The breath of a sigh escaped her half-open mouth. "Corfaire. Please."

"Don't." The word was sharp.

So much of conversation is punctuated by silence, and each silence has its own depth, and its own private meaning, for people on either side of its divide. Silence returned to them, given a deathly life by the sound of footsteps on every side. A wisp of other people's conversations filtered in without reaching Corfaire or Erin.

They were not friends; Erin felt they would never be so. And she could not say any of what she felt to one who was not.

The arches started their span above the head and beneath the sky. Great, rounded pockets of stone caught and carried noise, returning to it an echo and substance that an open sky could not provide. Above their heads, carved and worn, were thick, deep letters that Erin could not read. But she knew what they said.

Then she was through, and Rennath, the tight little circle of time, opened before her. The stone was cobbled and exactly as wide as she remembered. It forked immediately in three different directions—one to either side, and one that went straight as far as the eye could see. The arrogance of the city's builder was plain, for the road took no curves or bends as it reached openly for the palace. If any army entered here, it would find its task easy.

Easy yes, but only because the city's lord was no longer at home.

Beyond the palace the road stretched in a wide arc on either side of the grounds; it met again and traveled to the open market. Any and all who had wares to hawk there had to pass beneath the spires. This she could not see yet, but she knew it had not changed.

There—there, ahead on her left, was one of the many different guild buildings the city had boasted. It was squat, but not so ugly as the buildings outside of the wall, and she smiled at its dowdy exterior because it was familiar. She had seen the building go up over a three-year period. It had been a request of hers; she had become fond of the weavers' guild members, and many of her slaves had been sent there, to live as free a life as the Empire allowed.

Further up on her right another building stood. It was shabby; the windows were boarded shut. She wondered who lived there now, remembering; always remembering. That was the House of the Sick in her time; funded in part by the city's lord. By the Empire's lord. He had never understood why it held so much import to her, but he had allowed her to remove an entire document library and refashion it to suit the needs of the injured.

There were no injured there now, or if there were, no doctors or surgeons to tend them. She looked up at the high, carved eaves and ledges to see dry twigs and old grass jutting out in several places. A small head peered down at her, and a little beak opened in a squawk. She whistled up, and the bird vanished in alarm.

Halfway between the gate and the palace, eight tall buildings lined the street, four on either side. They were new—at least, newer in construction than most of the city—and they were tall. Narrow alleys broke them into neat, short blocks of nearly faceless, painted wood. She stopped in front of one, looking at the single door that sat recessed over four sagging steps.

There were numbers on it—at least there had been; the middle two were missing.

"Lady?"

She shook her head and saw that the wagons had traveled on. Very quietly she moved in to take up the last rank. To walk in the shadows that the spires cast. They had no blood, no magic—but the warmth of the sun was suddenly cut off, and for a moment she could see the black, pale skies of Rennath's winter. She raised her head, leaning further and further back, until she could see the ramparts that she had often stood upon while gazing out.

"Lady?"

Soft, persistent word. She knew it was Corfaire, but did not answer him. Instead, she let her eyes trail down until they lost sight of the towers for the wall.

As Corfaire had said, the gates were not guarded—at least not obviously so. But the red and black enamel of the crest that joined them glinted in the daylight. Beyond the black bars she could see the grass; it was cut, and no weeds seemed to grow there. But the flowers seemed out of season, somehow.

Who tends these now? She could see no one; the grounds were preternaturally still. No birds seemed to fly there; no squirrels made their mad dashes across the open ground. It was as if nothing moved at all.

At least, not yet.

The caravan moved, and she moved with it, following the bend in the road. But the gates she saw more clearly than she did the crowds around her.

There were guards in the city that bore no crests, not even that of the Church. She had not seen them during the caravan's march to the market, nor had they been at the market gates.

Those gates were new; Corfaire had said they were supposed to keep thieves out. There were other markets in the outer city that the poorer people could frequent; only people with house crests or house documents were allowed entry here. Slaves and nobles.

Still, the gates had not been guarded—neither when the caravan arrived to register its presence and leave an address to call upon, nor when they had left to find their rooms in the hotel of Hildy's choice.

Guards were out in the streets now. There were many, and they didn't appear with any regularity. But they had to be avoided, and she had come narrowly close to being discovered.

For the fifth time she checked her breast pocket. Paper rustled crisply between two layers of cloth. Good; she still had her documents. She hoped she wouldn't need them, but she had had enough presence of mind to take them in case of emergency.

The streets were quiet. There were more lamps along them than she remembered, each shedding a diffuse light out on cobbled ground. She avoided them, calling her blood-linked light to guide her footsteps. And then she stopped; here it still felt wrong to use her power.

Even if he was gone. Perhaps because he was gone.

The hotel she had slipped out of was close to the city center. It was a grand and glorious building, but it had not always been a hotel. At least one of the families that had been in power in the Rennath that Erin remembered had long since fallen upon poor fortune.

She was not even sure that the hotel was in noble hands. But the rooms were grand and large, even if there weren't many of them. Erin had wondered how they could afford their accommodation. Hildy had smiled.

"Do you think *I'm* paying for this?"

Which was certainly answer enough.

She shook her head and looked down the avenue. From any major road in the inner city, one could always see the spires. They towered above everything else, and careful planning had made sure that nothing was built to block any view of them.

She moved more quickly, as if dawn would suddenly come rushing in to steal these quiet hours. Hildy might barely understand, but Tiras and Hamin would certainly not. She *had* to go there for however brief a glance she was allowed of what had once been home.

The gates were closed, but no one stood ready to open them, nor to guard them from any who knew them well. Erin took a deep breath and then reached deftly between the bars. There was a click as her fingers found their hold, and then, arms still entwined with cold metal, she began to push them inward. They made no creak or noise of any kind, but she failed to notice this.

She took a step forward and closed the gates behind her. The path rolled out, like a rugged carpet, to the doors that allowed entrance into the great hall. The west hall. With a breath that was almost a sigh, she started forward.

And then she felt it; magic. Blood-magic. She looked carefully. She twisted her fingers in the still air. What normal vision could not see was now made clear to her. A soft, red glow touched every blade of grass, every tree, every stone.

Yet it did not hurt her; it did not cause her any pain.

Why?

She looked down at the path and then caught sight of herself; of the plain, unadorned tunic that had too many creases. Like the grounds and the palace, it too was glowing gently, surrounded by a halo that floated an inch away from her skin.

It did not surprise her after the initial shock. In his own way, and with his own understanding, he had tried not to hurt her.

This was something she might have forgotten to consider, but not Stefanos. Later, later she would wonder how he had accomplished this blood-magic.

She was very glad then that she had not asked Darin to accompany her. He was of the lines, after all. And this place was death to the lines. The thought coiled; memory made a subtle spring.

But I am not of the lines. Not here.

Stone curled in intricate crevices; water glimmered in shallow pools like trapped crystal. She knelt briefly, her hand skipping the surface of one pond. The water was cool.

She had never known the palace to be so still or so silent. Even in darkness, slaves had marked the hours, and the guards had patrolled the ground in their crisp, even step. She listened for word or voice, and caught an echo. Memory again. Any real sound would not have escaped her hearing.

She stood, wiping her hands against her tunic. It was time, now, to dare the palace proper. Like a ghost she drifted toward the main doors. Her feet crushed the grass as she was certain no other step had done in years, but they made very little noise.

The doors slid open before she could touch them. More magic. She smiled a little sadly as they rolled backward. They would have been difficult for her to open; they were heavy and sat stiffly on their great hinges. He would have known; must have known.

As she stepped across the threshold, she tensed. Her left foot was forward, her right back, and between them the thin line of past and present was taut and fine. With a deep breath, she brought her right foot forward. There. She had decided.

Shadow opened up beneath the high, peaked ceilings. No beams cut the eye here, but the stone above was perfectly carved and molded. There were frescoes on the ceiling, but the darkness hid them—and she had no Servant's memory to call them up in detail. It was better this way; she had never liked them.

Her mouth was dry, her throat tight. She took a step, and then another, but both were slow and measured. She did not look behind her, but she knew that the doors were rolling shut in the preternatural silence.

She was alone. He was not here. Not even here.

There were no words to describe the way her thoughts and emotions twisted inward, and if there had been, she would not have had the strength to voice them. Nothing was ever simple.

What did you expect?

But even to this she had no answer. Something was odd about it; familiar in a way that was different. She couldn't place it.

She made her way to her rooms, calling light to ease the passage. The stairs were clean, and the thick, cool rails betrayed no hint of dust or age. Insects at least must have made a home of this, but she could see nothing—no webs, no little movements. She had often felt isolated in Rennath, and knew now that it had been illusion; truly, she was alone here, as she had never been.

Her step quickened and faltered only once.

In the halls that led to her rooms, the tapestries that she had asked so quietly for still hung. She passed the woven scene of Gallin's death easily enough, flitted past the Gifting of God to his Servants and their kin, and walked by the investiture of the seven lines. These images were her history, but they held no pain for her, and no pleasure—not here.

There was only the Lady.

Flat and lifeless in the weave of a master, she sat at the head of delicately woven line history. Her legs were crossed and her hands open, as if in supplication or offering. But her eyes saw other futures, other possibilities. The Seeing.

"Lady," she said quietly.

There was no answer.

But as she turned, she understood why this ghostly walk felt oddly familiar. It reminded her of the times she had been in the Woodhall; it too had been trapped in time.

Do you come here, Stefanos? Is that why you preserved it?

Again there was no answer. She walked into her rooms, listening to the hollow silence. The fireplace was empty and cold, although the grate was immaculately clean. The two chairs sat by it, equally empty. The low table held a vase; there were no flowers in it.

She passed through quickly and opened the door that led to her bedchamber. Everything here was also preserved; the bed was neat, the curtains stiff and unwrinkled. She thought it had never looked so perfect. Even her closets were full. Dresses that she had worn centuries past stood in neat, seemingly endless rows.

Memories hung like curtains over a window into an uncertain landscape. She heard Tanya's quiet voice; Evvie's loud ordinances; Marcus' gruff, deep words. She saw where dinner had been laid in the late hours of the evening when she had chosen to forsake the dining hall, and saw further the place that Stefanos had often taken beside her.

And she knew, as she stood in silence, that these were not the reason she had come. Hesitantly, she pushed them aside, and they fell like layers of soft cloth around her, too fine to be completely forgotten, until at last only one image remained.

The last time she had woken here.

Light stirred in her, clear and sharp and hard. For a moment she felt the red around her as a weapon wielded by an expert foe; it hurt, and though no wound could be seen, it cut her deeply. She bit her lip and drew blood.

She knew why he had done it, but the question would not stay away; it haunted her like the strains of a blood-spell, catching her in the strands of a deep red web that her Light was powerless to break.

Oh, yes. She knew why she had come.

Derlak of Valens shifted before her, beckoning in a tense, heavy silence. She didn't want to believe him, but she followed where he led, out of her room and into the tall, shadowed hallways. The memory of that night was etched deeply enough that she lost her way only twice before finding it again, a hound to the trail.

She left windows and moonlight behind as she descended, at last, into the vault that Stefanos had called home. In every sense, the dead dwelled here, but sleeplessly.

Two doors she passed; they were small and tightly shut. She counted a third and wondered if she had once again lost her way. In frustration she stopped, and her teeth found the groove they were wearing in her lower lip.

This is so stupid. Her fist found a wall and scraped it, more to her detriment than its. *What am I going to do? Last rites?*

And then she saw it, a crack of light in the black hall, a light not cast by her blood—it was too far away and too precise for that.

She began to walk more quickly and more cautiously, wondering if someone else kept a vigil here. But she heard nothing; no words, and no movement that was not hers.

The door was open; light filtered around edges and hinges both. She reached out to touch it and drew back as she found sharp splinters. Violence had left its mark here, as it had on so many things. With only a hint of prayer on trembling lip, she swung the door wide.

For a moment she thought she must have the wrong room, and her legs bent at the knees. There was no altar here, no black marble slab, no touch of reddened shadow. The floors were clean and dustless, and here and there inlay caught torchlight that had been frozen between flickers. There were no pews, no chairs, nothing at all to break the line of a level floor.

Maybe that's why she didn't see it at first. But she walked in in silence and moved listlessly to the center of the room.

And there, in white marble and gold letters, was the answer to the question she had not even dared to ask.

Here lies Kandor, Third of Lernan, and four of the Line Elliath, who died this night that they might, unknowing, change the world. They died well, and they will not be forgotten.

Knees that were weak gave out completely; they fell to rest just beneath the edge of the plaque. Gold gleamed and twisted the reflection of the last of Elliath as she bent down.

Here.

It *was* real. All of it. She had known it, and yet . . . It had always been important to see a body, or at least to know where it rested. Stefanos, she felt, had never understood that. Nor, she was certain, would he ever.

Yet he had done this, had transformed a place of killing to a place where those killed might rest. They were here, with only stone and dirt as the wall that separated her from them. The marble was cold against her cheek, but she warmed it with her tears.

And although she knew it could not help them, she began to whisper the last rites. All that she knew did not deprive the words of meaning; they were not hollow or empty.

"I'm sorry. But I'm almost in Malakar now, and if you can hear me at all, you know that the Bridge is finally in sight for you." Her voice broke, and she touched the letters as if to draw strength from them.

"Belf—wait for me. Promise. We—we do everything together."

"Who is 'Belf'?"

Erin froze, but only for a second. She recognized the voice. The chill in the air was balmy compared to that contained in her next words. Even the tears seemed to turn to crystal, so suddenly did they stop their fall. "What-are-you-doing-here?"

"I might ask the same question." Corfaire raised an eyebrow, but he remained in the door, framed by it.

"How did you get in?"

"I followed you, Lady."

Impossible. I'd have heard you.

But she wasn't completely sure. She rose. Embarrassment struggled with anger, but it wasn't much of a contest; her hand strayed to her sword hilt and froze there, as if made of stone or white marble.

He crossed his arms casually, but Erin saw his fingers twitch as they rested inches above his sword. In a quieter tone of voice, he said, "Captain Hamin saw you leave. There was some small argument about it, but Darin held sway. He believed that you would return unharmed, and that you didn't wish company." He shrugged. "Darin is young, and perhaps naive. I took it upon myself to follow."

"And that was the only reason?"

Wary, white smile. "No." He bowed. "Lady."

There was no insult in the offered word. Not even a hint of it. If it had come from any other man, Erin might have thought she heard a hint of awe or hope there.

Her eyes lingered a moment over shining words and pale marble. Then she straightened herself and began to walk toward her unwanted guest. This, she would not share with him.

"It was true."

"Pardon?"

"That you lived in Rennath."

She could hardly lie now. Instead she nodded.

"What is this room?"

"Corfaire, enough. Please."

To her surprise he nodded and followed the gesture with a

bow. But his eyes found the room's center and lingered there over words that he could not read.

His eyes sought the heights of the spires with a quiet wonder. His face was pale and free from the subtle twist of lips that so often marred his expression. His hand never once pulled sword from sheath, nor did it dally near hilt after the initial meeting. He knew, without knowing why, that there was no threat here that could harm him. Is this what comfort and safety felt like, that it could resonate so deeply?

He did not speak until the palace gates were shut behind them. And when he did, he was almost surprised at the tone of his words.

"Lady."

She seemed suddenly small and fragile as her fingers curled around the bars of the gate just beneath the simple crest. Her profile was pale and still, her eyes wide and unblinking in the mask of her face. She nodded, but gave no other sign that she had heard him.

"When you travel to Malakar, I would be honored if you would accept my aid as your guide." His sword came out of his scabbard, and he held it out, hilt forward. It was not as awkward as it had been the only other time he had done it. In the dim light of the street, it hardly looked like steel at all.

Her face turned, but her hands still gripped the bars as if they were a window to a world she could not join.

He wondered what she would do. Would she take the sword? Would she ask that he blood it? Did she even understand what he offered? To make it more clear, he angled the blade up until the point of it was less than an inch from the throat that the proud tilt of his chin exposed.

"Put it away," she said softly at last. "Put it away or the guards in the street will come. We must get back."

His tongue stiffened, but it made no difference. He had no clever words to offer this rejection. He held the stance for a moment longer, and then his face hardened. Why should she accept an oath that the Empire had created? Only one other man had ever taken this from him, and in the end it had almost cost him his life. He had been foolish even to think that the Lady of Mercy could consider it worthy.

What did it matter, after all? He had planned his course of action in Coranth the eve after the battle. He would follow the

Lady into the heart of Veriloth, whether she accepted his pledge or no.

It didn't matter. It made no difference.

He almost believed it as he lowered the sword and stood before her. He jumped when her hand caught his. He flinched at the expression on her face and the width of her eyes. It was too close to pity.

"Corfaire."

"Lady," he said stiffly.

Her other hand came up, leaving the refuge of bars at last. Very gently, she uncurled his fingers and took the sword hilt from him. It shook.

Humiliation washed over his face as the blade slowly fell. He couldn't keep it at bay. "Lady, I can place the sword in the scabbard on my own."

"You have offered me your life," she answered. The words were cold and oddly accented.

He fell to one knee and wondered then if this is how the ceremony had come to be, for his legs would not support him. "Yes."

"I do not choose to take it now."

He lifted his face, and she lowered hers, until they were on a level. Her eyes were bright green. The wrong color, the wrong shape.

"But that choice is now mine."

He could not even breathe.

She leaned forward slightly, and the tip of the blade pressed against his exposed throat. It was cool as it trembled there. Absurdly, he thought it bad that her hands were unsteady.

"And this is proof of it." Steel pierced skin.

There was no finesse in the way she drew the blade back. There was little control in her nervous expression as her eyes sought the damage in the darkness. It did not matter at all.

He lifted a hand to the tiny wound and caught his blood with his fingers. "This is the mark of it, Lady." He answered, his voice much stronger and surer than hers. "I wear it. I will not forget what I have pledged. My life, and my death, are in your service."

"Then take back your sword and carry it thus."

He held out one hand, and she placed the hilt into it. Their fingers touched again, briefly. She drew back and began to walk down the street.

"Lady? Erin?"

"Yes?" Too quiet.

"Your permission to rise?"

"My—Corfaire, can't you hear the patrol? Get up!"

He did, but his feet, as they joined hers in running, were light.

chapter
fourteen

"Erin, dear, why don't you let one of the boys carry that?" Hildy stood, hands on hips, a frown wreathed across her cheeks. That frown increased as someone pushed past her in the market compound, and she made a little comment about rudeness under her breath. It wasn't very quiet.

Erin smiled and shook her head. "You're taking most of the boys with you. Tiras deserves a little rest, and Darin's shoulders aren't any broader than mine."

"Well what about Corfaire, dear?"

Erin looked over her left shoulder to see Corfaire. He was standing almost at attention, although no ceremony called for it. Neither of them had gotten much sleep the night before; she had spent much more time wandering the halls of the palace than she'd realized. But neither he nor she was willing to wait the day that rest demanded.

"I don't see how he could carry more," she said at last. "I think he's already more weighted than the horses."

It wasn't true, and Hildy clucked loudly before subsiding into another teary smile. "Are you sure you don't want any of the other boys?"

Hamin coughed. "Hildy . . ."

For about the tenth time, Erin shook her head firmly. "I doubt that Candy will be happy about the one I'm taking."

"I just don't want—"

Erin opened her arms and hugged the old merchant. "Any harm to come to me. I know." Her own smile was teary. She hid it against the breadth of Hildy's shoulder and took a deep breath. Hildy was clean and smelled a little of lilac and tea; later in the day these odors would be mingled with sweat. She had hugged Hildy often enough to know all the smells associated with her; they reminded her of Katalaan, of childhood. She knew she wouldn't have this again, and if she clung more tightly than usual, Hildy didn't remark on it.

"You've been a good guard, dear. When you come back, if you want the job, I'll take you on any time." She leaned forward conspiratorially, although her voice was no less loud than usual. "Between you and me, boys are fine, but it isn't the same as having another woman's company. Almost makes me miss the days I spent traveling with Candy." She sighed, straightened out, and moved on to Darin.

"You'd better make sure you eat more."

Darin almost giggled. It was one of the several phrases that were pure Hildy, and the guards often had betting pools as to who would hear it next, or who would hear it most often, on the route.

"Don't laugh like that, dear. I'm being serious. You're a growing boy."

"Aren't we all, Hildy?" Hamin chuckled.

Ignoring him, Hildy folded Darin into her ample arms. "Try to keep an eye on her, won't you?"

Darin's grip on the staff of Culverne tightened. "That's why I'm going." His words were very serious.

"Good." She stood back, looked at him, and shook her head. "We never did get you another set of boots. I honestly don't know how you could have damaged those ones so badly." And then she was on again, to speak a few words to Tiras, who even at his age was not spared much.

Erin watched Hildy move from person to person and stepped back so that Corfaire could be lectured in private. She watched the sardonic, affectionate smile curl round his lips, and heard the exasperation, equally affectionate, in Hildy's voice.

The scabbard of his sword hung loose at his side, and she wondered. How had she taken his oath? It was Empire born and bred, a ceremony the nobles oft used and abused. She had seen it once or twice when she had stood by Stefanos' side. In all of her years in Rennath, no one had offered the pledge to her.

Nor would she have accepted it if they had.

But Corfaire . . . she shook her head. What he offered had been so sincere and so intense that the importance of the answer was never in doubt. There was no politics in it, and it was no mere gesture.

True, she had hesitated, but in the end she had to accept the only expression of loyalty he knew how to offer. She only wished she understood better why. For her, the red and the green, the black and the white, had never proved themselves a good combination.

Maybe it was just Rennath and the echoes of all that she had wanted it to mean.

Again she shook herself and began to tighten the straps of her pack. The farewells had not been as hard as she had thought they would. Even knowing that she wouldn't see Hildy again didn't cut her as deeply as it had. For she was already distant here; stepping beneath the gates of the old city had brought her back to a time when Hildy had not yet been born.

Everyone waited in silence as she sent her gaze out and up toward the spires of the city proper. Quietly she said her last farewell. She wasn't sure, as she turned to follow Corfaire's steady lead, which of the good-byes she regretted more.

Lady Amalayna's fingers did not so much as shake. Her hands were dry and cool as she put down the pale, cream-colored lid of the powder jar that graced her dressing table.

She hesitated a moment and looked up to see herself reflected in the delicately framed oval mirror. Out of habit, she adjusted herself so that her face was perfectly centered. A proud, cold mask stared back at her. It was white, and powder and cream had been so perfectly applied that no blemishes marred her. Her hair had been drawn up into a smooth, black sheen, with only small strings of diamonds and platinum to break it.

"Lady?"

A frown started, and Amalayna took the pains to force it off her face. "Yes?"

The door stayed shut, which was only proper. The slave had been given no leave to enter. "Your father waits you."

"Good." She rose quietly and elegantly. "He is?"

"In the tower study."

She glanced out of the long, thin windows. The moon had stretched its way across the sky while she had risen and dressed. Time, in the evening, was much harder to judge than in the day; she hoped she was not late.

She walked quietly to the door and opened it herself.

An old slave waited her appearance, holding a silver tray with a brandy decanter and two heavy cut-crystal glasses.

"Ah, good. Leave that on the table and go back to your duties. I shall carry them to the lord myself."

House Valens did not keep ill-trained slaves. The old woman gave no hint of her surprise, and Amalayna knew the surprise was there. Instead, she did as her lady commanded. It was almost a pity that she would have to be killed, but it couldn't really be helped. There was much at stake here; too much for one slave to hold the key to, even if she never realized that she did.

Alone, Lady Amalayna looked down at the tray. Her face was frozen, expressionless. Now she hesitated, and this time for real. What she contemplated was almost unthinkable.

But what *he* had done was worse. She had not taken Lord Vellen's word alone, but after accepting that his words might be true, the evidence was trivial to obtain.

She crossed the room and pulled open a drawer. Pushing aside the vellum and quills, she pulled out one small bottle of ink and lifted the cap.

The liquid had a bitter scent, but the brandy would mask it well. Very carefully she twisted the stopper off the decanter and emptied the bottle. A clear liquid merged with the golden one until no eyes could have told them apart.

Then she straightened her shoulders and walked out the door. Five minutes later she returned with another, younger slave. He followed her wordlessly, and when she pointed at the tray, he lifted it.

"To the tower study," she said softly.

"Lady."

She waited for the slave to step into the hall. For one moment, her expression cracked, and her face lost the control that only years can bring to a person.

Dramathan of Valens was a tired man. The destruction of the temple's south wing had caused more than its share of unrest, and the captain of the Swords had made clear all he felt about the deaths of "his" men. The priests could be better controlled—or they would be, if not for the politics of the Greater Cabal.

When Benataan of Torvallen finally graced the altars, Lord

Valens intended to have a hand presiding in the ceremonies. He was certain that he could ask that much of the high priest of the Cabal. He was not going to settle for anything less.

The knock at the door took him away from his contemplations. He rose, bidding his daughter to enter.

Amalayna walked quietly in.

She was lovely, in the cold way that only nobility could be; distant, pale, and untouchable. She had been quiet of late, and from the set of her face, this night would be no exception. But at least she wore house colors, house cloth. Above the modest fall of burgundy neckline, the crest of House Damion caught the light.

She would serve the house well, he was certain of it.

"Father," she said quietly. She walked toward him and stopped, offering her cheek.

He kissed it; it was trembling. "Are you cold, Amalayna?"

Her smile was pained. Just a hint of white powder clung to his lips; half of her task was done. "I am not yet used to these evenings." But there was no complaint in her voice. "Why did you call me?"

He gestured to one of the chairs, and she took it. "Brandy?"

"Please."

The liquid was warm and rich and golden; it flowed down her throat smoothly, and she hardly felt the after-burn that lingered. But she noted that he drank after she did. Habit, not suspicion, but habits such as these were often difficult to break.

It didn't matter. Not now. If she had had any second thoughts, the time for them had just flown past.

"You heard of the trouble at the temple?"

She raised an eyebrow, studying his face. "There are very few who have not."

"Yes. Well." He drained his glass. "We need your help."

" 'We'?"

"Lord Vellen and I."

She was silent a moment. "Why?"

"The Torvallen alliance has gained too much ground due to the destruction. Lord Vellen is holding his position, but it has been weakened. Michaelas of Corcassus and Marek of Grimfaxos may prove to be a problem to us."

"Your sources?"

"Have indicated nothing, for the moment. Lord Vellen's have likewise returned with neutral news; Benataan has made an offer, but we do not know its nature. Nor do we know the disposition of these two lords to it." He sighed and ran his fingers through his hair. "I do not need to tell you, Amalayna, that we will suffer if Lord Vellen loses his seat. Keep this in mind and use your own network to gain information on the doings of the Greater Cabal."

She nodded quietly. "At once, Father. Regardless of what either you or Lord Vellen believes, His life is of great concern to me."

Dramathan's smile was a mixture of irony and weary affection. "I know. I have raised no fool."

The slave that answered the quiet, insistent knocking was the same old door warden that Amalayna had come to know well. He was dressed in house colors, and he wore them with a dignity that was almost too great for his station. The red and gold of the jacket seemed an impossible hint of sunlight in its full glory.

And of Laranth in his.

Her face was pale, but not due to powders or creams, and nothing hid the circles beneath her wary eyes.

"Lady Amalayna." The slave bowed very correctly. A little too much so. At his back, the bright crystal lamps of House Tentaris glittered in the darkness like an estranged friend. She shivered under her cape and cast a glance over her shoulder to where the carriage still waited in the narrow, well-lit drive.

"Please tell Lord Tentaris that I seek an audience with— with Lord Parimon."

The slave hesitated a moment, and the door opened a fraction of an inch. "As you wish, Lady Amalayna. Please enter and wait here."

A breach of protocol, that. But she was grateful for it; standing outside made her feel too exposed. She was not completely certain that she had not been followed.

Ah, well. If Lord Vellen knew, what of it? He would no doubt think it the weakness that it was. For a moment she leaned her back against the broad, solid doors and tilted her head to the light. She almost wished that she had never met Laranth, and failing that, had never been foolish enough to keep so little distance.

"Amalayna."

She looked down to see the lord of the house, casually attired, in the distant hall. He held something carefully in his arms as he approached her.

"Lord Tentaris," she murmured, moving away from the door. She pushed her cape to one side and curtsied. It was the gesture of a supplicant, and they both knew it well.

"Amalayna, why have you come?"

She looked directly at the red and gold bundle that he held so gingerly. Almost, her lips turned up in a smile. He was not a man used to the handling of children.

"To see Lord Parimon," she answered quietly. "To see my son." She swallowed as he stopped a few feet from her. He did not ask her to remove her cloak and enter. She hadn't expected it and was surprised at how it stung.

"Did we not agree that you were not to come here?"

A nod was the only answer she could offer in the face of his stern words, his stiff expression. She met his dark eyes directly.

And was surprised at the way the lines of his face changed. "I'm too old a man for this." He held out his arms. "Lord Parimon, I'm sure, would be pleased to grant you the audience you have risked coming for."

She needed no further encouragement; her arms were already under the back and head of her young son. His face twisted momentarily, and his eyes blinked open.

"Hello, Pari." No one save Parimon, not even Laranth, had ever heard such a soft tone to her words.

"Come, Amalayna." Lord Tentaris moved to her back and began to unfasten her cloak. It fell away, revealing the burgundy and gray of the house that now claimed her. But at her waist, trailing the length of her skirt, were twined black and white ribbons. She heard his breath, but did not see his face; her own was buried in the small neck of her child.

"Come," he said again, but softly. "The drawing room is being readied. There is a chill in the night."

Gentleness almost made her cry, where cruelty could not. She was aware of the arm around her shoulder and allowed Lord Tentaris to lead her through the halls that she knew well.

"Who—who is feeding him?"

"We have a wet nurse," Lord Tentaris replied. "Not a slave."

She nodded her approval, but could not take her eyes away from her son. He smelled of powder and soap. "Has he been well?"

"Amalayna," the lord's words were a drawl, "I am well aware that you still hold informants within my house. I daresay I know who they are. If your son were not well, you would probably know it before I."

She blushed, and he chuckled as they entered the drawing room. A small fire was burning in the grate, and tea sat upon the low table. He offered her a seat on the couch and took the armchair himself.

She did not speak for a long while, at least not intelligibly. But the half words and coos were of interest to Parimon, who joined in her senseless babble. One little hand flailed at the jeweled strands of platinum that hung from her face.

"I am old."

"Pardon?"

He smiled and shook his head. "I do not remember Laranth as a child. But I remember his mother when she first held him. She was not unlike you are now, and she was not very similar at any other time." The smile faded. "You would have been the daughter of my choice. I regret that my house cannot be as open to you as it was."

"As do I." Her words were stark and simple, but there was steel in each of them.

"Why have you come?"

"To see my son."

"I am old, child, but I have not grown addled. I know what your weakness for Laranth was—it was a mirror of his for you. But unlike other lords and ladies, I have never mistaken it for more. Why did you wish to see my grandchild this evening?"

"You will not be addled when you are in your grave," she answered, and her grip on her son tightened. She pulled a fold of cloth a little over his face, so that he might not see hers.

All trace of indulgence or amusement was gone from Lord Tentaris' face in that instant. He was a hawk, and the red and gold were the colors of his territory. Thus did he show the kinship that he felt with his grandson's mother.

"I wished to tell my son," she said quietly, "that I have begun vengeance upon his father's assassins."

The older man's eyes grew wide. "Who?"

She shook her head quietly and pulled the cloth away from Parimon's face; he had started to fuss. Her lips she pressed against his forehead. "Believe me when I say that it is better that you do not know."

"Amalayna, play no games with me."

"For the sake of my son, I would do more than play."

They bristled at each other, and Lord Tentaris rose, all age forgotten. "*Your* son? Remember, he is the son of *my* house."

"Do you seek to deny him to me, more so than you have already done?" Her grip tightened, and Parimon, aware of the tension, began to wail. The tight line of her mouth fell, and the edge of words blurred into the sounds of comfort she had not been able to offer him for too long.

"Amalayna."

"I'm sorry." She looked up wearily. "I have so little time." Even in defeat, there was still steel to her. "Yes, I know whose hand guided the killer. Laranth is ever in my thoughts, as he must be in your own.

"But there is no longer any danger to your house. Or to my son. And I can only be sure of that if you are kept in ignorance." Again she bent her face over her son's. "And only if I obey your dictate and do not come again.

"It is very hard."

"Who?" he said again, although he knew by now that she would not answer.

"What word can you give me that you will not interfere?"

"None, without your answer."

"Then there is no answer." She rose and very hesitantly offered her child up to Lord Tentaris and the care of his house. His crying was the only sound that marred the room's stillness.

"Amalayna—"

"Enough. Even with Laranth's aid, you could not hope to accomplish what you will try to without destroying my son's future. I will not allow it. What finances have gone into your trade war, only you alone can know for certain—but I can guess. You have lost several of your routes, and while House Wintare has not gained them, they are gone nonetheless. What resources have you left at your disposal? Already there are other houses at your door, and were you not so intelligent, they would have taken Tentaris down to bare stones by now."

He held Parimon awkwardly. Anger and respect warred with his face, and oddly, respect won. "House Valens raised no fool," he said quietly.

It was not what she did that surprised him, for she did very little. But her hands curled into tense, white fists—he could almost see the bone show through beneath translucent skin. "If you need my aid, or any that I can offer, it is yours."

She nodded stiffly.

"And should you wish to see your son, you have access."

That won a little expression from her face. "It—it is best that I do not."

"How long?"

"Pardon?"

"How long do you think you have left?"

She turned away from him and walked over to the grate until her skirts hovered inches away from the edge of the flame. "How long? Weeks. Weeks at best."

"And you are certain of it?"

"Certain that I will be caught?" Her smile was grim and fixed, although he could see only the edge of it. "I am certain."

"House Valens is powerful enough to protect you from much."

She had thought she could keep everything to herself, and even she was surprised when she turned to face Lord Tentaris. "I have no house."

Understanding flooded the lord's face as he met her eyes. They were blank and hard, almost transfixed. It was not much of a leap to guess at who else might be involved, but the horror he felt left little room for anger. That would come later.

Now, now what she had done—or would do—filled all of his thoughts. Once, Amalayna had been a cornerstone of her house, of Valens. Her father had been proud of her.

"He was my bond-mate." She said it almost mildly. "And I claim the right to vengeance."

"He was my son, and the house heir," Lord Tentaris replied. Very quietly he walked to her until they were almost touching, and for the second time that evening he gave over stewardship of his grandchild. "Ah, Lady." He shook his head. "You have my word."

"Thank you." She picked up her son and held him tightly.

"I will make sure he understands, when he is of age." He walked to the door and opened it. "I shall come back within the hour; have your privacy now."

"Thank you." The words were softer.

"And Amalayna?"

"Yes?"

"Laranth would have been proud of you."

He left quickly, without turning back; to do otherwise would have taken away her dignity. Only her child would witness her tears, and there was no humiliation for her in that. He would not remember them.

The only fear she had was that he would die too soon. Until the last moments of the rites, she needed her father to live; after that it was inconsequential. She had no illusions as to her importance to Lord Vellen; were her father to die early, he would call off the ceremony and be forever out of her reach.

These were her thoughts as she sat, alone, at the long dining table. Her father was elsewhere, on Church business, and her youngest sister—the only other lady of House Valens still to reside in the manor—was on leave with a group of her too-young friends.

Her only brother, and the heir to the house title, was in Sivari, tending to his duties as leader of the Lesser Cabal. He would not return home until the rites, and she was glad of it. They were not close, but he was canny and knew too well her thoughts.

She had no desire to see the house fall from its position and had taken precautions to insure his presence in Malakar at the death of her father; to do otherwise was to risk Valens overmuch. The traveling time from Sivari was measured in weeks, and Dorvannen could scarce afford those if he was not to lose the house titles.

Her fingers curled around her fork, and she cut listlessly at the slice of beef that lay before her.

What if, after all this, her plan failed? What if Vellen, suspicious and careful as he was, was too protected to be killed on the spot? She would almost certainly die, and the most important part of her goal would be left unaccomplished.

She pushed the plate aside with a grimace, and then set her jaw. She would eat; already her father had commented on her lack of appetite.

Perhaps tonight she would hear from her connections and discover what had been offered to Lord Vellen's allies on the council. She could not, herself, afford an audience with Benataan of Torvallen, but there were other ways in which to reach him.

She bent her mind to that. It always paid to have a contingency in case she failed at this plan.

* * *

Darin heartily disliked rain. Especially this cold, wet drizzle that seemed to have no end in sight. There was no sun, and the clouds themselves were an even pall across the sky, with no beginning and no breaks anywhere.

His outer coat, although oiled, was now quite damp, and the hand that held Bethany was shaking. Cold like this always seemed worse than the bite of winter.

He wished that any of the three of his companions would at least have the grace to grumble, but no. Erin, as usual, seemed immune to the effects of the weather; although her hair was matted to her cheeks and forehead, and her own coat was easily as sodden as his, she did not shiver and did not remark at the way her breath hung in clouds before her lips.

Tiras, all in black, was also impervious to the effects of weather—and, it seemed, of age. He walked in the same brisk, upright way, glancing from side to side at the slightest noise or movement, be it only from small forest animals.

Even Corfaire accepted the weather as if it made no difference.

Only the horses seemed to mind, and Darin was not going to sympathize with them, although the prospect of doing so was becoming more tempting as he walked. The only good news he'd heard all day was that they would stay at an inn on the road. And even for that, he'd had to listen to Tiras' arguments against it.

He began to fuss at the curling sleeves of his coat and scraped the mud off his boots against the undergrowth.

Erin, in quiet midsentence, looked back at the noise.

"It's Malakar, isn't it?" Her voice was very quiet; it seemed to fuse with the cold and the gray drizzle.

"No." His breath came out in a puff. "It's the rain." But even as he said it, his covered right arm began to throb. The drizzle grew harsher, colder—as if he were suddenly laid bare to it.

Erin stopped walking, and he caught up to her slowly.

He met her eyes; they were very green. "We're going to have to face Lord Vellen again." It wasn't a question.

She answered it anyway. "I don't know. I hope not." Her arm slid round his shoulder, and he felt her warmth through multiple layers of cloth. "But neither of us is what we were."

"What are we going to do?"

She shook her head, and water ran from her hair, splashing his cheeks. It too was warm.

"What *are* we going to do?"

Erin looked up from the dressing table and laid the brush down. She met Tiras' eyes across the breadth of the mirror, and saw Corfaire putting out the last of the dinner dishes. They had arrived late, but the innkeeper had seen fit to provide food for them in their rooms.

He should, she thought. They'd certainly paid for the privilege. She sighed and rose, turning to face the three companions that would see her through the last leg of a journey that had started too long ago.

"I don't know."

Corfaire frowned, but both Darin and Tiras looked resigned.

"Much of your plan," Tiras began, "and I use the word advisedly, has been your private concern until now. But we are less than a week from Malakar, and I believe it is time to make things more . . . exact."

"And if any one of us is caught?"

"So shall the rest be." The lines in his forehead deepened. "What is our goal?"

She closed her eyes and nodded slightly. "The Gifting of God."

Two sets of eyes looked askance at hers; Darin's eyebrows rose, but not in question. Bethany was glowing softly in his hand. Erin met his gaze, nodding, and both of their lips turned up in the barest hint of smile.

"This Gifting, as you call it, is in Malakar?"

"According to my maps and my understanding, yes. Where, I don't know." She frowned again, but this time more deeply. "Corfaire?"

"Lady?"

"Do you know of . . . a well? Large, but not ostentatious; old—possibly guarded. No, certainly guarded."

"No, Lady. And I do know Malakar."

"The Church would perform the blood ceremonies there."

"Ceremonies are performed in two places: either at the temple in the High City, or in the noble houses. Nowhere else in Malakar."

Erin seemed to sag as that hope died.

"But Lady, I was not among the slaves privileged to enter the High City temple; I have not seen all."

"You can find it, can't you?" Tiras said to Erin, his eyes so narrow they were almost closed.

"Yes. But not—not unless I use my power."

Tiras looked almost dangerous; his eyes glinted as if made of steel. "You fear detection?"

She nodded.

"The Church."

She nodded again, with just a trace of hesitation.

Tiras, no fool, caught it. "Erin, we must know what we face." He stopped and looked narrowly at Corfaire. "At least," he added, in a more moderate voice, "*I* must."

She held her breath a moment, weighing her words.

But it was Corfaire who answered the question. "She fears the Lord of the Empire."

"Nightwalker," Darin added softly, although it wasn't necessary. He remembered his Lord Darclan; tall, slim, and bearing an aura of malice that even the daylight could not fully disperse. He tried to push the image aside, choosing instead a younger one: the fall of Culverne. The shadow of death that walked among the survivors, searching for him. But the shadow had eyes now, and a bitter, haunted expression that Darin still could not fathom all of.

Is that where they were going, in the end? To face Lord Darclan in the heart of the Empire?

Yes, Initiate, Bethany said. She had spoken seldom on their journey, and her voice felt odd and hollow in his mind.

But . . . he'd never hurt her. If he found her, he'd never hurt her.

No. The reply reminded him of the Lord, but he couldn't say quite why.

The priests would. The Church.

Yes. But while I think she now fears death, I do not think it her strongest fear.

I don't understand.

Don't you? Darin, the Sarillorn of Elliath must carry the battle to its logical end. What she brings is war and death. Could you face him easily, with only that to offer? Could you face him so, knowing that he would not lift hand against you?

His grip on Bethany tightened. "No," he said, and three

pairs of eyes turned to look at him. He blushed. "Uh, just talking, umm, to myself."

Thanks, Bethany.

He expected no answer, and received none.

But why doesn't she just ask him to stop? Don't you think that would work?

Do you think that she has not tried? She is of Elliath; she is old in years, if not in experience. And even the latter, I think, goes beyond either of us. But do not ask.

Darin wouldn't have. He knew that any question about Lord Darclan only shadowed her and dimmed the light behind her eyes.

Corfaire did not know any better. Or perhaps he did; it was hard to know with him. "Lady, why should you fear the Lord? Can you not ask for what you desire? Would he not grant it?"

The breath that she drew was sharp and clean. She faced him squarely, although it seemed that she looked beyond his shoulder. "Corfaire, why do you think the Lady of Mercy left her Dark Lord centuries ago?"

"It was said that she would return."

"To the slaves. Not to the Lord." She lifted a hand, warding off further questions, and he subsided. The oath he had given her granted much.

She turned to gaze out of the window, seeing the blur of her own reflection. "Very well. Tiras, Darin, Corfaire—I go to Malakar to find the Gifting of God. The Bright Heart's power is weak, but it is not guttered; the Light burns yet.

"I must find it. And when I do, I will call on the Gifting. No more and no less. But I think it will have the effect of crippling the Church and the noble houses.

"It's imperative that you," she said, turning suddenly to face Tiras and Darin, "return to Marantine with word. Quickly. What Renar then chooses as a course of action will be up to the council.

"But it would be best if I was not detected at all until the Gifting is purged. The Church is a danger, and the Lord of the Empire more so. The power of God I can call cannot match the power that he can."

"Very good," Tiras said softly. "But *how*?"

"When we arrive in Malakar, I'll take the risk of searching. We don't have any other choice." She spread her empty hands out, palm up. "I've not been trained in this, Tiras. If I could give you a better answer, don't you think I would?" Her teeth caught her lip, and she stood there looking suddenly young and vulnerable.

Tiras stepped forward. "Perhaps you are right." He nodded to both Darin and Corfaire. "We will adjourn for this eve, Erin. Sleep; you look as if you could use it."

Nobody understood why her smile turned so bitter.

A thin sheaf of paper floated in front of Darin's eyes as he opened them. His hands were shaking slightly as they lay on either knee; his back and neck were stiff. Only a single lamp burned in the room, and the flame was already low.

"Good."

He nodded; he could not see Tiras, and even the shadow he cast was lost in the darkness.

"If I were a young man, I would learn this magic. If you could teach it." There was a creak as Tiras sat down. "Do you understand what I want you to do?"

"Yes."

"Good. The door is locked; the lock is simple. Nothing heavy need be lifted; the work is delicate."

Sweat began to bead on Darin's brow and palms as he concentrated. The paper flitted to the ground, forgotten.

"Open the door, Darin."

Dawn filtered in through the windows of the room that Erin occupied alone. She rose, stretched, and looked at the blackened fireplace. Hunger gnawed at her a little, and she got up quickly.

The sun was still low on the horizon; she hadn't overslept.

With a little sigh she sat in the room's sole chair and began to braid her hair, pulling it into three uneven strands. Frowning, she let her hair fall and began again, thinking about drill and the days when Telvar would have noticed even a hair out of place.

The day was already bright. She finished her braid and walked over to the curtains. They were a little threadbare, and she wasn't certain they had always been this dull, patchy shade of gray. She pulled them aside and looked up. There wasn't a cloud in sight.

That should help Darin a bit. Her lips turned up a little ruefully at the corners, and she traced a small circle in the air. Just a hint of green light flared before her eyes, fading into the grays and browns of the room.

She would have to do something to help him.

And for the first time in weeks, she felt up to it. She got dressed and packed her things, carefully tying the straps of her pack into neat, precise knots. She was halfway over the threshold when she froze; her backpack hit the door with a dull thud.

Oh yes, she felt rested.

She had slept the night through for the first time in too long.

A door swung open in the long hall, and a familiar face peered around its edge.

"Erin!" She barely heard the word. Stefanos had not called her into the darkness. He no longer rested in the hand of the Enemy.

Although walls were in the way, her eyes turned to Malakar. Any prayer that she was capable of fell from her lips.

Not in Malakar, Stefanos. Bright Heart, let him walk anywhere else.

chapter
fifteen

He was very hungry when the plane fell away.

Stone congealed around him in uneven, craggy blocks. Wood lay in splintered beams as the sky, pocked with starlight, looked down. He could see where the rubble had been cleared away, for marble, cracked in places, peered through the dust.

They had not done much to rebuild. Perhaps he had not been away for long.

Time.

He frowned, and his lips drew back over triangular teeth. None were there who could see it. How had his personal quarters fared? Not so badly as this, he was certain. He glanced around again, seeing no movement. But everywhere around him the evidence of his power was starkly visible.

Once it might have satisfied him in some small way. Now he felt nothing, save for the hunger. It reminded him of the amount of personal power he had used so recklessly.

Before the Twin Hearts chose their grave, the power to destroy so small a structure had been used merely to *move* the great distances the war had demanded of him. His Lord's power had been freely available then; there was no impediment in calling upon it. And he, who had been First, had never lost the voice of God.

He was tired of war now, and the hunger gnawed insistently at him. But he would not feed.

The ease with which he decided this did not surprise him. How many centuries had he gone without feeding for her sake? But the irony was not lost on him, not even now.

Feeding, he saw her. And fasting, he was reminded as well.

233

He reached out almost casually and crumbled a bit of carved stone between his fingers.

Ah Sara, Sarillorn. I cannot reclaim what I was.

You have ungently revenged the death of your Lady of Elliath. Even as he thought it, he called the last image of his oldest foe from memory. It spread before him in a quiet, weary defeat. He thought that now, centuries of mortal time later, he finally had a small understanding of how she could stand so, and fall so.

But he was still First of the Sundered; he would not dwell on this. Slowly he spread his arms wide, and red shadow claimed him. When it passed, he stood in the long, black hall that led to his rooms. He hesitated there a moment as if unfamiliar with the surroundings.

And then he gestured again, a red sweep of hand and lip. This too passed, and he stood in front of the well-kept gates of a castle.

They rolled open before him, with no hand but his to guide them. The grass was cut and clean; the flowers, not so plentiful at this time of year, were nonetheless neat and precise.

The master gardener's hand was still in evidence everywhere.

He inhaled to catch fragrance and hold it a moment. Malakar did not smell like this; it was not so green or so oddly wild.

Wild. Yes. He knew then why he had come here.

He began to circle the grounds until he found himself at the labyrinth. He knew the hedges well; no twist or turn they took could lose him. He chose, instead of blood-spell, the simple expedient of walking, although his feet barely touched the ground. Here, on nearly the first of days, he had walked with his Lady. He could almost feel her ghost at his side.

The hedges in darkness were neatly trimmed and clipped, but as he left their rigid, living confines, he saw the weeds and brambles begin to take hold. How the master gardener had objected to this unsightly growth! It almost brought a smile to him.

But the smile was lost before it started.

He could feel the call of magic—the blood of the Light. To his eyes, a green-white glow topped the ancient ruins of the well. It was pale, more pale than the blood of either of the Twin

Hearts should have been. But it, unlike the wound in Malakar, was still whole; still cleansed.

What was the use of it? The Bright Heart, even cleansed, had not been able to save Sara from the death that the Dark Heart had decreed.

Sara . . .

He walked to the edge of the well. It was uncomfortable, but he had expected no less.

"Can you hear me?" The words were a whisper. He raised one hand in a half circle, but let none of his power out. "Do you know that I have returned yet again?"

The water rippled.

"On the morrow, I will wake the master gardener." He bowed, and this too hurt. This he might have granted to Sara while she had been at his side to appreciate it. If the mortal Beyond existed, he hoped that she might yet be waiting and watching.

"You have lost your war. I have lost mine. And in the end, I do not know how much of an enemy you were to me." He turned hurriedly then, and walked away, for his blood still struggled to answer the call of the Light. Instead of the patient walk through the labyrinth, he chose to rise above it; to see it laid out, symmetrical and precise, a green crown to the enduring jewel of the well.

The bitter song of Light's power rang in his ears.

He accepted it; he could almost pretend that it was Sara's presence that he felt.

He straightened himself out to his full height, exhaled, and cast yet again. His eyes grew silver, not red, and when their light dimmed, they were a deep brown. Gray merged with pink until he once again wore the glamour of a mortal man.

From this height, he looked down. There was at least one grave here. He had made it himself.

In silence, suspended in the cool air, he bowed his head.

Gervin . . .

He had seen the well; it had not been enough. It was time for the building proper. He passed the front courtyard, pausing only a moment beneath tiered archways. He had built this, but none of God's power touched any part of it, not even the foundations.

He strode into the great hall of his castle, and after a few moments, a slave peered around a corner. It was gratifying to watch his jaw drop open, but Stefanos made no move toward him. His fingers curled into fists as he turned aside from the scent of fear.

Memory never really captured the feeling of the present. He had known the pain of denied hunger before, but it felt sharp and new.

"Lord!"

"Yes," he answered mildly. "I have returned."

"I'll get Ev— uh, the house mistress."

"Do."

The slave scrambled up off his knees and ran, banging at least two doors behind him. He heard the shouting clearly; it was likely a muffled bell.

Three more slaves, two very young, appeared out of shadow, adding light to the hall's many torches. They avoided meeting his gaze, and he did not interrupt them to give further orders. He waited, watching them as he had often done when Sara slept. Their fear was muted, but their excitement was evident.

His hunger ebbed away a moment as the Great Hall came to life.

The house mistress came up from the slaves' quarters looking both severe and newly awakened. Her dress was crisply starched and chafed at the ground as she walked.

"Lord," she said, wearing a voice that was as stiff and proper as her clothing. She bent to her knees and bowed her head to the floor before him.

"House mistress. Is my study in order?"

"Yes, Lord. As are your rooms."

"Good. Rise. No, do not bother with my cloak; I shall carry it myself." He brushed past her then and began to walk the halls of his castle.

He knew now why he had left it staffed. His study, with its row of books and its tall arched windows, waited in the pleasant darkness. His chair, and the ironwood desk that he'd purchased to grace the room, had been left empty too long. From here, he might reach a decision about the Empire, and about the future.

Perhaps, after some time, the taint of the blood-hunger would again be purged, and he might see a glimmer of the dawn without feeling her ancient vengeance. Sara had always loved the dawn, and if he were to dwell in the shadow of her memory, why not feel an echo of her warmth?

His stride grew more sure and more confident, and the voices of his slaves faded from hearing behind him.

Lord Stefan Darclan had returned home.

Sargoth looked up at the night sky.

His feet skirted treetops, but the moon was on the wane, and although her light was bright enough, he was fairly certain that he could not be readily seen.

Malakar lay fifty miles to the southeast, under night's blanket. But her streets were well lit and crowded as the houses went about their business.

Sargoth disliked this edict of the First.

To find the streets crowded with so much mortal chaff annoyed him, night or day. He now had no release from their noise and their pale flickers of life.

His power was a thin, red line that stretched across the province and beyond. It had taken many hours of searching thus, but he had finally found the thing that he sought.

The half blood of Elliath was on the move, and she was close enough now that he saw an end to his long labor. No, not an end. But the hope of one.

He wearied of the world; it held no mysteries for him to unlock. The bickering of the priests had amused him for a few days, but their struggles were pathetic echoes of grander, older ones.

She slept now, he was certain of it. Her light had ceased to move. At the rate she had been traveling, she would reach the city in long weeks. Long? He shrugged. It seemed that he, too, had been infected by the mortal awareness of time. What was time to a Servant? These weeks should have been a steady blink of an eye, no more.

His breath came out in a hiss as he spun slowly to face Malakar. As mortal cities went, it was grand enough, illuminated by shadow and the trace of power of the Servants who had deigned to lay foundations for the temple.

He hated it.

First among us, why do you stay so long from your capital?

He knew, of course, the moment that Stefanos had departed the Hand of the Dark Heart. He knew too the minutes that he had passed among the ruins of the temple's southern wing. It had taken many minutes of searching to find the source of red light that glowed at the heart of Mordantari, the "Lord's province" as it was known.

He thought that the First might have gone to see to the wound of the Enemy, but that light had not so much as flickered, and Stefanos had been there many hours.

Wind swirled around him, catching at the strands of dark cloak that he wore. But they did not disturb his thoughts.

Why, Stefanos? Why do you remain there?

He might have gone himself, but he knew that the power of the Enemy's blood would conceal the presence of the Sarillorn more effectively than spells of his own making. And in this, he was very much a Servant of Malthan: He had no desire to visit the site of a defeat.

Frustration was not a particularly pleasant thing, and he let it go for a moment, scorching the treetops with something that approached rage. If Stefanos did not leave Mordantari soon, the coming of the Sarillorn would count for little.

Only this once had he ever been strongly tempted to pierce the veils of time and see the possibilities that the future laid out before his immortal eyes. But no; he could not guarantee the time of his passage, and perhaps he too would lose the moment of the Sarillorn's ascendancy. He could not risk it.

All he could do now was subject himself to more human prattle, human wiles. He must talk with the high priest of the Greater Cabal, if Lord Vellen indeed had managed to retain his post there. He had grown bored with watching and listening and had perhaps not paid as much attention as he should have.

His claws unfurled and made an elegant pass at the air.

The treetops continued to blow in the wind, and ash fell like rain on the ground below.

Sargoth did his best to ignore the priests and acolytes that wandered to and fro in the busy halls. Fear underlay their every movement; the cold stone resonated with the warmth of its song. He was not tempted, however; he had fed at the beginning of the evening and was unwilling to waste the necessary time to do so again. If ever a Servant could be said to be bored of this enjoyable replenishment of power, it was the Second of the Sundered.

He stopped and frowned occasionally, looking up to the archways. He disliked them; they were too precise and too . . .

mortal. Perhaps when the game had ended, he would change them at his leisure.

Then again, he had had his fill of mortal lands for at least the next millennium. The imagination necessary to envision prolonging his stay was beyond him at this point, no matter for what reason.

The double doors—why was everything doubled?—to the high priest's room were guarded by four Swords. Not one of them challenged his entry.

Lord Vellen looked up as the door clicked shut behind the Second of the Sundered.

"Sargoth." He nodded and made to rise immediately.

Sargoth waved a hand, and Lord Vellen sat back, carefully setting aside a wet quill.

"What brings you, Second of our Lord?"

"News." The word hung sibilant in the air. "The plans of my Lord have almost reached their final stages."

Lord Vellen nodded quietly. He was weary; the letter before him, rankling in its anonymity, had brought no welcome news.

"She is not so far from Malakar," Sargoth continued. "Be prepared. Those of the priests in your control must keep all knowledge of her presence hidden."

Vellen nodded, and Sargoth turned to leave.

"Second of the Sundered."

He halted.

"I can see two problems with your plan."

"Yes?"

"The First is not among us; I do not know where he dwells, and I've not the time to search."

"He is in Mordantari."

"I see."

"Your second 'problem'?"

"I do not know how much longer I will maintain control of the priesthood." He sagged further into the chair as these most difficult words left his lips.

Sargoth shrugged. "Very well. Then perhaps I shall speak to your successor. Benataan of Torvallen, I believe."

There was a flash of anger in Lord Vellen's eyes, but his lips remained set. "Lord Sargoth," he began, drawing his hands from the desk and placing them in his lap. "I realize that you are involved solely in service to our Lord. Perhaps you have not had the time to observe the machinations of the Greater Cabal at length."

"Your point?"

"Benataan of Torvallen may well be my successor if my plans go awry. But I do not believe that he will aid you in yours."

Sargoth said nothing, but moved slightly closer.

"He has no grievance with the First of the Sundered, other than the loss of a member of his house—and at that, only a fourth child. Should he understand your plan, and I gather he must understand some of it if he is to work with you, what benefit does he gain by coming to your aid?"

"His life," Sargoth said darkly.

"Indeed? At the risk of much, I will say that you are the Second—and the Lord of the Empire is First. What is to stop Benataan from approaching the Lord of the Empire directly? The news he would bring would be welcome and would perhaps guarantee him freedom from more petty, political concerns."

"You are clever," Sargoth said. "If this man threatens you, kill him. I have taught you what you need to know to accomplish this."

Again Vellen's eyes flashed. "Indeed. And if it were that simple, I would. But Torvallen's house is not without power—and not without allies. Such a death would fall upon my house and upon me. My position is not so strong at the moment that I could accept this censure and be secure of my post."

"I see."

Vellen leaned back in his chair for a moment. "Second of the Sundered, I will guarantee my aid. But—I need your help." No one living had ever heard these words from Lord Vellen.

Sargoth said nothing at all. But his shadows grew deeper and more red in the silence.

Lord Vellen knew that he had been dismissed, but waited in his chair until all traces of the Second had vanished from his room.

Only then did he return to the work at his desk.

But his face was white, grim. He did not know how well the gamble would succeed. Sargoth was no fool, but he was not well versed in the politics of the mortal arena; he had no reason not to take the high priest at his word.

The lamp was flickering down, and Vellen cursed the need

to work in darkness. But perhaps, should Sargoth's plan bear fruit, he would once again be in control of the vast Empire of Veriloth. He would dispense immediately with the dusk-to-dawn edict.

First, he had to survive.

Lord Valens sat in silence in the council room of the Greater Cabal. His pallor was off, and he knew it—only with Amalayna's remarkable assistance had he been able to disguise it from all but the most privileged members of his own house.

It's just age, he told himself. Of this, he was not entirely certain. At any other time he would have chosen the simple expedient of remaining at home until the illness had run its course.

One glance at the slightly superior nod that Benataan gave across the table underlined the foolishness of that option now. He graced Benataan with a meager nod and surveyed the gathering. Only eleven of the Karnari had yet taken their seats, and the time for the meeting's start had long since passed.

It was a very bad sign when Benataan of Torvallen, replete in formal robes, rose and placed both of his hands upon the table. None of the Karnari were so formally dressed, but instead of looking pretentious, Benataan seemed already to wield the power he coveted.

It was a bad sign, indeed.

"High priests of the Greater Cabal," he began, his voice quite measured and reasonable, "it appears that we are to commence the meeting without the guiding force of Lord Vellen." The fact that he used the house title, and not the Church title, was lost upon no one.

Lord Valens looked at the other empty seat; it belonged to Michaelas of Corcassus. Amalayna had not unearthed any useful information about House Corcassus yet, but it seemed that it had become a moot point. He did not do himself the indignity of inquiring about Michaelas' presence.

That left it at five to six. And it left him, as the most senior of Lord Vellen's allies, to try to block the raising or voting of any important, central issues. He was already weary and not up to the game.

He looked at Lord Sorval of Kintassus and could not keep a grimace of contempt from his face. Five and a half to five.

"Gentlemen of the cabal—"

"Come," Corvair interjected. "Vellen is yet likely to show. And these matters go beyond politics for the nonce."

"Indeed." Benataan's glance was chill. "I had no intent to raise 'political' issues. The Church, and its fate, are what we must discuss this eve."

Sorval snickered, and even Benataan favored him with an ill glance. The man was becoming an embarrassment, and an expensive one, at that. His habit was not easy to supply, curse the merchant traders.

"What is there to discuss?" Marek of Grimfaxos said uneasily. He ran his fingers through his hair; he, too, had had some difficulties in the past few days.

"After the destruction? If you can still ask, perhaps you are not qualified to be a member of the Karnar."

Marek did not respond.

Irritated, Lord Valens raised a hand. "Make your point, Benataan. At least bring it to motion. If the high priest is not to be present, you can spare the endless aggrandizement; it does not impress us." It was not a wise comment, but Dramathan only realized this halfway through the sentence; his condition must be worse than he'd thought. Still, better to finish than to leave words hanging useless in the air.

Benataan did not even appear to be ruffled.

"If you do not wish to remain, the choice is yours. But there are matters of urgency to discuss. We are not in the position to immediately restore the south wing, and word of its destruction has already taken to the streets.

"The Lesser Cabals are becoming unwieldy. I do not have to mention the difficulty with the Halloran Cabal. We cannot afford any more uncertainty from the capital. It will cost us too much." He frowned, and this was not contrived.

"Agreed." Marek said, nodding impatiently. "But it is difficult; the Lord of the Empire is not easily predicted, and I daresay he is outside of our combined ability to control." His lips turned up in a cat's smile. "Or do you still counsel a form of concerted aggression in light of the destruction?"

This elicited several smiles from the Karnari. Benataan's face alone remained severe.

"It was not well thought out," Lord Valens added mildly.

"It is in the past," was the curt reply. "And it is the future we are concerned with."

"Come, come, Benataan," Morden of Farenel said, his gaunt

cheeks dimpled by a lingering, malicious smile. "Vellen offers you the seat of the council should you choose to stand against our Lord." There was mostly amusement in the words, however, and no practical sting; Farenel was still in close alliance with Torvallen.

"Enough. I do not know that the seat will be Lord Vellen's to offer for much longer, and it is of this that I wish to speak."

How surprising, Lord Valens thought. He straightened himself up in his chair and a wave of nausea dimmed the room's lamps. Damn Vellen.

"The Lord of the Empire cannot be pleased with Lord Vellen's leadership of the seat of the Greater Cabal. There is no other explanation for the south wing. We cannot afford to antagonize him further—what would be next? The east? The temple? Our position is already too tenuous among the nobles—they know well that the edicts most recently given out do not come from our hand, or from our choice."

Silence greeted the words, but there were many nuances to it. Agreement. Fear. Boredom. Contempt. Only the first two held any hope for Torvallen's position.

"We do not know what occurred when the High Priest Vellen left Malakar."

"Members of the Greater Cabal were assassinated."

"Thank you, Sorval." His words were tight. "Please. Your silence." The pause that followed was heavy with significance. "But I have been able to uncover his destination."

Dramathan raised an eyebrow. "This would be news," he said softly. He himself had no sources that could be moved to divulge this information, if indeed they did have it.

"He journeyed in secrecy and swiftness, to Mordantari."

Mordantari.

The word hung in the middle of the table like an unwelcome beacon.

Marek met Dramathan's eyes with a slight raising of brow, which was returned in kind. Both men were cursing silently, but only one was in any position to reconsider his options.

If this is true, Vellen, Dramathan thought, *you will rue it. This is not peripheral information.* "You have proof, of course," he said mildly.

"Of course."

A number of comments came to mind, but he uttered none of them; he knew that Benataan did not lie.

Morden cleared his throat and leaned slightly forward. "This is news." Not, apparently, to him; not by his reaction. "Mordantari is the Lord's domain."

"Indeed. Vellen returned in seclusion. He answered no questions. I believe we can draw our own conclusions from this." He straightened out his shoulders and stood quite tall.

"I believe we will need some time to think on this," Dramathan said.

"What time?" Benataan's voice was cold. "A few hours, perhaps? Long enough for more reprisals to take place?"

"What would you have us do?" Morden again.

Tirvale of Wintare moved his large girth in his chair and cleared his throat. It was a long affair. "I believe that we are presented with only one option."

"And that?"

"Vote," he replied. His hands were covered by a sheen of sweat, but it was hardly likely to be nerves; he sweated often. "The evidence stands as too great a warning."

"Seconded," Morden said.

Benataan's smile was almost beatific. For the first time since commencing his speech, he took his seat.

"Come, come, Benataan. This is too great a matter to be rushed into." But Dramathan's words sounded hollow even to himself.

"It was not my motion."

Very quietly, Dramathan rose and left his seat. "I will not vote," he said quietly. He looked around the table. Quorum here was seven members. Benataan had ten now.

"Nor I," Marek said, rising also. Nine.

Corvair rose quietly and pushed his chair in. Eight.

"I'm afraid I too must decline." Telemach nevertheless gave a graceful bow. There were seven.

Benataan smiled softly.

As one, he and Dramathan turned to look at Jael of Tirassus. The man had not moved. His dark eyes looked steadfastly down at the sheen of the table, and his hands did not rise above his lap. He was the color of mourning; deathly white against the pitch black of his robes.

"Jael?"

"I—will not vote against High Priest Vellen," the man replied. His voice was strained. "But I will vote."

"Gentlemen." Benataan nodded. "We are sorry to see you

leave the Greater Cabal." He smiled maliciously. "But we have a quorum, and we *will* see the motion through."

The four men who had stood looked at each other. To sit now was too much of an indication of weakness, but each considered the option.

Dramathan's smile was brittle indeed. He made no move to resume his seat at the council table.

The doors swung open with a bang, and a pillar of fire came up through the ground, eating away at the wood in the table's center. Ash floated in the air, light specks of black dust.

Benataan's face lost its smile.

"Gentlemen." The leader of the Greater Cabal strode into the room. He had not dressed in formal attire, as had his rival, but the power of the flames that still crackled lent him all of the aura of majesty that he required.

"High Priest." Marek bowed.

"You have not yet taken your seats?"

"Indeed we had. But the meeting was almost . . . finished."

"I am sorry to have been delayed. There was a carriage accident." His eyes met Benataan's coldly. "And also, other business I had to attend to."

At this, he turned to look at Jael.

Jael could not have paled further, but his face seemed more of a marble relief than living flesh. He met the high priest's eyes.

"As council is not in session," Vellen nodded to the seated members, "I will take a few moments to speak of private house matters."

"That is not entirely appropriate," Benataan snapped. "And council *is* in session."

Vellen ignored him, still watching Jael's face. "Lord Damion wishes to pass a message on to Lord Tirassus."

"It can wait," the lord of Torvallen said, this time more forcibly. "There is the matter of your small trip to discuss further."

"The message is simple enough," Vellen continued. "He wishes Lord Tirassus to know that Lord Evannen of Tirassus has requested leave to study in House Damion's libraries; he imagines the stay should last no more than a week."

"Evannen is at House Damion?"

"As we speak, old friend."

Jael rose quietly from his chair. "Then I believe the vote

cannot take place this eve." The look that he sent to Benataan was anything but gracious; his eyes, even at Vellen's distance, were flashing red. "You do not have a quorum." The chair that he'd occupied scraped against the stone of the floor. The stone was smooth, but the chair screeched nonetheless.

"He's lying," Benataan said, his voice quite cold.

Jael paused briefly as the possibility was evaluated.

At another time, it might have amused Vellen to play this out and make a game of his ally's uncertainty. This eve was not that time.

"Am I?" he asked quietly. He slid his hand into his robes and drew it out again; his fingers were curled against something. "Lord Evannen requested that I give this to his father's keeping."

Jael stepped quickly forward, palm up.

Everyone in the room could see the glint of gold and platinum that Vellen placed into Jael's hand: the crest ring of the sole heir to Tirassus.

Only Jael could see that it had not been cleaned; brown specks of dried blood still nestled in the inverse relief of his house. His brows drew together, and his face took on its first color of the evening—a red that was almost purple.

"It is," Vellen said mildly, "as we found it. Evannen is resting."

"My thanks to Lord Damion," Jael replied.

Benataan rose again, his face steady and composed. He had taken a risk; he had lost. Somehow, information of his foray had filtered into the hands of his rival. Tirassus was now an active enemy, and not a passive one.

"Perhaps," he nodded to the Karnari that had remained seated, "we will allow this to be raised at our next meeting."

Vellen frowned. There was no hint of defeat in Lord Torvallen's voice. He looked around the room and noticed, for the first time, that Michaelas was missing.

He did, however, incline his head.

At that signal, the remaining members of the Greater Cabal rose, and following in the wake of Benataan, began to leave the chamber.

Vellen was left alone with those who had stood behind his position. It had been, judging from the looks on their faces and the way they comported themselves, a closely called thing.

"My son?"

"Injured," Vellen replied curtly. "Our doctors are with him, but they do not fear for his life."

"Then I thank you."

"Do more. Where is Michaelas?"

Jael shook his head.

"High Priest," Dramathan said, interrupting their conversation with force of will where strength of voice alone would not serve.

Vellen's face was set and grim.

"Perhaps there are other questions that might be better answered. Why did you venture into Mordantari?"

Long years of practice kept the shock off Vellen's face.

Dramathan of Valens wore a look that he seldom did; there was danger in it, and it was worse for the quietness with which it was shown.

Vellen had seconds to decide, but experience helped here, too. "I will not deny it, but its nature is secret."

Marek snorted.

"Let me say just this: There is more than one Servant among us, and if my plans—our plans—hold to their course, there will soon be *none*."

"We cannot fight—"

"I am not Benataan, to even suggest so suicidal a course." He let anger edge his words—it was genuine.

"Then what?"

"You will have to trust me; the fight is not between us and the Lord of the Empire, but between the Lord and another Servant. I aid the other; he has no interest in our Empire."

There was silence as each man pondered Vellen's words.

Then Dramathan nodded mildly. "You are speaking the truth." At his words, his eyes lost their red tinge, and his shoulders curled inward as if he were exhausted. "It is enough. For now. But be warned; this will be raised in the next council meeting, and you had better have a good reply; Benataan is not so incompetent as he once was."

Vellen knew it well.

chapter
sixteen

The dress was red, lighter in color than new blood, but just as rich and nearly as liquid. Great folds of silk caught the light as it fell to the ground well below Lady Amalayna's feet. The sheen of the cloth looked bright and polished, but that was illusion; it caught none of her reflection as she gazed down.

"Hold still, Lady," the head seamstress said, crossing her arms and standing far enough back to survey her handiwork.

Amalayna smiled brittlely, well aware that she hadn't moved anything but her chin. The seamstress spoke from years of habit and wasn't likely to change her tune. Although she wasn't a noble, she was a free tradesman, and her services were enough in demand that she didn't have to force her matronly personality into meek subservience.

It was just as well; at this time it would serve as more of an annoyance than anything else. The lady sighed heavily and this *did* move the fall of the dress.

"Please, Lady Amalayna. The shoulders here *must* hang correctly. Lucida—pin the left now."

Lucida was young, but her face and the older woman's had a common heritage. The other girl, small and quite fair, began to hand out pins from the strap she wore around her neck.

"Cut it long, just to be sure."

"Yes, Mother," Lucida replied. Hers was the meeker voice, but it was meek more because of the force of her mother's personality than because she was in the company of nobility.

"When will this be finished?" Amalayna asked. It was perhaps the fourth time she'd done so, as it was the only relevant thing she could say.

"The ceremony's what? Two weeks away?"

"Yes."

"Ten days. The black velvet for the sash should arrive in two."

Ten days. Amalayna looked up into the long oval mirror. She was high enough off the ground, balanced on a sturdy stool, that she could not see her own eyes.

Her father's health was failing, perhaps a little too rapidly. She cursed silently, which added a few lines to her already dour expression. On top of that, she had had word that Benataan of Torvallen had almost succeeded in his move to unseat the leader of the Greater Cabal.

At another time she might have quietly wished him success. But no unseated leader in the last eighty years had been spared the grace of the altars—and that was not the death that she envisioned for Lord Vellen.

Nor did she wish Benataan to be so unsuccessful that he lost his own seat. If her plan went awry, she wanted some danger to remain to Vellen after her death.

"Right. You can come down now, Lady."

Her hands lifted folds of silk as carefully as possible. Little silver pins glinted up at the edges of the newly imposed hem, and she avoided pulling at them.

"Will that be all?"

"Yes. We'll be back in three days for the next fitting. The major work of the dress should be finished by then, and the beading for the crest as well."

Pieces of the dress slowly fell away, to be caught in the arms of seamstresses that cared much more for its fate than she.

Dinner was a solitary affair. She ate in the dining hall, as had become her habit, but did so alone. No place had been set for her father. He was not feeling well, she had been told, and would dine in his quarters alone.

Slaves came and went, bearing silver dishes and crystal glasses to and from her side. They were not much company at all, and she was surprised to find that she missed her father.

She set her fork down and picked up her wine goblet, staring into its burgundy depths.

Has it come to this? she thought bitterly, lifting it slowly to her lips. *Am I grown so used to House Valens, that I miss even your company?* She drank some of the wine to dispel the dryness that suddenly took her throat. Crystal shivered between her lips.

She did not want him to die too soon, that was all. Should he pass away before the ceremony, she knew well that it would not take place. Lord Vellen would have nothing to gain, and all chance of her vengeance would be lost.

A ghost of a thought flickered by. Why was it that the corner of the eye could oft catch things that a fuller view missed? She shivered, and for a moment the years fell away. She was young again, and her parents were the only two people in the world who could perfectly grant all.

She had loved him, then. She had forgotten.

I acted too quickly; he will die too soon. That was it. But it was not all.

She set the goblet down and stared at the closed doors beyond the table. Her throat tightened further, and she rose, putting the glass aside.

The doors opened quietly as she made her way into the hall. One slave tended the lamps that ranged across the wall in their neat, precise order. His shadow was twisted and distorted as it crept up the wall opposite his back.

She shook her head and found the grand stairs, taking care to walk slowly and in a manner that befitted her station. No one must conceive of the burden that pressed too heavily upon her.

The hall of the upper level opened before her, and she followed it past her rooms before she was aware that they were gone.

The double doors of Lord Valens' personal rooms waited in silence as she approached. Two house guards flanked them, swords drawn and pointed up toward the ceiling. They did not bar her as she knocked gently.

The door swung open, and Matteus, the house physician, peered out.

She met his eyes, and any question she had died on her lips.

"Ah, Lady. I believe your father will see you."

Nodding, she entered and closed the doors firmly behind her. Her head touched the back of the doors a moment.

"Come. He's in bed, but he's resting well."

"Is he awake?"

"Yes. He's eaten as well."

She walked across the sitting room and entered the left door. Lord Dramathan of Valens sat up in bed, pillows propping his back into a semblance of normality. His face was a peculiar shade of green and gray, but his eyes were bright and open.

"Amalayna." He nodded, and she approached the bed. "Do you have news?"

"Some," she answered quietly. "Lord Michaelas did not preside at the Greater Cabal's meeting."

"Of that," her father said wryly, "I am well aware."

"No children of the house are missing, but Michaelas has not left the house proper for a week. I do not believe that he was forced to miss the meeting, but I also do not believe that he desired to vote against Lord Vellen. Yet if the choice comes to it, I would not count on him."

"Reasons?"

"None yet."

Her father nodded tiredly, and she drew closer still, as if pulled. "Father?"

"Yes." His smile was weak. "I am not well. It's age, I think." He shifted on the pillows. "And I do not know how easily I will be able to attend the next session of the cabal."

"There is another session?"

"Yes." His breathing was labored. "Within the week. But come; you yourself look rather pale."

She bit her lip and caught his hand. Both shook.

"Amalayna, stop this nonsense."

"Why?" she countered, as her eyes began to grow brilliant. "Who is there to see it?"

"Lord Valens," he answered quietly. "And he does not appreciate this sign of weakness from a foolish older daughter." But he did not speak with his usual force, and he did not draw his hand away. "What is it, child?"

"I—I don't want you to die."

At this, his eyes drew up in genuine surprise. "Then I believe you will have your wish. I have no intention of dying."

She nodded quietly, and the tears remained trapped in the prison of her near unblinking eyes.

"Go, Lady. The ceremonies are taking their toll, and you look as if you need the rest."

She nodded mutely and left the room before the physician could see her face. Her feet carried her a little too quickly back to her own chambers, and there she sought the comfort of what little remained of the night.

She drew her covers under her chin, and as the tears fell

freely, she prayed for the return of Laranth's voice and of her own convictions.

What have I done? Was I mad, Laranth?

The answer came back. No. No.

She did not want her father to die, but without his death, there would be no peace. At least she took bitter comfort in the fact that she would barely outlive him.

She dreamed that night, as she often did.

The dream had two faces, two sides; it did not always end the same way, but it always began with Laranth.

She would have, if she were lucky, a few minutes of the company that she had grown so dependent on, the warmth of a living partner who was both lover and friend, with all the meaning those words could convey, and much they were too slim for.

Then next, his death, or rather, the garish, open casket of the mourning. His face bore no marks, no scars. She would reach out to touch him, and her fingers would feel ice and pain.

This part was always the same. His eyelids would roll open over cavernous, empty sockets and his hands would reach up to grab her.

For your house's sake, I was slaughtered.

She struggled, then, caught in a grip that not even death could break, and her lips formed meaningless sounds of denial.

You will not take rites with the man who murdered me for the sake of the house that aided him.

She woke crying out in shame and fear, and the colors of the noon sun comforted her enough that she could find sleep again.

The dreams returned.

She wore red, that glorious silk skirt over crinoline and lace. Her hands were in red gloves, her feet in black shoes. The beading at her bodice was all House Valens, and of the most expensive crystal and jeweled work. Around her slim waist was an expanse of black velvet.

The colors of joining, of power, of joy.

She walked down the long aisles of the temple, seeing out of the corner of her eyes all of the houses arrayed in their full colors and regalia. Here and there a head would nod at her passing, but she was not so improper as to acknowledge it. Nor would her father, who walked solemnly, in gray and burgundy velvet, at her side. Their arms were locked, and she could not have freed hers had she wanted to. She did not.

At the floating altar, Lord Vellen waited, Lord Damion at his side. Vellen wore red and black, a more severe robe than her own flowing dress. Ah, yes; the symbols of his office.

She smiled, as she always did, and bowed her head demurely, waiting for the ceremony to start.

Her father bowed to Lord Damion. Their hands met in almost a flash of light.

Still she waited. Her mouth said words, but they were devoid of meaning. Her hands itched at her side.

And then came the moment that she had been waiting for—that of the final joining.

A Karnar in red robes, with his high, imposing shoulders, handed Lord Vellen the blackened blade. Lord Vellen accepted it in steady hands, bowing over it and whispering the ancient words of the Church and God.

Silence reigned in the pews as the edge of the blade cut evenly into his palm. Blood welled there and even trickled down to touch both his robe and the marble floor.

"Lady," he said quietly, and handed her the knife.

She took it. Her hands were shaking, but not with fear. This was the moment that she had waited for. She lifted the blade above her palm, and then turned suddenly to catch Lord Vellen unaware.

The point of the knife she drove home into his waiting, exposed heart. She had time to draw it above the cries that were already filling the temple.

Time to plant it up to the hilt in his throat.

His blood spurted down her hand, and for the first time since Laranth's death, she felt warmth.

She knew the Swords were already coming. She could hear the scrape of metal against metal as their feet pounded up the aisles.

With triumph, and with fear, she turned to face them.

The Bridge to the Beyond lay open and waiting as she began to impale herself upon their blades.

She woke with a start to the setting sun, as the distant slice of the blades lingered in her chest a moment more. This passed, and she felt again the warmth of flowing blood. The smile that touched her lips was grim indeed, but not without peace. This dream had kept her sane for what seemed an impossibly long time.

It was all that she was to have, in the end.

For the death that she wished to cause was not, in her mind, murder. It was justice and vengeance; it was peace. She had not made a habit, even in the Empire, of killing anyone directly, and her lack of experience was to show in the worst possible way.

Lord Valens did not wake in the evening.

Matteus sent for her. She had dressed slowly and had even taken the time to pour one small drink before the slave came to her door.

"Go," she said, the word quiet but firm. "I have no need for assistance this eve."

There was a silence on the other side of the door, but no sound of retreating steps. She rose in irritation, wondering what the problem was. Her breakfast had already been laid, and it was cooling.

The knock came again before she reached her door. "L-lady?"

"Yes?" The word was ice and flew out of the door as it was wrenched open by her hand.

The slave was one of the younger housekeepers. She did not recognize him and knew that he was not one chosen to serve the members of the house. He cringed openly, something that they would have known better than to do.

"Lord Matteus sent me. It's—he says it's very, very urgent."

She forgot her anger at this impudence and forgot both her breakfast and her drink. She forgot her composure and the rules of comportment that the nobility live by. Heart in her throat, she ran through the halls of House Valens as she had not done since she was a child.

The guards that stood at the door to her father's rooms barely held their positions; their anxiety was clear for any fool to read should he care to do so.

Worse still, the door to her father's personal quarters was ajar, and she could see Matteus, standing before the black fireplace, his hand over his eyes.

"Lady," he said, turning slowly as she entered. His eyes

were veined with a rich red network that spoke not of tears, but of too little sleep.

"My father?"

Those eyes closed.

"Matteus!"

"I am sorry, Lady. I did what I could—but this illness is beyond me. He did not respond to my care." He waved a hand in the direction of Lord Valens' bedchamber. "If you wish to see him, do so now. I have not yet called—"

"You're *sorry*?" Two quick steps brought her to him, and her hands were on the shoulders of his shirt and the aged flesh beneath before she could think.

He looked back at the wild-eyed woman before him. Although she wore the burgundy and the gray in the style of Lady Amalayna, he barely recognized her, so changed was her face.

Ah, well. Grief was something she had proven herself too weak to deal well with. Had he expected grace or poise here? He tried to shrug her grip off and felt the hardness of nails bite into his skin.

"Lady," he said, trying to shake off his weariness. "You do your house no good by this display."

"You're *sorry*?" she shouted again. He was the bigger man, but she succeeded in shaking him.

He gave her no answer, and she pushed him back, letting go at the last moment. He made no move to stop her as she threw the door to Lord Valens' chamber wide. A flurry of color followed as she rushed to the bedside, and Matteus quietly closed the door behind her.

As the door clicked at her back, the fury left. Her breath rattled the whole of her body as if it were a weak, thin frame caught in a tempest of storm and violence.

Dramathan, Lord Valens, lay in bed. His arms were crossed neatly over his chest. His hair had been brushed and coiffed into neat, straight strands. His eyes were closed, and a sweep of gray lash lit against white cheeks. Those cheeks were sunken and hollow, the lips beneath them a compressed line.

Even in death Lord Valens could be pressed to show no emotion to his children.

She was close enough to touch him, but held her hands at her side. What point was there, now? The dreams of the morning became just that—as hollow as any child's impossible wish. There was ice on her hand, and her lips were sealed by cold as well.

There would be no ceremony, no joining of houses. Vellen would offer her no knife and no pledge that she could turn so neatly against him.

All that she had accomplished was this: Her father was dead, too soon, and he would never know why.

Her legs would not carry her, would not even hold her, and she sank with rumpled grace to her knees until her face was a foot away from the dead man's.

Laranth, her father, and her plans had deserted her completely. In the silence she began to weep, and there was no thought or hope of an end to it.

The road into Malakar was not so heavily traveled as Corfaire had expected. He frowned and slowed his pace as he looked to the gate house. Six men stood there, but at this distance he could see that none of them were of the elite. No red marked the dark surcoats they wore.

"Corfaire?" Erin whispered, keeping her sight trained on the gates.

"I don't know." He kept the uneasiness out of his voice, but not out of his movements. "Still, there were rumors in Rennath of a change—perhaps this is it."

"Are the roads so seldom used here?"

"Not at this time of day."

The sun was up, but not yet at midmorning, and merchants at least should have clogged the gate, holding both papers and soured expressions at the length of time they had to wait with their goods.

Still he had seen no signs of unrest on the route here. Farmers still tended their fields, and none of those fields had been razed.

Behind them, Darin and Tiras walked quietly. Darin's hand was on the papers that would grant them safe passage through the gates; they crinkled sharply, and Corfaire bit back the order to leave them be. The boy was nervous enough as it was.

Tiras walked with Darin's staff, using it as a cane. Age had settled onto his frame, bending his shoulders and lending them a frailty that even Corfaire would not have guessed possible.

Erin was dressed as a traveler, not a guard, although her

sword still hung beneath the folds of the cloak that Hildy had lent her for just this purpose. Her hair was unbound and unbraided. She looked the very image of cool modesty and distance.

Straightening himself out, Corfaire approached the gates. A guard halted him, as was expected.

"Your business?"

"We come from Rennath," Corfaire replied, handing him the furled papers. "We've traded there and are returning with goods for the High City market."

The guard raised an eyebrow and looked at his traveling companions: a young woman, a young boy, and an old man. The two horses stood solidly behind, heavily laden with baggage.

"You traveled alone?"

The glitter of suspicion in the guard's eyes was inevitable.

Corfaire drew himself up to his full height, and his voice altered subtly. "We are not from the northwest; we have little need of heavy guard, and they cost much."

"Rennath." The guard read over the papers, the boredom never straying far from his face. "I guess you haven't heard."

Corfaire waited patiently, unwilling to give the guard the satisfaction of hearing a question asked. It was not much of a gamble; he knew well the general level of the gate guards and was not about to be humbled in any way by one.

If Swords had been present, he would have taken an entirely different tack. It was odd; the only time he had ever seen a gate manned by just guards was in the late evening, when very little traffic came by.

The guard grunted and handed the papers back. He began a walk around, looking at each of the travelers in turn, until he came to Erin's side.

Corfaire smiled the wolf's smile, and his hand was already at his sword hilt. "I should not, were I you." He almost hoped the soft words didn't carry.

They did. The guard's face paled, and he stepped back, recognizing in the cadence and tone of the words the nobility of blood that Corfaire's profile claimed.

"Lord," he murmured. "Your papers are in order. But the city's changed some since you've been last. Edict from the Lord of the Empire—although there's some who say the Church did it—says that normal business starts at dusk. Normal days start at sundown. Market's not open now, but you'll probably be able to wake an innkeeper." His eyes brightened a little. "If you're looking for a place to stay—"

"Thank you. I know the city well." He turned to Erin and bowed slightly. "Lady?"

She took the arm he offered almost gratefully, as it moved her farther away from the city guard.

"We are about to enter Malakar, the capital of the Empire." He paused and looked over his shoulder to see that Darin and Tiras were following. "Come on. Let's get to an inn; we can have lunch and find out what's been happening in the city."

His arm trembled as he said the last few words, and Erin looked furtively at his face.

With the exception of Tiras, they all had reasons, beyond the obvious, to fear this visit. Corfaire's past was here, and he had not yet done with it—nor it with him.

The Lady Amalayna was a noble of Veriloth, and she struggled to remember it as she sat, very still, in her father's sitting room. No slaves had been called, and no house guards either, although it was inevitable that the house guards would know of their lord's death. It was, after all, to his person that they had sworn their lives.

Her youngest sister, Maia, had come, and even now sat by her father's deathbed in the privacy of his closed bedchamber. She was not so young that she did not realize the need for secrecy, nor so foolish that she would allow her grief to show in public areas, and Amalayna had not seen fit to lecture her at this time.

But the rhythm of her quiet sobs could be heard even through the closed doors, and they distracted the acting head of the house. She glanced up at the doctor, who was resting with his eyes closed in the winged chair.

He knew, of course, and she had no choice but to trust him. Still, she would feel better if he might agree to be detained for the next few days.

"You look tired." Her voice was soft. "I took the liberty of having one of the guest rooms prepared."

An eyelid creaked open, and a faint, grim smile touched Matteus' cracked lips. His hand reached down, seeking and finding his drink. "When does Dorvannen return?" The words were too weary to achieve the casual effect they aimed for.

"Six days."

"For the rites?"

She laughed. She couldn't help it. "Even so."

"Perhaps, Lady, it is not I that needs rest." But he nodded, falling further into the chair. "It's been a difficult few days. I think I might take you up on the offer."

She relaxed. "I'll send for a slave to lead you there, then. Have you eaten?"

"Not much."

"Good. I've already arranged for a meal."

He rose quietly and gave her a little half bow. "Will you allow me to send a message to my daughter?"

"But of course. I wouldn't want her to worry." She, too, rose, and caught his free hand in hers. "Matteus, I'm sorry, but I've no choice."

"Sorry?" He shook his head. "Your father would have done no less. And I've been in this situation a number of times before. You see it as a physician in the High City." He chuckled wryly. "Besides, my own home has one slave and not nearly the array of comforts and services that House Valens will provide to a humble visitor. Why should I overburden my daughter when I can live at your expense?"

She hadn't given him leave to speak so freely, but didn't mind. He had good tact and wisdom, and she was grateful for both. She could not face another death today, especially if it were one that she would have to order.

Reaching out, she pulled a long cord and then walked him to the door. When the slave answered her call, she quietly gave directions to him. His bow to both her and the doctor was exact and precise. If she did not go mad in the next few days, it would be because of these perfect little details of normal life.

Only when the physician turned the far corner did she retreat into her father's sitting room. She had much to think on, and she did not flinch from doing so.

This morning had seen the ruin of her ill-made plans. With Dramathan of Valens dead, Lord Vellen had no reason to carry on with the rites; he had nothing to gain, and little to lose, for though Dorvannen was competent, he was not that high in the Church hierarchy. One day he might rise from the ranks of the Lesser Cabal to the heights of the Greater, but not soon enough.

She could hide her father's death for a few days at best, and if there were spies in the house, which she felt certain of, any measures she took would be crippled.

A deep breath filled her lungs, and she sat down, hard.

The Greater Cabal convened in two days. If she could keep word of her father's death from Lord Vellen and his allies, then perhaps Benataan of Torvallen would win the seat he coveted.

That would be a swift and sure guarantee of Lord Vellen's death—and the death would be less pleasant than the one she had planned to grant him.

But it would not be at her hands.

She gritted her teeth over the cry of frustration that she longed to make. It was not what she had wanted, but it would do. It would have to. Rising, she walked through the room to the door on the farthest right. She walked in it to her father's study, and took a seat at his desk. On it, a quill and inkstand stood. The seal and the wax were in the uppermost right drawer, and she found vellum there as well.

> *To Benataan, Lord Torvallen,*
>
> *A matter of import to us both has come to my attention, and I believe you will find it to your benefit to examine the information contained herein before you dispose of this document.*
>
> *I am well aware of the disagreement between yourself and Lord Vellen, and while I regret it, I find that I too have a matter that must be resolved with him, be it humble compared to your own.*
>
> *Dramathan, Lord Valens, will be unable to attend the convening of the Greater Cabal in two days hence. This matter is not known publicly, although I fear it cannot be concealed for long.*
>
> *He has given no proxy and no vote, if vote is to be taken. Please use this to your advantage.*
>
> *No reply is necessary.*
>
> *—Lady Amalayna of Valens*

Were there time, Amalayna would have started a form of written dialog and barter with Lord Torvallen. Indeed, she knew that she ran a risk in revealing as much as she did. But Benataan was likely to be a very busy man soon; he would not, she hoped, have the time to take advantage of a house that, for the moment, had no head.

She sealed the scroll and rose with it. Once again she pulled on a cord and made her way to the sitting room. When the slave came at her summons, she asked for a courier to be sent.

Richard came quickly.

"Lady." He bowed and held out one hand.

"Have this taken by route of Kelso. Tell him to pass it on twice. Use the courier that is often used by the merchant House Kallaxas. The letter is for the eyes of the addressee *only*. If he is not available immediately, the courier is to wait. If he is, no reply is necessary."

"Lady." He bowed again and was gone.

All that was left was to wait.

"I don't understand this." Corfaire hit the bell at the desk with his fist and glanced around at the almost-deserted lobby. The sitting room, with its ample fireplace, was completely empty, and beyond it, the dining tables were clean. No settings had been placed on them, and the chairs rested upon the table-tops.

"The edict," Erin said quietly. But even she felt uneasy. At midafternoon, Malakar looked like a city deserted by all life. Curtains were drawn along the various windows in the merchant quarter, and no wagons moved in the streets. Not even a single carriage had passed them by.

A door slammed open, and a man in a rumpled jacket came stumbling out. He squinted slightly at the light.

"Aye, what is it?"

Corfaire's hand stopped a hair's breadth from the bell. "We've come from Rennath, and we seek lodging and a meal."

"From Rennath?"

"Yes."

"Well then." The man got behind the desk and pulled out a heavy ledger. This he threw open and flattened under a heavy palm. "Haven't they had word?"

"Of the edict? No, obviously."

The innkeeper, or a substitute, as Corfaire was beginning to suspect, yawned loudly. "Right. How many rooms?"

"Three. Preferably in the same wing."

"Three. Right." The man's eyes narrowed, though whether it was from suspicion or sleepiness was hard to tell. "We don't have a dorm here; we've only got real rooms."

"I'm aware of that." Erin's fingers curled suddenly around his arm, and he forced a fixed smile onto his face.

"Good. How long will you be staying?"

"Probably a week. We have goods brought to Rennath from the north, and our stay will depend on the speed at which we sell them."

"Week? That'll be, what, twenty-eight silver crowns. We want payment in advance."

"Half."

"All of it."

"Half."

The innkeeper yawned again.

"Or we can go to another inn. There are enough in Malakar." Erin's fingers reminded him to level his voice. He had been a slave here, yes—but he had always served as personal guard of House Sentamos, and he was used to respect from the merely free.

"Half then," the innkeeper said grudgingly. He held out a palm, and Corfaire dropped the money into it. He made a point of counting each coin. The innkeeper returned the favor by counting each key, but somehow managed to take longer even though he only had to go to three.

"Won't be a meal until dusk," he muttered as he turned to leave the desk. "And it's extra."

"Of course. We're sorry to have troubled your sleep."

"I suppose it doesn't matter." The large man said, not even bothering to look over his shoulder as he headed out the door.

The problem with sarcasm, Corfaire reflected as he lifted the packs, was that it required an aware wit to appreciate it.

"Uh, Corfaire?"

"What?"

Darin shrank back at the force of the word. "You forgot about our horses."

Corfaire's fist hit the desk squarely—but it didn't touch the bell. "The stables are at the side. I'll see to the horses myself." It was a wise decision, although he didn't particularly have any desire to visit the stable. He was not sure he could face the sullen innkeeper again without losing his temper thoroughly—and even if the Lady weren't with him, it was something that he wished to avoid in this city.

* * *

The walls to her room seemed faceless and gray. Even the tapestries and the life-size paintings that ranged from floor to ceiling did nothing to dispel this effect.

She sat by the curtained windows, the surface of a drink trembling in her listless hand. Dawn had already driven back the darkness without. Within, it touched nothing.

She had not even tried to sleep. The bed, with its sheets unturned, waited in the other room. The wild, proud face of her ancestress stared down in heady contempt, not even bothering to demand an explanation for failure. Looking beyond it, she could see gray stone, unfinished and undecorated. All that was needed were bars, and the illusion would be complete.

How long had it been? Five hours, six?

Her temples pulsed with a beat not unlike the grand clock in the great hall.

And then the knock came at the door. She was almost across the room before it sounded again, quietly.

No lady of House Valens would throw the doors open so quickly their crash would echo in the halls, but she had much on her mind. Amber liquid sloshed around the rim of her crystal glass, finding refuge on the dark carpet below.

Richard stood on the other side of the door. His face was quite pale.

"Lady." He bowed formally and lifted his hands.

There, seal unbroken, was the letter that she had penned.

"The messenger was to wait for Benataan to receive the letter," she said quietly, taking the scroll in an unsteady hand.

He could not have known all his words would mean, but he hesitated for a moment and looked away from her pale, strained face. "Lady, he would have had long to wait. Andrellus is Lord Torvallen now." He took a deep breath and waited for her to speak. When she did not, he continued. If he could not deliver this message in time of crisis, he could at least provide her with information.

"Benataan, former Lord Torvallen, passed away last evening, a scant few hours before the dawn."

"How—how did you gain this information?"

"The entire house cannot speak of anything else, with the exception of its lords and lady. Benataan was taken by a Demon of the Dark Heart. There is enough of a body left for ceremonies."

She did not have the strength to dismiss him, but he left anyway, his tread on the carpet light and even.

The door swung shut as she walked to her sitting room and the curtained windows.

Benataan of Torvallen was dead.

And with him, her last hope of peace.

The trap of her room closed around her like a coffin, and she stared, sightless, into the quiet shadows in front of her glimmering eyes.

chapter
seventeen

"Have you tried yet, Lady?"

"Hello, Corfaire." Erin's voice was a whisper against the cloudy glass of her window. The curtains, such as they were, were drawn wide. Dying rays of sunlight hit the floor behind her feet. Her face looked whole and healthy, but Corfaire knew it was due to the pink the sun cast off in its last spin for the evening. Her fingers, small and slim, curled around the pocked wooden sill.

It was disturbing to see her look so vulnerable. The power that she sometimes wore was invisible and untouchable now. He cleared his throat.

"Lady?"

"Yes." She turned from the window and the empty streets below. "Yes, I have."

"You found nothing, then."

"Not what I was searching for, no."

"Are you hungry?"

She was, but there wasn't any food that she felt like eating. The day had gone past as she stood at this window, unfurling the smallest strand of her power and sending it out. It should have worked. She should have been able to sense the Gifting from much farther away.

Was I mistaken?

The map lay on the bed, a pale ivory sheet against the dark blankets. She had looked at it time and time again, comparing it to the newer one she had taken from Dagothrin's vast library. The Gifting had to be here, locked from sight in the maze of silent buildings.

But she couldn't sense it at all.

265

Her power had only seen red, the color of the Church and its working. Most of it was clustered in one central area of the city itself, and she had taken care not to disturb it or examine it too closely.

She bowed her head. "Do you know Malakar well?"

Corfaire had answered this question many times, and each time the answer had been the same. But he did not grow frustrated or impatient at the repetition she forced from his lips.

"Well enough, Lady. I grew up here."

She walked over to her map and placed her finger firmly down in the center of the city. "What is here?"

"Did you not see it as we walked up the Westway?"

"One tall building, or perhaps two, behind shorter ones. Nobility?"

"In a manner of speaking. The Heart of the Church rests there. It is a full fifth the size of the city proper. Just east of the Upper City—we're in it now—on the far side of the temple complex, is the High City. The estates of the houses are found there, provided the house is politically powerful enough to claim land in Malakar."

"We're in the Upper City?" There was a faint hint of disbelief in her voice, and she turned to glance out of the windows once more. The street below was narrow, and garbage rested against most of the tall, old buildings.

"Yes. It's more commonly referred to as the merchant quarter. If you find it distasteful, be glad that you aren't in the Northern City. The docks on the Torvallen are there." He picked up a chair and brought it to her, but she sat as if the action were an afterthought.

"We will have to go nearer to the temple, then."

"Are you afraid of it?"

"I don't have a choice. They can find me, Corfaire, if they're looking. The priests, I mean."

He knew who she meant. "How close?"

"Pardon?"

"How close do we have to be?"

"I don't know yet." She seemed to shrink further, and as the sky darkened, so did the circles under her eyes.

"We have to go to the High City market to dispose of our wares. It's just off the Eastway, and it passes quite close to the temple walls." He walked over to the door. "But you need sleep, Lady. Let me talk with the others and arrange our evening. I will return in a few hours."

She nodded, but her eyes were drawn to the window, not the closing door.

There was so much power in the temple. Thousands of priests might account for it. Thousands—or one Servant of the Dark Heart.

If he were here . . . She could not use her power so close to his. It would be just as wise to walk up to the gates along the Westway and demand an audience. She would be found for certain.

"Second of the Sundered." Vellen bowed low, the red of his robes whispering against the stone floor. He held the bow for a long time.

Both knew why.

"High Priest." Sargoth turned quietly from the altar of the temple proper, drawing his shadow with him.

"I have news, Lord."

The use of the title did not amuse Sargoth, but the words that Vellen presented made him stand more tall.

"What news?"

"She has arrived."

"What have you done?" The sibilance was lost to the sharpness of the words.

"Nothing," was Vellen's neutral reply. He stood, gaining his full height, the torches glimmering off the back of his red collar. "I did not wish to alarm her, or otherwise notify her of our presence."

"She is well aware of it. The spell that would hide *my* presence from her blood would build ten of your little cities."

There was only so much arrogance that Lord Vellen could take, and he bridled, although his expression did not change at all. "She has made no move to flee."

"No, it is not I that she has come for."

"Is she aware that it is your presence she feels?"

"Probably not. She might think me the First of the Sundered."

There was no hiding the fleeting frown that transformed Vellen's lips. But it did not dally long on his face. Indeed, it was difficult to refrain from smiling broadly. Benataan of Torvallen was a corpse, fodder now for the worms and the carrion insects that dwelt below ground. None of the Greater Cabal could now question his right to the seat. The manner of the former Lord Torvallen's death had made certain of it. Of course, the killing had been attributed to the wrong Servant. What of it?

"Have her watched, High Priest. Have her followed should she choose to leave her current dwelling. But it is your responsibility to ensure that she is not detained or harmed by the patrols of the city, without making this known to her. She is not alone?"

"No. She is with an old man, a soldier of some sort, and a young boy." His eyes widened and then narrowed as he looked into the darkness beyond Sargoth's shoulder. "A young boy . . ."

"*None* of them are to be detained without my leave."

"But it is only the woman who interests you."

"After my business with her is finished, you may do as you please. Do not think otherwise." He did not utter any threat, as he did not feel the need.

"What would you have me do, then?"

"Wait." Sargoth raised his arms in a high arch over his head. Blood-power trailed down them in a bright, liquid stream, and he began to fade even as it grew. "I will be a day, perhaps two; I have my own matters that must be attended to."

There was no one to pray to. The Dark Heart granted no favors to one who was not a priest, and Amalayna had foresworn that option many, many years ago. She was cold but sent for no slaves; the ashes that rested in the fireplace were not yet to be disturbed.

She was not drunk; she had not touched a drop since receiving her courier's word. But she had not eaten, either, and both sleep and rest had eluded her.

The door to her closet was half-open, and the shadows revealed a glimmer of color, red and gold. Burgundy and gray were too drab to stand apart from the darkness.

She rose and walked quietly to the door, swinging it full open. It creaked while she supported her weight against its hinges. Happiness had never had such distinct colors before. Her fingers curled around red silk and gold thread, and she drew the full skirt of this one old dress to her face.

She wanted to go home.

Her hands shook as she realized that she had nothing to offer her young son now, and nothing to offer his grandfather.

Maybe Dorvannen will let me go home.

She could not be certain of it. Of all of the children of House Valens, she knew best the political workings of Malakar—and her brother would need the knowledge she had for many months to come.

And after?

It was strange to think of it: She would live, and so would her enemy.

I want to go home.

The dress fell back into the closet like a secret.

Shaking, she walked to the door of her bedchamber and pulled the heavy cord. She could almost imagine she heard the distant ringing of a bell as it pealed into stillness while she waited.

Lord Tentaris was working quietly in the study. His desk was a neat mess of papers that had to be signed and sealed before he could attend to the diversion of funds. The trade war with House Wintare had slowed in the past month, which was good. The mercenaries that he had been forced to hire to guard his route against bandit predations had eaten heavily into the profits those routes generated.

But even so occupied, he heard the quiet knock at his door. Perhaps he rose too quickly to answer it, although he expected no callers. He was tired of working in this dim light and closed space.

She stood in the door like a ghost, and for a moment she was one—her feet hardly seemed to touch the floor, and her eyes looked beyond him at a distant tragedy that had been sealed within them, as if at a moment of death.

"Amalayna?"

The word seemed to cut strings that held her, and she sagged against the door frame, pressing her cheek against cold brass. Beyond her, Lord Tentaris saw two slaves at their early cleaning duties. He frowned, but instead of ordering them away, stepped back himself.

"Come."

"I'll not be long, Lord Tentaris. I just—"

"Amalayna." He was disturbed. Words had seldom had much power over her, but just the sound of her name seemed to ease her now. "I gave you leave to come here as you pleased." Not, perhaps, the wisest of decisions, but it had been granted, and he would not stay that grant.

"Would you like something to drink?"

"No." The word was soft. "I've been drinking overmuch lately."

"Then at least sit." He held out an arm, and after a minute hesitation, she took it, allowing herself to be led. "Do you have news?"

"Dorvannen is Lord Valens now." The words sounded like a litany too often repeated. She collapsed into the chair and buried her face into shaking hands.

Although he felt the words like a tremor, he was experienced enough to wait for her to speak, although the moon edged across the sky as he did so.

When she looked up, her eyes were ringed red, the power of emotion, not blood. "I—I don't know what to tell my son."

"Lady," he answered softly, "you may tell your son whatever truth you deem fit. He will listen because it is you, and he will not be disappointed. Let me send for him. He is sleeping at the moment."

Kindness did what loss could not.

Lady Amalayna of Valens began to cry. Only her eyes showed it at first, but soon her whole body shook. Some part of her mind must have known it was foolish, but the intellect did not reign here. She was in Tentaris, and it was the only home that she had really known.

Lord Tentaris watched from a distance for a few moments, and then he moved closer to her, extending one hand until it rested firmly on her shoulder.

She was a ghost again. The Lady Amalayna that House Tentaris had so valued had passed with the death of his son. Laranth would have been pained to know that, inadvertently, he had destroyed her, and his father did what he could to offer comfort.

Sargoth was curious. This was not unusual. What was was the uneasiness that moved just beneath the surface of his thoughts. It had been a simple matter to use his Lord's power to travel to where the First stayed, but now that he had arrived, he was almost at a loss.

Before him lay the doors to the castle that Stefanos had built in Mordantari. Behind him, the gates rose, cutting the moon into even, straight slices. There were no slaves at all, no mortals toiling in darkness or running errands.

Indeed, the castle seemed to be . . . sleeping.

He drifted toward it, and both his curiosity and his uneasiness grew. He had little pride to speak of, and certainly none compared to the rest of his brethren, so he hadn't the option of lying to himself. It was not because he had met one defeat here that he traveled cautiously.

He did not know what to expect.

It was difficult, and the moon trailed across the sky in a gentle arc as he stood in shadow.

Stefanos, you surprise me. I thought that the Sundered held no mystery. Very slowly he began to move toward the castle's main doors. *Why did you destroy so much of the temple?* As a display of power, he could understand it—but the First had not remained to reap the fruits of his demonstration. He had come—fled, even—to Mordantari. Sargoth was not completely certain that he was aware of the rubble that he left in his wake.

If not for the interference of his Lord, the Second would have approached this question with a cold glee—and he would have asked the First of the Sundered all the questions that he desired answers of.

Who knew? If not for the Dark Heart, he might even be enlightened. He passed through the doors without bothering to open them, although it was a spurious use of power.

He felt the rumble of power that suddenly surged to life in the castle. The First of the Sundered was aware of his intrusion.

This, at least, was not surprising. Sargoth straightened and began to walk down the long halls, following a power that stone, wood, and distance could not conceal from his immortal sight.

At last he came to the study. The door was already ajar.

"First among us." His voice was a sibilant whisper.

Stefanos sat in a human chair, behind a large, human desk. Human wisdom, ephemeral and superficial, lay bound in numerous tomes that stretched from wall to wall. His shadow was likewise bound under a mortal countenance.

"Sargoth." A little flicker of red glowed at the center of brown eyes, and the fingers on the desk froze as if anchored by claws. They were.

"You are far from Malakar."

"By whose standards?" The smile on his face was a pale glimmer in the poorly lit room. "Are you becoming bound by mortal time? I will tell you, Sargoth, that it is a dangerous gamble."

Although he was unique among the Sundered, Sargoth was part of them still, and he bridled at the implicit suggestion that anything mortal was a danger.

"There is no danger to me, my Lord," he replied. "I have no more interest in the mortals than they have in the cows that they eat." He drew his shadow tight as he continued to speak. "Only one of us has ever felt their pull."

Eyes flickered again, but the red there burned more brightly. "More than one, surely."

"The others, only because they hoped it would lend them an advantage against you."

Stefanos shrugged and turned away. "Why have you come? These are my lands, Sargoth. You are not welcome in them." The words were a dismissal, but the tone behind them wavered, and Sargoth chose to risk remaining.

"I have come to give you fair warning."

"I am not interested in warning," was the unexpected reply. He rose, finally, but instead of facing the Second, he turned to look out the window. Stars and moonlight paled beneath the glow of the Bright Heart's blood.

"But—but what of the revolution? What of the fall of Illan and the army that is gathering for Verdann?"

For a moment the guise that Stefanos wore flickered, and there were two open shadows standing in the room. His hands shivered in the light, and his fingers grew longer and paler.

This, Sargoth understood.

"Indeed," Stefanos said, and the shadow was gone. "What of it?"

The Servants of the Twin Hearts did not sleep, and any dreams that they partook of were human. Yet tonight, for the first time in his long existence, Sargoth understood what a nightmare was. He had seen, and prepared for, every possibility, but he had not prepared for the unthinkable.

A low, quiet sound filled the room, and it took Sargoth a moment to place it: the sound of human chuckling.

"Sargoth, Sargoth—you are unusually transparent. It amuses

me. I think I will even listen now to the words you have brought this far."

He turned suddenly, and shadow filled the room, erupting in a dark fury. Red, glowing lines ran through it like fine wire, and the Second of the Sundered was caught in its net before he could lift a finger. Gone was human seeming, and the torches on the walls were a faint hiss and tinkle in the distance. This shadow, this Servant, was First among all of the Sundered, and if he had changed since the dawn of their awareness, Sargoth had no time to discern the subtleties of it.

"And I will listen to the reasons for it. I have had *enough* of your games!" Each word was harsh and solid; each syllable, formed by a precision of power, mouth, and tongue, caused the fine, tight web to shudder.

Sargoth grimaced and threw up his own magic, but it was not enough. He had used his power too much over the last few human months.

But at least he felt none of the curiosity that had so disturbed him. Stefanos' flight had been a ruse to lull him, nothing more.

He cursed himself, and Stefanos, in painful silence. He had not thought he would fight for survival this eve.

Fear was an effective antidote to weariness.

From the moment that Erin left her dingy room, she could feel her heart pressing against the thinness of skin with its insistent beat. The walls of her throat seemed to collapse and cling together in dryness. Every step that she took felt significant and irrevocable, and her feet trembled as if they were on the verge of a scaffold.

Here, in Malakar, the last test came. She could not call upon the power of God to aid her. The incident in Coranth had shown her clearly that the Bright Heart was dimmed. Even were it not so, she could not invoke Him in this place.

She had only herself, and her companions, to rely upon. And she had proved often that failure was no stranger to her.

Fear of it grew as she walked down the hall to where Darin, Tiras, and Corfaire were waiting. Corfaire wore a pack, and his sword besides, but neither Darin nor Tiras was visibly armed.

The staff of Culverne lay in the bowels of their room at Tiras' insistence. To carry it, even when its nature was known to so few, was too great a risk. The High City was close upon the temple's outer wall.

She stopped ten feet from her companions and looked at them carefully. What she saw was not really suspicious: A well-dressed, older man in the black that had ever been Empire fashion; a well-dressed young boy who looked uncomfortable in the high collar and stiff cuffs of his shirt, and a suitably attired guard who would have looked at home in the service of any imperial house.

She herself wore, instead of stiff jerkin, a long, full-skirted dress. It had two slits, lost to the folds of falling red cloth, that would make a hasty retreat more convenient—but she had no sword, and the single dagger that she carried at her waist seemed a jeweled accoutrement and not a weapon.

Hildy had made certain that the four would not look so out of place as solitary traders in the High City market.

"Erin?"

She shook herself and forced a smile to adhere to her lips. "Sorry. Just looking."

"Are you ready to leave, Lady?"

"Yes."

"Good. I have a lamp that might be lit should we need it, but the innkeeper—who is a good deal less surly in the black of night—assures me that the way to the market is well lit. And guarded." The last two words evoked a shadowed grimace. He stepped forward, offering his arm.

"Take it, Erin," Tiras said quietly, as she stared down. "And come. The market opened for business almost an hour ago."

The streets were crowded, but the presence of people only reminded Erin more of the desert, where life bided its time in the sun to emerge in full force at dusk. Several lamps lit the wide street that Corfaire called the Westway, but most of them seemed new and at odds with the buildings behind them.

The walk through the crowd reminded Erin that she hated the city—everyone was too tall and too tightly packed together. All the usual courtesies prevailed, but if someone nearly sent her flying, his brisk apologies were lost to the surrounding chatter.

Darin walked at her side, and he, too, seemed ill at ease in the crowds. Only Tiras and Corfaire followed the rhythms of motion dictated by the city as if they were born to it; the older man looked bored, and the younger slightly irritable.

But it all fell away as she walked along the Westway. Walls rose above the heads of the people to her left; they were tall, and at their fullest height adorned with closely planted iron spikes. As if the temple were a small fortress within the larger city, guards roamed freely across the wall.

No, not guards. Swords.

The wall was well lit, and as one black-clad man passed beneath a heavy torch, light glinted off his surcoat. Red light—a thin, broken band.

"This is where the Westway becomes the Eastway." Corfaire's words were loud. He spoke them only an inch from her ear.

She nodded quietly, but continued to watch the wall. Beyond it, blurred by night and lack of focus, rose a single, thick tower. This she had seen entering the city.

He looked at her, raising only an eyebrow in question, and she shook her head involuntarily.

"It's very crowded, Lady," he mouthed.

She still shook her head. It was too close.

His shrug was answer enough, and she almost felt ashamed. How had she thought she would arrive in Malakar prepared for any conflict?

If Erin had had any hopes that the crowds would thin as they walked, she lost it. The High City market had its own set of gates, guarded by men who were much better armored and armed than those that stood watch at the brink of the city. They were not normal city guards, but they were not Swords either, and they wore breastplates instead of the usual chain. There were four men in all, and they stood quite tall as they watched the crowd with impassive eyes.

But they were not so intimidating as the guards at the outer gates had been. They made no move to stop the flow of traffic into the market.

"This way." Corfaire pulled her neatly between two people. She mumbled an apology as her elbow connected lightly with somebody's chest. If the apology was acknowledged at all, the words were lost to the shouts of merchants hawking a variety of wares. In this respect, the High City market was no different from any other that she had been to.

The crowds thinned after they had gone thirty feet, and

Corfaire's arm was no longer a harness that pulled her along. She had time both to catch her breath and to look around at the others who had come to market.

She was underdressed. Full skirts of velvet brushed by beneath fitted bodices of lace and silk; pale skin, colored by powders and scented with a mixture of perfume and sweat, seemed the order of the evening. There were wigs, although they were not common, and one or two parties had come arrayed with slaves and palanquins.

These slaves did not have the hungry, hunted look of many that she had met in her life. They were dressed in house colors, and the clothing, while much more simple than that the nobility wore, was nonetheless costly and well made.

"House Stentos," Corfaire whispered.

She blushed. She was not often caught staring.

"Lady Eilia." His expression was neutral as he too looked carefully at the splash of deep blue and brilliant green the woman wore. "She's known for both the amount of money she has and the speed with which she spends it. Our wares will most certainly fall into her hands within a two-week." He shrugged, adjusting the straps on either of his shoulders. "If we manage to make it to the gem master's ahead of her."

There was an etiquette to market travel, and Erin was pulled to the sides of stalls every few feet to allow some large party passage.

"If the group wears house crests or colors, they have priority," Corfaire explained. "They also tend to have guards that enforce it." His smile was odd and quirky, but it was also completely mirthless.

Erin noticed that his hand did not stray from his sword, and although he left it bonded, she would not have been surprised to hear the scrape of steel against steel while her attention was elsewhere. For that reason, she stopped watching the moving human mass.

Corfaire noticed the expression on her face.

"Yes," he said, shortly. "I'm not comfortable here." His eyes skittered across the surface of the crowd, and he nodded. "Come. We've a way to go yet."

She followed, her grip on his arm now as tight as his on hers. The crowds up ahead seemed to be thinning. She took a deep breath and moved quickly between two rather large people.

Then she stopped.

"Lady?" Corfaire's eyes were narrowed. "Is there a problem?"

She could not speak. Her eyes were locked upon the sculpture that stood at the market's center. Behind her, she heard a sharp intake of breath, and recognized Darin's voice.

Corfaire cursed quietly. The statue had held little meaning for him, and it was so much a part of the market's landscape that he had not thought to mention it.

The Lady of Mercy looked down upon them, her face almost beatific in its white perfection. A smile that was not entirely human was lit upon her lips, and her arms swept across the air in a gesture of welcome.

"Even here."

Corfaire barely recognized his Lady's voice.

"In every market of every capital in the Empire." In the darkness, he could see a small brass bowl and a wreath of dying flowers. "Sometimes the slaves are allowed to adorn the idol—particularly if the house that owns them is displeased with the Church." He grimaced. "I imagine that enough of them are at the moment."

His glance jumped between the statue and Erin, and although both stood immobile, no one would have recognized the one in the other. He relaxed, but only marginally.

"Lady." His voice was soft. "We attract too much attention by standing here. Later, if you like—"

She shook her head. "No. Come on." But her gaze lingered backward on that unearthly countenance. She saw, not herself, but the Lady of Elliath in full glory.

It—it is almost finished with.

The gem master's stall could hardly be called that, even by one with a sour imagination. No wood and canvas would do to announce the value of the wares that this man sold. He had, instead, two tall columns of stone, a roof of slate, and a sign that obviously took much work to maintain. It was inlaid with gold. Three or four people had stopped in front of the stall, but several slaves were in attendance on both the north and south sides.

Corfaire stood back and removed the pack from his shoulders. He seemed to stand straighter for lack of the weight, and

Erin wondered, for the first time, what the pack contained. Jewels, yes—but how many had Hildy sent with them?

One well-dressed man looked over his shoulder in mild curiosity. The state of Erin's dress dispelled it, and he returned his attention to the wares beneath glass that had first caught his eyes. The grimace he gave at the sight of them standing in line was so impersonal it was hard to be offended. Or, Erin amended, as she saw Corfaire's jaw tighten, it was hard for a stranger to the houses to be offended. She caught his arm and shook her head very slightly. His face relaxed. His arm did not.

Erin did not mind the wait. Here, in front of what were obviously expensive goods even for the High City nobles, there was little traffic. For the first time since entering the market, she felt she had room to move and breathe. Darin stood to her left, and Tiras was a shadow at her back, but these two she did not mind in close quarters. Her eyes wandered no further than them, and she hardly looked at the slaves at all—they were both a reminder and a distant accusation.

"I think a thousand crowns is a fair deal, Lady Mistria. You will not find better workmanship anywhere in the Empire."

A thousand crowns. Erin's brows rose as the words drifted back.

"A thousand crowns? It is pretty, Waldreth, but it is merely a trinket. Surely you ask too much. The market in Sivari is not so dear."

"The mines of Erentil are not the equal of those to the northwest," was the terse reply. "Only the unknowledgeable feel that the lesser price for poorer gemstones is the better deal." There was the decided clunk of heavy glass. "*My* gems come from a dealer in Rennath who is not disposed to the Sivari stock."

A better introduction would not come again in the course of bargaining, and it looked likely that Lady Mistria, in her mauve and green house sash, was not going to close the deal she had embarked upon.

Corfaire stepped neatly between her and the lord who was gazing through the glass. He pulled out a letter from his inner jacket pocket and waved it to catch the merchant's attention.

"Master Waldreth?"

Master Waldreth's balding head bobbed up and down in a slight acknowledgment of his name. He held out one large, stubby hand, caught the letter, and pulled it toward his chest.

A pair of heavy, wired glasses was then perched upon the bridge of a wide nose, and he stared down at the words on the paper as if they made less sense than the wares in his case. His round eyes narrowed, and then widened. With a deft little flip of the hand, he reoriented the paper so that the words were right-side up.

"Master Nostrum?" he asked, and extended a hand. "You're earlier than I expected, but that's all to the best. What have you brought?"

Corfaire removed a glove and returned the jeweler's grip firmly. "I'm not the gemsman you are," he said as his hand was released, "but Hildy is rather good at what she does. She's given me a list of prices for each of the items sent, and I'm afraid there are strict guidelines I'm forced to follow."

"Was I expecting something different?" Waldreth sighed. "At least I don't have to deal with the old vulture herself."

"No. Malakar isn't to her liking."

Master Waldreth spit cleanly to one side, which evoked a little snort from the lord at the case, who was listening as intently as one can when one is pretending that all proceedings are beneath one. "Vanelon." The word was a curse.

Corfaire smiled. "The same. But we don't expect problems from that quarter for some time."

"What's that?"

"Never mind. Vanelon, after all, is not of the High City, regardless of its pretensions."

"Well then, bring the pack and come inside." He stopped and squinted into the darkness. "These people with you?"

"Yes."

"Fine then. Bring them along." He ruffled through his pockets, pulled out a brass key, and set about locking his cases. A sign came out from under the counter and was placed down at an odd angle.

Erin corrected it before she followed Corfaire's lead.

The negotiations that followed in the long narrow room at the back of the shop were not of interest to Erin or Darin. Tiras, on the other hand, joined Corfaire and Waldreth at the table, and after a few interruptions on his part, Master Waldreth pulled out an extra eyeglass and shoved it into Tiras' hands.

Things were spirited, and debate replaced conversation as

Erin and Darin began to drift away, looking at the tools and benches in the shop itself. Here and there, unfinished works lay beside intricate drawings and odd bits of metal. Erin had never seen the inside of a jeweler's shop before, and she marveled as much at the process involved as she had at the cost of what was produced.

None of the three at the table seemed to notice, and another hour passed before the proceedings wound down. Gold was exchanged, and some sort of note, so Corfaire's pack did not end up lighter than it had been when he'd arrived.

Master Waldreth, on the other hand, looked quite pleased with himself.

"I'm just on for tea if I can find the cursed pot," he said cheerily. "Would you care to join me?"

"Not this evening, I'm afraid. We've other business to attend to before we leave the city." Corfaire stretched his shoulders as he stood. "How do you get used to this infernal darkness?"

"Same as anybody does. Doesn't do to question the Lord of the Empire. Not even if you're noble, and a priest to boot." He lowered his voice a little. "Have you heard the rumors in the market?"

"Some." Corfaire shrugged. "Which one are you talking about?"

"The second of the Greater Cabal."

"That one I'd missed. What news?"

"Taken. By the Lord of the Empire on a nightwalk." Waldreth shook his head. "Seems he'd done something to argue against all these dictates about the night hours. It's enough of a lesson to give to any of us below."

"It is that." Corfaire looked at Erin; she was frozen by a bench. "Lady?"

"Yes?"

"We leave now."

Her nod was terse. He walked over to where she stood and offered her his arm. The strength of her grip came as no surprise. Very slowly, he walked to the swinging door. "Shall we return to the inn?"

Any answer she had to give died on her lips.

As the door started to swing, it was yanked, hard, from the outside.

Corfaire and Erin stopped short as they stared down the

points of four drawn blades. They did not move. The swords were too close for it, and only one of them was armed.

But Corfaire looked up to see house guards. They wore the orange, yellow, and black of House Sentamos.

"Well, well, well," the foremost of the guards said quietly. "I think we've found a runaway slave."

chapter
eighteen

"What is going on here?"

Corfaire's eyes did not move from where they rested. He met the eyes of a tall, wide-chested man with a scar that ran the length of his left cheek partially hidden by a thick beard. It was Yarvele, blessed with the signature of Corfaire's personal fighting style in House Sentamos.

"I see you finally made your rank." Corfaire's voice was quiet, and not even a hint of fear made itself known above the contempt he put into those words.

Yarvele's smile made it plain that he had no intention of dignifying a slave with a response.

"What is going on here?" Master Waldreth forced his way to the front of the door and stopped his bulk short of impalement. He squinted at the glint of lamplight on steel, and then his frown deepened.

"Sentamos?"

"Indeed, Master Waldreth. We are sorry to trouble you, and will endeavor to be out of your way as quickly as possible." He pushed his sword gently forward until the tip made an indentation in Corfaire's plain surcoat. "Move forward slowly."

Corfaire released Erin's arm and did as ordered.

"I would hate to have to bring back only a body, but the price for it is almost as high." The sword pushed further home, but it hadn't the strength to cut.

Erin watched quietly. Her fingers skirted the edge of her sleeves as she crossed her arms slowly. She had only a dagger.

Behind her, she heard the movement of black velvet and knew that Tiras was also preparing for trouble. Still she remained motionless, almost paralyzed. Trouble was the one thing that she could not afford in Malakar. The house guards seemed intent on Corfaire; he was their quarry and their target.

He had served well as both guide and guard. He had brought them to Malakar unharmed, seen them through the gates, and even pointed out where the temple was safest to approach. She owed him loyalty.

But she owed others much more. He was just one man, no matter how well she knew him, if she knew him at all. How much claim did one man have?

If even one of the house guards had threatened her, the choice would be made; she would have trouble, whether she wished it or no, and she could stand by her companion. For once, they showed no interest in anyone but Corfaire. And Corfaire, knowing her position, did not so much as glance back as he walked out of the doorway.

The end justifies the means.

Telvar's words, rusty and quiet, came back to her. They had been said coolly, but their effect did not engender icy resolve. They burned.

Even here, with everything at stake, Erin found that she did not have the strength to be more than the person she had become. She drew a breath.

"The slave is mine." She made her voice sharp, haughty, and cool. Years of listening to the prattle of the nobles had at least given her this ability.

Five sets of eyes stared at her. A loud curse against the Church in the middle of a service would have had no less an effect.

"What House Sentamos could not keep, I have claimed." She stepped out of the door and moved forward with a surety she did not feel. The clean, sharp steel of drawn swords was more clear to her sight than the men who held them.

"Garbage." It was Yarvele who spoke.

"Those are the laws of the Empire," was her icy answer. "Should Lord Sentamos wish to regain what he lost, he might make an offer of purchase. Until that time, the slave is mine." Her words had been true in the Empire that had existed four centuries ago; she prayed they were still true now. She had never missed her sword so much.

"You wear no house colors."

"I bear no brand," she countered smoothly, "and I have sworn none of my life to another's keeping." Her eyes pointedly looked at the crest across his surcoat. "If your lord is indeed here, I would speak with him. If he is not, you might wish to avoid embarrassing him by dealing with the market guard." She turned to Corfaire. "Come."

"Hold." A new voice said, and Erin's heart nearly stopped its quickened beat.

Yarvele immediately bowed, as did his comrades, and the downward motion gave Erin a clear view of a man dressed in oranges, yellows, and blacks. He was older than she by at least twenty years, perhaps more. It was hard to judge by his face, for a scar cut across the forehead and left cheek, twisting the corner of his left eye into a downward squint.

Corfaire's harsh breath told her more than she needed to know, and she used the momentary silence to shore herself up. This was the worst thing that could happen, but it had, and she had no choice but to deal with it as best she could.

"Lord Sentamos?"

The man's eyes burned with flecks of red as her words drew his gaze from Corfaire. There was no madness in him, but the anger that was there was so intense it would be easy to mistake him for a reckless fool.

Nothing in Erin's life had been easy; she made no mistake now.

"I am." He bowed, but the bow was awkward, and Erin realized that at least one leg was partially crippled. "It appears that you have recovered a thing which was once in my keeping. I am grateful for it." He straightened out, approaching his full height with a grace that belied his old injury.

The guards were no longer at any loss. Their lord spoke for them, and Erin knew that while the one law, such as it was, was on her side, Lord Sentamos had the greater strength—and this was the unspoken law on his.

Without her sword, she didn't have a hope of robbing him of his advantage—there were four fully armed men here, and Corfaire would be given no opportunity to draw his weapon. Tiras might help—she was certain he knew all that had transpired—but if he felled these guards, and Lord Sentamos chose to call in the market unit, they would all be guilty of the minor infraction of murder.

It would be worth the risk, if she thought there was a chance of carrying it through quickly.

"Have you an offer?" Her voice was quiet.

"Offer?" He raised an eyebrow, which distorted his face further. "Yes. You may keep your life. After all, there are laws associated with aiding an escaped slave, and each is less pleasant than those associated with keeping one." His face lost its exaggerated politeness. "Take him."

"I don't think so, Lord Sentamos." The voice was new, although the person that uttered the words was obscured to Erin's sight. Swords being drawn underlined the man's meaning.

Erin frowned. Something in the disdainful tone was uncomfortably familiar.

Yarvele glanced at his lord, and the older man lifted a hand slightly. The guards moved to one side, to give their lord a clearer view.

And Erin saw three men in the brilliant reds and golds of yet another imperial house. Two carried swords and wore fine-mesh chain beneath long surcoats. One of them was a giant who stood nearly a head above the entire crowd. He wore a helm, but the faceplate was turned up, and no one could mistake the expression on his face for anything but danger. The other man who stood beside him was less impressive, but he held his blade with a surety that spoke of years of experience.

The third man was actually quite short: He carried no sword, and his dress was both elaborate and fine. His jacket was clean, rich velvet, and the ruffles that protruded beneath it, numerous to the point of absurdity, were nonetheless the work of the finest of seamstresses. He carried himself with the indolent arrogance that only assured power knows.

Erin didn't know whether to cry, scream, or laugh, so all three sounds compromised and came out in an audible choke—which was silence itself compared to the sudden noise behind her. She knew all three of these men very well.

King Renar of Marantine stood slightly behind his personal guard: Gerald of the royal guard, and Cospatric of the Happy Carp.

"Oh, Amelia. *There* you are. I should have known I'd find you here." Renar sniffed disdainfully and brought one heavily ringed hand to rest on his hip. "What *is* all this fuss about?" He stepped forward, barely deigning to notice the house guards. "You aren't going to lose one of our slaves, are you?"

"No, indeed," Erin replied stiffly. "Hello, Gerald. Hello, Cospatric."

"Ma'am." Gerald nodded curtly. Cospatric's reply was non-vocal, and Erin could only hope that everyone but she missed it. He winked.

"Good. Lord Sentamos, do you have some business with my house member?"

The lord raised a hand to his chin and studied Renar carefully—only a little less so than he did Gerald. "Perhaps I might. Which house do you come from?"

"Dark Heart, don't you recognize the colors? A man of your station? I must admit, I'm surprised." And slightly offended, to judge by the expression of outrage that had already turned his cheeks pink.

"I recognize the colors quite well. Tentaris." Each word fell more curtly than the one it followed. "I do not, however, recognize you."

Renar sniffed. "Gerald, do be good and fetch the slave. Be careful with his pack."

There was a moment's stillness before Gerald complied, and another moment before the house guards received Lord Sentamos' unamiable nod and moved aside.

"You are?"

"Reggis of Tentaris. I hold the house's eastern estates."

"I was not aware that Tentaris had any eastern estates."

Renar's chest rose. "Well, Lord Sentamos, it seems you aren't overly aware, but I hardly see that that constitutes a problem."

"You carry papers?"

"*Pardon?*" The drop of the jaw that emphasized the word was followed by a quick snap. "I imagine *my* papers are as much in order as *yours.*" He shook his head. "Amelia, dear, do come here. Oh yes, and bring Peter and Jardonis with you."

Erin carefully threaded her way around the statues the House Sentamos guards had become. She looked once over her shoulder to see that Tiras and Darin had followed.

"Very well, Lord Reggis. You own property which I would be interested in purchasing. Perhaps we might come to an accommodation."

"The price," Erin said softly, before Renar could begin again, "would be very high. This particular slave has been well trained at arms and is less costly to maintain than regular guards would be."

"Your price?" was the even reply.

"At this time, we are not interested in selling him."

"Oh now come, Amelia dearest. Surely we could just listen to what Lord Sentamos would be willing to offer?"

"Indeed, that would be prudent." Lord Sentamos stepped forward. "Ten thousand crowns."

Renar was taken with a sudden fit of coughing, and Erin slid her arm extremely firmly around his shoulder. She looked coolly at Lord Sentamos.

"We will consider your offer carefully," she said, raising her voice more than she would have liked so she could at least be heard over Renar's choking. "But for this eve, we have business elsewhere that we must attend to."

"And where might that be?"

"Elsewhere."

The answer was too quick and too sharp, and Erin nearly bit her lip seconds after she'd said it.

"Perhaps, Lord and Lady, I *will* see your papers."

She looked at Renar, who shook his head very shortly.

"What's the trouble here?"

Yet another voice entered the tense tableau. Erin swiveled her head to the side and froze. She felt Renar's fingers bite solidly into her arm; they gave her the support her knees refused to.

Arrayed just in front of the jeweler's stall were eight armed and armored men. They carried swords that were readied for trouble, and the visors of their helms were down.

But their surcoats were no ordinary market wear; they were solidly black, except for the broken circle that glittered at their chests and the red thread that embroidered their hems.

She had used none of her power since she entered the market, none at all, in fact, since she'd left the inn.

"Let me handle this," Renar whispered. The sound reached her ears alone. He opened his mouth to speak.

"Is there a problem here?" The Sword who had first spoken said. That he usually did not have to repeat himself was evident in the tone of his voice.

"There is some question as to the identity of this man." Lord Sentamos' voice was smooth and slightly malicious. "I was in the process of asking to see his papers."

The Sword's gaze swiveled to Renar. His eyes could hardly be seen in the dim light, but everyone knew where they were aimed. "I see."

Erin tensed further. No sword. No Heart-cursed sword.

"Is there a reason for the request? He bears Tentaris' crest."

"I am familiar with House Tentaris and its two branches. I do not recognize this man at all."

The Sword shrugged. "It happens."

"I do not believe he is of Tentaris."

"That is a serious accusation."

"Be that as it may, it is still true." He stepped forward, limp pronounced.

The Sword was silent a moment, then he nodded. "Where are you staying?"

"At an inn for the moment, sir, but it hardly matters. You can't possibly give credence to—"

"Can't I?" The Sword thrust out a mailed hand. "Papers, please."

"I'm hardly a common peasant; do you think I carry these things with me to satisfy the whim of rather rude nobles? I've never been so insulted—"

"Silence!"

"Oh, I'm terribly sorry, were you trying to say something?"

Erin cringed. But she'd seen Renar in action before and knew that there was still some small chance that he survived his flowery stupidity.

Not a good one, though. The Sword stepped forward and pushed her to one side. She stumbled back, and another set of arms righted her.

"I'm-going-to-kill-him-if-the-Sword-doesn't." Tiras was also capable of a whisper that went only inches from his lips.

"Please—do you have *any* idea of what this jacket cost?"

There was a small shriek as Renar was lifted, without difficulty, off the ground. "Shut up."

"You only had to ask."

His eyes rolled, and Erin was certain she heard the rattle of teeth.

"Enough of this! If you're Tentaris, there's a sure way to prove it. Halison, Morete!"

Two of the Swords moved into position on either side of the beleaguered Renar.

"Take him and make sure he stays quiet!" He turned to look at Erin, Tiras, Corfaire, and Darin. "You're with him?"

"Yes, sir."

"Follow."

"Uh, my good man, do you mind telling me where?"

An elbow was planted into Renar's soft stomach, and he folded.

"Tentaris, of course."

Almost as one, the Swords formed up. They marched in order. Erin and her companions fell somewhere in the center of the group, and not by their own volition.

Gerald and Cospatric sheathed their swords and took up step in the back rank. The difference in their training showed, for where Gerald's step was crisp and even, naturally falling into the beat of the Swords, Cospatric's was more obviously wary and individual.

Behind them, Lord Sentamos returned to his litter. But his orders were clearly heard even above the din of the market and the grinding step of well-heeled boot.

"To House Tentaris, quickly!"

Lady Amalayna of Valens sat quietly in the darkened window seat that overlooked the garden's glowing lamps. Pale light had been trapped in carefully blown glass, and even from this distance she could make out the delicate form of an eagle with a heart of fire.

Lord Parimon of Tentaris was snuggled quietly in her arms. He was not a small child, and she had never been in the habit of carrying him for any length of time, but she found the ache of her arms a comfort.

The wet nurse had come and gone, and he had fallen asleep shortly after.

Her lips brushed his forehead before her eyes sought the garden again. No other house could be seen, and she almost imagined she was on a private island with only her son for company.

Lord Tentaris had been very kind, and that brought an ache of a different sort. He had no daughters, and his wife had died early, two months after the childbirth from which she had never fully recovered. Perhaps, when her brother became lord of Valens, she might petition to once again return here and support her son and his grandfather as she was able.

She thought of asking, but remembered that Lord Tentaris was out on business in the merchant quarters. It was a good thing. She knew what his answer would be, and she was not certain she could face it yet. She would have to soon; she had stayed here for the day, and House Valens was suffering for her absence. Duty demanded her return to its halls and its politics.

She sighed and gingerly shifted her position. Parimon murmured, but his eyes remained closed. His breath was a soft, delicate sound; in sleep as even as a heartbeat. Not even a rustle of curtain disturbed it, and Amalayna listened intently. Were she never to hear another sound but this, she thought she might be content.

And it was not her fate to be content.

"Lady Amalayna! Lady?" Knock. Bang. *Bang.* "Lady?"

She rose swiftly, recognizing the voice as that of the door slave.

"Enter." Her own voice was loud; it had to be, to be heard over the knocking. Parimon stirred, and his fists flailed at the air, catching strands of her hair.

The door swung open, and the elderly slave hesitated at the edge of the carpet. He fell to the ground immediately, and his knees made a distinctly unpleasant sound.

"Lady."

"Yes?"

"There are people to see the lord."

"He is not here at the moment."

"Yes, Lady." The slave swallowed. "But I think they will see you instead, if you will speak with them."

"Who are 'they'?"

"Swords, Lady."

Amalayna's jaw snapped shut, and her grip tightened. It was enough to wake Parimon and to start him wailing. "No, Pari. I have to go downstairs for a moment." He couldn't understand, of course; all he really heard was the tenor of her voice, and it offered no comfort.

She walked to his cradle and set him down as gently as she could. His crying became louder as the distance between them grew.

Swords. Here.

"Why have they come?" Her voice was casual and calm as she walked to where the slave waited. Stiff fingers straightened out the wrinkles in her skirt and sleeves. At her nod, the slave rose.

"They've escorted someone who claims to be an eastern cousin to the house."

"Pardon?"

The slave swallowed again.

"Speak freely and do so quickly."

"Lady." He bowed. "They've come with an old friend of—of Lord Laranth."

Curiosity grew as fear receded. They had not come for her, then. They did not know. "Old friend?"

"Yes, Lady. He's—he's wearing house colors and the crest. Calls himself Lord Reggis."

"Reggis? I don't believe I know the name."

"No, Lady. Neither do the Swords."

"Then we'd best go down and quickly. The Swords have enough power to wait poorly."

She smoothed the last wrinkle from her brow as she left the room. Reggis? An eastern cousin? Impossible. When she and Laranth had pledged their vow and joined their houses, she had met all of his kin. What friend of Laranth's could possibly be so bold—or so stupid—to masquerade as such?

She closed the door on the cries of her child and quickly followed the slave to the front doors. From the top of the grand staircase, she could see eight Swords in the hall. Mingled among them were seven people, and even though the front vestibule was large, it looked quite crowded.

An odd smile lit on her lips as she stopped at the third stair from the bottom.

"Ah."

The captain of the Sword unit looked up. His bow was neither deep nor held for long, but it was enough.

"Lord Tentaris is absent at the moment," Amalayna said coolly.

"Yes, Lady." If he noticed the burgundy and gray that she wore, he forebore to comment on it. "But our business does not necessarily need his attention. I believe that you were once associated with House Tentaris, and for some years."

She nodded.

"Captain?"

"What?"

"There's somebody at the door."

The captain's frown was deep, but the annoyance in it had nothing to do with surprise. Amalayna guessed that he had expected some sort of interruption. "Clear a path for the slave, then."

The man so referred to took a breath and began to weave his

way through the gathered crowd without even the slightest hesitation. Even before his hand reached the door, he had assumed his proper position, and the angle of his chin and shoulders was enough to please the woman who had once been lady of the house.

"We've come to see Lord Tentaris."

"I'm afraid that the lord is not available for interviews at the moment."

"Then we would be pleased to wait."

The old man bowed rigidly, and the depth of it told Amalayna that she was dealing with a house guard. She could barely make out the orange, yellow, and black the guard wore.

"Please leave your slaves outside." He stepped back, almost ran into a Sword, and somehow managed to retain his composure as six more people entered the vestibule. There were four house guards, one attendant, and a man who walked with an odd gait.

Amalayna took two steps backward and up so she could clearly see all those assembled. Her eyes lingered longest on Lord Sentamos; he was obviously not in a pleasant mood.

She forgot weariness then and forgot failure for long enough to use the skills she had honed in the political sphere of the Empire.

Sentamos was angry, and his gaze was almost entirely reserved for an uncrested guard. That guard was nervous, but there was anger in him as well; only his companions seemed to be free of it. The old man was difficult to read—which meant he was dangerous, experienced, or both. The young boy and the young woman, both in nondescript clothing, were frightened, although at least the woman was careful enough to keep it off her face.

The two guards who had the audacity to bear Tentaris crests were stiff and ready for trouble. They seemed quite used to the job they had taken and obviously had been called upon more than once to protect their counterfeit lord.

And Lord "Reggis" himself . . .

Her smile deepened. Here he was, once again the very heart of trouble.

"Reggis." Her voice was almost velvet.

"Ah, Lady Amalayna!" He started to walk forward and was intercepted quickly by two of the Swords. He looked disdainfully up his nose—down would have been impossible, given the disparity in their heights—at one of these Swords.

"My dear, you wouldn't *believe* the abuse I've been subject to tonight. Why, just look at what they've done—" The rest of the sentence was lost to yet another elbow.

Her frown was very real. "Captain, I see no need for this. What trouble is Lord Reggis in?"

"Lady Amalayna."

"Lord Sentamos?"

"You—you don't recognize this—this buffoon? Surely Tentaris cannot possibly claim one such as this?"

"I am not of Tentaris at present," was her calm reply, "but I do know the house and its lines. Reggis is perhaps not the ideal example of nobility"—Lord Sentamos' expression twisted his face terribly—"but he is on the eastern flank of the Empire, not in the capital. Has he managed to offer you an offense?"

"*I* offer *him* an offense? Do you know that this man demanded to see my *papers*?"

"Reggis." Now her voice held a note of warning. She didn't actually expect him to heed it.

"Lady, if you are willing to authenticate this—this lord's claim, our business here is done." The captain of the Swords nodded briefly, and Renar landed hard, and not exactly quietly, on his feet. "We would appreciate it if you did not bring this matter to the attention of Lord Tentaris."

"I will not," was the slow reply. She turned to Lord Sentamos. "Do you have a claim to register?"

She had never seen a house leader so near apoplexy.

"No, Lady, I do not believe he does." That it was the Sword who answered spoke volumes. "Lord Sentamos?"

Sentamos did not have the grace to reply. He shook his head and transferred his glare to Lord Reggis. Without a word, he nodded to his guards, and his attendant aided him out the front door.

The Swords were quick to follow, and the hall once again took on its proper, lofty dimensions.

Amalayna took the last five steps and reached the floor, brushing her feet gently against the long carpet.

"Well then," she said quietly, looking at no one but the fake lord, "you seem to be in trouble again, Renardos. What on earth have you stolen this time?"

The only thing that surprised Erin more was Renar's reaction. His smile was a mixture of the sly and the childlike as he gestured.

"Just the type of thing that Laranth has always been interested in."

"Laranth?"

"Well, yes, you know Laranth—he's your bond-mate."

Erin wasn't close enough to kick him, but it didn't stop her from trying. She had never seen the lady before, but the way she had said the name spoke of a loss that was not nearly distant enough.

Red, wide eyes stared out like a colored window from a white wall; slim, soft hands tightened around the stairs' railing.

Erin waited for tears that would not fall.

"Laranth was assassinated." Her voice quavered; her body did not. The corners of her lips turned up in a tremulous smile. "But we—we can talk of that later. Lord Tentaris is not in the house at the moment, but I can't imagine he'll be happy to see what you're wearing. Come, my chambers are upstairs. You'll be able to change there."

"I think I need it." Renar looked down at the wrinkled mess of his shirt; the bottom edge of it hung crookedly over his sash. His expression was perfect, and very much in character for the personality he had chosen to wear—but the eyes that met Amalayna's were hard and distant.

"Who?"

Amalayna looked up from her chair. She was sitting beside her son's cradle, and her hand rocked it gently, automatically. The question did not take her by surprise, but the single word that contained it did: Renardos had never been one for brevity.

Or for an anger such as the one she sensed. No, he had been all arms and words and pretty posture. There were times in the past that she had wondered if he knew the meaning of the word *quiet*.

She continued to rock the cradle, although she knew that he was aware of her attention. After a moment, she spoke, but her voice was quiet, a lull for her sleeping son.

"Who are your companions, Renardos?"

"My companions?" He shrugged. "These two are personal guards; that one—" His gesture indicated a very quiet Corfaire. "—is a former slave of House Sentamos."

Although most slaves were beneath her notice, she put aside long years of habit to look more fully upon him. "Sentamos?" He certainly looked the part of a guard; his armor showed wear, but his sword was obviously very much a part of his dress. A slave? Something tugged at the strings of her memory, and she followed it until her eyes widened. Lord Sentamos had not been born crippled; he would not have survived his youth.

"Are you the one who—"

"Yes, Lady."

The quiet malice in those two words made her freeze for an instant. She wondered how one slave could have been so dangerous, so treacherous. The thought almost kept her from realizing that Renardos had made no mention of the other three companions that stood so very still.

"The others?"

"Traveling companions." He shrugged and pursed his lips. Then, as if remembering himself, he added, "People that I met on the road, Lady. You know the sort; I believe they had business in the High City market."

It did not fool Amalayna.

"Renardos." She rose then, leaving her son altogether. "You are changed since last we met. I begin to wonder if I ever really knew you."

Her eyes were dark, and darkly ringed, as she walked across the room to stand before him. She had the advantage of height—Renardos had ever been sensitive about this—and she used it to look down her nose.

He met her eyes.

"Who?" he asked again, his voice as soft as hers.

"Two." The word almost surprised her, coming as it did from her lips. She squared her shoulders, knowing that she would tell him much of the rest. "One is dead. The other—the other is beyond my reach."

"No names, Lady?"

"Of the dead, I will not speak. What difference would it make?" Her eyes were a shattered plea, and she closed her lids on them briefly. Her shoulders curled inward, and her face paled further until even Erin felt pity for this lady of the Empire.

All in the room were silent; if they breathed at all, it could not be heard. They watched Lady Amalayna as her hands fell down to clutch the folds of her skirt and shake there, half-hidden. She seemed on the verge of something; her lips opened slowly, and she swallowed.

Erin stepped forward, ignoring Renar's sudden frown. Her boots left gentle indentations in the carpet until they came to rest a few inches from Amalayna.

"Lady?" If it was weakness that made her hold out her hands, she was hardly aware of it. "The name?"

Amalayna turned to face Erin, her face almost blank. They stood watching each other, with a wariness that spoke of fear or anticipation.

"Lord Vellen."

With two words, Lady Amalayna had crossed the threshold.

Sargoth was ever curious. Even now, surrounded by a purity of red-fire that he had not seen in millennia, that did not change. As his shadow wall parted, and fine, sharp power cut into him, he wondered if pain was universal, if all of his victims who died had felt a tenth of this visceral agony.

He knew the sound of immortal pain, but still it was new to hear it from his own lips. His eyes caught the thrash of claws at night air, and he knew them for his own. The surge of power that flowed through his hands was automatically called—and the pain ebbed, if it did not pass entirely.

Above everything, he heard the First of the Sundered—the voice of thunder over the storm.

"What game do you play, *Second*? I *will* have your answer!"

The net closed again, this time sprouting little teeth around all of its intricate edges. It stopped less than an inch short of cutting its victim into shards of darkness.

"Stefanos—"

No other word escaped him. Had he wished to prevaricate, he knew the time for it had passed. He felt pain again, but this time it was not new enough to catch his attention. He put the force of his remaining power into a cry that touched even the mortal world—and beyond.

Sargoth.

Loooorrrrd. Like a human sigh, the word escaped him, touching the bounds of the Dark Heart. Immediately he felt a surge of power at the core of his shadow, enough to push the net away, if not to break it.

The pain was gone. At leisure he would examine it. Stefanos remained.

For a moment, the net pressed inward, and Sargoth was impressed anew at the power the First could wield when he wished it. And then it was gone.

They stood as if nothing had passed between them, and after a moment, Stefanos turned away to look at the light outside of the window.

"I should have known." His voice was soft. "You belong to your Lord."

"We all do."

"Do we, Sargoth?" Inexplicably, the anger was once again gone, and Sargoth's curiosity was a bitter ache. "You have called, and he has answered. The game is still with him." A shadowy arm was raised. "Go, Sargoth. I will no longer play."

"And the Empire?"

"I do not care for it." He shrugged. "Keep it or destroy it as you wish; give it to the Church and its priests."

He spoke only the truth, and Sargoth felt each word as a physical blow. This, then, was the end of the Dark Heart's plan; all of the power and planning, the deception and humiliation of working with mortals, had come to this pass. He did not understand why. Every detail should have been perfect.

The Dark Heart would not be pleased. If anything had the power to frighten Sargoth, it was this.

He had to think, and quickly, had to pull some partial gain from the ruins of his plan. His voice went out to the darkness like a whisper. It carried his uncertainty, but that could not be avoided.

Sargoth . . .

Lord? Yes; I will come.

The Second of the Sundered raised his head, and the glitter of his eyes was reflected in the window that Stefanos stared through. Long after he had faded, their afterimage marked the air—a symbol of confusion, frustration, and fear.

chapter
nineteen

Renar was weary when Amalayna at length dismissed them. He had always held her in high esteem—inasmuch as one could any noble of an imperial house. She had been so cool and competent. Her political struggles had been completely veiled, and more potent for it. To be truthful, she was a beautiful woman, if one liked ice and distance. She was haughty and as perfect as a flawless gem—with just that hard clarity and those sharp edges.

Or she had been.

Laranth's death had shaken him greatly, much more than he cared to admit. He grimaced, knowing his reaction had been admission enough. Even grieving, Amalayna was keen and perceptive. Nothing, he was sure, had escaped her notice.

A house slave with an almost deplorable lack of curiosity led the way to a set of large guest rooms that they had been given permission to use for a short while. Renar was happy with the terse offer. It gave him a chance to get out of his gaudy costume.

He stood aside at the door, entangled with the bother of thought, and let everyone pass him.

What were they going to do now? House Sentamos, while not Church bound, was extremely important; to offend it at this point was the act of fools. On the other hand, to be in Malakar at all was easily as foolish—but Lord Sentamos would have them followed no matter where they chose to bide. Judging by the man's expression, being tailed was the least of his intentions.

I knew, Renar thought, with just a hint of angry hubris, *that I should have just come with them.*

He turned sharply on his heel and caught the swinging door, sliding quietly into the room.

It was an interesting room, especially seen as it was: A flurry of color—red, gold, and deep browns—passed by his eyes as he sailed through the air. The ceiling and the floor seemed to be doing a happy tailspin that ended with the sumptuous paneling of a wall. He barely had time to grunt at the impact before hands picked him up by the back of the collar.

Lace and frill might be delicate; the double-lined velvet of the house jacket was not. Seams cut into his underarms as he was yanked to his feet and spun round.

"What-in-the-hells-are-you-doing-here!?"

It was hard to remember, especially when the contents of his skull were being shaken with extreme force, a time when he had seen Tiras look quite so angry. He considered ordering Tiras to stop, but thought the better of it. His teeth might take out his tongue before half a word escaped.

"Your pardon, Master Tiras," Gerald began gently. He didn't bother to finish the sentence as Tiras' baleful glare hit his face. It was enough of a distraction for Renar, who grabbed his former master's hands and wrenched himself loose.

The young king looked around the room. Erin met his gaze, but only briefly, before finding something of interest on the bedside table. Darin, who had had his share of Tiras' rather sharp tongue, suddenly started looking at his hands as if they were new and surprising.

Cospatric shrugged and grinned.

If there was anything that Renar hated, it was the I-told-you-so expression that Cospatric wore.

"Well," Renar said, straightening out his collar, "I rather thought I was saving your lives."

This got about the reaction that Renar expected—although he was still a little taken aback to see just how livid Tiras could look.

"You *fool!*" Tiras drew closer, and Renar retreated, hitting the wall with his back. "Don't you have any idea of what a king *is*?"

Renar showed a little wisdom: He kept his mouth shut.

"Do you have any idea what kind of risk you take with Marantine? What if you're killed here? There is no proper line of succession! Do you think Marantine, so recently liberated, will easily survive a struggle for power?"

"I left Lorrence in charge."

"Lorrence *is not the king!*"

"He may as well be—he runs almost everything. I won't be missed, Tiras."

"Lady?"

Erin turned almost unwillingly. Her slight shoulders looked smaller than ever as they shrugged. "The lines never mixed with normal politics."

Tiras snorted. "You know I'm right."

She shrugged again and sighed. "Yes."

"Erin!"

"You probably should have broken both of his legs before we left." She smiled halfheartedly at Renar.

"I've half a mind to do it now."

"Tiras, for the Bright Heart's sake! She's just joking!" He slid sharply to the side and rolled low—both movements in less than five seconds.

"Renar, you have a duty now that supersedes all other plans. Marantine's heart is your life."

"Then we'd both appreciate it if you didn't end it on the spot." Renar's cheeks were flushed, but it was hard to tell whether the stain was from shame or anger. Erin thought both.

Tiras opened his mouth to speak, but Renar's tongue was faster.

"I'm here, and we don't have much time in Malakar. We have to find what Erin is searching for and quickly. Sentamos is no house to be trifled with; if our throats aren't slit while we sleep it will be no small miracle.

"And we can't stay here. Lord Laranth is dead, and his father was never the biggest of my admirers." He shrugged. "I *know* Malakar better than any of you, save perhaps that one—" he pointed at Corfaire. "I can lead you almost anywhere." He paused and drew himself up to his full height. His hand flew out dramatically. "I *know* the floor plans of the temple."

Erin, Darin, and Corfaire all gaped.

Tiras, ever the master, was not impressed. "And what makes you think that that knowledge is useful?"

"Erin's face, for one."

Tiras looked back with an economy of movement that indicated a simmering temper, not an explosive one. "Lady?"

She closed her eyes, sagging a little. "I'm sorry. It's the only place I haven't really checked. What I search for is there, or the power that conceals it from me is there. We have to—to at least get closer."

"And you want him to lead?"

She shrank further, although it hardly seemed possible. "I know you're right, Tiras, but more than Marantine is at stake."

"You aren't saying all, Lady."

"No." She drew a deep breath and turned her gaze to Corfaire, who had remained silent throughout. "But if Renar leads us in, Corfaire can leave the city."

"Leave?" Seldom did Corfaire's face express emotion so clearly. "Lady, I cannot leave. You've accepted my oath; I am life-sworn."

"You can't stay in the temple when we—if we find what I'm looking for."

"Why?"

"It will kill you."

He was silent as he weighed her answer, knowing it for truth. Erin had not yet lied, at least not successfully, and she spoke with the quiet force of conviction.

"Why?" The word was soft, almost gentle.

"It is the Light of the Bright Heart—and it knows only one enemy. The blood that you carry. The Light will destroy it."

He turned and let his head drop. His eyes slid over the sheath of his sword and came to rest on his right forearm. There, beneath layers of linen and leather, lay the mark that had robbed his life of true power.

"Oh Lady, Lady," he said, and Erin recognized the tenor of his chuckle, "there truly is no mercy in you. Do you still have no miracles to grant?" His hands, still gloved, curled into taut, slim fists as his voice changed. "I have never been afraid of killing. I have seldom thought it important which life I took.

"But I am life-sworn to you, and I know the Swords. We are not so different, they and I. You will go to the temple, and I will follow."

"Corfaire—"

He held up a hand that was still mostly fist. "I never chose my parents. I suppose this is true of any of us who live. But I have worked for most of my adult life to expunge my father's influence and control. Perhaps your Bright Heart will do it in the only way possible.

"And perhaps, Lady, you will prove true in that way to your

title." He turned, fully, to face her, and his eyes were almost black. "To order me away would be no mercy."

She was silent under the weight of his words.

"Well then, if that's settled, we might come back to the question of me." Renar's hands fluttered in the air and came to perch firmly on his hips.

"I think Tiras should break your legs." Cospatric was grinning widely.

"No one asked you."

"Lady?"

"I think we—we need him."

"Well good. Now that we've decided that, I think it's time to start moving. I'll just go out for a moment and speak to Amalayna, and then, if you're all prepared, we can leave. Oh, and Gerald, Cospatric—the two of you should get out of what you're wearing."

"Your Majesty."

"Don't sound so snide about it."

"What did you have in mind?"

"Evening dress. Full jacket, frills—stop being idiots. You know very well what I had in mind."

"They might, but I would be interested to hear it."

Renar froze. "Erin, that didn't sound like you. Have you learned to throw your voice lately?"

She shook her head, but her eyes stared over his shoulders.

"Damn. I didn't think so. Cospatric, you didn't smuggle any of your lady friends in with you?"

Cospatric was also staring past him. If he thought the comment humorous, it didn't show.

"Which means—" Renar sighed theatrically. "—that Lady Amalayna has a way into the guest chambers." He turned and spun into a low bow. "Lady."

She walked quietly out of the study, her skirts rustling oddly in the stillness.

"I searched it," Gerald whispered.

"I'm *sure* you did." Renar's voice was honey and vinegar.

Corfaire drew his sword. The sound rang dully in the silence. Lady Amalayna did not deign to notice the threat.

"So," she said quietly. "You are the reigning Maran monarch."

Renar shrugged. "At your service."

"I doubt that. I doubt it very much."

She stepped fully into the room and shut the door behind her. They were seven to her one. It almost made the situation even.

"I don't suppose you've called house guards?"

"Not exactly."

"What are you waiting for?" Corfaire took a step forward, and Tiras caught his arm. He pulled, but the older man's grip was deceptively gentle; the fingers were not dislodged.

"Then you've come to bargain." Renar gestured at the large, winged chair in the room.

"I prefer to stand."

"Suit yourself. I, on the other hand, am quite exhausted; with all the abuse I've suffered this eve, it's no surprise. You don't mind?" He had already seated himself and planted his elbows on the armrests.

"No. It isn't to you that I want to speak." So saying, she turned her black, hollow gaze upon Erin. "I don't know who you are, but I think I know what you're looking for."

Erin jumped slightly, but held herself firm. All sign of fear or fatigue had been erased from her features. "And?"

"I can help you get there."

"Then you don't know what I seek." Erin's fingers itched. "Or you would make no such offer. Renar—she's stalling."

The lady held up one thin, fine hand. A solitary ring glittered on a finger. Her voice was soft. "Should it become necessary, I will indeed stop you and see an end to your plan. But it may not be necessary."

"You are of the Empire, Lady, you—"

"I don't care about the *Empire*." The vehemence in the last word took even Renar by surprise. "If it stands or it falls, what difference will that make? I had already planned my death— and I lost it, because I was foolish. I want only one thing, and I believe you can give me that."

"Lady Amalayna—"

"Renardos, *be silent!*"

Erin stared, and as she did, she felt a familiar pull. The song of the blood rang in her ears with the melody of Lady Amalayna's pain. It was wild, black, and almost incoherent. She lifted her hands, then looked at them as if they were someone else's. They fell stiffly to her side. Even had she chosen to, there was nothing she could do to soothe this woman.

"What can we offer?"

Lady Amalayna leaned forward, and the walls surrounding her noble face crumbled. "Vellen."

"The high priest?"

"No other."

"Why?"

Amalayna hesitated for a moment, and a haughty expression flitted across her face. It vanished in the wake of a desperate hope. "He killed my bond-mate."

Erin's silent pause was an agony for Lady Amalayna, but she bore it well. "We can't promise that. If all goes well, we will never see him."

"If you are looking for what I suspect is the Enemy's Wound, you will meet him."

Erin's eyes widened. "Yes," she said softly. "That *is* what I seek."

"Then take me with you. Give me only the opportunity to avenge myself, and I will be satisfied with whatever bargain we make."

Erin still hesitated, and Amalayna offered the only other thing that she could.

"I can get you into the temple."

Erin bowed her head. When she raised it again, her face was pale. "Lady, how much of our conversation did you overhear?"

"Enough."

"If you are with us, you will perish."

"If I were not, and I succeeded, I would do the same."

Corfaire snorted. "How can we trust her?" His words, edged and cold, were for his Lady's ears alone. "If she should somehow manage to assassinate the high priest, would she not then turn against us? She could claim his death as our responsibility."

Erin waited for Amalayna's answer, but before it was given, Corfaire spoke again.

"You have a child." His face was impassive. "Will you risk his life in this?"

Amalayna was quite alone in the room. No one, not even Renardos, could speak for her. No one offered her their trust. Nor would she have done so, had their positions been reversed. She swallowed, and turned not to Erin, but to Renardos himself. Her hands she held out in a gesture that was almost supplication.

"Renardos."

"Lady?"

"I— You asked who the other assassin was. I told you he was dead."

Renar nodded carefully.

"That man was my father, Lord Valens."

Renar's elbows embedded themselves in his chair. He did not speak.

"I—I will do anything that I can for Laranth. He—he does not rest peacefully. Please—your lady is not of the Empire. Tell her."

"Erin." Renar's voice was the king's voice. "The lady's offer is good." His skill as an actor was not up to the task of hiding his horror and his awe at what she had revealed, for he knew Veriloth well enough to know the cost had been enormous.

Amalayna was very tired. The rush of hope that had all but thrown her into the room had robbed her of any true strength. Even so, she managed words. They were almost as natural as breath.

Erin lifted a hand, and Corfaire obeyed it, stepping forward with his weapon. This time, Tiras made no move to hinder.

Amalayna saw the halo of gentle green that suddenly sprang to life around Erin's body. She shivered; it was wrong and dangerous, this light—a pale mask of war.

"You know of the Wound which we call the Gifting." Erin's voice was full and yet distant and sharp. "You must know what its power is, if it is invoked. I will go to the temple, if that's where the Gifting is. I will do what I must to cleanse it.

"The Church will almost certainly fall, if not immediately, then in the coming weeks. The land will lose the Greater Cabal and much of its most powerful nobility.

"We will do everything we can to take advantage of this."

Renar left his chair and walked quietly over to where Amalayna stood. He encircled her shoulder with his arm and drew her gently back. "Sit."

There was nothing in her that resisted. As the chair enfolded her, her hands enfolded her face. They were cold; everything was. When she was a small child her father had often counseled her to be careful of loyalty. *You must only have one,* he had told her, and his words echoed. *If you have more, you will be torn by them; they will be able to destroy you. Come, child of Valens. Where does your loyalty lie?*

Where?

"Lady Amalayna?"

She knew loss. She understood betrayal; she had suffered it and had repaid it in kind. *Laranth.* One of his assassins was dead at her hands; it should have eased her pain; it should have given her the strength to continue. Her hands shook as she withdrew them; her fingers glistened with more than jewelry.

What did it matter if the Greater Cabal fell? What did it matter if the nobility were thrown into turmoil? In the history of the Empire, it had happened at least once before, and the great civilization of Veriloth had survived and grown. "I told you," Amalayna said, her breath very shallow, her words steady. "I don't care about the Empire."

"She's lying," Corfaire said.

"Is she?" Erin did not look back; she knew well the expression Corfaire's face had donned.

"How could she do otherwise?"

"Lady?"

"I have little that will convince you; you must believe as you choose."

"Choice," Erin said with a bitter grimace, "has often failed me."

Amalayna looked up to meet Erin's eyes. Were it not for the bright green glow, they would have been almost the twin of her own. "Who are you?"

"Erin. Of Elliath."

That name had meant nothing to Corfaire. But Amalayna was learned and knowledgeable. She rose, gathering the shreds of her dignity about her. "That's impossible."

"Is it?" Erin's voice was light, but the timbre had changed. "Is it so impossible?" Her hand found the dagger sheath of her left inner sleeve, and a bright blade swept steadily across her open palm.

Tiras muttered a curse under his breath as he wheeled to face the windows. They were curtained heavily.

The cut was shallow; there was very little blood. Erin slid the dagger back into its sheath before she started the wide, circular gestures of the True Ward.

It was easier than she had expected. Perhaps this was because she was so close to death. Her choice of pathways had come, finally, to an end. There was only one road to follow.

God's power was weakened, and it came to her slowly, but come it did.

The weariness of the day faded from her limbs; the cold teeth of fear pulled away. For a moment she hesitated, frozen on the threshold between light and life.

And then she heard it; the whisper of a familiar voice.

Great-grandchild . . .

Lernan.

You are almost at the crossroads. Walk with care. I will be waiting for you. Look for me, child.

She threw her arms wide, and her eyes gazed upward, beyond the confines of the ceiling. There was only His voice and His power.

Amalayna cringed backward at the sight of this stranger, this walking legend. All that she had read, and all that she had been taught, paled beside the visceral truth of this moment. Elliath had once been the greatest of the lines—the first to emerge and the first to fall.

She shielded her eyes as she looked, but it was her blood and body that truly saw the Light. Her spine shrieked in protest, and her hands sought a weapon, any weapon. She clamped her jaws together to stop her teeth from severing her lower lip.

This woman, this one, was her enemy. Compared to her, Lord Vellen was nothing. She moved forward, and something caught her, pressing her arms to either side.

This was blood-call. This was death, here. She drew breath, gasping as if her lungs could never be filled. She looked up to see the ecstasy writ across Erin's simple features.

"Lady of Mercy." The slave said it. Amalayna turned to look at him for the first time since entering the room. He was on one knee, and his head was bowed. His gauntlets were curled around fists, and the hand that held the sword was shaking.

And Amalayna understood all that had been said in this room. She stopped struggling, although her captor did not release her. *The Lady of Mercy. The Dark Lord's consort.*

As if the words were said aloud—and they might have been—the Lady looked down. Amalayna could only watch as the light began to fade. But the image of Erin, surrounded by the Enemy's fire, had burned itself into her memory. She could not forget it, and could not see Erin again as a mere companion to Renardos.

"Do you understand?"

Amalayna nodded. "Have you—have you come for the Dark Lord?"

"I have come for those that he rules. And I—we all—must move quickly."

Amalayna's throat was dry, but she managed to speak. "I—have spoken only the truth. If you will have me, if you will grant me my one request, I will lead you into the heart of the Church." She bowed her head.

"Lead us in?" It was Renar's voice, but it sounded thin and pale to her ears.

"Yes," she answered softly. "That much I can still do."

"How?"

"I have some authority there, although it is unofficial. Lord Vellen and I are promised to the rites." Even so shaken, she could still find amusement in the sudden silence of shock that pervaded the room. She savored it a moment before it was broken.

"Then we had best leave; we must return to our inn and retrieve items of necessity." Tiras' voice held a sharp edge. "That was foolish, Erin."

"Yes," Erin said. "It was. Lady Amalayna—Lord Vellen is yours."

Dinner.

Lord Darclan looked down the long, empty table. The seats around it were evenly spaced, and dull light glinted off their dark, high backs. Only before his occupied chair was the table properly set; the silver showed no trace of the passage of time. Lamps lit along the walls flickered low, as per his instructions. In time, weeks perhaps, he would have them burning at their full capacity. Thus would the dining hall be restored to its former familiarity.

The door that led to the kitchen swung open on its hinges. Three slaves entered the room in full serving dress. He could hear the rustle of one starched skirt.

They were nervous, these slaves, but their fear was only the most minor of scents. He could read their stiff, straight faces clearly. There was no necessity for words. A full year had passed since last he dined, and he imagined that they had gotten used to life without his presence—or the presence of his Lady. The uniforms they wore smelled vaguely musty.

He lost the smell of them when they brought their dishes forward and began to serve him. As always, they did so in silence, and he did not choose to break it with words.

The last slave, and the oldest, stepped forward after the plate had been laid with its main course. He held a bottle wrapped in linen.

Lord Darclan nodded, and the old man removed the bottle's cork. Red wine; an older vintage. The lip of the bottle touched the lip of the cup, and the liquid trickled out.

The slave stood back, waiting. Lord Darclan smiled and lifted the cup to his lips. It was ceremony and ritual; no matter what the wine tasted like, he knew he would nod in acceptance.

But he froze before the cup had reached his lips.

The shadows of the room were suddenly fuller and darker than they had been. There was no subtlety in it; in mere seconds the red glint of power touched everything.

The shadows parted, and to his right he heard the sound of shattering glass, the trickle of wasted wine. He did not look at the slave. His eyes stared ahead, and the red glint that began at their depths was no mere reflection.

Sargoth, Second of the Sundered, had once again entered his private domain.

He rose, pushing his chair back with only enough force to leave it. "You dare?"

Sargoth said nothing. Instead he drifted closer until the shadows he wore did not conceal him. No longer did he stand so tall or straight; in mere mortal hours he had been so leeched of power that he could not manage it.

And yet . . .

Stefanos glanced around. Everywhere there was red, but this was no Servant's net. The light, crimson and raw, pulsed solidly. It was whole.

"Sargoth."

"Stefanosssss." The word was chill, hardly a name at all. The voice that uttered it was changed. Stefanos recognized the fragments of it that were still Sargoth's—but the timbre of it, the coldness, these were too great to belong to a single Servant.

He knew, then, whose power filled the room.

"Why have you returned?"

"To tell you that I have lost my gamble." Twin voices spoke out of a single mouth. The words gave him no comfort. "What was planned has failed. You have claimed a victory that I do not understand." The frustration and rage inherent in these last words were entirely Sargoth's.

"What gamble?"

"We had hoped to derive some satisfaction from forcing you to bring your folly to its final end. We have failed in that and must settle for less than we had hoped."

Silence now held too much menace, but Stefanos could not be moved to fill it. Instead, he heard the breath of the slave as it cut the air in short, tense gasps. Fear; oh yes, there was fear here.

"Your Sarillorn is not dead. Had all worked out, she would be soon—and by your own hand." There was silence again, and then a dry, brittle chuckle. "You did not even guess."

Stefanos found no words to say. His feet lost the sensation of the firmament beneath him. Had he been in battle, the shock would have cost him eternity. He struggled against it, finding a voice that was almost his own.

"You—cannot be—speaking the truth." He felt weightless; his hands gripped the table before him and held his suddenly insubstantial weight.

"It is." This, too, was almost pure Sargoth, dry and pointed. "I would not kill her."

"Not if you knew, no." Sargoth bowed, out of necessity and not respect. "But it is out of your hands. You have chosen to remain, and we will see that you do."

"She—is—alive." Hope fought with anger, and between them there was numbness. The First of the Sundered had never been so finely trapped.

"She is now in Malakar. She searches for the Wound of the Enemy as we speak. We knew this would come to pass, and we waited for it for naught.

"But we will take what we can from this knowledge, *First* of the Sundered. You will not be prepared to greet her—but we shall. She will die, unaided, and without human hope. The Bright Heart is weak now."

Stefanos raised his arms then, a wide, swift motion that even immortal eyes could barely discern. He whispered softly, sibilantly, each syllable punctuated by urgency. Power blazed down his arms and around his body.

Nothing happened.

"Oh no. You chose to remain here, and you *shall*." Sargoth lifted his arms in a poor mimicry of Stefanos' spell. "But we shall not. Think of us, Stefanos. Think of what we will do, hours from now."

Stefanos leaped then, with a cry of rage that words could not articulate. His claws were extensions of hard, red power, and his eyes were fire.

Sargoth was already too insubstantial to hinder. The First of the Sundered hit the wall and embedded his hands in stone. He snarled, pulling them out. He had no time to turn and see the last of his once-subordinate. But the words that came at his back were heard very well.

"This has cost me much, Stefanos. The Lord is very angry."

Sargoth was gone. But the walls that had come with him remained. And Stefanos knew, with certainty, that he could not breach them; they had been set by God.

He tried, though. He summoned his power, concentrated it, and began to force it out at the walls themselves. This manifestation would cost the Dark Heart dearly, and it could not be held forever.

But it could be held for long enough.

"Sara!"

Lord Vellen stood in the central temple's empty confines. He wore red, red robes that were new and fine—a fitting accoutrement for his office. That office was undisputed now, and it would be for a long time.

The moon was waning, and precious little of its pathetic light filtered through the dark, stained glass. This eve, he would preside over a special sacrifice: his thanks to the Dark Heart.

His only regret was that the ceremony would be so small, but it was necessary. He could not now assemble all of the house nobility to fill the cathedral. Benataan's death had been too sudden.

Benataan's seat would have to be filled; already he had come up with three candidates that would suit him well. At the right moment in the service, the man he finally chose would be called upon to join the Greater Cabal. Scant hours had to pass before that moment, and although he had all but decided, it amused him to let the three men hover in uncertainty.

The temple slaves went about their business in silence, and he watched as they prepared the room. The ebony box that contained the sacrificial blade lay closed in the center of the altar; at its west edge, a silver bucket that had been polished to a warm, soft glow awaited the ceremony's end.

He was not impatient now. He could savor each passing minute in the knowledge that he was prepared for anything.

Or almost anything.

The shadows behind the altar shifted and suddenly erupted in a fanfare of black and red, lapping around the edges of the rounded stone recess. He froze a moment, but did not summon his own power. If it could be avoided, it was for the best—he would need it for the evening.

Out of the shadows a thin form lumbered.

He did not recognize it at first. It was bent and seemed both insubstantial and frail. He could not prevent the widening of clear, hard eyes as the figure straightened out.

"Second of the Sundered?"

"Yessssss." Even the voice was different, thinner and more sibilant. Were it not for the aura of power, unseen but not unfelt, Lord Vellen would have thought it a priest's game. "The Dark Heart requires your service."

Vellen fell to one knee and bowed his head. "What is his command?"

"There has been a change of plans. Do you know where the woman now resides?"

Vellen nodded again. A report had come in not two hours ago.

"Good. Send Swords for her now. She is to be brought to the temple, alive."

"Unharmed?"

"I do not think that possible. Alive will do."

"The others?"

"They are yours." Sargoth looked around at the silent temple. "I must prepare." His voice was very cold. "It seems that you had planned a service here that you will not perform. *I* will preside."

The news was not so bitter a blow as it might once have been. "The First of the Sundered?"

"Will not interfere. My Lord has seen to that."

Vellen turned at once, but not before his lips folded into an expression too exquisitely unpleasant to be called a smile.

chapter
twenty

The crimson walls followed him. They were not so grand or so large as the dome that had once threatened Sara, but they were infinitely more powerful. No hand of dilute Darkness had had any part in their making.

He had not expected anything different, but the desperate ache of the *need* to escape had driven him across the castle grounds to this one spot that might have offered hope.

The stars were very bright. The sky was clear. Moonlight was no less powerful for the fact that it radiated from so slender a crescent. And all of these were as nothing to the Light of the Wound. Even surrounded as it was by crumbled stone, it still had the power to sting as he stood by it.

Here, the walls seemed thinner and perhaps a bit less impervious, but that was all. Seeming. He could not break through them.

But he thought, just for a moment, that they might break him. He had learned much in the last year, and had accepted limitations and changes in himself that would have been unthinkable at any other time in his past. His regret had been the timing: He had changed too late for Sara; dead, she could take no joy or peace in it.

And now, to know that she was not dead was a bloodless pain that could almost drive him mad. His power was low, but he called it yet again to assault the walls that held him. It was not his nature to accept defeat—no matter how much he might change, it would never become so.

He closed his eyes, for the Light distracted him. In the darkness behind his lids, he could see her face more clearly than any of the power he summoned.

"Lord?"

It was not her voice. He drew his shoulders up and raised his head before turning. And then he lowered his eyes.

Kneeling before him on the damp grass—the newly cut, newly laid grass—was the single slave who had remained in the room throughout his encounter with Sargoth and the Lord that he served.

He was an older man even by mortal standards. His hair was peppered snow, his face and brow were a subtle map of years and experience. And he still wore the starched jacket and neat pants that the dining hall demanded.

"Yes?" Stefanos had given strict, terse orders to make sure that he was left uninterrupted in his struggle.

The slave knew it well; it was from his lips that the orders had been relayed. Yet he knelt so, against all orders, completely free of any fear.

"Lord." His voice shook, but only slightly, and even Stefanos was not sure that it was not due to age. "I witnessed the coming of the nightwalker."

One brow arched into a pale forehead.

"I—I heard his words. Forgive me." The breath drawn between sentences was shallow and came quickly. "I carried your orders to the house mistress." He glanced over his shoulder, and Stefanos did the same.

The darkness would have confounded mortal eyes. He saw, near the final row of intricately cut hedges, the warm radiance of life. Many people had gathered there, many slaves. They waited, but for what, he was uncertain.

"She—we spoke, Lord. And we've come with what help we can."

"Call the others out."

The "others" came in a single file. Their feet were heavy against the ground, as their Lord's had not been, and they left a trail of flattened grass that was certain to annoy the master gardener.

Or perhaps not, for among those who waited was the gardener himself.

The house mistress knelt at his feet. "Lord." She gestured, and the rest of the slaves did the same, surrounding him in a semicircle of obeisance.

"Why have you come?"

"The Lady." The first slave answered. The two words hung

in the air, so strong in their starkness that they were almost visible. As if aware of this, the slave spoke again. "We thought her dead."

Lord Darclan did not reply. What was there to say? But he nodded, waiting.

It was the house mistress who spoke next, sparing a second to frown at the slave from the dining hall.

"We might have known that your plan would save her. The slave master spoke briefly of it before he ordered us to send our people away."

"Gervin."

There were nods, but none of the slaves spoke the name. If the Lord willed it, he alone might break law.

"Why have you come?" There was more insistence in the words, but no menace.

The house mistress raised her head and straightened out, although one knee still crushed the damp grass. "You saved her life then, and you might do so now."

"I cannot." Very bitterly he looked above them to see the walls of hovering red. "I have tried."

Now the faintest trace of fear passed through her. He felt it quivering in the distance. "The slave master hid much from us, Lord. But not all. We—we older ones know what you—you might be." She swallowed, and then her words came in a rush; to wait too long might give an opportunity to deny them. "You need lifeblood for your power. We—we can be spared, and we have come to offer what little we can."

He had thought he would never know surprise again. He looked at them, counting maybe twenty in all, and felt their silence, weighted and hushed, as they stared up at him.

Laughter was no fit reward for what they offered, but he could not help it; a grim chuckle left his lips. He turned his back to them and stared at the open sky.

"You honor your Lady," he said, when he could speak again. "And if it would help, I would accept your offer gladly. But that is not the way of the power I wield. Only the unwilling death yields what I need." There were many slaves still sleeping in the castle. He did not have time to slaughter them all, and he knew that had he the time, he would not. Was it only Sara, now? He could not be sure.

The sigh that came was uttered as if from a single mouth. And then one of the oldest men rose, leaving his pose of servitude. The house mistress grabbed his leg as he passed her, walking to face their Lord. He reached down gently and pulled her hand away before continuing.

It was the master gardener.

"Lord." He bowed. "Gervin was not the only man among us to have served, however distantly, with the lines. Not the only one who understood the nature of the Bright Heart." His eyes were squinted slightly as he stared past Lord Darclan. "I studied with a master scholar of Meron. We had much in common, he and I; a love of living things, and an understanding of how to encourage them.

"I built this garden for you with the knowledge he gave me. I did not know who you were—but I guessed it. Who else might claim Mordantari as his own? But I slaved here. I thought I might still bring life, and its beauty, to the world that the Dark Heart claimed.

"Days ago, maybe more, you gave me leave to finally change this last part of the garden; you made it mine." He smiled. "I set the slaves to work here, digging and laying. I had them weeding through all of the sun's sojourn. And I saw the well. I saw its light.

"The Dark Heart must have unwilling blood; the Light, not so. I do not know if the Bright Heart can accept what we offer—but if it strengthens the Light, might it not weaken the Dark?" He reached out then, suddenly and swiftly, and caught Lord Darclan's hands in his own. The difference of texture was more than just magical; the gardener's hands were callused and warm, the Lord's smooth and cold—the contrast between the mortal and the immortal. "Give our lives to the Dark Heart as we have willingly offered them. If it gains you no strength, will it not weaken his?"

Stefanos did not pull back. Instead he gripped the callused hands tightly as if discovering just now the reality in them. The solidity. "Are you all agreed in this?"

"Yes." The house mistress answered.

"Why?"

"Because she is the Lady of Mercy, and the Dark Heart will destroy even that hope." The house mistress smiled, but it was shaky. "Besides, when we reach the Bridge, we'll have our own tale to tell to our parents and some of our children."

He stared at them all, weighing what they had offered against the hope that it would make any difference. It had never, in all of the Dark Heart's history, been tried. The blood of the willing . . .

Yet he knew, too, that it was so slender a chance. He knew what Sara would say, could she accept or refuse what they offered. She would be very angry, very hurt, to know what his decision was.

"She will never know," he said quietly. "I could not tell her."

The house mistress smiled sadly, but nodded just the same. "She doesn't have to."

He closed his eyes, feeling the rough, slow pulse of the gardener's wrist beneath his fingers. *She* would say no. It would be just one more death on her hands, above her head.

They were still very different, she and he.

"Yes." His voice was soft and attenuated, like an echo. "I accept. But not in her name. In my own."

There was a surge of fear, a wildness beneath the perfectly still surface. It kicked, hitting some harder than others, and it twisted at them.

"But it *must* be willing; I will take no life otherwise."

"And it's got to be quick." The old slave from the dining hall rose and walked to join the gardener. "I might as well be the first, then. It was mostly my idea."

Lord Darclan looked into his eyes a moment, and then nodded. No one alive had seen such a nod. There was admiration in it, almost awe. He released the master gardener's hands and offered his own to the slave.

"Come, then. Walk with me. But I will ask you one thing: Your name. Who are you?"

"Reanis," the man answered quietly. He said it with pride. There was nothing of the slave in him. The hand that gripped the Lord's was strong, and if it trembled, it bothered no one. They walked quietly past the Well of Lernan, and out of sight of the rest of the slaves.

"Lord?"

Lord Darclan turned to look at the master gardener.

"I—I want to walk about the grounds for a bit. I'll return."

"You do not have to do this."

"No, I know." The gardener shook his head. "It's just—all of this, it really is mine. I wonder who'll care for it when I'm gone, but I always wondered that." There were tears in his eyes, and Stefanos realized that they glimmered in the darkness like the Light of the well.

The innkeeper was far less surly in the presence of a crested house member than he had been the previous day. Corfaire noted this without any amusement at all. Lady Amalayna was obviously a woman with important business to attend to; when she placed her coin on the counter, it was taken with a great deal of bowing and scraping, and no argument whatsoever.

They did not entirely empty their rooms; much that was there could be left behind. In their pockets they took some of the gems the jeweler had not bought and some of the coin he had paid with. Backpacks and spare clothing were discarded. Weapons were not.

Erin alone took the time to change from her Empire dress to her guard's gear. The one concession she felt she could make to subterfuge was the large, dark cloak she draped over her shoulders. Beneath its heavy folds, the Bright Sword hung at her side, its weight a comfort. She and it would not be parted again.

The streets were busy, but not so crowded as they had been in early evening. At least that was Erin's impression, but she wondered if their ease of passage had something to do with Lady Amalayna's presence. The noblewoman was tall, and her step was the practiced gait of haughty contempt. She rarely looked to either side, and the set of her lips was cold and fierce. Nobody really spared half a glance to her companions; one look at her told them it was none of their business.

In the anonymity of timid crowds, they came to the turning point of the Westway. A wide road ran perpendicular to it, and Amalayna halted them there.

"Now," she said softly, "be careful. Watch your demeanor." Her cheeks were flushed, and her breath came quickly. "This road leads to the temple."

The last was not necessary—even in the darkness, no one could miss the massive sprawl of grand buildings that rose above the stone walls.

"Guards?" Tiras asked sharply.

"Swords." She shrugged. "There are not many buildings along this road, but it may be best to avoid the Swords in their patrols, at least until we come under the scrutiny of the walls themselves."

"Ready?" Tiras turned to look at Erin. Erin nodded grimly and turned a similar look upon Darin. His fingers were white against the wood of the staff of Culverne, and his nod, although almost as brief and forceful as Erin's, spoke more of anxiety than determination.

Erin was struck yet again by his age and forced herself to concentrate on the staff he carried: his office. He was patriarch of Culverne, and as she, had his duty.

Amalayna gestured, and Gerald and Cospatric stepped forward. They no longer wore Tentaris uniforms, but they did bear a crest: House Valens. Corfaire was likewise attired, but he moved less quickly, glancing back at Erin for permission.

She nodded, understanding.

Renar and Tiras, robed now in shadows, seemed to melt away. Amalayna's party consisted of Darin, in Valens colors, and Erin—who wore a cloak of a midhigh station; a favored slave. The "guards" she now ignored.

"Do you understand what to do if we're halted?"

Nods again. Only Corfaire bristled at the assumed note of command in her words.

There was irony in this situation that was not lost on Erin. To have learned so much and traveled so far just to turn the last few steps of her path over to an imperial house noble was something that she could never have predicted.

But it was not the first time that she had walked in the darkness, with the blood of the Darkness for company. She only prayed that this noblewoman would be as false to her heritage as Stefanos had strived to be.

Had, in the end, failed to be.

It wasn't cold, but she shivered and drew her cloak more tightly around her shoulders. Even though they moved quickly and tightly, there was still time for doubt to gnaw at her.

No. She took a deep breath. *If I've made mistakes, they've led me here. And here is where I* must *be.* She had no time for doubt.

"Lady," she said softly, and bent down. "Your hem."

"Fix it, then. But be quick."

The Swords met them in the road.

That they were no ordinary guard patrol was evident in

many things, and Erin took stock of them all at once. They were armored in black, and the ringlets of fine chain showed beneath Church surcoats. Dark gorgets rose to meet the back ends of closed helms, and weapons cut the air with hard, clean lines. Sixteen in all walked in four rows; the front men obscured those that followed, but Erin thought she glimpsed crossbows.

More telling was the fact that not one man carried a torch. There was light enough in the city for their half-blooded sight.

Lady Amalayna stiffened, and a single word escaped her; it was not a pleasant one. Her hand curled momentarily in a fist, and she whispered quickly out of the corner of her mouth.

"Patrols are usually eight." She clapped, briefly, and Corfaire halted; long habit. Gerald and Cospatric followed his cue, but nervously. Where Corfaire's gaze was stiff and formal, theirs were wary; while his hands remained in position at his sides, theirs flitted above their sword hilts.

Darin halted, and his knees locked. He was grateful for it; his early years in the Empire shouted adamantly in his ears, and he almost hit the ground in obeisance. It would have been a breach of protocol; there were no priests present.

Amalayna murmured a harsh "stay" at her attendant and then stepped forward. The Swords had stopped in the street, and the hindmost two ranks had merged with the foremost; there were eight men abreast in two rows—little hope now that they would just pass.

"Lady." One of the Swords stepped forward and bowed. He was no mere captain, no nervous youth. Had there been any edge of ambition in him, she might have played upon it, but he was older and wiser. This was very bad.

"Major." She inclined her head; a curtsy was not, strictly speaking, necessary.

"What brings you from the High City?"

"I have come for an audience with Lord Vellen, the high priest. I would have stated as much to the temple guard."

"It is odd," was the man's reply. "For we are leaving now to visit your former residence."

"Really? Odd indeed." Her words were polite and slightly bored. They impressed some of the Swords, but not the one that mattered.

"Yes. We've been sent to retrieve visitors to House Tentaris. If they still remain there."

"Visitors? Ah—you mean the people from the market."

"Indeed." His gaze passed her shoulders, and his face altered subtly, the lines of it becoming hard and fixed. "Is there anything you wish to tell us?"

It was his offer of amnesty to her, and the only one he was likely to make. Nor would he have made a similar offer to any who was not the betrothed of the high priest. Any stain upon her would reflect poorly on that lord and be costly to the Sword who had caused it.

Amalayna's jaw snapped shut. *Yes,* she wanted to say, *there's a lot I want to tell you.* How could she come so close, not once, but twice, and have it all unravel in her hands? Reality washed over her, and its touch was very cold. What had she been thinking, to come this far? Where was the levelheaded woman that had once been the prize of two houses?

Even masked as they were by the pale tint of powders, her cheeks glowed red. Her head remained tilted up, and her lips remained closed. She had this one chance to step aside and wash her hands of this whole affair; even prolonging her answer as she now did carried the taint of treason.

Treason.

That one word, cold and sharp, slid down the back of her spine. Her head sank, and her hair brushed her cheeks.

"Lady?" the major said, the word a little less arrogant.

No act of treason had deprived her of the thing she valued most in her life. That was lost to her under the direction of the leader of the Greater Cabal—the man who gave orders to the Swords that stood arrayed before her. Her head snapped up, and her eyes were rimmed. "No," she said softly. "I have nothing to say."

And her hands cut the air between them, her lips running silent over ill-used invocations. Her left hand found one dagger, her right the other.

Of the twenty who had come, twelve served. The old slave from the dining hall was but the first, and he had died gracefully and quietly. No power of the Sundered that Stefanos held could mask or comfort pain, but the First knew the ways of mortal death, and he dealt the quickest blow that he could.

It was difficult. Habit and more than habit tried unsuccessfully to force his hand to slow or stay the descent of the knife, to linger in the shadow of human pain and human dying. Had he been hungry, he doubted that he would have been able to control this urge—not when he stood so close to death and the shedding of lifeblood.

But he prevailed. And as he touched each of his willing victims, he sent their message out across the void that separated him from his Lord. The touch of their peace, their love, and their hope was uncomfortable to him—and he knew it would cause more than discomfort to Malthan.

But how much? How much more? The taunting whisper of God was stilled; he felt nothing of his maker.

The starlight blinked, and the moon burned at his back; the velvet of near-cloudless sky could not contain them. He had no time to bury the bodies that remained behind when the life fled, and he knew that it became more difficult for the last few that followed.

Some, indeed, could not give fully what they had promised. Not among these was the house mistress that had served him faithfully from the beginning of his reign in Mordantari. She too died, although less gracefully than Reanis; her lips were frozen in the grim rictus of her own silent struggle with life and death.

Twelve had died. A dozen bodies lay in a neat row beyond the hedgerow. In the shadows, their throats looked swathed in dark cloth. He looked at them all and felt each death more strongly than any he had personally caused before. His bow was all he could spare them now, but if their sacrifice succeeded, he promised them more in silence. There was only one man left to come, and he waited in patience, although time was once again his greatest enemy.

The master gardener came around the hedges, the tread of his step light and firm. Stefanos moved to greet him, leaving the dead to their rest.

"Lord," the gardener said, bowing quietly. He saw what the shadows did not fully hide, and turned his face away. "I am ready." Fear tingled in an aurora around him, commingling with shame and determination.

Stefanos drew his dagger for the thirteenth time and held out his hand. The callused fingers that met his palm were no seeming; they were old and slightly bent. And they were wet.

"You do not have to do this," the Lord said quietly, as he drew closer. "I will not take what cannot be fully offered."

"I know," the gardener replied. "I saw the others. They're

relieved, but they're ashamed. Don't think I could live like that." He stiffened and stepped forward, as if to embrace too tightly this offered death.

"Besides, I think thirteen is a fair number; pit us, one for one, against the Greater Cabal. But please do it quickly."

The knife was a flash in the darkness; it spun through the air and ended with the skin of the gardener's throat. But it did not penetrate; it drew no blood.

"No." Stefanos drew back. "I will not take this."

"But I am ready," the old man replied.

"I am not." He turned away. "You are a giver of life, in your own small way. I am a taker. But we both have choice to exercise. I cannot tend your garden; there is no one here who could." He set the knife down against the grass, unblooded. "She loved your garden."

The row of dead lay beyond him, like small trees or seedlings that had not yet been planted. "Go now and tell everyone that I *must* be left in peace." He gestured, drew in his power, and began to concentrate. Now he would see if these deaths bore the fruit that had been hoped for.

Lady Amalayna stepped forward, her tongue caught in her throat. The major waited, his blade ready to greet any deft movement, any quick strike. Of the two, he was the more powerful—he was trained in the ways of death, and the steel he carried was the work of several years.

The major's eyes were wary nonetheless. To strike at a noble not named by the Church was risky, and as any risk, carried a great price if made in error.

Amalayna suddenly returned to herself. She looked down at the daggers in her hands with a grimace of distaste, and when she looked up again, her eyes were ice and steel.

"Fool," she whispered, taking care to let no sibilance halo the word. "Do you think I came to the Church without reason? No! Don't look back. They already trust me little enough."

The major did not lower his sword. Behind him, two of the younger men had already started to do so, but their leader was not so inexperienced.

"Do you not know who they are?"

"We aren't concerned with that."

"You should be." Her reply was cold; the force behind the words was not noise, but a quiet assurance of power. "I was to lead them to the Church and gain an audience with the high priest."

"So I see."

Amalayna stiffened. "If you wish to play at swords, do so. It is your life, after all. But think on this: My way would deliver them to the Church, where the Greater Cabal has most of its power, without loss." She leaned forward slightly. "It is the proof of my loyalty to the man who would be my lord. Do you seek to deprive me of this? Think carefully; we of House Valens do not forget."

The major studied her face and found it not so blank or disinterested as his own. If intensity were heat, he might be seared; if it were ice, he would surely never move again. He looked beyond her to see those that waited tensely; only one had drawn a blade, and that one was the image of Veriloth; pale and dark, with eyes that glowed the faintest trace of red. There were five in all, but only three of these seemed a threat—what harm could a child and a woman do?

What harm indeed. It was the woman they had been sent to capture, and they numbered not eight, but sixteen.

Yet he did not trust the Lady Amalayna herself, although her words rang almost true. He hesitated a moment longer, and then lowered his weapon. His orders were only to see that the woman was delivered to the main altars, and if the party passed through to the temple, that was certain to be the case.

"Very well." His voice was quiet. "You may pass."

"Follow," she replied, equally quiet. The daggers found their sheaths again, and her empty hands curled inward. "But at a greater distance. Try not to be seen."

He nodded again, more curtly, and signaled his men. They split their ranks, moving seven and eight abreast to either side of the roadway. It was certainly wide enough to allow it.

Lady Amalayna turned and walked back to the rest of her companions. With her eyes, she tried to allay the terrible brilliance contained in Erin's face. She could not speak for fear that the words would carry; the major had blood-power about him equal to her own.

"Come," she said. "There was a—misunderstanding. We may pass through." But her eyes widened, her lips trembled. *Please,* she thought, *please understand. I have saved us for the final stretch; do not endanger my plan.*

Erin remained standing, her eyes wide and green. The

breeze caught her hair, and the lamps lit it from behind until it seemed dark filaments shot through with fire. Except that there was no breeze, and the lamps were too far away to cast such a light. The air was still and chilly; the shadows long.

Amalayna reached out and grabbed one of Erin's hands. She was prepared for the jolt that slammed into her arm, but even so she staggered. Her blood burned at the contact, and her lips moved almost of their own accord. She bit them and looked away—at the ground, at Darin, at anything but the woman who stood before her—the woman who was her ancient enemy.

"Please."

The Swords shifted uncomfortably in the streets; their hands hovered over their now-sheathed swords. Battle was in the air, and its call was strong. But they did not yet see what the source of that call was.

Be careful, child. Heed the offered warning.

The voice was the softest tickle in the back of her mind, but it was cold. Erin's eyes dimmed, and she seemed once again a mortal woman. Her fingers bit into Amalayna's, but whether in comfort or in warning, neither woman could have said.

"We wait your orders, Lady."

"Then follow."

No one spoke until the booted march of the Swords faded from earshot. Even then, the feeling of enemy eyes lingered in the air. Corfaire stepped forward and caught Lady Amalayna by the forearm.

She turned only her head, and although she could not look down at this man dressed in her house uniform, her gaze was haughty and cold. Before words escaped his open lips, she slid her own into the silence.

"We will have a fight, and if we're unlucky, it will start the moment we enter the temple. Are you prepared?"

Corfaire's hand fell away as he met her eyes. There was no love between them, and any respect given was grudged, but they had some goal in common. He nodded brusquely.

"And you, Lady," Amalayna continued, "hide your light. It is difficult; it will almost certainly call too much of a battle, too early." She turned away, but her last words, though softly spoken, were nonetheless clear. "The Swords will follow us; we dare not linger long in the main courtyard, or we will be overwhelmed on both sides."

"Can we fight our way through to our destination?"

"You ask that of me, Lady? How should I know for certain what *you* do not?"

"It is your Church," Erin replied.

Amalayna thought a moment before answering. "If we are lucky, there will be no fight. But you *must* follow my lead and be prepared for it to fail. I carry the weight of my house for a day or two longer. Let us pray that it suffices."

Corfaire suddenly began to chuckle; there was no warmth in the sound. "Pray? To whom?"

The two dark glances he received were almost enough to silence him. Lady Amalayna began to walk forward quickly, forcing the others to follow.

Erin glanced back to the shadows, but she caught no sign of Renar or Tiras. They were well hidden; she hoped that they could manage to follow Amalayna's lead before the doors were sealed. If that had, in the end, been their plan. They had not told her; she had not asked. Now, there was no time to consider it.

The Church was grand, and as the shadows fell away at their approach, it loomed higher, brighter, larger. The tower—all that could be easily seen over the walls—was sparse and simple; large blocks of stone placed seamlessly together rose to the parapets over which four flags curled around their flagpoles. Statues adorned those heights; human, perhaps, and a little larger than life.

Corfaire's brow wrinkled as he missed a step.

"Corfaire?"

"It is nothing, Lady. But I thought—I thought there were two towers. My duties brought me seldom to the temple. I may have been mistaken."

"No," Amalayna said quietly. "You have made no mistake. The southern wing—and its tower—were completely destroyed by the Dark Heart's demon."

"Why?"

"I'm afraid I didn't think of asking him."

"Maybe the priests displeased him." Erin's voice was quiet and distant; her eyes were turned momentarily inward as she remembered what his displeasure had often meant to the Church.

"It may well be. But they must have angered him greatly, then. The wing was destroyed in an evening."

"Is he—is he there?"

Amalayna paused and looked back. There was something in the tone of the words—in the words themselves—that caught her attention. Fear, which only a fool would not have felt, but more than that. Anticipation? Sorrow?

"How old are you, Lady?"

"How— Old, Lady." She sought the tower and the flags. "But I'll answer your question, if you can answer mine."

Amalayna nodded quietly and bent her head. Her hands fluttered in the air before a face that was tense with concentration. To Darin, she seemed to echo the gestures of Erin herself—the other face of the coin of war. Power, in a thin red line, arrowed outward; it touched the walls and seemed to end there, although Amalayna did not stop her whispered murmur. The hair on the back of Darin's neck rose, and he wondered how Erin could bear this use of blood-magic. But he waited, and after a moment, the line faded from view, leaving only an afterimage in the night air.

The lady of no house turned to Erin; her face was pale and taut. "I can answer your question. He must be there. There is too much power for it to be otherwise. Did you expect this?"

"Yes."

"Are you—can you—be prepared for it?"

"I don't know." She seemed to shrink inward under the battery of Amalayna's eyes. "Four hundred and thirty, maybe a few years less, maybe more."

Amalayna's eyes widened. "Is there some truth to the lore of the slaves, then? Are you the Dark Lord's Lady?"

"I am his bond-mate." It was simple, really, to let this last of her secrets fall away; to stand revealed by these few words. She was cold, and her heart was thrumming with a life that did not seem to be her own. Maybe those who heard her now would understand her better if things somehow went awry. Maybe.

Only Darin was not surprised by her words. And because of this, only Darin could see the rising pain beneath them. He reached out and touched her gently with the tip of the staff of Culverne.

"No more questions," he said quietly, striving to lower his voice to give it some ring of authority.

There was no time for them; they were upon the gates.

chapter
twenty-one

Erin felt it as she approached. There was a wrongness in the air
that cost her no spell to detect; it was heavy, dark—loud in a
way that ears alone wouldn't catch. She wanted to turn back,
but held her ground; the temple was the end of her road. All
she had to do was enter it. Did it matter how? If the Gifting of
God was truly here, it would be well tended by the blood ceremonies. All she had to do was get close to it.

Don't let me fail, not now. Not here. This is the last chance.
Her fingers pressed tightly into her palms, but not enough to
draw blood. Blood she would need later. Now she needed hope.
Lady Amalayna's plan had seemed so good to her in House
Tentaris. She would not let fear deprive her of belief in it.

The gates were wrought-iron bars, decorated on either side
by a broken red circle in a field of black. Both were spotless
and seemed to glimmer with a light that the street lamps alone
could not explain.

There were Swords on either side of the gate; two in front
and four behind. They stood erect, but not fully at attention;
they showed no wariness at the approach of the lady of House
Valens. Their uniforms were only partly practical, and Erin
frowned briefly; such a display was not in keeping with . . .
with the Lord of the Empire's standards. She straightened the
line of her mouth, remembering that the Church probably dictated the Swords' dress. Perhaps it impressed somebody.

There were houses, and then there were houses; Valens was
one of the few that any Sword would recognize immediately.
Both of the men at the gate bowed at Amalayna as she stopped
just a foot from them. No torchlight was needed to see her bur-

gundy and gray; indeed, the Swords needed little in the way of light at all.

"Lady Amalayna of Valens."

She nodded regally.

"What is your business here?"

"I have come to speak to Lord Vellen, the high priest of the Greater Cabal. I bear a message of some urgency."

"Does he expect you?"

"No. But the news I bear has relevance to him, and it is a timely matter."

The Sword considered this a moment, and not only for display; his furrowed brow spoke of indecision. "The high priest has left orders that he is not to be disturbed. Might not this news wait until morning?"

Amalayna was silent in return as she studied both his face and the face of the second Sword. Neither even glanced beyond her shoulders to look at her companions; neither seemed suspicious in the least. It was almost too much to be hoped for.

"It would be best not to wait."

She thought he might order her to do so anyway, but he turned to the closed gate and motioned one of the Swords forward. They spoke in quiet tones for a few moments, and then the Sword beyond the gate departed.

Amalayna stepped back. She did not turn her head and barely moved her lips at all. "Be ready."

Minutes passed, and Erin counted each second, listening intently for the sound of steps approaching from behind. The streets were mercifully silent and remained that way until the Sword returned to his post. He did not speak, however; nor did he open the gates. Instead he peered out through the bars for half a minute before once again disappearing.

Be very ready, Lady.

They waited until the Sword returned for a second time. He nodded sharply, and the gates began to roll open. Even this was not done quickly; the gates themselves were older and complicated. Very few had desire to enter the Church quickly.

"You may enter."

Amalayna nodded and walked steadily forward. The passage from the first gate opened up at the second, but the courtyard was empty. She did not turn as the gates were closed behind them. She needed no final glance of the outside world, seen as it would be, from behind bars. She wanted no reminders and no gestures that even remotely spoke of regret.

Erin was not so complacent. She glanced back over her shoulder to see that the four Swords had turned to face their retreating backs. Their weapons were drawn and readied, although they did not leave their posts. She looked above them, her eyes trailing the heights of the walls. Along the curtain wall, Swords also stood. Even in the dim shadows she could see that they had readied crossbows and longbows. They too no longer patrolled the streets below with their eyes.

But the courtyard itself was empty. No rush of Swords came pouring out of the main doors to greet them. No priests stood in the thrall of spell and imminent battle. It looked peaceful. It felt deadly.

Erin said nothing. She could hardly accuse the lady of leading them into a trap, could she? The fact that the temple existed at all was trap enough for her. But she wondered as she walked. The high priest had left orders that he was not to be disturbed. What task kept him occupied? This was no quarter, with its blood sacrifice and its required death. And if he had allowed himself to be disturbed, was it only because he now knew she was coming?

Or was it because Stefanos knew it?

She stopped just behind Amalayna as the doors began to open. They were not so complicated as the gates, and even Erin hardly noticed the slaves that pulled at either side of the heavy, adorned wood.

The doors had opened only a foot's width on either side when she saw who stood at their center.

He was robed not in black now, but in the deepest red, with sleeves that trailed to the edge of his hem. From his shoulders, a red collar rose, its edge visible above the pale platinum of his hair. Only his sash spoke of the darkness that was his power. At his brow, gold glittered in a thin, bright line that was broken only by a solitary ruby. And all around his tall, straight body was a pale, thick halo—red mist, captured and held by spell.

The high priest. Vellen.

There were two levels of fear in the six that saw him. Corfaire, Cospatric, and Gerald touched swords in the instant that they saw his smile. But Erin, Darin, and Amalayna did not even move. Theirs was the deeper fear, for they had all felt his touch upon their lives, and they still bore the scars.

"Lady Amalayna." Vellen bowed. There was a majesty in the movement that belied the gesture; it left no question of his power. "You choose an odd moment to ask for an audience."

"My Lord." She in turn bowed, but less fluidly, less charismatically. Her throat was too dry to allow her to speak forcefully. "Please—accept my apologies for interrupting you. I had a matter of import for your consideration. Something that I wished to deliver to you personally."

"Oh, indeed." Ice-blue eyes swept out beyond her back. "And you have arrived most opportunely. Come, will you not enter?"

The doors were fully open now. Lord Vellen stood at the forefront of his own personal guard, but their naked blades held less threat than his smile.

Only Darin had ever seen one quite so warm or amused on the high priest's face. It was a mask to seal in the screams of the dying.

"Ah, Lady, Lady." Vellen shook his head in mock annoyance. It was not to Amalayna that he spoke. "Should such a one as you come dressed in the garb of slavery? You have stooped low indeed from your previous position."

Suddenly the smile was deep, sharp, all-encompassing. Lord Vellen threw back his arms and his eyes silvered. "Enough! Away with this disguise!"

Before Erin could even move, her cloak was ripped from her shoulders by a powerful wind that touched only her. The clasp caught a moment at her throat; she felt its cold, metallic bite before it, too, fell away.

"And thus do the shadows fall away from the Sarillorn of Elliath. But for a moment, Lady. Come. I have bid you enter. Was it not for my hospitality that you came?" His eyes pulsed again with silver frost. "Oh, no," he said softly. "Draw no weapons. I do not recognize you three, but you come with the Sarillorn, and that is knowledge enough."

Cospatric bit back a cry as his sword hand blistered in the wake of a fire-flash. Gerald might well have been mute again, and Corfaire showed nothing, nothing at all.

"But you, little boy—I recognize you. And I recognize the thing that you carry." He laughed for the first time. "Do you think to use it against me here? Do, please. It will amuse me. It will avail you nothing."

Erin caught Darin's hand in her own. She squeezed his shaking fingers.

"Come, Amalayna. You have my gratitude. You have led them to me and have saved my Swords effort and possibly lives."

"Lord." She bowed quietly and began to walk forward without a backward glance. But she was not allowed to stand near the lord of the Church. Two Swords moved politely to stand on either side of her; an honor guard.

Vellen gestured again.

Darin pulled his hand away from Erin's and swung Bethany around. White light coruscated down the length of the staff, crackling audibly over Darin's wordless shout.

Another, stronger light joined it as it flew across the courtyard and up the steps.

The high priest of the Church staggered backward. But his smile never dimmed as his eyes traded silver for red. His counter was quick and smooth—but not fast enough to block Bethany's strike.

Or it shouldn't have been. Erin knew ward and counterward well. And she knew that the power that shielded Vellen was not his alone. For he stood, taller and more menacing, framed by the Light.

Beyond him, the Swords flinched, but they, too, were protected by their Lord.

Only Amalayna screamed.

Vellen gestured, and her scream was cut short, but she sagged visibly between the two Swords. They caught her, before her knees crumpled, and held her rigidly.

"Unwise," he said, and gestured again, his hands flying and plunging in one final motion. "You will need what power you have, Lady."

The Light faded, leaving an afterimage across Erin's eyes. Before she could move again, the ground was pulled away from her. Her feet flailed a moment a foot above the flagstones.

"Now I tire. Come. All of you." They rose, instruments to his will, until they, too, were suspended in midair by the power of the high priest.

Sargoth had, after all, been a very good teacher.

Darin wanted to call his power then, but the gates would not form in his mind. He had forgotten what it felt like to stand in the wake of Lord Vellen's power. He was shaking, and all he could do was retain his grip on Bethany.

The five drifted forward in silent struggle; they could not even turn to see the doors of the wing close quickly behind them.

Renar's lips made no sound as he mouthed a curse. Years of practice kept him silent—that and Tiras' hand biting into his shoulder. He reached up and caught the fingers of his teacher. He held them a moment before frantically and deliberately gesturing.

There was not even a tremble in the older man's grip. He waited until the young king finished, and then began his own discourse. It was, of course, shorter and more precise.

When he had finished, they both looked to the walls of the temple and the closed gates. The Swords that patrolled the curtain wall still looked inward, as if no threat from without could equal the excitement within. If they were good, they would take up their duties again, and soon.

Renar's previous experiences here told him that they were good. That had not prevented his entrance before. It would not do so now. He had seconds, and he used them, sliding across the ground like a moving patch of velvet or shadow. No sound followed in his wake, but he was aware of Tiras dogging his steps.

The master was older, but experience told what age did not; he was all grace and supple movement.

If they were lucky, they would be undetected; if they were unlucky, they would have to kill two Swords. Renar's mood was such that he didn't know which of the two to pray for.

Hold on, Lady. We're coming.

Stefanos stood above the grass in the center of two circles, one bright and one dark. The first, and the closest to him, was one of his own making; thin, fine, and sharp. The second was the will of his Lord made manifest: thick, rigid, immovable. Where they touched, they merged, but when they separated, they remained unchanged. There were no breaks, and no flaws, in either.

And yet . . .

Stefanos drew his circle in and looked about him slowly. The almost unreasoning urge to throw all of his power against his Lord's was gone; in its place was a tense rationality. He wanted no pain, no despair, no anguish to flow from him to the Dark Heart; it would only strengthen His power.

But was there a difference, now? Was there a slight thinning, an odd mutability?

His Lord spoke no words; the whisper of the darkness had been stilled. This gave him hope. He moved through the paths of memory until he found what he sought: the raising of the wall. His eyes, turned inward, studied it carefully, examining each detail.

On high, shadows hid the frescoes on the curvature of the vaulted ceilings. Light pooled in sparse circles around torches and lamps, but its soft halos did nothing to make the details above more clear.

"Feel free to examine them more closely," the high priest said. His words filled the hall with the grandeur and depth of power. Erin alone began to rise. She made no move and no struggle; there was no point in it. The power that Lord Vellen used now was not blood-magic, and she had nothing to fight it with. The red-fire, he hoarded carefully.

Her flight brought her above the reach of the light, where the shadows took her coldly. She stopped an arm's reach from the heights. There, surrounding her in a downward fall of color, death reigned. Caught, timeless, protected from the ravages of the sunlight, rich, stark images struggled free of the darkness. To her left, resplendent in armor that was almost certainly an added detail, the host of the Dark Heart rode triumphantly through the lands of Elliath. Their horses were all of a color, and their banners were shadow and blood. Light gleamed oddly off their open helms as they surveyed what their horses did not avoid stepping on: the fallen.

She bit her lip and decided. The last light fell away from her, and her eyes lost their ability to pierce the darkness.

"A pity," Vellen said softly. "But perhaps it is not necessary after all. You alone need no education in the glories of our past."

But he held her aloft in midair. She heard the soft scrape of metal and felt a tug at her shoulders.

"You are not a warrior here; there is no battle, no question of it." His voice was velvet, so soft that she wondered if she heard it with her ears. "What use have you of weapons?"

There was another scrape of metal; another buckle opened. Her hands fought against the power that stayed them, but with no effect. The Bright Sword drifted gently away from her body.

"What use have you of armor?"

The hard leather was peeled away and the underpadding followed. Both fell almost beyond her vision. Compared to the loss of the sword, these were nothing.

"Better, Lady. Come. We are ready for you now."

She floated downward. Without her light, and without her armaments, she was an ordinary woman; small, and in seeming, delicate.

She could see Vellen clearly now. At his side, a Sword held her possessions. The sword he did not even pull; it was a short sword, not a great sword—and with no one behind it, it held no menace for him, and very little interest.

"You aren't even afraid yet," the high priest whispered. He stepped forward, reached out, and caught her chin in his fingers.

She said nothing, did nothing.

But he was wrong; she was afraid. Behind the set neutrality of her eyes and mouth, thoughts trembled in a struggle to come to the forefront. Why had she thought it would be easy? Why had she thought they would not be prepared? Why had Lady Amalayna's offer seemed so foolproof? She had failed again, and yet . . .

It was not over.

"Come." He did not even release her face; she was dragged the last few yards to the new, plain doors of the temple proper, her feet resting on air. There was no question at all of where he was taking her.

Yes.

There was a difference, so faint and subtle that even he had not recognized it at first. He smiled, the first real smile of the evening. No one could see it, and he had no idea of how it transformed his face—but he would remember in detail the feel of the corners of his lips and the moment in which they rose.

Had he been mortal, or of mortal blood, he would have willingly offered the taint of it to his Lord. In his mind, he did so, and his offering was a silent roar that the Dark Heart could not ignore.

Stefanos, cease this.

The inner circle closest to the First of the Sundered faded out of sight, absorbed once again by the Foremost Servant of the Darkness.

Lord.

The Dark Heart did not respond. Stefanos looked carefully at the walls and then began an assault of a different sort.

There were forty Swords in the temple proper. Forty men, armed and prepared for any ensuing conflict. Beyond the safety their numbers represented stood five high priests, also garbed in their most ceremonial attire. They formed an open half circle and watched in silence.

Erin barely noticed them.

For at their head, farthest into the room, stood shadow personified. Her breath escaped her then in a sharp, short gasp.

It was not Stefanos who waited.

She did not recognize the Servant who did, not for several minutes. But as she approached in the silence, as the Swords created a tunnel through which their lord passed, she saw beyond the bent back and the pale darkness, beyond the brilliant red of magic that could belong only to a Heart.

"Sargoth."

The Second of the Sundered raised his head. She saw two red points in a mask of shadow. "Did I not say we would meet again?"

Not Stefanos. Not Lord Stefan Darclan. Not the darkling bond-mate that she had so dreaded facing in her final hours.

Sargoth did not look away from her. "Vellen, you have done well. Our Lord will be pleased indeed. But the Lady is now in my care. Bring her forward."

"The others?"

"Yours, as agreed upon. But they will have to wait." He stopped a moment and looked just beyond Vellen. "Who is this?"

"My promised mate." The high priest held out a hand. He spoke no word of command, but none was needed; his personal guards knew him well enough to judge his wishes. They took a step away from Amalayna, bowed, and let her go. She stepped forward and placed one icy hand in Vellen's.

"Come, Lady. Enjoy the fruit of your endeavor." He smiled. "After this eve, there will be no dictate from the Church that is not mine. We consecrate the altars to a new Lord of the Empire."

If Sargoth thought this presumptuous, he was not inclined to comment. He waited as Erin was dragged forward through the air. She came, her eyes wide and unblinking.

"You cannot know what trouble you have caused me, half human."

Something was wrong with his voice. The tenor of it was too strong; the sibilance absent.

"All my plans have gone awry. I serve my Lord in this moment, but I shall find some satisfaction in it for my losses."

He gestured, and his eyes flashed silver and red, silver and red.

Erin fell to the ground at his feet. She began to roll before she was caught once again, this time by a surer, more ancient power. Her hand froze a hair's breadth above her dagger; her fingers had already curled to grip it.

"Oh no. Did you think we would allow you to invoke our Enemy's power here? I have prepared long, and I am no mere priest. I have the ability to keep you from your God."

Fire suddenly burst around her—not red-fire, but not normal fire either. She saw the hand of Darin's teacher and would have bitten her lip, but her mouth would not move. In an instant, all of her clothing was consumed by the hiss of those flames, and she was jerked to her feet. Not even ash remained to conceal her.

"So that you might see her and know all that the last of our Enemy is." He gestured again, and she began to rotate, bound tightly to an invisible stake. She could not even close her eyes, and they began to smart and water.

"Tears, Sarillorn?" Sargoth drew her closer and lifted one clawed hand. "How pathetic. But I believe . . . yes. Kerlinda of Elliath died just such a death as you will." He smiled, but the glitter of his teeth was red. The surge of her anger, her pain, and her fear all but enveloped him, so close was he to his God.

Then he gestured. Red plumed outward from his arms. She felt its foreign sigil strike her skin and sink until it rested so close to her she too was red.

She had not heard her mother's name for years. But the screams returned to her now.

The death of the slaves had opened the way for him. Their offer was foreign, almost unthinkable, to what he had been. But what he had become could grasp and understand it. Barely—but enough.

Power he needed, yes—but the power was kin to the Dark Heart, born of the Darkness, and alone was not enough.

Did you wish to hear my *voice, Lord? Then* listen.

He lifted his head an inch, but otherwise did not move. He opened his eyes, and beyond the haze of red, he conjured up a single image so strongly it was almost flesh.

Her image.

But she was not sleeping, was not dead, was not angry with him, hurt by him, or confused. She was not armed, not armored, not caught in the Light of her heritage. No; she was simply dressed in a robe she herself had chosen because it lacked frills and the excess of finery. Between her cupped hands, she held a single lily that one of the slaves' children had picked for her out of the garden—risking the wrath of the groundskeeper and master gardener both. Her eyes were turned down, her lips turned up, her shoulders curved inward.

Sara.

She looked up, across the years, to see his face. And what she saw, he could not say, but the smile grew deeper both on his lips and her own. He did not even remember where or when this was—and neither were important enough to cause him to cast through memory for the answers.

She was now.

She had always been part of the now of human imperative. And she had caught him in its web.

Sara, love. What do you have there?

A flower, Lord. For you. Her cheeks dimpled. *Only you can pull one from your gardens with impunity.* She held out a hand; it passed through the barrier. The faintest scent of lilies touched his mind.

And the Dark Heart growled.

She could draw no blood, make no offer to her silent God. Even her lips could grant her no prayer, and she wondered if Sargoth would release her enough to allow her to scream. He drew closer, and she felt the chill of his claws caress her thighs.

His hands shot up and in at the same moment, but with such a deliberation and care he might have been an artist working with clay. Blood came, rushing to fill the depth of the open, white wound.

Blood was what she needed. Her arms were not free; the gesture of the open circle was lost to her—but it wasn't necessary. She concentrated and lost God's name as Sargoth struck again across her open breast. It was slow, this strike; she felt her skin resist him a moment before giving way to the greater power.

She could not scream; her throat would not allow it. But the tears that trickled down her cheek were no longer those of mere discomfort.

Her eyes cast around the room beyond her tormentor's back, and she saw the black altar, clean and shining, that rested upon a web of red. Beneath it, so close it was a subtle torture, lay a stagnant, muddied pool.

Then she lost the use of her left eye.

Choking, she struggled to remember the name of God.

He saw her more clearly than he saw the red walls. He heard her more clearly than he heard the Dark Heart. And he opened some part of his mind, of more than his mind, to the gentle pressure of her words.

He allowed for no loss; he would not think of it. Not when he could remember the other sensations that only she had ever brought forth. Warmth. Love. Hope.

These had ever been a private secret for the Lord of the Empire; he had shared them with Sara alone. Until this moment.

Love, with its depth of faith and hope, had become the sharpest of his weapons.

Stefanos! Cease this!

Lernan.

There was a scream in the auditorium that was not hers; it was too high, and too young. But the pain behind it did not touch more than her ears; she was too involved with her own.

Lernan. God's name.

Blood ran down her throat from the ruin of her lips.

Lernan! God, I grant you this willingly!

The Second of the Sundered laughed aloud. "He cannot hear you, half blood. He will never hear you again." His eyes flashed, and her lips were free. The breath that passed them came out in a whimper and grew into a full scream. "But we hear, Sarillorn. We will hear this for hours yet." He looked up. "Do you all have a good view?"

Darin of Culverne screamed again with the voice of an eight-year-old boy.

Stefanos gathered the remains of his power the way a father will take a child into his arms: gently, lovingly.

This redness, this warmth, this part of his life—it had been the one thing he had denied Sara while she had remained at his side. He had rarely let her see it and had never let her touch it.

He offered it to her now, with a warmth of love that denied its essence. Held it out, in strength and with conviction.

The wall shuddered as his hands touched it. It shivered, growing hard and brittle. This one thing that Stefanos offered, it had never been able to contain.

Almost at a distance, the First of the Sundered watched his only victory against his Dark Lord. The wall was fraying.

Too late!

Sargoth's hand stopped; it froze in midair.

Erin's screams died into choked sobs, and her one good eye traveled the length of Sargoth's shadowed visage. He seemed to be struggling with something that she could not see.

The room became silent; there was not even the sound of breath to interrupt Sargoth's quiet whisper.

"As you command, Lord."

He raised one claw, pulled it back, and then tore out half of Erin's throat.

Red light flared like an inferno in the chamber. Shadow surged forward and back; clouds, dark and heavy, held a crown of red-fire. The hells of legend might be more pleasant than this and infinitely less dangerous to the damned.

The Lord of the Empire had come.

Do you see, Stefanos? You are too late. She is beyond you.

The voice of the Dark Heart had never been so stark and so clear. The whisper of words barely contained what lay beneath them; the darkness was stronger here than it had been since the Awakening.

Sara hovered above the ground in an awkward parody of life. Her arms were stiff at her side, and her feet jerked spasmodically beneath her. He barely recognized her face beneath the network of welts and wounds that had destroyed it. Her naked body was slick with the blood that rained down from an open jugular.

This was not what he had dreamed of. This was not what he had offered the Dark Heart as the key to locked walls.

"Welcome, First of the Sundered. Welcome to the altars of God." Sargoth bowed awkwardly. "Have you come to claim what is *yours*?" The laughter was strong and double-edged; sibilance skittered across the surface of a shadowed, ancient power. "Take it, then."

No one moved in the crowded chamber. All eyes were upon Sargoth and Stefanos, waiting an outcome that they could not hope to influence.

The Lord of the Empire had no words to offer. There was suddenly nothing beneath his feet, and the shadows that surrounded him seemed to go on and on into an infinity of empty hopes and memories.

"Kill the others," a new voice said. Lord Vellen's. The high priest. He spoke to his Swords, and for the first time in all their years of service, they hesitated at this high command.

Stefanos roared. His voice, inhuman and immortal, filled the temple and traveled beyond the locked doors. He threw his arms wide in a gesture of denial, and his eyes flashed, not red, but silver.

At a distance, he caught Sara in the arms of his unblooded power. He could not feel her, but he could see how each invisible tendril that came from his opened gate jarred her body.

Thirty seconds had passed.

He turned her to face him and saw the empty socket, the empty eye.

Stefanos, who is your master?

The laughter of the Dark Heart shuddered through him; he could not turn from it and could not deny it: It was that close. Light, even pure Light, would be a welcome alternative, a merely physical death.

Light . . .

He leaped forward then, toward the Second of the Sundered.

Sargoth did not move, did not even brace for the charge, so sure was he of the Dark Heart's protection. Radiating outward from him, so strong it was almost clear to the mortal eye, was a solid sphere of blood-magic, the finger of God. Not even Stefanos could breach it—not now.

Yet Stefanos stayed true to his unpredictable nature. Instead of attacking, he caught the half-blood's dying body in his arms and pulled it close.

"You cannot save her. You cannot even breach the walls that keep her from her God."

"No," Stefanos said, fully accepting the import of Sargoth's words. "I cannot." And then he leaped again, carrying his dangling, precious burden. He seemed suspended a moment in midair, and he had cast off the last of the red-fire that had been his mantle. Were it not for the height of the jump, and the speed with which he traveled, he might have been mortal.

His feet landed upon the altar, black against black. He spoke a single word. It was quiet, soft, and undeniable. The color of his open eyes was silver, a flash of incandescent lightning that drove away, forever, all memory of redness.

The great altar, the pride of the Church of the Dark Heart, shattered. Marble shards flew everywhere, sharp projectiles that spoke of the wrath and power of he who had once been the chosen of his God.

"*I* cannot."

Sargoth wheeled suddenly, bringing the power of the Dark Heart to bear as he realized the intent of the First of the Sundered.

And Stefanos surrendered his Lady to her Lord. He had no time for gentleness or care—no time to see whether any spark of life remained within her. No power of darkness or of magic aided him at all as he plunged her into the waters below. The putrid surface of the Wound of the Enemy gave way before the last of Elliath, closing sluggishly over the top of her head.

Sara, please. Sara . . .

He heard Sargoth's scream. He saw a shadow of red power slowly taking shape. He had lost all sense of time and nearly all sense of place; there was only the poisoned Wound and the body of his Lady. He wondered if she was dead, and if this last defiant gesture only served as a fitting burial. Mortals were so frail . . .

Sara!

And then he felt it: a faint, painful tingle that began at his fingertips. His eyes could not pierce the surface of the water, but he felt no movement beneath his hands. He wondered, briefly, if he imagined the sensation. Until it began to grow.

For the first time, he truly understood what the blood of a God of Light could do.

All there were privy to his screams as the water lapped at his hands and arms. He could not contain his agony, but he did not pull away while anything remained of his hands.

His pain fed the darkness.

Erin could not breathe. She tried, and water filled her mouth, traveling a quick path down her throat to mingle with the blood in her lungs. She wanted to struggle, but couldn't. The nerves of her spine had been badly damaged. There was hardly even room now for thought.

She did not see the water that surrounded her, did not feel the clawed hands that gripped her skull and forehead. Instead, she saw mist. Soft, gray mist that seemed to contain a hidden light of its own.

And she knew where she was. She had been here once before. *This* was her final path. It led to the Bridge, beyond all pain, all guilt, all loss. Her parents would be there, across the odd and endless river. Her grandfather. Telvar. Katalaan.

She started to walk, if walk was the word, but something would not let her go. This time she did not struggle. She knew what it was. Erin of Elliath had not yet earned her place on this path; there was something left to do. But the doing would be hard. Never in her life had she truly imagined all that a Servant of the Darkness was capable of inflicting. Pride, anger, confidence in God—all of these things had somehow conspired to keep her free from the pain of a slow, bloody death. Here, in the mist, she felt no pain, no fear.

But *there*, there it would all return to her. And yet dead— she could say that now—dead, she could not accomplish anything of value in the living world.

She drew a sharp breath and held it, although it made no difference here. And when she expelled it, it carried a voice that was almost unearthly.

"Lernan, Great-grandfather, I give you my dying blood freely."

The mist suddenly thickened and grew cold; it swirled

around her, battering her as if she were a mountain and it a rushing current. The gray light grew stronger and stronger still, until it was blinding white, with the palest touch of green life.

Great-grandchild. I bid you return awhile. You have almost reached the end of the road that I set you upon, but not yet, not yet. I cannot expect your forgiveness, and yet I ask it. Return, dearest of all my descendants.

His voice was so sharp and clear that it resonated throughout all of her body with the glory of its song. She had never been so close to the voice of God, had never been touched so strongly and so completely by His presence. She felt His blood swirl around her as if it were two strong arms; two beloved arms that could offer a comfort nowhere else to be found. Invisible lips pressed themselves against her forehead, smoothing away all traces of pain, past or present. She felt overpowered by warmth, she could no longer remember a time when she had not known His Love.

The Bright Heart of Elliath had been cleansed.

chapter
twenty-two

The waters began to rise.

Even through his pain, Stefanos felt the sudden change in the depths. There was no stillness or taint of death. He closed his eyes, but the green light growing before him—almost around him—could not be shut out by mere lids.

Torn between reluctance and profound relief, he hesitated a moment before he finally released Sara's face. It was almost too long.

The light began to coruscate as the waters rose in no natural pattern. Like a pillar, they came out of the Wound of the Bright Heart, rising ever upward in the long reach of the Enemy. Only the vaulted ceiling seemed to halt their progress—but even of this, he could not be certain. The Light that burned him was pure enough, strong enough, to splinter the dead shade of gray that was stone.

He could not see his lady. He lifted his arms and opened his mouth before he realized that his response was a gesture of war, of eternal battle. Of the Dark Heart. What other response was there to the Light?

His own choice. But no choice had ever been so difficult to make. He was burning in white-fire and death. He could not see his hands and wondered if any of their flesh yet remained.

But he did not act, not even to stop the pain.

"Sara!"

The pillar of light suddenly opened. Layers of water, of the blood of the Light, peeled away slowly to reveal the very heart of the column. The Lady of the Lord of the Empire lay nestled within, her legs curled to her chest, her arms folded around

346

them. Her skin was very white, very pale. How long had it been since she had seen the sun?

He shook himself, wondering at the irrelevance of the question. Perhaps the Light had burned more than just his flesh.

"Sara?"

She lifted her chin slowly. Her lashes were pressed against her cheeks, and they came away as if she were afraid of what her eyes would see.

There was hardly any distance between them at all, but he dared not cross it. All he could do was touch her with his own eyes, eyes that were now just blackness in the shadowed gray of his long face. He had not the power left to pretend to be human.

"S-Stefanos?"

His knees would not support his weight, although the weight was almost insubstantial. He sank to the marble floors and felt shards of the shattered altar bite into his legs.

"Lady." He bowed his head before her, unable to meet the growing brilliance of her not-quite-mortal eyes. "I was wrong. Can you forgive me?"

She opened her mouth to speak, but it was not her voice that answered.

It was cacophony, heard from within and from without.

I-will-not.

"Kill the woman!"

"Destroy the Enemy!"

Thus did the Dark Heart, his Second Servant, and his high priest declare themselves.

And the First of the Sundered raised his head almost wearily. He was alive, although he did not understand why, but that was all: He had none of the power necessary to face any but the most trivial of foes. Not even Lord Vellen could be called trivial now.

"Sara! Call your Light!"

Her smooth brow was almost a child's as it wrinkled into wide-eyed confusion.

"Stefanos?"

If he had been mortal, he would have wept.

The leader of the Greater Cabal swept his arms wide. His eyes, normally icy blue, were the heated red of the fires. The wildness of the call of Light was upon him, and he could barely contain its urge.

"Come, Jael, Marek, Telemach, Corvair—we are the Greater Cabal, and this is the last battle we will ever have to fight. Come!" He held out either hand.

They needed no further urging, for they too were of the blood. One by one, each of the four came to stand beside their leader. The differences of their heights, their ages, their complexions, and weight paled into insignificance as their eyes burned brighter; they could have been one man, with one purpose.

"Captain—prepare. You are the Swords of the Dark Heart— His weapons. Concentrate all that you have upon the Enemy!"

Again, no further words were needed. For the Swords, however weak in blood, were still Malanthi. Their weapons were already drawn, and they glittered in the light like long, dangerous teeth.

"What of the others?"

"Others?"

The Sword gestured, and Vellen turned his head slightly to see the prisoners who had been the Sarillorn's companions. They had almost been forgotten. He sighed almost regretfully. He had so wanted to offer the boy to God at his own leisure. His eyes silvered slowly, for the red was reluctant to let go.

"Kill them."

Darin, Gerald, Corfaire, and Cospatric were suddenly dropped the fifteen feet that separated them from solid ground. They had no time to brace for the impact, but in only one case did that make any difference. The three guards, still in Valens uniforms, had already started their rolls into recovery.

Darin was stunned.

Bethany, held up until this moment in white, taut fingers, suddenly rolled away, clattering as if she were only another stick of wood. She disappeared beneath the tread of fast-moving boots.

Darin raised his eyes from the floor to see the Swords, with weapons that he could not hope to counter, running toward him. He had screamed so much this evening that he hadn't the voice to utter even a quiet curse.

But he had seen Erin rise, whole, from the Gifting of God. She looked like no priestess and no Sarillorn of legend, curled as she had been in the blood of the Bright Heart. No; she had seemed almost helpless, like the youngest of children waking from nightmare. He shook his head and began to struggle to his feet.

Bethany was not his only weapon, but the Swords were close and moving closer with every breath he took.

If he could have seen his own face, he might have stopped in shock—but he was the patriarch of Culverne, and though weak of blood, Lernari by birth. He too felt the call to battle take him, and his eyes were the deepest, clearest, brightest of greens.

There were three in the room who heard the call as clearly and more strongly than Darin did. But they had the advantage of age and experience to stay their hands momentarily.

Amalayna, once Lady of both Valens and Tentaris, had encountered this Light brief hours ago, wrapped like a cloak around Erin. Then, she had thought it powerful and pervasive; now, she could barely stand against its imperative. *Light* was the enemy. Light was the reason that war had been invented. She clenched her hands tightly and felt an alien coldness in their grasp. Looking down, she realized that she had already pulled her daggers. They gleamed, reflecting death incarnate in sharp, painful green.

Her mouth was open, and the words that left her lips were a declaration of war and purpose. She was burning; she felt the warmth of life struggle against this glare of death. What chance had she, after all? No desire, no purpose, no determination had ever been as strong as this. She began to move forward, twisting the daggers in her hands until they appeared to be miniature swords.

Corfaire had his sword out; he had gained his feet more gracefully than either Gerald or Cospatric. He had no shield, but he did not miss it—it would only slow him down. His lips were bloody; he tasted the trickle of warmth and salt that made its way through clenched teeth.

Light burned at him like fire. His skin, both exposed and armored, tingled with the pain of it. He, too, shouted until his throat was raw, and the words were a declaration of death to any who might hear.

He had come this far for a purpose that now eluded him. All of his skill and training had been honed to *this* fight. He had been a slave for most of his life; he was used to following orders and imperatives without thought of death. He laughed wildly and swung his sword through the air without fear. What was there to be afraid of, after all? He had never lost a fight.

In front of him, rising to a pathetic height, was the boy whose very blood was anathema. Of their own accord, his feet carried him to that boy's back. *This* was an Enemy. He had never truly understood what that word could mean.

His blade rose in an arc; he could almost hear it whistling in the air.

Stefanos rose as quickly as he could. The Light of the Bright Heart, which he would never acknowledge as Enemy again, was almost blinding, but he did not need mere sight to see the gathering force of Darkness that entered the room to answer the summons of the Light.

But the First of the Sundered had spent four centuries denying the call of the blood—four centuries and an eternity of hunger and desire. This call to battle was stronger than any other moment he had faced since the Awakening.

And it was not strong enough.

Other hungers and other desires had taken root with deceptive softness. He was tainted by them, pulled by them, and in the end, commanded by them. His Lady's face was changing; confusion was being replaced by some other emotion. But it happened slowly, and he had no time to watch the transformation.

Sargoth was upon him.

Darin started to concentrate. It was hard; opening a gate required an intensity of thought that would not come. The Swords grew larger; he could see the expressions on their faces, for they were mostly unhelmed now.

He dared not close his eyes, but the sight of the enemy did not give him the moment of peace that he needed. He stood almost rooted to the ground, and then his arms shot up, cutting the air with a speed that was dizzying.

In front of him, the sigil of the Greater Ward took shape in the air.

The Sword at the forefront of the unit of eight screamed in pain and anger as his headlong rush carried him through it. But he did not stop, did not even slow. His sword came up, and

Darin's arms rose again—a poor shield to the blow that was certain to follow.

He heard the whistle of metal's contemptuous disregard for air, and his lids slammed tight over his eyes.

The blow never reached him.

Instead, he heard the clang of steel against steel and felt an arm shove him down and aside. His eyes sprang open as death retreated.

Corfaire and the Sword formed an artist's visceral tableau of combat. But this was no fresco, no tapestry; they began to move almost instantly, seeking the weakness that strength concealed.

"Don't just gawk, boy!" Corfaire said, although his lips hardly moved. Sweat was running from the ridges on his forehead to the edges of his jaw. He strained as he lifted his weapon and danced neatly out of the edge of his foe's reach. "Move!"

Darin still stood frozen for a moment; he could see the glow of red that signaled the Enemy within Corfaire.

"Damn you!" he shouted as he lunged. "Get out of my range! Get-out-of-my-sight!" Swords clattered together and fell apart as Darin's ward began to fade.

A hand clamped down on Darin's shoulder and dragged him away as the Swords once again surged forward to help their captain.

It was Gerald's hand.

"Patriarch!" he shouted. "Take cover!" He could not see as Darin saw, did not understand that Corfaire's concern for Darin's presence had nothing to do with Darin's safety. "Aid the Lady if you can—this battle is beyond you!"

Gerald's voice, free from the taint of either blood, filled Darin's ears and brought him back to himself for a moment. He turned on his heel and raced for the far wall, stopping only once his hand had reached it.

Then he turned to see three men standing abreast—Gerald, Cospatric, and Corfaire—Corfaire who, by his actions and choice, had declared himself a slave no more.

Three men against eight Swords. Damn it, where was Bethany?

All plans had gone awry. Vellen, the leader of the Greater Cabal, gloried briefly in that knowledge. It should have been a sign to him; he had never taken well to defeat or deviation of any sort before. A red arch, of which he was the center, sprang out from either of his hands, finding struts and supports for itself in the members of his cabal. He had no need to call for God; God was in the very air and had no intention of ignoring him—not now, not in the face of the Enemy.

The clang of swords sounded at his back like the tinkle of bells that announced the presence of greatness. He threw back his head, and it seemed that he had three eyes; the ruby of his office burning with the colder light.

The power of the Karnari gathered like a hand above the five. All around it, the shadows and darkness began to dissipate. The glove was gone; the first remained. The reach of its arm was long.

Red-fire burned so brilliantly in the air it almost had the power to blind. Unerring, it sped toward its target.

God's voice filled her suddenly with its absence. She felt the ripple of the waters around her grow momentarily cold. The pillar shifted, and she lurched downward. Of their own accord her legs unfolded, and her arms reached out to grab something—anything—that would brace her for the fall. It did not come; the waters shored her up at the last moment, and she stood inches from the ground, encircled by the stone mouth of the well itself.

She saw Stefanos, his lips frozen, his fingers curled, and wondered what was wrong.

And then the fire suddenly touched her skin, and she had no time for more.

Even bent and seemingly crippled, Sargoth was a power. He did not dare the fires of the Enemy; they would come too close to his frail form. Instead, he concentrated on the Servant who had once been his superior.

Power made him feral, power and the hand of God. It did not make him careless.

Any other enemy would not have been able to hold so much control. Stefanos was already leaping; not backward or sideways, but up. He felt the Second of the Sundered whistle past him and bit back a cry of pain where claws raked his side.

There was redness and fire in them, but there was no death; not yet.

"Sara!" he shouted, *"Sara, ward!"*

He cut himself free from the air, once again moving too slowly to avoid Sargoth's reach completely. Another bloodless gash appeared to keep company with the first. Sargoth was toying with him.

She heard the call at a distance; it twisted in and out of the crackle of fire and fire's pain. She tried to retreat into the Hand of God, but His comfort was gone. He had pulled her from somewhere warm to somewhere hot.

There was nothing to protect her skin from blistering and buckling, no clothing, no armor—no ward. No ward. She bit her lip and struggled to make some feeble gesture, but when her lips moved it was only to allow a scream to escape.

No fire had ever been so intense and so binding.

The ululation of her cry was musical, higher and sweeter than almost any other sound of battle that reached Lord Vellen's ears. He watched her as she writhed in pain and thought it even more beautiful a sight than the interrupted ceremony of the Second. High above her, the First of the Sundered fought a losing battle—one of retreat, one of weakness.

Even the cleansing of the Enemy's wound had granted nothing. The Dark Heart would soon be the only one that beat, and it would beat with the pulse of His victory.

He cried out his wordless praise, and the red-fire grew brighter, carried by the cabal that would soon freely rule the entire world.

Darin did not dare to approach the fighting. He drew one dirty sleeve across his forehead; it came away wet. His skin was tingling, and his eyes were bright, but battle lust had broken for the moment, and he was free to think.

He gestured, calling up the Greater Ward with an ease that would have made the Grandmother proud. And then he looked through it, at a world tinted green. The eight against three had become six; two Swords, still twitching, lay upon the cold ground, offering it their blood.

He needed Bethany, and now might be his only chance to find her. He scanned the ground beyond the Swords, seeing in a way that was new to him. She was not very hard to find, limned with the power of the Bright Heart, isolated in a sea of red.

He started forward and then stopped himself, taking deep, deliberate breaths. She wasn't reachable, not by foot.

He brought his hands to his ears to drown out the noise and began to concentrate as if his very life depended on it.

Come on, gate. Open. Open, damn you.

His eyes saw only blackness as he struggled.

Lady Amalayna moved slowly past the Karnari. Her daggers were almost extensions of her hands, and her eyes were wide and glassy. Never in her life, in her long experience, had she felt so much that was both alien and inescapably *right*. She heard the screams of the Lady in the Light, and they were impossibly musical. Everywhere around her, her heritage had sprung to bloody, glorious life.

So intent was she upon these new sensations, that she only saw it out of the corner of her eye. Whirling, daggers forward, she saw one of the Karnari crumple, a dagger embedded in his throat.

She shouted a warning, but it came too late. Another Karnar fell to some invisible enemy.

Her eyes sought the heights in desperation.

"There!" she cried, swinging one arm up. "In the galleries!"

Bethany lurched up from the ground as if held in clumsy, shaking hands. So intent were the Swords on their battle that they did not see her. Sweat had already started to gather in the wrinkles at Darin's brow.

Come . . . here . . . now!

She straightened, and the grip on her became sure. Like a spear seen through a memory-walk, she came slowly enough that he could follow each inch of her passage. He lost all sensation and all hearing—the room became eerily silent. Only the whisper of the gate could be heard, pleading for more power. He had made that mistake once before, and although he could not imagine what this gate could do given free reign, he did not let his concentration or control lapse.

She came to his hand, and he curled his fingers tightly around her. Her light was once more his, and the two would not be parted.

The gate almost closed before he heard her whisper.

The Bright Sword, Initiate. Find it. It is here.

Bethany had never been given to completely reasonable requests. *I can't—it's too heavy.*

You can. The Light needs what power you can lend it.

He started to search the room, and her voice once again pulled him short.

Not with that *sight. Seek the Light, Darin.*

He nodded, but he was a little afraid of all that came with that vision. He opened his eyes, trying to hold his gate, as the world turned red.

There, just in front of him, Swords carried fire, *were* fire. Beyond them, there was darkness. To their left was a crimson that made his teeth ache. He could make out no faces now, no crests, no insignias—they were insignificant compared to the glow that they carried. He followed its trail and saw what it ended with: Lernan's Light. Fear cut his breath, and the gate almost spun away. He could feel Bethany burning his fingers with necessary warmth.

Not there, she said urgently. *Not now. The sword.*

What light could a sword cast when compared to God's blood? He struggled to look away, and by some miracle, succeeded. And his eyes lit upon a small glow in the shadow. With relief, his sight returned to normal.

Cast away, along with Erin's armor, lay the short sword she had carried. Gallin's sword. The Bright Sword. He began to concentrate anew.

A crossbow bolt slipped neatly between what might have passed for ribs in a mere human. It did not pain him, or cause him mortal injury. At any other time, he would have merely used it as a pretext to destroy the aggressor.

But this was not another time; indeed, another time might never come to pass for the proud immortal who had once been First among the Sundered. The bolt struck him in his downward dance in midair, with enough force to send him upward. The Second of the Sundered wasted no given advantage—and unlike small sticks of pointed wood, his claws caused pain and injury.

Stefanos let out a snarl of rage and lashed out himself, losing some of the control that he had always prized so highly. His arms, slowed by lack of power and injury, fell short of their target. His eyes flashed silver as he called pure fire to his aid. A column flared momentarily to life, consuming a Sword entirely before it was guttered.

Sargoth.

He should have killed Sargoth years ago.

The Bright Sword came. It was not as heavy or difficult as Bethany had been; it was light, and it moved as if meant for the air. Darin tore it from its sheath as it traveled, easing the load that he carried.

Green light glared in the darkness, and the background rumble of red and shadow did nothing to suppress it.

Below, Swords looked up at this new foe that had entered the fray. That helped Cospatric; he had, for a moment, only one foe to contend with.

But these Swords were good—possibly the best he had ever encountered. He bled, and there were rents in the armor that should have served as better protection. He countered, countered again, and then thrust forward.

They were fast. Speed and skill should have counted against him by now. Long minutes had passed, and he had still managed to keep to his feet. He could not know that speed and skill had been subject to a battle lust that unbalanced control or thought—but he took advantage of it just the same.

The room barely existed for him, although he was aware that marble made a poor fighting surface by now. He could not see Erin, and her screams were not the attenuated music that other ears heard. He could not see the two Servants who fought for supremacy of air, or survival in it.

But he did see the preternatural gleaming of a short sword as it descended to the level of his hands.

The Sword that had left off his attack made a grab for it. His first mistake. Cospatric had no compunction about ensuring that it was his last. The sudden scream of the Sword was cut short, and the short blade once again began to hover in the air, inviting Cospatric's attention.

In the heat of combat, his reaction was all that could be expected: quick, intuitive, his own.

"Not a God-cursed chance! This stinking magic got us into this mess in the first place!" And he slashed under it, sidestepping the handle that tried to worm its way in his direction.

The Bright Sword, thus shoved aside, still hovered until another hand reached out to take the power it offered to a wielder.

There was a scream of pain, but it was muffled by teeth that were clenched and a body that was braced to feel it.

Corfaire dropped his own sword and struggled a moment with this alien, enemy force. He felt fire in his hands, although they did not burn; he felt his arms lock in pain, although he could still swing them. He opened his mouth and let out a feral cry that caught all ears for a moment.

"*Lady!*" It drowned out her screams for a merciful second before he began a new assault. He moved awkwardly, even clumsily, given his usual grace and speed—but the Bright Sword made up for it, finding its target almost unerringly.

On either end of its blade.

Fire consumed him, but he dared not let go. Blood trailed down his lips as his teeth cleared his skin. To either side, Gerald and Cospatric were left behind to deal with those not immediately killed.

Half-blind, Corfaire began to cut a path to the woman who held his life—or what little remained of it.

"Hold the red-fire! Concentrate on it!" Lord Vellen's voice was ice; he barely looked at the jerking bodies of those who had once been Karnari. "I will deal with this!" He followed Amalayna's arm until he saw what she had seen: two black-clad men in the galleries above. They had no light; neither red nor white—at any other moment this evening, they would have been beneath his notice.

"Do you dare?" he shouted.

"Oh hells!" replied the shorter of the two. They dove to either side as lightning split the air, cracking the stone rails that had served as their cover.

One slim dagger clattered uselessly against the wall beyond them. It bore the crest of Valens.

Amalayna's arm was pulled back as she aimed the second dagger. Her eyes followed the darting shapes, picking them easily from the shadows.

She recognized Renardos and the old man who was obviously a friend. Her dagger froze in midair; they were quick, and she had only one more throw. But they hardly stayed still, and there was enough of the gallery left to provide them with too much cover.

"Lord!" someone shouted.

"Don't be a fool!" was the angry reply. Lightning stove in another rail. "Concentrate your strength upon the First of the Sundered! Do you think you can reach them before they flee, where *I* cannot?"

She heard the mail jingle of a stiff salute. Turned to see the back of a Sword and his waiting unit. Turned again to look at the profile of the lord of the Greater Cabal, with his silver eyes and his flushed face.

His was nearly the greatest power here, next to those that had no business with mortality. He still bore the brunt of the red-fire as it streamed around his head and shoulders. He stood so tall and so straight in the light of God that she knew she had never seen so beautiful a man.

Her heart stopped beating then.

No. Not never.

She turned, hearing the battle and its call, feeling the bite of light and the burning of blood as it rushed up and down her taut arm.

"Laranth." Her voice was a whimper. She bit her lip, drawing blood. *Help me. I need strength. Laranth . . .*

Her blade cut through the air, ending with Vellen's throat. Steel rose once, twice, and almost a third time before the Swords reached her.

The pain was suddenly gone.

Erin gasped. The walls of her throat clung together. She opened her eyes, blinking tears away as rapidly as she could. Her vision was all of the Light—no Stefanos remained bent before her, and not even his long shadow was visible.

She knew where she was now, knew why she was here and why she had twice been denied her passage over the Bridge. She raised her hand to her lips, baring them to expose the white of teeth. She had no daggers and very little else that would pierce her skin and draw her blood.

But she raised her head as her hand found her mouth, searching for some sign of Stefanos. Lord Darclan. Her bond-mate.

It was odd; she had been so afraid to meet him again, and now—now she wanted the chance to bid him farewell. To tell him, *yes, I forgive.*

He was gone, and she had her last duty. Her bleeding hand

left her mouth, and she plunged it into the rippling blood of God. Let the red-fire return now, for all the good it would do the Enemy.

She was no memory-walker—although she had once been privy to the use of the Gifting, all that remained in memory was the stark, pale image of the Lady of Elliath.

The Lady's warning echoed in her ears.

Do not touch the Gifting, Grandchild. You do not know how to control what you draw, and you will be consumed by it.

Yes.

"Fools!" Sargoth roared at the Swords below, his prey momentarily forgotten. *"Kill the woman!"* His skin tingled and ached, presaging the future. He looked across the room to see what remained of the Greater Cabal and cursed again, more strongly.

The Swords rushed toward the column at his command. In seconds, they, too, would feel what he felt, but until then, they might have some small chance.

Erin absorbed the first quarrel that struck her. She did not even feel the separation of flesh that was left in its wake. There was no pain, no injury. Not now.

Instead there was warmth, a sweet rush of power that traveled up her hand until it filled all of her.

Another bolt hit her, this time in the throat, and it, too, left no mark.

She rose, higher and higher, until she was almost at the peak of the ceiling. There, seconds stretched out into infinity as she raised her face. She was the perfect vessel of an ancient power's will.

Her arms swung wide and in full circle, crossing over her chest; the gesture was all fluid perfection and cold grace. She said nothing; there was no need of words.

Lernan's Light had found its focus.

Great-grandchild, forgive me. For you have been my hope, but I am still of the Light.

Her power—His power—flared outward, an undeniable rain of green brilliance and pale death. She felt its surge, and warmth became heat; pleasure and comfort gave way to a slowly building pain. Its like had touched her before, but that memory was no match for reality.

She could not withdraw now, could not move. Light held her captive, by her consent. She heard screams and saw red-fire billow incandescently upward to touch her face. It never reached her.

The Bright Heart was here; the Dark Heart could only watch. He had never been as open to His followers of shadow, had never offered so direct and weakening a power as the Gifting. And only once in His long existence had He ever felt need to regret it.

She took some small pleasure from this knowledge, but it was small indeed. The pain was growing so strong she was not certain that the red-fire did not eat away at her very blood.

She tried to think of Belfas. He would be free, soon. She would be with him. Maybe—maybe they would have much to say to each other at the Bridge.

She opened her mouth to scream, and the scream was a name that lingered in the silence.

"Stefanos!"

And the pain suddenly dwindled.

The Gifting of God let her slowly down, without ever releasing its precious burden.

She looked down at her body and saw it, incongruously whole, and turned to see that her hand still rested within the waters of her God.

Look. Look now, Great-grandchild.

She did, as the waters opened before her. The dead were everywhere. No, not everyone was dead. For among the armor-clad bodies that seemed to lie like a carpet across the cold floor, she could see Darin, standing with his staff in one hand and his mouth agape.

She nodded, and her eyes moved to Gerald and Cospatric. They, too, stared at her, but Gerald blushed and turned away. He cuffed Cospatric on the side of the head, and Cospatric found something interesting to look at near the region of his boots.

She saw two dark shadows, but they were dark to mortal vision only, and once again she smiled. Renar was shaking dust off his jacket and frowning. Tiras was standing quite straight and proud. His eyes alone looked completely beyond her, and she caught her breath, hardly daring to follow the line of the old weapon-master's vision.

Stefanos.

The First of the Sundered stood in silence upon the ground before her. She could see him fully. He wore no magical guise and did nothing to drive away the shadows and the bloodred mist that even now were his nature.

"H-how?"

My will, Great-grandchild. Will you not speak with him? Will you not take this last chance? I understand what he has become to you; I cast no blame.

She started to step forward, but the Light did not release her.

No, child. Speak from where you are, as the Sarillorn that you are. I will keep watch.

She wanted to tell Him that He had no need to do so, but arguing with God, after this miracle, was not within her. "S-Stefanos?"

"Sara." He bowed, formally and with the greatest of dignity. She saw his injuries clearly as he moved, and her heart fell; it was not within her power to heal him.

The red light around him grew stronger, brighter.

"Are you—do you call the Dark Heart's power?"

His smile was grim and cold, with just a hint of the pain her question invoked. "Can you think so of me, even now? No, Lady. I do not call it, but I cannot deny it fully. I have not the strength."

"Will He strike—through you?"

"No." There was no doubt in the word. He looked up at her and tried to smile. Failed. Very carefully he walked toward the Light that he should shun. He held out one clawed hand that fell just short of the hand that she offered in return.

Stefanos met her eyes. "There is always something, Lady, that stands between us." His voice was so soft she barely heard the catch in it. But around his limbs, the red was growing stronger.

"Darkling."

"Sara."

Tears began to gather at the corners of her eyes.

Bright Heart—please . . . Your power should have ended all of this . . .

No, child. Four of my descendants still await their freedom from the First of the Enemy's binding.

But—but my death—

Alone will not grant it. Speak. Say what you must.

Her lips opened, trembled, and closed again on a heavy

breath. *I have come all this way; I have cleansed You and called Your power down upon our—Your—enemies. But this . . . Don't make me ask this. Not of him, please.*

God gave her no answer, and that was answer enough. She tried to struggle free of the Light, but it remained a warm and loving prison. She had dreaded a confrontation, had feared that her actions in battle would not prove true to her determination. But this, this was worse.

"Lady, what would you, or your Lord, have of me?"

"S-Stefanos . . ." Her fingers trembled as they strained toward his, falling just short of contact. Her eyes were round and wide, glittering palely. And then she drew herself up, swallowed, and accepted the last, and the hardest, of her tasks.

"Darkling.

"I—I loved you. Hated you. Love you still. I've seen you in the realm of the Dark Heart; I know what—what you felt there.

"But—" She drew ragged breath again. "But we are still what we are. Look at you. Even now the red and the shadows are growing stronger. Look at me—I am still *of* the Light. That won't change. It can't really, no matter what we do.

"You rule, and are ruled. I serve, and I am also ruled. Maybe—no, don't say it." Her hand came up in a soft gesture of denial. "You loved me as much as you could; I loved you as much as I was able. And it—it was almost enough."

"Sara." He shook his head softly, and even through the harsh red light that had grown like a mask over his face, he was beautiful to her. "Don't. I have changed. I do not need this." His arm took in the grandeur of the damaged temple. "I do not need my Empire any longer. Only stay with me, and I will change it for you, as you require."

Her laugh was soft and brief. "*You* will change it? Can't you hear what you say? It is still yours.

"And even if what you say is true, I cannot do as you ask. Stefanos, Darkling, I have walked in the hand of the Dark Heart, and I know why I haven't succumbed to age and death. Carla, Rein, Teya, and—and Belfas are trapped there and will remain so for as long as I live. Don't make me, don't ask me, to live with that burden. I—I want to, but I know it would—" She wiped the tears from her eyes without closing them or looking away from his still, pale face.

"This world is gray now, and I think it has no place for the black and the white. We two can rise above what we *are* at the best of times, but not always—and always is what we would need. We have too much power, and there is too much conflict between our different blood. You've said that you love me. Show me. Don't ask me to bear this. Release me now."

He stepped forward and winced, drawing back.

And as he did, he heard the voice of his Lord.

So. In the end, I win, Stefanos. What the Second of my Sundered could not manipulate in his shadow, this half blood of my Enemy has succeeded in bringing about.

I hear you very well, First of my Sundered. And your voice serves only me. Do you know how much power you send?

The Dark Heart was very close. His voice was no longer an attenuated whisper. It was strong and full.

Stefanos was angry, and his anger almost served her as answer enough—but he saw her face as she waited and knew every word she had spoken for truth.

"Sara, I cannot do this."

"Then no one can." She closed her eyes, shrinking from him. Her voice was quiet and distant as she spoke. "They hate it there; it has almost destroyed them."

And he knew, then, that her love for him—the light that she alone could bring with no cost—had survived the memory of the sacrifice of her line-mates, but it would not survive indefinitely. Once, once only, had he seen that light guttered. To lose it, even if she remained alive, would be too great a price.

But to lose it to her death . . .

His memory was sharp and cold and empty. Images flickered past, disregarded as he found what he sought for and examined it closely. There. And there. Beginning and end of the spell that had robbed him of the decades she might have remained at his side. Seventy years? Eighty? One hundred? They seemed, for the first time, significant.

And the long wait, while he solidified his world, meant that he would never have even those. Nor would she.

"Lady. If I— If I do as you have asked, you will die."

She nodded.

"Those years—they will take you at once, and I cannot prevent them."

She nodded again, not bothering to restrain the tears.

"If I ask you not to . . . No. I am sorry."

He brought his arms up and delved into the red mist that

pulsed all around him. God granted the power he asked for willingly. He saw what he had to do to release her; it was simple, really. It would not even give him many more minutes of her time. His mouth moved over the words as his hands clawed at the air in the deliberate turmoil of her request. He could not wait another minute longer; he would lose the strength to grant it.

But as the last of these bindings began to fall, he leaped suddenly toward her, unmindful of Light and the total destruction it would bring.

An immortal never saw the Bridge; there was no Beyond that they would ever share or know. But this last minute, this last gesture, would be his, no matter the cost.

Light, red and white, crackled and thundered as he both sought and offered her the comfort of one final embrace.

And his Lady Sara, his Sarillorn, knew at that instant what he had decided. She pulled open her arms and caught him, holding tightly through the pain of red and the heat of white and the fear of the death that would take her.

And the Hope of the Bright Heart at last reached the end of her road.

Lost in the crackle of twin fires, the beat of Twin Hearts, and the cacophony of voices bright and dark, she freed both her hands and caught him, injured, between them.

She felt the change take her, over the roar of odd voices, heard something rumble in her ears, and something crawl along her body like a wave of harsh sand, digging and twisting at flesh that withered and buckled at its touch.

She heard his whisper, his plea, his pain—and heard something strange: the voice of the Bright Heart, that she would never hear again.

Come, brother!

Brother? What—

Come! We two who have never truly met may yet know each other. Come!

Light surged around her—through her—but it was a Light of a type that she had never felt. It hurt, and yet it carried with it some hidden triumph that eased the pain it caused.

She felt the Darkness, and for the first time, heard its voice. And the sound of it, in the end, was not so different from what the Light had been: ancient, powerful, and inhuman.

What is this? What do you do? No!

But Stefanos would not pull back, and the Dark Heart did not have the time. The Light, strange and shimmering, passed from its Sarillorn into the Servant of the Darkness. He thought it would be his death—but he, too, felt its strangeness and the thing beyond the pain it caused.

He felt his skin tingling and felt a change take him. His grip grew tight, with wonder and with hope.

His spell—the spell he had cast to bind his Sara—she had interrupted it. A smile took his lips, transforming it in the mottled splash of color that was the boundary of Light and Dark. She had been bound by his life, yes. He had not realized, until this moment, that he had been bound by *hers*. It was fitting, in the end, that he die as she did.

And this, this was the end.

Sara held Stefanos tightly, or at least she thought she did. As the magic swirled around her, inside of her, through her, she lost the sensation of hands. She was lost in the feeling of his desperate words as he tried to tell her everything in the rush of seconds that remained. All sound was washed away beneath the roar that was emerging from where the Dark Heart and the Bright Heart finally saw and knew the essence of each other: Sara and Stefanos.

She cried out, denial, acceptance, and loss mingling in a way that words alone could never convey. Pain grew; she felt herself curling inward, ever inward, as the age he had promised transformed her strength into the weakness of the very end of life. At the last, she surrendered to it.

The Light became dim, the Dark brighter. The red and the white were lost to a shade of gray mist that she felt she knew well.

She could not see her feet for its thickness, but the pain of transformation was gone. Her hands found her face; they were slim and smooth. She sighed and knew that the Light had left her. She was now near her Bridge, and all of her dead awaited the final reconciliation. No one would call her back, yet she waited a moment to see if the whisper of God could be heard.

Silence.

I am finished. At last. She turned, but her steps were heavy, almost wooden. The mist, so gray and all-encompassing, had not yet cleared to show her the path.

"Sara?"

She stopped, raising her head. That voice . . . "Stefanos?"

"I hear you, Lady. Where is this place?"

"Stefanos!" She leaped forward, stumbled into him, and bounced back. "Darkling . . ."

He caught her, held her, and they stood as one in the eddying gray that cast no light and no shadow. Her fingers trembled against his back, his arms, his chest—and then stopped suddenly as they reached his cheeks.

He heard her gasp and wondered at it, but let her pull away enough to look up.

"Stefanos—you're crying."

"As are you, Sara." His voice was gentle, soft. He drew her back into the circle of his arms and buried his chin in her hair. There was nothing that separated them, nothing.

Death didn't matter, and the Bridge—it could wait. Or maybe not. Erin, Sara, the Hope of the Bright Heart, tilted her head back and laughed.

"Why do you laugh, little one?" Stefanos' voice was quiet, almost with awe.

"I just thought—when we cross the Bridge, you—I'll—we'll have to meet my parents." Her smile was giddy, radiant—young. "What am I going to say? Mother, Father, this is my bond-mate. You might remember him, he was the First Servant of the Enemy?"

"Meet your parents?"

"Didn't I tell you?" She caught his arm tightly in hers. "No, I guess I didn't. When we performed the ceremony, it wasn't important. I certainly didn't want your parent there." She laughed again, swung around, and hugged him tightly. Then she pulled back. "Darkling, what is it? What's wrong? Nothing can hurt us here."

"Sara—I can't see your light."

"My—" Her smile gentled, and for a moment, she was the older of the two. "There is no Light here, no Darkness."

"Not Light. Light. Yours. I—I saw it often when we were together. It was—it was your love."

"Maybe you don't have the sight to see it with anymore. But can't you feel it? Don't you know it's there?" She caught his cheeks in her hands and marveled at the feel of the warmth beneath her fingers. "This is—this is what normal people must do."

Yes.

They both froze then and looked around, trying to pierce the veil of gray fog. Mist swirled in circles around their twined bodies, moving sluggishly at first, but gathering speed.

My son.

My great-granddaughter.

You were both my hope.

The words tingled along Erin's spine, passing through her body.

L-Lernan?

No. But have no fear, child. Part of what I once was remembers you and what you have suffered. Yet there is no real peace for you yet; no Bridge, no Beyond.

The world has changed; the body houses not two Hearts, but One. You and he were the only door that would ever open for the two that we were. I needed you both because you were of Light and Darkness, and only you two could ever reach this point: containing the essences of the Twin Hearts and binding it awhile by a love that should never have been possible. Only at this moment, caught in death and dying, could you be the . . . bridge that we could cross. And as you are now together, so it is with me.

The half of me that was once Light understands now the anger, the loneliness, the hatred, of the Darkness. I understand when pain is beautiful; I understand that suffering will always exist. And I understand that hope and love will also prevail, in their time. Just as you two did.

I grieve for your suffering, and I revel in it—both. But you followed what the Lady of Elliath saw; you were true to things that you could not understand.

And my son.

Stefanos did not speak.

I have taken from you all that once made you great. You betrayed a part of me, and I will not forget it—but I forgive it as I can. You forsook the Darkness for the gray—and gray indeed have you become.

My children, leave me now, and when you do, tell them: There is no Bright Heart and no Dark Heart; there is the gray alone—the Heart of Man.

Already I hear voices, smaller and more insignificant than yours once were—but with their own odd powers, their own unpredictabilities.

Go in peace; remember this day.

The voice began to dwindle, and the mist to thin. Erin stared in bewilderment as marble appeared beneath her bare feet.

"But—but the Bridge?"

It is not for you yet. A whisper now.

"What of Belfas? What of the others?"

A laughter so full of affection that it could not be hurtful echoed in her ears.

All that you were was not blood alone, great-grandchild. He waits for you. He is free. And you—you, too, are merely mortal. Arrive at his side in your time; he will understand. He tells me to tell you he'll understand if you are late; you always were. And now, hush, child. I have a world to touch, and I see all the possibilities of life, of choice.

I cannot contain myself longer here.

And the Hand of God, of the One Heart, withdrew from the temple. Sunlight shone down through the hole in the ceiling, and filtered through the cracks and missing panes of the stained glass windows. The Gifting of the Bright Heart was empty, a deep, long tunnel through rock beneath the floor.

At its side stood two people, one tall and one—although she would have hated to acknowledge it—quite a bit shorter. One wore dark clothing that was tattered and torn as if from great battle; the other wore nothing at all.

She felt the breeze skirt along her upturned face as she closed her eyes and smiled.

"Sara."

"Mmmm?"

"Take this."

She looked up at Stefanos—at the face that had once been magical guise, but would now know the passage of time—and blushed. Her fingers caught the edge of his cloak as she wrapped it around her shoulders.

"I am human." His voice held a wonder. "But you are still mine."

"And we're very happy to hear it, but do you think we could hear it somewhere else? Look at this!"

Renar was shaking his jacket as if it were a dead rat. "Completely destroyed."

"Erin?"

"Darin!" She threw her arms open, realized that she'd dropped her cape, fumbled with it a second, and then laughed.

He laughed as well and came running as quickly as he could, only to stop a few feet away.

She looked down, sensitive to his expression, although his pain called nothing, nothing at all.

At his feet, nearly lost among the bodies of what had once been Swords, was a guard clad in the gray and burgundy. His fingers, or what remained of them, were locked in a tight grip around the handle of a short sword.

"Corfaire." She knelt and placed her fingers at his throat. She started to push and realized that it was useless. Nothing happened. So had the Bright Heart—the One Heart—warned her. She had been taught to doctor in the regular ways, but even had she not had that skill, she would have known he was dead.

Her eyes filled, and Darin shook his head fiercely.

"It wasn't—it wasn't the Light that killed him, not when you called on the Gifting."

Gerald walked quietly up. It still surprised her that so large a man could make so little noise. He bent down, shoving bodies aside, and carefully picked up Corfaire. "He fought for you, Lady. I think this was the death he would have wanted."

Renar had slid into his jacket and was now looking at the doors. "Uh, do either of the two of you know if we're going to have trouble getting out of here?"

Stefanos raised an eyebrow. "No," he said tersely. "But shall we not find out?"

He gestured, and his eyes flashed silver.

Silver.

Not all of the magic had been lost, then.

With an accusing creak, the doors opened. There was no one in the hall. "Lady?" he said, bowing formally.

She smiled tremulously and took his arm. Beginning together, as they meant to stay, and followed by their companions, they began their walk into a new life.

epilogue

"Isn't this a little selfish?"

Stefanos, in the common clothing of a merchant traveler, grunted as he pulled tight the strings of a bedroll. His hands, once immune to everything, were calloused. Scars he'd received on his first day as a mortal had barely faded. It had taken time to realize that the strength blood had granted him was not the only thing he had lost.

"Selfish, Sara?"

Crossing her arms, she looked out the window. There were royal guards in the courtyard below, practicing their drill. She never understood what such drill was supposed to accomplish, but had to admit that it was an impressive sight.

"Yes, selfish."

He finished shoving things into a pack and then began his search for boots.

"Quite probably."

She shook her head and looked up, seeing the castle walls on the horizon. Beyond them, the city of Dagothrin was flourishing. It was far from the heart of the kingdom, if indeed kingdom it was, but many, many people had made their trek to the northern capital.

It had not been easy for the last several years. There were any number of times when she wondered if she—or her bond-mate—might not have been better off in the Beyond. She remembered his first combat—were it not for the silver of his eyes and the speed of his magic, he would be dead. He had reacted so automatically, and so arrogantly, that he had forgotten for an extremely dangerous moment that weapons, mere steel and wood, could now kill him.

And she, too, had forgotten that with no Light behind her hands, she could not save the injured or the dying. The first time it had happened—

She shook her head. Why these dark musings? It had been difficult, but the One Heart had promised as much.

There was a new religious order that had swept the land, but she had shied away from it, although she was central to its legend and genesis. Twice she had tried to change her name, and three times had tried to abdicate her responsibility to the people.

Cospatric's stinging words shadowed her face, but they brought a weary, affectionate smile as well.

Oh, poor child. The great Lady Erin can't rely on her blood-magic anymore, and now she's just useless. It doesn't matter that everyone trusts her. It doesn't make a difference that she still knows how to doctor and how to fight—'cause she doesn't have her magic.

Well, don't bother feeling sorry for yourself in my *bar, Lady. Either get off your duff and start* living *a life, or get out.*

How his words had hurt, then! And how they had helped. She still drew them out of memory and kept them as a reminder of the renewed responsibility she had earned. He'd even apologized for them later, but far too late; they'd done their work.

And she thanked him for it silently, almost every evening.

"Are you sure about this?"

"Sara, why is it that when *you* have doubts, it is *my* certainty that you question?" He walked up to her and encircled her waist with his arms. She tilted her head back against his chest, and he saw the lines that had deepened around her eyes and had etched themselves into the corners of her mouth.

He loved those lines. They were the engraving that years of laughter and smiling had placed there, and she did not wear them heavily or with regrets.

"Renar of Marantine has been a good king, no matter how he railed against it. The crown for now is not under any threat; the two-year war saw to that quite effectively."

"I know that, but—"

"*But?* When we reach your Bridge, I shall have to have words with the person who taught you to say that!" He tightened his grip and kissed her gently on the neck. "Tiras, even old, will never be doddering, and he's just the adviser Renar needs. Darin is up and coming; he's grown into someone that you can justly be proud of, and he's here to aid."

"But—"

"There are no buts, Sara. We were given a life of our own, free of the constraints that almost destroyed us both. What is the point of that, if we can take no time for ourselves? You are important, love, as am I, in the king's council. But we are both only human now. Come, let us go. Hildy will be waiting."

She sighed and pressed her back against him.

"Darkling?"

"Yes. I'm here." He lifted her gently then and turned her around. "Have you really changed your mind?"

"No." She shook her shoulders, straightened herself out, and smiled. "But I'm almost afraid to go there."

"Don't be. Hildy says it hasn't changed much."

"Hildy was never in Mordantari before the Cataclysm. She wouldn't know."

"I would. Not as well as I once did, alas, but more than the mind remembers. I wish to see Rennath. I wish to see Mordantari and the castle that I once built for you. There are . . . old friends there that I once promised to pay my respects to. If we do not go now, when shall we?"

Leaning down, he kissed her lips.

"Come, Sara."

She rolled up the sleeves of her simple tunic and smiled wistfully. With deliberate care, she shed the burden of her office and became, for an instant, the private woman that he loved so much.

Hildy was waiting, after all. And this time, the journey was theirs to choose. No fate shadowed it, no war undermined it, and no blood set them against each other.

Yes, perhaps he was right. They had helped to build this new world, from the ashes of the old, and there were many shoulders who could now carry its burden. It wasn't perfect, and some part of her naively regretted that—but it was full of choice and promise.

She caught his arm, beginning to tingle with expectation and the foreign sense of complete freedom.

"All right," she whispered. "But we'd better hurry. Tiras may have gotten older, but if he breaks our legs, I won't be able to heal them."

He chuckled, put on his pack, and then suddenly swept her off her feet.

And if they didn't live happily ever after, they had enough happiness to make that living worthwhile—which is all, in the end, that they had ever dreamed of on the long road of which the Sundered were the beginning, and their children the end.